# BANKRUPTURE

# BANKRUPTURE

RUSSELL H. WALTERS

ISBN Paperback: 978-1-7326638-1-7
ISBN eBook: 978-1-7326638-0-0

Printed in the United States of America

Book Cover and Interior Design: Creative Publishing Book Design
Cover Art: Bogdan Maksimovic

*Cover photo credits:*
Philadelphia PD cruiser: Zuzu (CC BY-SA 3.0)
Dodge Ram: RL GNZLZ (CC BY-SA 2.0)
    Artaxerxes (CC BY-SA 3.0)
    John S. and James L. Knight Foundation (CC BY-SA 2.0)
Store:  Paul Sableman (CC BY 2.0)
    Stuart Grout (CC BY 2.0)
Buildings and street: Paul Sableman (CC BY 2.0)
Barrel fire: Lewis Clarke (CC BY-SA 2.0)

*For Wendy, my sandpaper.*

"We must not let our rulers load us with perpetual debt."
—Thomas Jefferson, 1816


"When the levee breaks, mama, you got to move."
— Kansas Joe McCoy and Memphis Minnie, 1929
[Led Zeppelin 1971]

# PROLOGUE

*Sunday, October 15ᵗʰ, 2028*
*5:00 PM*

Aaron had been responsible for many deaths since his return from the front, but so far he hadn't been the one to pull the trigger. That would change today. Adrenaline was starting to course though his body, focusing his mind and sharpening his eyes. It was always like this right before a mission. But now, instead of riding in an MRAP (a Mine Resistant Ambush Protected vehicle) in the hellhole that had engulfed the Ukraine when Russia decided to mount an all-out assault, Aaron was riding shotgun in the lead van of three. The vans were painted to match the Philadelphia Police Department's special tactics unit and were filled with twenty-four of Aaron's foot soldiers from his organization, the Southwest Militia. Most of the men were veterans of the Ukraine or the cauldron of the various wars simmering in the Middle East— Iran, Turkey, or Egypt; where the United States was either choosing a side in a mindless civil war or enjoined in the endless fight against Islamic radicals. None of his men were from the Alaska or Taiwan fronts. Those conflicts were too fresh and the body counts too high for many veterans to come home.

1

Except for Wilson. That crazy bastard went absent without leave from the front lines just outside Anchorage and showed up in the hood just a few weeks ago. He'd be the first man out of the lead van on this raid.

Aaron shook the macabre memories of war from his mind. The vans were now on Oregon Avenue heading east toward the Packer Avenue Marine Terminal. That's where his property was coming in. Usually when a shipment like this came into the terminal, it was a matter of sending a driver in with a thick envelope stuffed full of the bribes needed to clear the terminal with no questions asked.

But this time was different. Aaron's connection at the terminal had told him that the feds were poking around the manifest for the ship carrying the container with his shipment from the Ukraine. That could only mean one thing: Aaron had stretched too far. Usually, Aaron and his partners in the Ukraine smuggled rations, uniforms, general supplies, some small arms, and rifle and pistol ammunition. He kept a small percentage of the goods to make sure his organization was the most powerful on Philadelphia's streets.

The rest of the shipments he smuggled to his brother in Texas. The separatists needed all the weapons they could get in their fight for independence from the federal government. Aaron sold drugs, ran prostitutes, and extorted the weak to generate cash to buy weapons.

This time, his partner in the Army's logistics unit had told Aaron he could put together a more potent shipment. Through several encrypted cell phone apps and message boards, Aaron had brokered bringing in Barrett fifty caliber semi-automatic rifles, M249 squad automatic weapons, a couple FIM-92 stinger surface to air missiles, several AT4 anti-tank recoilless rifles, and a bunch of old M79 forty-millimeter grenade launchers with ordinance, in addition to the usual mix of M4, M16 rifles and old handguns.

Every shipment that came in inched Texas closer to independence and moved Aaron closer to his goal of getting away from the cold, ugly streets that had created him to a new start in Texas with his brother. Yes, his militia controlled the Southwest section of Philadelphia. But now he considered it enemy territory—to be abandoned once his mission was complete.

Before the caravan got to the terminal, they pulled into an empty lot along Oregon Avenue. Aaron turned to remind the men in the back of his van of the briefing everyone had received before they left his headquarters. "Listen up. We're gonna' hit these suckers hard. Once we're in the terminal, you gotta' secure the shipping container and load its contents into these three vans. You are 'weapons hot' once you exit the van. They're all federal agents. Most will be wearing ballistic vests. If a tango goes down, do not assume they are done. Make sure you finish them. No witnesses. Any questions?"

There were none. These were hard men. They knew what working for Aaron meant. Many of the men had body armor from previous shipments that was far superior to what FBI and DEA agents wore.

Aaron was waiting for a three-letter text from the crane operator, also on Aaron's payroll, to tell him Aaron's container was being lifted from the ship. It was critical they hit the terminal the second the container reached the ground, before the feds could access its contents.

Aaron's cell vibrated. He read the text: "NOW"

"Go!" Aaron yelled to the driver.

The driver mashed the accelerator, kicking gravel and lurching the van forward. The other vans followed quickly behind.

Aaron keyed his two-way radio. "Thor One, Thor Two. The package is in the air, Loki's coming in hot."

"Thor One, confirmed." Aaron's first sniper was set up under the decking on the Walt Whitman Bridge.

"Thor Two, confirmed." The second sniper called in from the rusting hulk of a compressed natural gas tanker parked on the New Jersey side of the Delaware River.

The three vans breezed past the police cruiser regularly stationed on the corner of Oregon Avenue and Packer Avenue just before the terminal. The cop in that cruiser owed a gambling debt to Aaron that would be forgiven if he kept his butt planted in his cruiser with his radio silent.

The three vans approached the guard station. If the painted vans and uniforms didn't get them past the guard, plan B would.

The guard opened his window and asked, "What's going on, gentlemen?"

The driver looked at Aaron; Aaron responded, "Feds called us in to back them up on an op this afternoon."

The guard replied, "No problem. I just need to confirm with the FBI agent in charge. He told me to—"

Before the guard finished his sentence, the driver ducked down and Aaron drew the silenced twenty-two caliber pistol tucked under his right leg and fired three rounds into the guard's torso, neck, and forehead.

Plan B.

Aaron's driver floored the accelerator and the van smashed through the gate. More noise than Aaron would have liked but right now, timing was everything.

Thor One called in from his perch on the Walt Whitman Bridge, "Loki, the feds are unaware of your forced entry. Proceed to gantry crane to intercept container."

Aaron was pleased to hear his entry hadn't caused the feds to change their plans. "Thor One. This is Loki, provide tango count."

A brief pause and the sniper responded. "Thirty."

Aaron grimaced. Even though his men were slightly outnumbered, the surprise they had installed on the front of all three vans, with the added advantage of his snipers, should make this a decisive operation.

The three vans cleared the lanes of stacked shipping containers and made a sharp right, heading north along the docks to an area secured by the federal officers. There were two FBI agents about twenty yards south of where the bulk of the agents were standing. They were providing perimeter security for the other agents who were waiting for the container, which was about sixty feet off the deck and descending slowly.

These two FBI agents paused when they saw the Philadelphia Police Department paint scheme on the vans. However, once they realized the vans weren't slowing down, they started to bring the M4 carbines they had slung across their chests to their shoulders.

The FBI agent to the left was about to fire on the first van when his chest exploded. A tenth of a second later, the right shoulder of the other agent disappeared into a red mist. Both agents were done.

Bringing the snipers had been a good move. Aaron nodded in satisfaction. *Thor's hammer is a bitch.*

The three vans flared out and approached the group of federal agents. By this time, the agents had started to take cover behind vehicles and were drawing their side arms.

As the vans screeched to a stop in a near line with about 5 yards between each van, Aaron depressed the plunger on a radio frequency transmitter. A thundering clap was released and all three vans vibrated from the blast.

Each van's bumper had two claymore mines attached to it.

The C4 explosive in the six mines propelled over four thousand, one-eighth-inch balls in a deadly cone of destruction thirty yards wide. The effect was devastating. The deadly cloud of shrapnel immediately felled more than half of the agents. Those who survived the initial blast, shielded behind vehicles, had their backs exposed to the two snipers.

Aaron got out of his seat and leveled his M16 on the frame of the van door, looking for any targets. His men swarmed past him, moving in a deliberate pattern and shooting any agent who moved, whether they were standing or on the ground.

Both snipers, Thor One and Thor Two, were now shooting every five seconds or so. Enough time to cycle the bolt on the Barrett Model 98B bolt-action rifles he'd bought for his snipers on the black market. The few remaining agents knew the situation was hopeless. One dropped his pistol and was trying to make a phone call when a sniper round severed his spine.

A Latina DEA agent dropped her carbine and put her hands up, meaning to surrender. Aaron sighted his M16 on the small patch of skin just above her ballistic vest and pulled his trigger.

The bullet slammed home and killed the agent, eyes wide open at the shock of being shot after surrendering.

"No witnesses!" Aaron shouted to his men.

As the shooting slowed down and trickled to a stop, the container finally reached the ground. Aaron shouted, "Target is on the ground. Let's go." The men mobilized immediately.

Eight of the men set up a perimeter to make sure no one else showed up. The other men stowed their weapons, opened the container and started loading the crates into the first van.

Aaron spoke into his radio. "Thor One and Thor Two. Maintain positions during loading. Make sure no backup shows up. Once the third van is loaded, exfiltrate immediately." Two reports came back of a simple "Copy."

The loading proceeded without incident. The men got back into the vans, cramming themselves on top of the crates of weapons and ammunition from the shipping container.

On the way out of the Packer terminal, Aaron saluted the patrol officer, who was still parked in the same spot. The officer nodded to Aaron while keeping his eyes low to avoid looking him in the eyes. Then Aaron watched as the officer took a deep breath, grabbed his radio, and made the call for a disturbance at the marine terminal.

By the time the responding officers arrived, Aaron would be well clear of this part of the city on the way back to his headquarters with the most expensive and dangerous shipment he had ever received.

# CHAPTER 1

*Monday, October 23rd, 2028*
*1:00 PM*

Julianne had just finished her workout when she got the text from her boss.

BR: "My office. ASAP."

Her reply: "10-4. 20 minutes."

Lunch was her hour-long oasis in the middle of her day to work out. She was a long time removed from playing basketball at Temple, but staying fit was important to her. Usually, her workout was easy to schedule around. Her boss was a morning guy and was known for either having long business lunches with local power brokers or being out on the golf course by noon. Today was obviously an exception.

Julianne's hair was still damp and her cheeks were slightly flushed from her workout and fast-paced walk back. She breezed past the receptionist, who barely looked up from her computer monitor to wave her in. "The Big Guy is in a mood today, tread lightly Jules."

Julianne smiled without breaking stride, "Thanks Rhonda. If I don't come out in ten minutes call SWAT."

That garnered a chuckle from Rhonda as Julianne grasped the large brass handle on the door, swung it open, and slipped into Mayor Bill Rhodes' office.

Julianne noted that he was gripping a printed report in his hand. He was clearly upset. There was a plethora of problems in the city right now. But since he'd cancelled his usual afternoon forays and called her into his office, she assumed he had finally read the report she'd written last week.

Mayor Rhodes raised his eyes from the report and glared at Julianne, "I just read this report from your office—"

Julianne's hunch was confirmed. She decided to stay quiet until she could see what avenue of attack the mayor would take.

"—and I *believe* it is telling me that the City can't make its payroll next Friday? Whose fault is this?"

*So*, Julianne thought, *he went right to accusations*. She approached his desk and said evenly, "Sir, we just don't have enough cash in the operating account to make a full payroll payment. It's simple math. As far as whose fault it is, that's a big question with a long answer. It started with—"

Mayor Rhodes interrupted her. "I don't need a history lesson, just tell me what our options are and how you're going to fix this. I appointed you as the Director of Finance to take care of these kinds of issues, not throw them on my plate."

Julianne's latte complexion darkened another shade as she took a moment to compose herself. After taking a deep breath, she said, "Mr. Rhodes. As I pointed out in the report you are holding, I recommend the City file for Chapter Nine municipal bankruptcy. It would—"

For a second time, the mayor interrupted her, "No, never. Not on my watch. Ms. Barnes, I have sixteen months left in my second and final term. There is no way I am having my legacy destroyed by being the mayor who bankrupted the city. Give me other options. Raise taxes? Take out a loan? Raid the pension funds? Give me something!"

This time Julianne's eyes softened a bit and a look of pity crept onto her face. "Here is our status with each option. One, raise taxes. Problem here is we have already raised both the wage and the sales tax. In fact, in the past fiscal year, we generated less revenue from those taxes even though the rates went up."

Mayor Rhodes asked pointedly, "How can that happen? A higher tax rate should result in higher tax revenue."

Julianne responded, "Well, sir, two things happened. Employers relocated jobs to outside the city limits and people stopped buying things inside the city. In fact, if we tried to raise taxes anymore, we would approach the point where the people and business would be idiots to live or work in the city. This would lead to even lower revenue and the City would try to raise rates again, causing a vicious circle of lower revenue and higher taxes that economists call the 'death spiral.'"

She continued. "We could try to issue another bond to raise cash, but the debt markets might not lend anymore to us. If they do, it will be at such high interest rates that the City will never be able to make the coupon payments. A large part of the reason we are running out of cash is recent interest payments on bonds that you and your predecessors issued."

Mayor Rhodes interjected again, "Are you telling me we wasted our money paying some Wall Street fat cat holding our bonds and now we can't make payroll? What kind of office are you running, Ms. Barnes?"

Ignoring the accusation, Julianne straightened her shoulders and leveled her stare directly at the mayor's face. "Again, it's not that simple. As the Director of Finance, I act as the chief financial officer for the City. As you know, The Office of the City Treasurer is directly responsible for managing the City's debt and paying vendors and employees."

Mayor Rhodes interjected again, "I don't need a civics lesson. Get to your point."

Julianne nodded and continued, "Hopefully, you recall that the man who ran the Office of the Treasury committed suicide three weeks ago."

Rhodes admitted, "Yeah, that's right. What a shame. Jerry was good guy. I went to high school with him."

Julianne said, "He didn't leave a suicide note, we don't know why he killed himself, but I have a feeling that his struggles to pay interest on twenty-six billion dollars of debt may have had something to do with it."

Mayor Rhodes stared at Julianne with a bored expression as she continued, "I dug into the Treasury department once Jerry was gone and found what he had been hiding. For all intents and purposes, the city is bankrupt. It has very little cash left. So little that, based on my findings as you read in my report, we can't make next week's payroll."

Mayor Rhodes steepled his fingers under his chin and stared at the ornate finish on the ceiling. In a voice that Julianne thought was more for himself than to be shared with her, he said, "I just can't believe we have been paying Wall Street fat cats bond interest payments instead of our police and fire fighters. I can't wait to see that headline."

Julianne didn't want to interrupt Mayor Rhodes from his thoughts, but she felt compelled to point something out. "Sir, those bonds are held by every day Americans, not fat cats on Wall Street.

And if you miss a single payment on a bond, you are in default and the credit markets close up to you. No more loans at all."

Julianne was surprised to see Mayor Rhodes chuckle and lean back in his mahogany and red leather chair. She noted the sense of power Rhodes exuded seated in it and the way his dark skin matched the tone of the wood on the armrests. *But,* she thought, *a sense of power isn't worth much when you're bankrupt.* "Okay, Ms. Barnes, I give up. Please explain option three—getting operating cash from the pensions."

Her eyes grew big as she took a deep breath. She hadn't thought he was serious about that. "Sir, what you are suggesting is illegal. We cannot access the municipal pension funds without breaking several laws. Also, as the Director of Finance for the City, I am the Chairperson on the Board of Pensions for all the municipal workers in the city. It would be a breach of my fiduciary duty to the fund to allow any money to be withdrawn for non-pension uses."

The mayor scoffed at her reply. "You're worried about your fiduciary duties? I'm worried about the very social fabric of the city being ripped apart! If we can't pay our workers, this city will cease to exist."

The mayor continued, "If it's breaking laws you're worried about, who's going to enforce the laws? The feds? They're busy fighting a three-front war right now. Not to mention the ass-whupp'n the local feds received at the docks last week—the Philadelphia field offices of the US Customs and FBI were decimated. It's all hands on deck in DC right now. They won't even have the resources to find out what we are doing, much less the capability or will to enforce any penalties right now. So, tell me. Are we making payments into the pensions? And how much money is available to use in the pensions?"

The implications of the last barrage of questions stunned her. After a moment, she recovered and responded, "Sir, most of the pensions are currently sixty to eighty percent underfunded. We are currently making the required payments but at the current burn rate, the pension will be out of money in three years. Even without breaking any laws, we need to announce a serious reduction in payouts now."

Julianne let the information sink in without saying anything more. She noted that the mayor turned his eyes to look out the window to the streets below. He began speaking in a deliberate tone without looking at her.

"Here is what we are going to do. Immediately stop making payments into any pension funds. Go to the New York City bankers and get bonds issued. I don't care when they come due as long as it is after I am out of office. I also don't give a crap about what the interest rates on the bonds are; we can use some of the principle to pay the coupons. You can tap the pension fund if needed for short term cash, but make sure there is at least enough money there to keep it solvent until I am out of office."

Julianne shook her head in silence and listened at the mayor continued.

"No reduction in pay-outs for pensioners. I don't need the media running stories about some old widow eating dog food because I cut her pension. Plus, the unions would go crazy if they caught wind of this. I'm more worried about them than the Federal government. The unions can act like animals if they think someone is threatening their futures, and I don't want those knuckle-draggers turning on me. Fudge the numbers on the accounts until I leave office. Also, cut any non-essential service out there. Use your discretion. If for some reason you run out of cash for something, issue IOU's to the non-essential staff for payroll. Whatever you do, don't mess with the police or fire fighters. I need them fully in the game and don't want them calling in a blue flu when I need them most."

Julianne was dumbstruck. "Sir, what you are asking me to do is highly illegal. I don't want to be any part of this, Chapter Nine is the only legal—"

Mayor Rhodes turned to look at her. He was smiling. "Oh, you are part of this. No backing out now. Imagine your life if you joined the twenty percent of the city's population that's out of work. I know your mother is living in one of the assisted living properties run by the housing authority. I would hate to see her out on the street."

Julianne gasped, "You wouldn't dare—"

Without pausing he continued, "Go write a memo outlining your plan in my name. I'll sign it and you can use it as a get-out-of-jail-free card. If it comes to that."

Julianne paled as she nodded and left the office, closing the door behind her.

Rhonda glanced up from her screen and said, "Girl, you look like you just seen a ghost."

Julianne tried to summon a smile to her stricken face. "More like the devil himself."

# CHAPTER 2

*Thursday, October 26ᵗʰ, 2028*
*7:00 PM*

Jimmy was enjoying dinner with his mom when his cell phone buzzed, alerting him to a text message. Mom loved cooking and this was her signature dish. Corned beef and cabbage and of course the best side dish in America: mashed potatoes. Mom's were so good, Jimmy had named them "love potatoes" as a six-year-old, and the name had stuck. Tonight's potatoes were no different—she knocked it out of the park.

Before sitting down for the meal, Katherine had confided in her son that she had been saving small slivers of her arthritis pills and taken them this morning so that she would be able to prepare this meal for him. Usually, her medicine would only make it three weeks of a typical month, even with Jimmy cutting the pills in half for her. Her arthritis kept her from working and his health insurance only paid for the smallest dose of medicine available. Sometimes it was hard for her to get out of bed, but she always did.

Jimmy didn't want to look at his cell phone. But he was on call. He glanced down at the message.

Just as he'd expected. A service dispatch into the city.

Jimmy looked up from his phone and saw the sadness reflected in his mother's eyes. He really didn't want to leave her tonight. It was Thursday night. Their routine was to clean up the kitchen and walk—or drive, depending on how her joints were doing—to Saint Dorothy's Catholic Church, better known as Saint Dot's, for a night of bingo. Jimmy was by far the youngest in attendance, but he didn't mind. His mom was his best friend, and he didn't want her going out by herself anymore.

Jimmy said gently, "Mom, I need to go into the city tonight. There's a building with both elevators down."

Katherine looked at her son and said, "Finish your dinner first. Those people in the city can take the stairs for a little while. Lord knows most of them need the exercise."

Jimmy sighed. "Mom, you know most of them don't have cars? That they walk everywhere already? The public transportation's getting worse, along with everything else in the city."

Katherine continued, unfazed. "You know what I mean. Those black people are all lazy and violent. We give them food and housing for free and all they want is more free stuff. God forbid they go and get a job. And if we don't give them free stuff, they get violent and steal it from people who worked for what they got. It's just not right, Jimmy."

Katherine's attitude toward the largely African-American population within the city limits had never been good, but it had gotten worse in the past two years since she had stopped working. While Jimmy was growing up the comments were mostly veiled, but nowadays she made herself perfectly clear.

Jimmy rubbed his mother's hand while he tried to think of a response that wouldn't immediately turn her off. Every time it came up he tried to say it slightly differently, hoping maybe somehow she'd eventually get it. "Mom, people are people, no matter their skin color. One of my best friends at work is African American. Assuming that people are lazy or violent based on their skin color is as ridiculous as—as assuming that someone's kind just based on their haircut!"

Katherine shook her head and said knowingly, "Jimmy, you don't read what I read on the Internet. Those people are dangerous. I don't want you getting hurt going to those neighborhoods after dark."

Jimmy gently held her hands in his and looked into her eyes. "Mom. It's okay. I'll be fine. Everybody in those neighborhoods knows I'm a repair guy just trying to fix their building. They know if they started attacking people like me, they could have trouble getting things in their buildings fixed."

Katherine's eyes softened. "Okay Jimmy. But be careful. I love you."

Jimmy got up from the table and grabbed his company uniform jacket from the back of the chair. Shrugging it on, he said, "Thanks Mom. I love you too. I'll have Colleen check in on you tonight if I'm running late."

Katherine looked at Jimmy slyly. "You should be checking in on Colleen, not bother her with checking in on me! I'm perfectly fine."

Jimmy laughed and said, "You know what, I have been thinking about asking her out on a date. But I don't know if she'd be interested."

Patting his rather soft midsection he continued, more seriously, "I'm not nearly the specimen Jack was. Also, it's just barely been a year since he was killed on the Alaskan front. Is that enough time? I don't want to disrespect his memory. He was like a big brother to me."

She replied, "All I can tell you, son, is that you can't hit the ball if you don't swing the bat. Jack was a good man and so are you, just in different ways. Colleen is starting to put her life back together with that job she got at the YMCA, but I also heard the government cut the payments to military widows. She could use a good man with a good job, and those two boys will need a father in their lives." She paused. "You should know that more than anyone. Someday you'll need to look in the mirror and realize you have more to offer the world than fixing elevators for those lazy people in the city."

Jimmy leaned over and kissed her forehead. "That's enough out of you. I will see you later tonight or for breakfast if it gets too late."

The comment she'd made about the boys not having a father cut Jimmy much more than he thought his mom could imagine. Jimmy's dad had left when Jimmy was eight years old, and he died from a blood clot just before Jimmy graduated high school. For the first couple of years after the divorce, Jimmy got to see his dad once or twice a month. But then his old man moved out to Lancaster County and took a job as an over-the-road trucker. Jimmy only saw him a couple of times a year as a teenager.

Jimmy knew there was a hole in his life from not having a father around to raise him.

He could have really used a strong male role model during his teen years. Someone to show him how to be a man. His mom tried to help, but it wasn't the same. She didn't know how and when to push him to do things like play sports or ask a girl on a date. Consequently, perhaps, Jimmy had done neither in high school.

Looking back, he regretted not pushing himself, not trying new things on his own, rather than waiting for his mom to allow him to try new things. He understood that she didn't want him to get hurt playing sports, or get involved with a girl too early; but he couldn't help but wonder if maybe those were the kind of mistakes you're supposed to make, and then talk to your dad about, and learn from.

In the six years since he graduated high school, Jimmy was proud of his accomplishments. He graduated at the top of his trade school class then went right to work repairing elevators. His work helped people live safely in buildings, kept food on the table and a roof over his and his mom's heads; and maybe most importantly, exempted him from the draft since his job was considered "infra-structure critical".

But Jimmy felt in his heart something was missing. He loved his mother and enjoyed her company, but she was right, he needed something—or someone—more.

Shaking off his brief reflection, Jimmy grabbed his van keys and trotted next door to Colleen's house. It didn't take long; the houses in this area of Upper Darby were almost on top of each other. The lawns were so small it was a toss-up whether to use a lawn mower or a weed whacker to trim the grass. Jimmy knocked on Colleen's door. He could hear the TV in the background and two young voices arguing about which show to watch next.

Colleen answered the door with a harried, annoyed look on her face. Even though her light brown hair was coming loose from a ponytail and she was wearing a mismatched and oversized sweat suit, Jimmy found her stunning. She had her first son, Jack Jr., when she was eighteen—only a few months after she and Jack were married. Now eight, Jack Jr. was the same age Jimmy was when his father left him.

When she saw that it was Jimmy, she released a sigh and raised an eyebrow—a silent means of asking why Jimmy was at her door. Before either could speak, the argument about the TV program flared in volume. Colleen held up a finger to Jimmy to give her a second, turned around, and shouted, "Dougie! Just deal with it, it's your brother's turn to watch his show." Colleen took a step out, keeping the screen door propped open, and tucked a stray strand of hair behind her ear.

"What's up, Jimmy, are you on call again?"

Jimmy stood a little taller and made a show of brushing the non-existent dust from the sleeves of the uniform jacket he wore for work and responded, "Yeah, you know the drill, gotta' make a living. Could you do me a favor and keep an eye on my mom if I have to stay out late?"

Colleen nodded and said, "Sure, once I put the boys down, I'll bring the kiddy monitor over and do the crossword with your mom until her bedtime. She's helped me with the boys when I went out on errands, so I'd be happy to return the favor."

Jimmy nodded and responded, "Thanks Colleen, I appreciate it. Hey, I have . . ." He paused, his mother's advice ringing in his ears and conjuring a mental image of a baseball being thrown at him as he stood holding a bat. In his mind's eye, he lifted the bat off his shoulder and started to swing towards the incoming ball. He tried to ignore the mental baseball game and continued, "Yeah, I have another quick question. Tonight is bingo night at St. Dot's. Would you ever be interested in going with me sometime?"

Colleen's eyebrow peaked again. She tilted her head slightly. A moment later she replied, "I don't know, Jimmy. Bingo isn't really my thing."

Jimmy imagined the ball arcing towards the inside of the plate in a wicked curve. He knew he was in danger of having the ball speed by his bat without a hit if he didn't do something fast.

He smiled and said, "Yeah you're right. Bingo does sound lame once I say it out loud. Maybe some other time or place?"

Colleen reached out and patted the embroidered American flag on his jacket's shoulder, "I don't know Jimmy—maybe."

"Is that a 'maybe-yes or a maybe-no'?"

Colleen smiled, "It's a 'maybe-yes'." Jimmy heard his heart pounding. Tried to ignore it. She continued, "But right now I need to make sure Jack Jr. doesn't have Dougie in a headlock. Be careful in the city tonight. I hear things are going downhill."

"Okay. Sounds good. Thanks again for looking after Mom. Yeah, it seems like every time I drive in on Market Street, I see more and more storefronts boarded up. I've never had a problem though; I think the company uniform helps. Take care." Jimmy turned to walk back to his van.

As he walked to his service van, he imagined the bat completing its swing and the ball chipping solidly off the bat. *A foul tip is better than striking out*, Jimmy thought.

Jimmy climbed into the cab of the service van and fired it up. It idled a little rougher than normal. He guessed it didn't like the bio diesel that his company got apportioned. The engine ran better on real diesel, but there wasn't much of that since the President banned fracking a few years ago.

Banning fracking had led to a drastic reduction in the supply of natural gas, which increased the consumption of fuel oil, which led to a shortage of diesel fuel.

And then about two years ago, just when the economy was starting to stabilize after the fracking ban, Russia invaded Alaska. Jimmy remembered they struck on December twenty-first, the darkest day of the year up there. Over thirteen hours of pitch dark and the other hours dimly lit by various shades of twilight. The Russians had spent years building up their Arctic army and navy, which included dozens of icebreakers. At the time of the attack, the United States had two operational icebreakers.

The Russians invaded by sea and by air. They secured the entire North Slope area of Alaska, where most of the US crude oil production had been located. Thousands upon thousands of US infantry troops met an early, icy grave trying to dislodge the Russians. The government didn't want to use heavy bombs to fight the Russians because of the damage to the infrastructure it would cause. That meant the troops had to slug it out with a highly trained, securely entrenched enemy on the ground. The result was a meat grinder that killed soldiers at an unprecedented rate—including Jimmy's neighbor and mentor, Jack.

Jimmy shivered in his driver's seat, partially in an unsuccessful attempt to shed his deep thoughts and partially in reaction to the chill in the cab of the van. Since Jimmy's job as an elevator repairman designated him an "infrastructure critical" worker, he was exempt from the draft on that basis. He also acted as the caregiver for his mother, which would be a factor in his favor even if he had a different job. Not having a criminal record also helped. Instead of going to prison, many convicts were being conscripted into penal battalions. Based on the astronomical casualty rates of those battalions, their main function seemed to be depleting the Russian ammunition stores.

While Jimmy was thankful he did not have to go to war, it felt like sometimes his job took him into a warzone anyway.

It wasn't the profusion of normal-looking businesses, bars, and churches along his route into the city that made it feel like a warzone. It was the abrupt shift from normalcy to desperation that you felt just before entering the city limits. As Jimmy passed Cobbs Creek Park, a thin strip of woods on the outskirts of the city, he couldn't help remembering the stories he'd heard as a kid of the DMZ (demilitarized zone) between North and South Korea, back when they were still separate countries. Every time he drove past the line of trees he thought of the DMZ. A no man's land of tranquility between enemy territories. That's what Cobbs Creek Park was—a neutral barrier between the quietness of the suburbs and the danger of the city.

But the DMZ had failed. Now the whole Korean peninsula was a tyrannical nightmare. And with how much Jimmy went back and forth between the city and the county, he sensed more and more that the quietness of the suburbs was masking a deeper fear, and that underneath the turmoil of the city was something much more concrete and dangerous.

Jimmy passed through the DMZ and wound his way through the streets without confrontation to the government-funded apartment building that needed service. It was overcast and quite chilly for late October so not too many people were out. There was also a kind of street truce that extended to maintenance workers, nurses, and other folks who came into the city to make it work. The gangbangers called those workers "civilians." Like in video games where you lose points if you shoot the civilians. Same concept. Jimmy was happy to be a civilian. He was also glad that most of his work was during the day when gang activity wasn't too bad.

Jimmy liked to start working at six a.m. and get out by three p.m. Then most of the bad actors were still asleep from the night before and the high schoolers, whom Jimmy found extremely aggressive at times, were still in school. Jimmy's theory on the high schoolers was that since they were still juveniles, they figured now was the time to do the crime because the punishment was a joke.

But every once in awhile he got after-hours calls like this one. He'd never had any problems, though, and since so few people were out tonight, he didn't have any reason to worry.

That's what he told himself, anyway.

# CHAPTER 3

*Thursday, October 26ᵗʰ, 2028*
*7:45 PM*

Jimmy pulled his service van into the parking area in front of the building with the elevator problems and cut the engine. He saw a group of men hanging around the side entrance but they seemed busy on their cell phones. The glow from the screens illuminated their faces. Some looked like youth and one could be in his late twenties, but Jimmy couldn't tell at this distance or lighting. But they didn't look up and didn't seem too threatening.

Jimmy grabbed his tool bag from the passenger seat and headed in to see what was going on. Upon entering the foyer, where the security guard sat behind three inches of plexiglass, Jimmy was accosted by two sensations. The first was the temperature.

*Holy crap, it's hot in here.*

Jimmy had noticed that the folks who lived in these buildings typically liked it about ten degrees warmer than he found reasonable.

The second sensation was the smell. A mix of various heavy, fried cooking odors intermixed with an undertone of decomposing trash and a hint of feces. Typical, but disgusting nonetheless.

Jimmy didn't recognize the guard and it took him a while to look up from the video playing on his smart phone. Jimmy stood there for a full ten seconds before he couldn't take it anymore. *Shouldn't this guy be more aware of what's going on? What if I was a threat? Shouldn't he be at least glancing at the video feeds from the surveillance cameras?*

If the guard had looked at the camera feed for the parking lot, he would have seen the men slowly begin to saunter towards Jimmy's service van.

But since the video monitor for the camera system was facing away from Jimmy, he was not aware of this development. Jimmy cleared his throat and said, "Good evening. I got a call that the elevators were out of service."

The guard looked up, grunted an acknowledgment and pushed a button to unlock the inner door of the vestibule granting access to the main lobby.

As Jimmy was making his way to the elevator machine room, he had to maneuver around a tenant blocking the hall with her walker. Her front basket had a few items in it from the corner store.

"You gonna' fix that elevator?" She asked with a glint of mischief in her eyes.

"Yes ma'am, that's what I do. Get you up to your home in no time." Jimmy responded with a smile.

"Shee-et son, that ain't no home, it's a shithole that the gov'ment pays for 'cause they don't know what else to do with me."

"Well, whatever it is, I'll fix these cars so you can head up in no time. Excuse me and I'll get to it."

The tenant decided the bench in the hallway was a good place to park so she backed into the seat and retracted her walker with her. Jimmy walked a few steps past her and opened the door to the elevator machine room.

The first piece of good news for Jimmy was that the building, only four stories tall, had hydraulic elevators. A hydraulic elevator has a reservoir of hydraulic fluid in a tank in the elevator machine room. A pump in the machine room pumps fluid into a big cylinder that the elevator car rides on. Pump in more fluid from the reservoir, the car goes up. Pump fluid out of the cylinder and back into the reservoir, the car goes down. Of course, there was a lot more to it than that, but the present advantage for Jimmy was that the elevator machine room was on the first floor. If it were a traditional cable driven elevator, the machine room would be on the roof and that meant humping himself and his tools up and down a flight of stairs. Not fun.

The second piece of good news was the smell in the room. The pungent, singed smell of a burnt fuse permeated the air.

Jimmy thought back to the first time he ever smelled that smell. It was summer break, and he was at his dad's place in Lancaster for a weeklong visit. Jimmy was about twelve years old and he had found an old radio in his dad's closet that hadn't worked for years.

Jimmy took it apart and found what he thought was a bad resistor on the printed circuit board. A bike ride to Radio Shack for a pack of replacement resistors and two hours of trying to solder it back onto the board and he was convinced it was fixed. When he plugged it back in, it did make some noise, but before he could adjust the tuner, a loud "pop" came from the circuit board and a puff of smoke rose out of one of the components on the board. That smoke had the distinctive burnt fuse smell. His dad had told him that electronics must run on smoke because once you let the smoke out, they stop working.

Back to the task at hand. Jimmy fished out two 50-amp fuses from his bag. Since the sweeping brownouts this past summer, these fuses were failing at a rate Jimmy had never seen. Even though the news hadn't reported on it, Jimmy thought the power company was having trouble regulating the power on the grid as well as they used to. More electricity spikes blowing more fuses. But he was the guy to make the repairs, so at least it kept food on his plate.

Once both fuses were replaced, Jimmy restored power to the elevators, listened to the pumps fire up, and walked out to the hallway.

The tenant was still there staring at Jimmy. She was doing her best to give him the stink eye, but Jimmy figured she was a softy. "Come on over, I'll reset the elevator and you can be the first one to try out my handiwork."

"Boy, you are quick. I guess you don't get paid by the hour." She groaned out loud as she hoisted herself up and off the bench.

"Oh, I do, but I have a special lady at home who I don't like to leave alone for too long. You and her would get along like peas in a pod," Jimmy added as he led the elderly tenant to the elevator.

Getting out his key he opened the elevator door and reset the operation of the car. He held the door open and the tenant shuffled in.

The tenant grabbed Jimmy's wrist as he was about to exit the elevator car.

"You're a good boy. You be careful of these ruffians around this building. They are up to no good tonight." She warned.

"Yes ma'am." Jimmy countered with a smile as he exited the elevator car to allow the doors to close.

Jimmy took a minute in the lobby to document what services he'd performed and what material he'd used. The tablet figured out when he arrived and left, so he didn't need to fill that info in. Jimmy re-approached the guard desk.

"Excuse me. Your elevators are all good now. Please sign the tablet." Jimmy said as he slid the tablet through the slot in the safety glass.

The guard looked at the tablet, looked at Jimmy, and said, "I'm not signing anything, you got to get maintenance or management to sign this."

Jimmy replied, "It's nine at night. You know as well as I do, they're not here."

The guard shrugged and handed back the tablet, "I'm not signing it."

Jimmy smiled as he received the tablet through the slot, "That's okay. I had the tablet recording the video and audio before I handed it to you. That's proof enough I did the service. My office will be good with that."

The guard looked back at Jimmy with a dead stare. "That's just not right, man."

Jimmy shrugged, tucked the tablet back into his tool bag and headed out into the cool evening air.

# CHAPTER 4

*Thursday, October 26ᵗʰ, 2028*
*9:00 PM*

Jimmy was halfway across the parking lot to his van when he saw the group of three men leaning against the side of the vehicle. In the split second it took him to take the next step, two choices flashed in Jimmy's mind.

He could keep going to the van and sweet talk them into letting him leave without a confrontation, or run back to the building and call 911.

As his foot was meeting the concrete, the choice was made for him. The men pushed off the side of the van. Three on one. Jimmy knew when to run. Using the foot he had just planted, Jimmy turned a full one-eighty and ran back to the building.

Jimmy had the advantage of distance. The men were about twenty feet behind him. Jimmy was only sixty feet from the entrance of the building. As he built up speed, he figured he would make it, no problem. Two first downs and he was back to safety.

But Jimmy had two disadvantages. One was he didn't exercise much. At all. He figured he was on his feet doing mechanical work all day plus the occasional up and down a stair tower. It was all the exercise a man needed. The second was his tool bag. He didn't even think to drop it.

The two negatives outweighed his head start. As Jimmy opened the front door of the building, one of the younger boys slammed his body into the door, banging it shut.

Immediately, he felt hands pulling his jacket back and twisting him around. As he was forced to turn he saw a blur coming in from his left aimed straight at his chin. Clinching up and ducking his chin, the blow struck above his temple. Not a damaging blow, but it hurt.

The next punch came from the man who spun him around. It was an uppercut right into Jimmy's gut, just below the sternum. Jimmy's breath left him and his knees buckled. He fell into a fetal position, helpless.

Jimmy watched as the boys started to go through his tool bag. The eldest of the trio said to his younger cohorts, "Just grab the whole tool bag, we'll get good money fencing his tools and I know a guy who can wipe the tablet."

Then the ringleader squatted next to Jimmy and grabbed him by his jacket, pulling Jimmy's face to his own. Jimmy was finally catching his breath but the smell of cheap alcohol and fried food emanating from the thug's mouth added to the nausea Jimmy felt from being hit in the gut.

The man holding Jimmy said, "You need to give me your wallet now. If you make me search you for it, I'm gonna beat you."

Jimmy protested, "C'mon man, you got my tools. I'll give you my cash, but don't take my whole wallet, it—"

Jimmy didn't finish his thought because the thug threw a sharp jab to Jimmy's face. Jimmy's nose exploded in pain and his head snapped back. He gathered his senses enough to exclaim, "Okay, okay—here, here it is. Just take it."

Jimmy was still on his hands and knees as the thug took his wallet and stashed it in his jacket pocket. Then he looked at Jimmy and said coldly, "Ain't nobody tell Dante what to do."

With that Dante drew his right fist and swung it in an arc down towards Jimmy's head. Jimmy tried to lift an arm to block it, but he was too slow. Dante's fist impacted the left side of Jimmy's face just below his eye socket and his vision exploded in a rage of red with white streaks. Jimmy fell flat and struggled not to lose consciousness. He stayed in the fetal position until he heard the laughter of the men fade into the distance.

After a few minutes, Jimmy slowly propped himself into a sitting position and did a systems-check of his body. Breathing was okay, though his upper abdomen area was sore. But his head didn't feel so good and his vision was blurred. He moved his head side to side to make sure his neck was okay. No problem there.

Jimmy waited until his vision cleared. He checked his pockets and found he still had his van keys and for some reason, the muggers didn't take his phone. Sitting in the middle of the parking lot, Jimmy dialed 9-1-1. After being put on hold for three minutes, he gave his name, location, and a brief explanation of what happened to an obviously bored and dispassionate operator.

Not trusting himself to stand, he crawled across the desolate parking lot and sat on the ground in front of his van, supporting himself against the front bumper while he waited.

# CHAPTER 5

*Thursday, October 26<sup>th</sup>, 2028*
*9:05 PM*

"**M**ama, the whole city is about to implode. The pensions are bust, contractors haven't been paid for months, and I don't know if we can make payroll next week. It's too much for me to handle and my boss is asking me to break the law instead of fixing it the right way. I'm thinking about resigning. What should I do?" Julianne was sitting in the small kitchenette in her mother's apartment.

Her mother pursed her lips together and tapped her finger on her chin. Julianne knew that expression. It meant serious wisdom was about to follow. Julianne took the moment to lean back in her chair, loosen the tension that she had been holding in her shoulders, and let her eyes wander over the letters and accomplishments on the walls in her mom's diminutive apartment.

The framed documents chronicled Margarette Barnes' adult life. Her certificate of graduation from the first ever class of police officers for the Southeast Pennsylvania Transportation Authority (locally known as SEPTA) in 1981 hung above the television in her adjoining sitting room, the left-most frame on the wall. SEPTA did not have a dedicated police department before that year. In the same frame was a picture of Margarette on graduation day in her crisp, new service uniform. Her bright, wide smile formed a beautiful contrast against her smooth chocolate skin and jet-black hair pulled back into a bun atop her head. Julianne always thought the most striking element of the photograph was her mother's eyes. She may have been smiling in the photo, but her eyes were all business.

To the immediate right of that frame was a case holding the Medal of Valor that she'd earned for successfully combating an active shooter on a SEPTA bus in the Mayfair section of the city. She suffered a gunshot wound during the melee that collapsed her right lung.

The next frame held Margarette's thirty-year service award and her retirement certificate of appreciation from the SEPTA police department. This frame also had a photo of Margarette in it next to the certificates. The uniform was the same with the exception of the addition of dozens of colorful bars on her chest, awarded for various achievements and merits during her career. Her skin had faded and moles that had been invisible thirty years ago dotted her cheeks. Her hair was completely grey and her smile was reserved, barely showing teeth stained from years of coffee consumption, a far cry from the platinum white on graduation day. But Julianne was still fascinated with her mother's eyes in this photo. They had the same penetrating intensity compared to the photo thirty years previous.

The final frame held a letter of appreciation from the non-profit food bank Margarette had worked for until her health problems landed her here five years ago. She'd worked as the security officer in the pickup area of the food bank. She held the distinction that, in her twelve years at the food bank, she never even had to even raise her voice to diffuse a situation. Julianne suspected that even the tweaked-out drug users who frequented the shelters knew what Julianne learned as a little girl: *Nobody messes with Mama.*

There was only one picture missing from the wall: One of Julianne's father. Margarette never spoke about the man, nor had Julianne ever seen any documentation that he existed. Julianne's only clue as to her father's identity was her own skin. It was the color of a latte coffee while her mother's was Kona brown. That meant, in all probability, her papa was a white man.

When she was younger, Julianne fantasized that her father had dated her mother in a wonderful relationship. When she learned of her pregnancy, he did the right thing and proposed to her on the spot. Then a week before the wedding, her hero father was killed in the line of fire defending an elementary school from a deranged gunman.

In middle school, Julianne shared her theory—or rather, fantasy—with her mother. Margarette laughed until she cried then told her child that the biggest mistake in her life had become her biggest blessing. That was all she ever said about her father.

Margarette cleared her throat and Julianne refocused her attention on her mother.

Margarette reached out and gently held Julianne's hands. Her dark, age-spotted skin stood in contrast to Julianne's smooth, latte-colored skin. "Julianne, honey. You have been put in the place where you are for a time such as this."

Julianne felt her eyes moisten. It'd been awhile since anyone quoted Scripture to her. Somewhere deep in her soul, she knew her mother was right, but she was scared. "Mama. The things my boss wants me to do could put me in jail."

Margarette shook her head and squeezed Julianne's hands, "If things are as bad as you say, going to jail is the last thing you are afraid of. You aren't afraid of that. You're afraid that you aren't up to the challenge."

Julianne nodded as tears silently streamed down her cheeks. Margarette continued, "I know you. Sometimes even better than you know yourself. I'm telling you that you can do this. You can do anything your put your heart, mind, and soul into. I raised you to do anything and I know you can handle this."

Margarette took in a deep breath of the oxygen-enriched air provided by the tubes below her nostrils.

Julianne protested, "But Mama—"

Margarette cut her off, "But nothing. You think I wasn't afraid wrestling that three-hundred-pound crack head on the bus back in 2002? After he shot me—with my own gun—all I wanted to do was lay down and die. But I knew I was the only thing between that beast and the innocent people on that bus. I fought with everything I had. I can't even remember getting that gun back from him and putting him down."

Julianne said, "Mama, this is totally different."

Margarette responded, "I know. It's different and it's the same. Your beast has a different name. But it's just as mean, and it will destroy innocent people unless you do what you have to do to stop it."

Julianne took in a deep, shuddering breath and wiped the tears from her cheeks. She leaned across the table and planted a kiss on her mother's forehead. Looking her mother in the eyes she said, "You're right Mama. I'm going to fight this beast."

# CHAPTER 6

*Thursday, October 26ᵗʰ, 2028*
*9:15 PM*

After Jimmy had been waiting ten minutes, a police cruiser rolled into the parking lot with its red and blue lights flashing but no siren sounding. During that time, Jimmy had gotten himself off the asphalt and was leaning against the hood of his service van. The trickle of blood from his nose had stopped, leaving a crusty layer of dried blood on his upper lip. No one had come out of the building since his mugging.

Jimmy had placed a call to his supervisor, Nick, to let him know what happened. The hand tools were his own, but Nick was going to be pissed about the tablet. Nick's phone went to voicemail. *That sucks,* Jimmy thought. If Nick had been available, he could have logged in to the company's dispatch software and tracked the location of the tablet before it got wiped.

The police would have been able to use that information to catch these guys. However, if Nick followed his usual patterns, he would check his voicemails on his ride into work the next morning. Those thugs would be long gone and the tablet wiped clean by then.

Two officers exited the police cruiser and walked over to Jimmy. They didn't seem to be in a hurry to meet him, so Jimmy pushed off the hood of the van and walked towards the officers with his hands clearly empty and where the officers could see them.

The two officers were a study in contrasts. The driver was petite Latina with her hair pulled back in a ponytail. The officer riding shotgun was a man at least six and a half feet tall with skin as dark as night. He was holding a tablet in his left hand. Both officers had their right hands resting lightly on their service pistols as they approached Jimmy.

The female officer was the first to speak, "I'm Officer Rodriguez and this is Officer Williams. How can we help you?"

Jimmy responded, "Yeah. I got mugged by three guys. I was called here to—"

Officer Williams, clicking on the tablet with a stylus, interrupted Jimmy mid-sentence. "Please state your name and reason for being here. I gotta' put it in the form before we can take any other info."

Jimmy took a deep breath and let out an audible sigh, "Okay, no problem. My name is Jimmy, well, actually, James Brennan. I was here tonight to repair the elevators in this building that were not operating. When I left the building, three men assaulted me and stole my tools, the company tablet, and my wallet."

Officer Rodriguez asked, "Any witnesses?"

Jimmy looked around at the empty lot and asked, "Are you serious? In this neighborhood?"

Officer Williams clicked on the tablet again and said without looking up, "I'll take that as a no."

Jimmy looked at the two officers as they assessed him. Neither officer showed any interest in being there or talking to him about the crime.

Officer Rodriguez finally broke the silence by asking, "Any other details you want included on the report?"

Jimmy shook his head. He couldn't believe that these cops were trying to wrap this up already. They hadn't asked a single question about the number or description of his attackers. Jimmy remembered what the leader of the thugs had said to Jimmy right before he hit him the last time.

Jimmy said to Officer Rodriguez, "Yes, there is. The muggers were three African American men and their leader called himself Dante."

Jimmy watched as a flicker of recognition flashed in the eyes of both officers.

Officer Rodriguez asked, "Like the inferno?"

Jimmy responded, "Yeah, like the inferno. Do you know this guy?"

Officer Rodriguez told Jimmy, "Stay by your vehicle, we'll be right back."

Jimmy did as he was told and leaned against the hood of his service van. He watched as the officers stood near their cruiser and held a conversation. Officer Rodriguez seemed more animated than Officer Williams, who looked down at his partner and shook his head several times. Finally, Officer Rodriguez roughly grabbed a slip of paper printed out from the tablet Officer Williams still held. Officer Rodriguez approached Jimmy with the slip in her hand.

Jimmy asked, "What's going on? Are you going to pull the video from the camera covering the parking lot? It probably recorded the whole mugging." As Jimmy spoke, he pointed out the video camera mounted on a light pole on the perimeter of the parking lot.

Officer Rodriguez glanced to where Jimmy was pointing then looked back at Jimmy. Handing him a slip of paper that resembled a receipt from a self-service kiosk at a restaurant, she said, "Sir. Thank you for calling the Philadelphia police department. On this slip of paper, you will find an incident report. A detective will be assigned this case. Please reference the case number when you call the phone number on the bottom for the status of your case. Thank you and have a great evening."

Jimmy looked down at the paper and up at the officer twice, incredulous. He said, "That's it? That's all you're going to do?"

Officer Rodriguez looked around at the surrounding buildings. She stepped closer to Jimmy, lowered her voice, and said, "I think it's best you get in your van and drive home now."

Jimmy was about to continue his protest but the intense look on the officer's face gave him pause. He didn't know why, but it was obvious from the officers' behavior that upon hearing the mugger's name, the game had changed.

Jimmy nodded his thanks to Officer Rodriguez and retreated to the safety of his van. His ride home to the suburbs through the dark and quiet city streets was uneventful.

Jimmy didn't know who this Dante guy was, but if something about him made the police nervous, he just wanted to get home.

And never run into Dante again.

# CHAPTER 7

*Thursday, October 26ᵗʰ, 2028*
*10:15 PM*

Jimmy hung his jacket on the coat rack next to the front door. The combination family room/ living room/ dining room, which Jimmy just called the front room, was tidy and dimly lit. There hadn't been a table in the dining room area since Jimmy could remember. Instead, the space was filled by a couch and two reclining chairs facing the front wall of the house, where a large wall-mount television hung. The steps to the upstairs bedrooms and bathroom were on Jimmy's right as he shuffled toward the back of the house and the kitchen.

The kitchen was located at the rear of the house. While cozy, it was in dire need of a facelift. The linoleum floor was nearly rubbed bare in a few spots, the cabinets were a dark brown, and the appliances as old as Jimmy was. The laundry area was tucked off to the left side of the kitchen; no wall separated the cooking and sitting area from the washer, dryer, and slop sink.

The only light in the front room spilled from the gap under the door that separated the kitchen from the front room. This indicated that Jimmy's mother was still awake. Jimmy had mixed feelings about coming home in this condition with his mother still up.

His nose was swollen and tender to the touch. He had never been hit in the face before or had a broken nose, but he didn't think his nose was broken. While it was tender, it didn't explode in pain when he moved it like he thought a broken nose would do.

He was more concerned about the blow to his head and the condition of his left eye. It was swollen shut and he could feel a pulsing ache from it with every heartbeat. He could go to the hospital, but the co-pay for an emergency room visit would set him back two weeks in pay and by the time his primary care doctor could see him for an appointment, the bruising would be a distant memory.

He thought about going upstairs to the bathroom to wash up first, but the allure of an icepack on his throbbing eye made his decision for him. His plan had been to fill a bag with ice, lay it on his eye and nose, and go to sleep. The light coming from the kitchen meant his plan was scuttled and he would have to explain this to his mom right now. He braced himself for the concern—and racism—he was about to hear from his mother.

Holding the door open, Jimmy was surprised to see two women seated at the table.

He recovered quickly and smiled at the ladies sitting at the kitchen table enjoying a cup of coffee. Probably decaf. Katherine was careful not to drink anything caffeinated after dinner. Colleen's agreeably inert kiddie monitor was on the kitchen table and she and Katherine were working on the crossword his mom loved to do.

Neither woman noticed him, so Jimmy sheepishly said, "Hello ladies," his voice cracking.

Colleen was the first to look up. She gasped.

Katherine put the paper down when she saw him and cried, "Oh my dear Lord! James Paul Brennan what happened to you?"

Jimmy sank into a chair at the table. "Three guys jumped me as I was leaving my service call."

He then turned toward Colleen and added, "I wanted to fight back, but it was three on one and they were quick." He lowered his head down and looked down at his hands. His fingers and palms were rough and calloused from his work repairing elevators. He made his hands into fists and turned them over. His unscathed knuckles were a physical reminder that he hadn't fought back against the mugging.

Relaxing his hands, he shrugged and looked up. "There wasn't anything I could do."

Jimmy took a deep breath to calm himself. His anger against the muggers was slipping away. He couldn't understand what would make a man lash out and hurt another man. Jimmy didn't think he would hesitate to inflict violence on another to defend himself or a loved one, especially his mother. But to attack someone for money? No way. He could never see himself lowering his morals to that level no matter how desperate he was.

Desperation. That's why he couldn't stay angry at Dante and his cohorts. They were desperate. Jimmy saw it in the shuttered storefronts and the blank stares of the youth in that part of the city. How could he stay angry at men whose situations were unimaginable to him? While he was upset at their behavior, he found it hard to hold a grudge against them. Especially since he would, hopefully, never see them again.

No, Jimmy was upset with himself. Upset that he hadn't been more aware of his surroundings when he first pulled up to the building. Upset that he didn't find some way to fight back. Upset that

Colleen was seeing him this way: weak and beaten. If she was unsure about going on a date with him before, this surely wouldn't help her think of Jimmy as a provider and protector for her and her boys.

Colleen had put her crossword puzzle down and was observing Jimmy with a concerned expression. She reached her hand out and placed it gently on Jimmy's shoulder, "Jimmy, not everyone should be a fighter. Fighting leads to death and we can all see where that got our country." She paused, looking down, and said, "Where it got my family."

Jimmy reached for Colleen's hand and replied, "It's okay Colleen. I miss Jack too."

Before either of them could continue, Katherine pulled her chair between Colleen and Jimmy and asked him, "Did you call the police? Did they find the men who did this to you?"

A scowl darkened Katherine's face as she pursed her lips and continued, "Were the muggers black? Where they Jimmy? I told you—"

Colleen inhaled sharply and asked, "Katherine, what does it matter? Criminals come in all colors."

Jimmy couldn't handle a racist tirade from his mother right now. He pushed himself away from the table, retrieved a Ziploc baggie, and started to fill it with ice cubes from the freezer.

With his back turned to his mom, he answered, "Colleen's right, it doesn't matter what color they were, Mom. They were desperate men and I should have been more aware of my surroundings."

Jimmy continued, "And yes, I called the police and no, they didn't catch the muggers. The muggers took almost everything. My wallet, my tool bag, and worst of all, the company tablet. My boss is going to be pissed about the tablet. I'll probably have that docked from my next few paychecks. The tools are no big deal; I have another set of just about everything around the house. But I am not looking forward to going to the Department of Motor Vehicles to get another driver's license issued. I would just as soon take another beating than rot in line at the DMV."

Jimmy's comment about the DMV elicited a chuckle from Colleen. Jimmy smiled, momentarily distracted from his pain. He liked to make people laugh. Hopefully, it was an ample distraction from his mother's comments. It was hard for Jimmy to reconcile the blind hatred of racism with the love and care his mother had always shown him. It just didn't make sense. And while he could love her anyway, he knew most people wouldn't see anything but her racism.

Katherine watched Jimmy with a scowl on her face. He knew she had more to say about the incident. He hoped she would at least choose her words carefully with Colleen in the kitchen.

As Jimmy sat down, Colleen took the ice bag from Jimmy and gently placed it on his upturned face. He made sure not to wince, as the pressure of the ice bag against his wounds spiked the pain in his face. However, within seconds the numbing effect of the ice overwhelmed the discomfort from the pressure. Jimmy leaned further back in his chair, his face to the ceiling so the bag would stay in place without him having to hold it.

The ladies discussed the danger of the city for a few minutes as Jimmy rested with the bag of ice covering most of his face.

Finally, Katherine patted Jimmy's shoulder and asked, "What are they doing to find your stuff and put those men behind bars?"

Jimmy slightly shrugged and answered, "Probably nothing. That part of the city is run by a gangster, Aaron, who formed what he calls the Southwest Militia. You can tell 'cause every building is tagged with SWM. Once I told the police the name of the leader of the guys who mugged me, they couldn't get out of there fast enough. My gut tells me that those guys are in the Southwest Militia and the cops aren't going to do a thing against them."

Colleen stood behind her chair and asked the question that had been bothering Jimmy the whole ride home. "I thought you told me they didn't attack people who repaired their buildings? Why did this happen to you? Didn't they know who you were?"

Jimmy nodded, "You're right. I've been thinking about that. The folks in that part of town call us 'civilians' and usually Aaron and his militia enforce a zero-tolerance policy on any kind of attack on us. These guys either went off the reservation, in which case they have more to fear from Aaron than the police, if he finds out; or, maybe things are getting so bad that the SWM is allowing its people to branch out. I don't know this Aaron guy, but from what I've heard, he is smart. I doubt he would allow his folks to hurt the people that keep his neighborhoods running, so I don't know why this happened."

Katherine was clearly agitated by this turn in the conversation, "Jimmy. I don't care who those hooligans are. They need to be punished. I am going to call Lieutenant Brady and make sure they are dealt with."

Jimmy, who was relaxing to the point of falling asleep, slowly responded, "Okay Mom. Call Brady. But it won't do any good. He's a township cop in Upper Darby, not Philly. I'm as big a fan of John as you are, but there is nothing he can do."

Not to be deterred, Katherine responded, "Well that won't stop me from trying."

Nearly fading into sleep right there in the kitchen chair, Jimmy said, "Okay, Mom, stand down. I'll call John and see if he can help me. If nothing else, maybe he knows someone at the DMV so I don't have to waste a whole day down there."

Katherine was gearing up to ask another question when Colleen cleared her throat, "Katherine, how about letting Jimmy get up to his bed? He is about to fall asleep right here in the kitchen."

Jimmy grunted in approval and slowly rose from his chair, "That's a great idea." Seeing his mother about to grab his arm to help support him, Jimmy stood up taller, ignoring the pulsing beat of pain in his face from the sudden movement and the removal of the ice bag, which he was now holding by his side. He continued, "I'm fine. I'll just take this ice bag with me upstairs and call it a night. I need to get to work early tomorrow to deal with the tablet issue. Nick is going to be pissed. Good night, ladies."

Jimmy gave his mom his customary peck on the top of her head. Then he paused, looking at Colleen. After a moment of indecision, he reached out towards Colleen with the arm not holding the ice and leaned in for a hug. Colleen leaned into Jimmy and reciprocated. They pulled back simultaneously after a moment.

The pain in his face forgotten, Jimmy smiled and nodded at Colleen as he left the kitchen and headed through the front room and up the stairs to bed.

# CHAPTER 8

*Friday, October 27ᵗʰ, 2028*
*3:35 PM*

Reggie thought of himself as a simple man. He liked his job and was proud of the work he did. Driving a trash truck for the City was his dream job. Eight hours a day, five days a week. He'd been running the same route for the past six years. He knew some people looked down on him, considered him the low man on the totem pole in life. But they didn't know shit. He thought to himself, *I gotta' job where I get to see all kinds of different things every day, know when I start and when I'm done, know where I'm going, what I'm doing, ain't got nobody telling me what to do, and I get to listen to the radio all day.*

Reggie also liked that what he did made a difference in the world. In his mind, he wasn't a trash man. He was one of the blue-collar warriors that kept the streets from going to shambles. It wasn't glamorous work, but it needed to be done and he was happy to do it.

And today was the best day of the week. Friday. Payday. *Getting paid a fair wage for a fair day's work is what life is all about,* Reggie thought. *I think that's even written in the Bible somewhere.*

Reggie parked his truck. He liked the sound of that—his truck. The City owned it but he had over twenty thousand hours on it, all his from the first day the truck was delivered. It was one of the first models with the automatic bin loader on it, making a second person on the truck to load the trash bins unneeded. It had also been retrofitted with a GPS tracker soon after he got it. The air brakes were a just a bit soft on today's route. He'd tell the mechanic about it when he got back to the office.

Reggie climbed out of the truck's cab and headed over to punch out and pick up his pay for the week.

Strange to see guys gathered in front of the office. Usually, guys got their pay and hit the bricks as soon as possible. No need to hang out around the yard, especially on Friday.

"Hey Burt. What's happening, Mick?" Reggie said as he approached two other drivers.

Burt looked up from the paperwork he was holding. "Beats the hell outta' me Reg. You best just go in and see for yourself." Mick looked at Burt and said, "This ain't right man. It just ain't right."

Reggie patted Mick on the shoulder as he passed him without breaking stride. "You'll be alright. It's Friday, what could be so bad?"

Reggie found out when he walked into the office. A hulk of a man was blocking the service counter where the pay clerk sat. Reggie knew the man well—the yard mechanic, Jackson. He was yelling at the pay clerk and the shift manager, clenching his pay envelope in his right hand. "I didn't just fix half the trucks I was supposed to this week! I fixed all of them. Now you gotta' pay me all the money you owe me for my work!"

The pay clerk looked like a doe in headlights. The manager, Mr. Cannon, walked up behind Emily's chair at the service counter, cleared his throat and said, in as a calm a voice as possible, "Look Jackson. This isn't our doing. We got a memo this morning from City Hall. I'm sure this will get sorted out in due time. Just keep the IOU and when we get more instructions, I'm sure we will all get paid."

Emily jumped when Jackson's meatloaf of a fist slammed down on the counter. "This is bullshit! I'm going to all the TV stations. Screw that, I'm going to the mayor's office myself. He oughtta' know better than to fool with people like me."

Reggie had never seen Jackson so revved up before. He had known the mechanic since high school when Jackson's family moved to his block, two doors down from his row house. Jackson ran with a tough crowd back then, got himself in a jam, and his choice was jail or the Marines. From what Reggie heard, Jackson did a tour in the Syrian conflict fighting ISIS, Syria, and Russia all at once. Freakin' mess. Jackson was sent back to the US for some special training and then did a tour in the Ukraine in one of the Marine's force recon units. Jackson's dad used to brag about his son, telling Reggie that Jackson was one badass Marine, even if there were some disciplinary problems during his service.

Reggie didn't like to see anyone this worked up, especially someone capable of so much violence. He walked to Jackson's side. "Jackie. Calm down man. Don't do nothing you gonna' regret. We'll figure this out. We are the people that make this city run. They'll come to their senses right quick."

Jackson took a huge breath and straightened his frame to his full height, well over six feet. He slowly turned his head toward Reggie. In that instant Reggie had no idea if Jackson was going to clobber him or talk to him. Luckily for Reggie, Jackson spoke. "Reggie. I know you a peacemaker and you done right by me and my family with all the shit I put everyone through back in the day. But you don't know what you're talking about here, man. This is fucked up."

Reggie looked Jackson in the eye and could see the rage dissipating. "I know Jackie, you're right. You okay if you wait for me outside and I'll figure out what's going on, then we can talk it out?"

Jackson smiled at Reggie as a parent would smile at a child offering his piggy bank to help make a mortgage payment before the house went into foreclosure. "Sure Reggie. You figure things out then let us know the deal." Jackson turned and took two quick long strides to the door. He grasped the handle and flung it open. The knob buried itself in the drywall. Then he stepped through the doorway and grabbed the door on the way out, slamming it so hard part of the molding on the frame popped off.

Emily jumped again and let out a frightened squeal. Without saying a word, she fled to the ladies' room.

Reggie looked at Mr. Cannon and said, "What the hell was Jackie talking about? IOU's?"

Mr. Cannon found Reggie's check and handed it to him. "I honestly don't know Reggie. We got a memo from City Hall this morning before we ran payroll that everybody, me included, is to be paid half our wage and get other half in the form of IOU's."

Reggie took the two documents out of the envelope. The paycheck had about half, actually a little less than half, of the usual pay on it, because of taxes and union dues; and the other half of the pay was an official-looking financial document that said, "By the Good Faith and Standing of the City of Philadelphia, this warrant will be paid by the Treasurer of Philadelphia . . ."

Reggie and Mr. Cannon locked eyes before Mr. Cannon finally lowered his. "Look, Reggie. I appreciate you keeping Jackson from doing something stupid. But what am I supposed to do? I'm in the same boat. The memo was specific about one thing though. Take real good care of them IOU's. There will be no replacements issued if they are lost or stolen."

"Alright, Mr. C. Thanks for being straight up with me. Like I said, I'm sure this will get sorted out right quick."

Reggie left the office and expected to see his co-workers out front where he left them. Somewhat to his relief, they were gone. He didn't really have a handle on the situation anyway, so he'd been a little worried about what he would have said. But it didn't matter now.

*Oh well.*

*Time to catch the bus home.*

# CHAPTER 9

*Friday, October 27th, 2028*
*4:10 PM*

Reggie's four-mile bus ride home was nothing out of the ordinary. Most people were using their smartphones with audio buds jammed into their ears. Forget that. Reggie liked to hear the engine working and the gears whining. Music to his ears. He did pick up a few snippets of the word "IOU." But there was none of the passion displayed back at the yard office.

The bus let him off at Woodland Avenue, at a shopping plaza. About a five block walk from his home on Springfield Avenue. This was the best part of Reggie's routine. Cash his check, get some lottery tickets, and an ice-cold bottle of beer. Well, not quite beer. Reggie took pride in the fact that he hadn't had a drink since his beloved wife Malynne succumbed to cancer. He knew right there and then after the funeral that it wasn't about him anymore. He had to tighten the ship and get on the straight and narrow. So instead, Reggie enjoyed a Friday afternoon old-fashioned root beer.

Reggie never drank his root beer on the walk home. Not until he was comfortably in his favorite Barcalounger would he crack open the root beer and work on his lottery tickets. Sometimes waiting for something a little bit makes it a little sweeter than it would have been chugging it the second he bought it.

As Reggie approached the check cashing storefront, he was amazed to see how many people were in the place. Usually only a couple of old-timers like him were in there; most people nowadays went to the bank or just used their phones. But after the crash of 2020, Reggie didn't trust the banks anymore. He figured three crashes in his life were enough, thank you very much.

This last one in '20 was the worst. They actually told everyone how much money a day you could take out of your bank account. Right here in America. That was enough for Reggie. Now he got his cash every week and took care of things that way. It was more troublesome to pay some bills, but at least he knew his money was safe.

Reggie opened the door and was immediately met by the shrill voice of an upset woman at the counter. "What do you mean? You're going to give me fifty dollars for my one-hundred-dollar IOU? That's against the law!"

The proprietor responded in his musical middle-eastern voice, "No, it is not against any law, Madam. I am not making you sell me your IOU. It is your choice. You can keep it and the City will pay you back when it can, or you can sell it to me today for fifty cents on the dollar. That is my offer."

The woman, still visibly upset, responded, "But I need to eat now. I can't wait for the City to decide to pay me some weeks or months from now."

"I understand, Madam, and I want to help you. But if I buy that IOU from you today, I am accepting the risk of when and how much the City will pay back on its IOU. What if they pay it back two years from now? What if they only pay back sixty cents on the dollar? I am giving you cash today and accepting the risk. I need to be compensated for this." The proprietor spoke evenly but firmly.

The woman placed the IOU on the counter and signed it over to the check-cashing store. "I don't know what the hell you're trying to say. Just give me the money." She slid the IOU through the slot in the bulletproof Lexan window.

The proprietor grunted in agreement, inspected the signature on the IOU, then counted out fifty dollars and slid it to her.

After a few more patrons, Reggie stepped up to the window. "Hey Mr. Gupta. The usual please. Although, my check is smaller than usual too."

Mr. Gupta smiled and replied, "No problem Reggie. Would you like to cash in your IOU also? As you heard, I give one dollar for every two dollars on the IOU."

"Hell no Mr. G. That there is a sucker's play. I been savin' some beans for a day like this and I don't spend much on stuff anyhow. The City will make this right. You just watch."

"Alright, Reggie, here is your money. See you next week."

Reggie pocketed the money and walked next door to the package store. He bought his root beer and his usual line up of scratch-off lottery tickets. Reggie knew the lottery tickets were a waste of money, but it was fun to do the scratch-offs and sometimes he won some money. He knew he would never hit it big though. No way "the man" would allow him to win that much money. Reggie figured they had it rigged so he would win a little every now and then to keep him playing. Just like a casino.

The walk home was usually uneventful. Reggie was always friendly and said hi to everyone he met. He never had problems with the kids hanging on the corners. *Well,* thought Reggie, *guess that's one benefit of my son being a gangbanger.*

He sighed. It was Friday. No time for agonizing over things he couldn't change. He was determined to enjoy his walk home as much as possible.

He pushed the thought of Dante as much to the side as he could.

# CHAPTER 10

*Friday, October 27th, 2028*
*4:35 PM*

Julianne perched her chin on her steepled fingers, elbows firmly planted on her desk. Cell phone silenced, desk phone forwarded to a voicemail box that was too loaded to accept new messages, office door closed. She closed the financial portal software for the City while a local news website played, low volume, on her computer screen.

From this vantage point, she could look out of her office window in the Municipal Services Building and see the Schuylkill River to the south and the Delaware River to the east. She couldn't quite see where the two rivers merged down near the old shipyards, which didn't really bother her, since they weren't much to look at. It was enough for her to know that the two muddy, polluted rivers did indeed merge before opening up into the Delaware Bay and then the Atlantic Ocean.

She imagined herself on the water, looking up at the buildings and overpasses as she silently floated by. How sweet it would be to let the current carry her away from the city with its noise, filth, and problems.

Shaking her head to clear the daydream, she focused on the three framed photos on the wall opposite the entry door to her office. Mama in her service uniform, the mayor of Philadelphia, and the President of the United States. Julianne only respected one of the three—a great statistic for a batting average; not so good for influential people in her life.

Mama would point out the foolishness of her floating daydream. Too many dead people in that river to bump into, and the toxins and bacteria in the river would eat her alive and require intravenous antibiotics for a week to fight the infections.

Typically, Friday afternoon at work was a time to wind down and plan her activities for the following week. Not this week though. Her brain felt like what she imagined a prize fighter experienced after winning a fifteen-round slugfest. Not physically, of course, but the mental blows felt just as damaging.

But Julianne was still on her feet. She recalled the conversation with the mayor at the beginning of the week. So far, she had implemented most of what the mayor had ordered. The one thing she had not done and would not do was to "fudge," as he said it, the numbers. Her mother had raised Julianne with a zero tolerance policy on lying, cheating, and stealing. They were the three prongs on the devil's pitchfork, Mama liked to say.

Tuesday had started with an emergency meeting of City Council. Julianne scared the seventeen members into a passing a twenty percent cost reduction mandate, to be implemented by Julianne's office. Since the city spent most of its money on payroll, that meant furloughing or laying employees off. The measure only passed by a one-vote margin, but a win is a win. Julianne walked the ordinance from the council chamber to the mayor and he signed it without even reading it. The ordinance exempted police and fire, but everything else was fair game.

By Wednesday, all the department heads and union representatives were screaming bloody murder. Death threats barraged her by the dozens. The death threats were frightening at first, but she wasn't going to let them deter her. Julianne viewed the death threats and the loud, angry, sometimes hysterical calls from the various city department heads as a counterpunch from her opponent. She knew that this fight would not be without casualties. She knew these cuts were hurting real people. But if they didn't make the cuts, many more would be hurt.

While the reduction in payroll costs would get the city's finances on a sustainable footing, those benefits wouldn't take place overnight. It would take three to four weeks for the full effect of the savings to kick in.

And then yesterday, Julianne had dropped the second major bomb in this conflict: The issuing of partial IOUs to city employees for their paychecks. Her plan called for most employees to get half of their normal paycheck and the other half in an IOU. Julianne projected being able to make full payroll and start paying back those IOUs about six weeks after the cuts. Hopefully, a short enough time frame that no one would lose their home, rental, or car because of a missed payment.

To say it was a quick turnaround was an understatement—the IOUs were being sent out today, just a day after she announced the decision. She'd made the announcement yesterday afternoon at a stand-up meeting of as many department heads as she could muster, considering she had only called the meeting that morning. Twenty or so long-time civil servants who had risen through the ranks to leadership positions filled the seats and lined the wall in the finance department's large conference room on the upper floor of the Municipal Services Building. The reaction of the leaders upon her announcement of the IOUs was not what Julianne had expected. She had expected anger, rage, and possibly even physical confrontation. She was girded and ready for anything.

Instead, her announcement was met with laughter.

That response scared her more than the spectrum of irate responses she'd prepared herself for. It reminded Julianne of a parable she heard as a child of a king raising the taxes on his subjects to bring in more money. The first round of tax raises was met with disapproval and resentment. The king wasn't concerned by the response, so he ordered a second round of tax increases. This caused an angry and indignant response from the people, who stopped just short of rioting.

Then, against the advice of all of his advisors, the king ordered yet further tax raises. This time, his subjects took to the streets in laughter. He finally began to realize he had pushed too far when he saw the people laughing at the ridiculous and unrealistic burden his latest tax increase had imposed.

Julianne wondered the same thing. Had she pushed too far? Was the tough medicine she was implementing too strong? Would she end up killing the patient before her efforts could turn the situation around?

She looked at her watch. It was nearly five p.m. All of the checks, IOUs, direct deposits, and pay stubs should have been distributed to all of the city's employees. She glanced down at her laptop once more before closing it. The headline alert banner on the local news website splashed an emergency alert that the city was now issuing IOUs to its employees. Julianne was about to click the headline to see how wrong the reporter got the details of the program when she heard shouting outside her office.

Julianne closed her laptop and stood up from her desk. She didn't know what the commotion was, but she wasn't going to deal with it sitting on her ass. She was about to step toward her office door, and the shouting, when the door slammed open.

In rushed Larry Roosevelt, the Managing Director of the city and the mayor's right-hand man. As Managing Director, all the departments responsible for the operations of the city reported to him. That meant parks and rec, police, fire, transportation, licenses and inspections, the streets department, etc. If Julianne was essentially the city's Chief Financial Officer, he was its Chief Operating Officer.

Larry was the only white guy on Mayor Rhodes' cabinet. He was about average height but had broad shoulders, a thick neck, and a nose that had been broken a few times. Julianne recalled an interview he once gave, where he shared how he'd grown up in the row house next to Bill Rhodes and they were childhood friends from day one. Bill the smart one, the schemer, the planner; Larry the one who made sure no one messed with Bill. Larry then got a scholarship to wrestle at Drexel while Bill went to school next door at the University of Pennsylvania. When a news photographer was taking some shots of the mayor's first cabinet meeting, where Larry was sitting to the right of Mayor Rhodes, he remarked out loud that the two made an "Odd Couple," and the name had stuck.

That memory brought a shade of a smile to Julianne's lips even as Larry approached her desk. Veins pulsed in his neck and there was white spittle on the corners of his mouth. Larry balled both hands into fists, landing them both on the edge of Julianne's desk so that his thick arms looked like pillars. He leaned his red face forward and spat, "What in the hell do you find so funny? Do you know what you have done to me, to the city? IOUs? Seriously? What's next, bartering? I've got half a mind to jump over this desk and wipe that look right off your face."

Julianne could feel the adrenaline coursing through her body as her fight or flight instinct kicked into overdrive. Her throat constricted, vision narrowed, and sweat started to bead on the skin along her hairline. Just as she was about to respond to Larry, her administrative assistant, whom Julianne had just told that she would be cut down to thirty hours next week, popped her head around the door jamb leading to Julianne's office and tentatively asked, "Ms. Barnes? Should I call security?"

Julianne knew it was a risk to take her eyes off Larry; it might give him an opening to make good on his threat. But she also knew that she needed to diffuse the situation. Julianne calmly turned to address her assistant and said, "No, thank you, Nancy. Please close the door to my office so that Mr. Roosevelt and I can have a private discussion."

Turning to the agitated pit bull across her desk she said, "Larry, I know I don't need to explain to you how we got here or what mistakes were made over the years. But you need to trust me that the changes we are making will keep the city from total collapse."

Larry snorted in response, "Trust you? I barely know you. You've been on the job for six months. I have no idea why the mayor appointed you in the first place. And 'we' didn't make these changes, you did. I am going to make sure that every worker being laid off or getting an IOU knows your name when they can't feed their kids or make rent. Just because you wanted to save some money."

Larry's accusation fueled an anger that Julianne had been feeling ever since she got her promotion and began digging into the City's finances. The years of negligence and the cavalier attitude of those preceding her regarding the financial train wreck that the City was heading towards disgusted her to the core. If any of the preceding administrations had made some tough choices years ago to implement fiscal discipline, the draconian measures she was taking now would not be needed. They'd just left it to her to clean this mess up.

She leaned forward to mirror Larry's aggressive posture and responded, "I know that we will all face hardship because of what I'm doing. Do you think I want to fight this fight? We couldn't have made payroll this week. The cuts in personnel I implemented will right-size the city government so that its expenses match its revenue."

She took a breath and Larry interrupted, reaching into the breast pocket of his suit jacket. He pulled out a city-issued IOU with his name on it. With the exceptions of his name and the promised amount, it matched the IOU on Julianne's desk. Waving the paper in front of Julianne's face he said, "Then explain this? What the hell does issuing IOUs have to do with right-sizing the government?"

Julianne didn't back down. "The cuts don't save money immediately. We had to issue these IOUs until the costs savings kick in and we can build up cash. I am trying to do this without borrowing more money, but that still may be necessary to bridge our short-term needs."

Larry pocketed his IOU and turned away from Julianne. He strode past the small conference table in Julianne's office and stood in front of the window, looking out over the city. Speaking into the glass he said, "So instead of taking out more loans, you decided to destroy the lives of hundreds if, not thousands, of city workers. Great move Julianne."

Julianne considered walking around her desk and joining Larry at the window. She decided against it, instead using the bulk of her desk to provide a physical barrier between them. She wanted to tell

Larry that he didn't know what the hell he was talking about. That issuing bonds and taking out loans was what got the city into its current mess. Julianne had called a couple investment banks in New York during the week to feel them out on what terms she could get on behalf of the City. The interest rates on the quotes for issuing the city more debt were sky high. The City would never be able to make the payments, even with the cuts Julianne had enforced.

Instead Julianne countered more mildly, "I called New York to get quotes on loans, Larry, and if we took their money now, with the interest rates they would charge us, it would leave us in worse shape within months."

Julianne watched as Larry rolled his shoulders and cracked his neck twice by leaning his ears one at a time to each shoulder. Julianne was reminded of fighters getting ready for a bout. The menacing action caused Julianne's heart to pump frantically and she found herself glancing at the door to see if she could make it out before Larry acted. Larry took one final deep breath and turned on his heels. His face was calm but his eyes burned into Julianne with murderous intent. Julianne's breath caught in her chest.

Larry walked back to the front of Julianne's desk. He slowly raised his right hand in a fist and brought it within inches of Julianne's face. It took all of Julianne's inner strength not to flinch or look away. Instead she straightened her shoulders further and locked her eyes directly with Larry's.

Larry extended his pointer finger so that the tip was within an inch of Julianne's nose. Slowly and barely above a whisper he said, "You are going down for this. Watch your back."

Abruptly he withdrew his hand, turned, and strode quickly to the door, letting himself out.

Julianne released the breath she had been holding and placed her hands on her desk to keep herself from crumpling into her chair. Her earlier satisfaction of "winning" the first round of this fight was a foolish indulgence. She hadn't won anything. She might not agree with Larry, but she didn't blame him. And he was right. She would need to watch her back.

There was going to be a full cabinet meeting at the mayor's office Monday morning. Usually, she looked forward to the meetings as a way to get to know the other leaders in the city, especially Police Chief Braxton. But now her thoughts about the meeting were colored with dread and the uncertainty of what Larry would have waiting for her there.

# CHAPTER 11

*Friday, October 27ᵗʰ, 2028*
*5:05 PM*

Reggie unlocked the door to his row house and entered his home. The acrid smell of burnt chemicals hit him once he was halfway to the kitchen. His smile, leftover from his pleasant walk home, quickly faded. His temper rose. He knew what that smell was.

Dante, his son, was here. And he was smoking crack cocaine.

Channeling his anger, he called in a loud, stern voice, "Dante, I told you not to bring dope into my home and I can smell you been smoking it in here too."

Silence. Reggie continued to walk back to the kitchen, his grip tightening on the root beer. Not much of a weapon but better than nothing, if he had to use it. Reggie pushed open the swinging door to the kitchen and saw his fool son sitting at the table with ear buds in, listening to music on his phone. He had also poured himself a huge bowl of cereal, though the spilt flakes and milk on the table threatening to cascade to the floor betrayed his limited success. Reggie looked at the bottle in his hand. Not that he would ever actually hurt his son, but he did briefly fantasize about breaking the bottle over the dumb-ass boy's head. Would be a terrible waste of root beer though.

Instead, Reggie walked to the opposite side of the small round table, pulled a chair out, turned it around, and sat down straddling the chair back to face the table. None of this caused Dante to look up. Reggie sat and stared at his son.

Finally, Dante raised his head and their eyes locked. Reggie noticed his son's pupils were dilated, a sure sign the boy was high as a kite.

"Dante. Dante! Take them damn things out of your ears and listen to me."

Dante slowly reached a hand to each ear and removed the ear buds. Reggie could hear the tinny sound of ghetto rap emanating from the small speakers.

"Son," Reggie said, trying to maintain a calm and measured voice, "What are you doing here?"

"Hey Dad, I got hungry so I helped myself. You alright with that?" Dante replied.

"Dante. I want to know why you are here and why you are smoking your dope in my home." Though still measured, his tone was edged with steel.

Reggie noticed an instantaneous flare of rage in Dante's eyes before it was replaced by the cunning look of a car salesman trying to sell a coupe to a family of six.

"Dad, ain't nobody on the street talk to me like that—"

Reggie cut Dante off mid-sentence and said, "Boy, you are in my home. Not on the street. I need to know why you are here and what you were thinking bringing—and then *smoking*—dope in my house." His voice rose slightly. "You know neither of them things are allowed under my roof."

"Alright Pop, you win. Me and my crew jacked a civilian last night near Market Street and I figured it would be smart to get off the street for a little while."

Reggie's eyes bulged and his jawed tightened. He looked at his son until Dante looked away.

When he spoke, Reggie's voice was quiet, "Son. You know I love you and I did what I could for you after your mom passed away." His tone hardened. "But you crossed the line this time. You brought dope into my home and you are using my home as a shelter for you to hide away after you jacked somebody. And not just somebody. A civilian!"

Reggie leaned back, rubbed his face, then continued, "You know that's going to bring heat down from the police. And if they don't catch you, your man Aaron and his enforcers . . . I don't even want to think about it. You know Aaron don't allow no one to go beating or stealing from civilians. Everyone knows that. You need to clean yourself up, get a job like the rest of us. Stop living off the government. Where do you think the government gets its money? From taxes of working people. Like me."

Reggie watched as his son's dope-saturated brain tried to process the conversation. A cunning smiled emerged from the fog and Dante replied, "Dad. Aaron ain't going to find out what I been up to. And I served my country, did you?"

Reggie replied, "You know I never served in the military if that's what you're saying, but I serve the people of this city everyday."

"Dad, that ain't the same. I got hurt in the Army in the Ukraine. Now the government owes me and I will take what they're giving. I got disability payments coming every week. I'd be a fool to go to work and kill that."

"Son, you and I both know you hurt yourself when a crate of MREs fell on your foot. Now I ain't trying to downplay your service, but there is dignity in work. I seen you walk. Heck, I seen you run! You can do any kind of job you want. I can call some people I know to get you in somewhere. You got to stop jacking people and living on the street. It ain't going to end well."

"Dad, I ain't never going to be like Rose and you know it, so don't try to put that on me."

Reggie paused for a moment. It was true he was proud of his daughter Roseate. Her mother named her after a bird she saw in Florida on their honeymoon. Rose was in her junior year at Chestnut Hill College, across the city in a real nice section. Reggie liked to visit Rose at school and encouraged her to stay there on weekends or travel to a friend's home on longer breaks to steer clear of the bad influences in this neighborhood.

Finally, Reggie spoke. "You're my son. I don't want nothing bad to happen to you. But you can't stay here bringing drugs and crime into my home. You get yourself cleaned up and get yourself a job, and you can stay here as long as you want. But right now, you finish up your cereal, grab your stuff, and get gone."

Dante dropped the spoon in the cereal and stared hard and long at Reggie. Reggie returned the stare, boring his eyes into his son's. Dante finally broke the standoff, slowly stood up and shrugged on his jacket.

"Alright old man. If that's the way you want to play it. Kick your own flesh out on the streets when he needs your help the most."

Before Reggie could say anything, Dante opened the back door of the kitchen, stepped through, and slammed it shut.

*Damn*, thought Reggie. *That's the second door been slammed on me in one day.*

Reggie hated the thought of throwing his only son out of his home and onto the streets. Part of him wished he could give his son a long enveloping hug and make his problems go away. But the time for that was long past. He knew if he kept giving his son handouts, Dante would never learn. Reggie just hoped nothing bad would happen to him in the meantime—the street was a hard teacher.

Reggie looked around at the mess Dante had left in his kitchen, then proceeded to clean it up before he retreated to the family room. He sat in his favorite chair, took a swig of his root beer, and started in on his lottery tickets.

# CHAPTER 12

*Sunday, October 29th, 2028*
*9:00 PM*

Aaron stared at the blank screen of his smart phone. It was almost time to make the call.

Turning the phone over in his hand, his mind wandered back five years ago to his barracks in Corpus Christi, Texas. He was back in the states from four straight deployments in the Ukraine for advanced weapon systems training.

He had just finished a set of sixty pushups, thereby winning a bet with a bunkmate, when a lieutenant colonel in the Army walked into the musty dorm unannounced.

Aaron's initial reaction was annoyance—as a newly minted Marine Sergeant, he was the alpha male in this barracks. Officers wisely stayed away from the enlisted quarters, especially officers from a different branch in the military.

Aaron snapped to his feet and stood at attention, sweat glistening on his light brown skin. As his eyes met the colonel's, his hand, arcing towards his brow automatically for a proper salute, stopped abruptly before reaching its destination.

Aaron was looking at a face he had last seen fifteen years ago when resource officers from the Philadelphia police department were pulling him and his brother apart, their mother dead on the kitchen floor, their father in handcuffs.

He'd barely had time to register the face before his brother had him in a bear hug.

The night of their mother's murder by a father they barely knew, the foster system separated the brothers. Randall, Aaron's elder by four years, won the lottery: placed in a nice neighborhood with a caring family who began the adoption process almost immediately—nearly unheard of for a twelve-year-old boy from a tough neighborhood. Once the adoption was complete, Randall's new family moved to Texas, where Randall eventually attended college on an ROTC scholarship. Randall's exemplary service in several theaters in the Middle East, along with some fortunate wartime promotions, allowed him to attain the rank of lieutenant colonel in a time span unheard of during times of peace.

Aaron was not so lucky and bounced from one abusive fostering situation to another until when he was eighteen and faced a choice—ten years in prison for assault with a deadly weapon, or join the Marines.

Aaron's reunion with his brother, Randall, had been brief—Aaron was slated to leave the base in Corpus Christi in two weeks for his return to the war in the Ukraine. The brothers used what time they had to fill in the missing years and to come up with a plan for their futures.

Looking at his phone again, Aaron noted it was time to make the call. He opened the encrypted app that the secessionists had developed and entered in a string of twenty-four characters. If Randall did not enter the exact same code within two minutes of Aaron inputting his code, the app would not connect the call.

Aaron assumed the NSA listened to every call in the United States (and beyond, for that matter). But he'd been assured that this app would make the conversation undecipherable. While the federal government was hamstrung with all of the international wars and internal turmoil, Aaron didn't want to attract more attention than he was already getting from the government after the siege at the docks to retrieve his most recent shipment. If they found out where those arms were going, it could make his goal unreachable.

The status indicator on the app turned green. Randall had logged in over seventeen hundred miles away. Randall hit the "connect" button and waited. The app took about half a minute to establish a secure connection and there was about a five second delay in the audio, making conversations slow and frustrating. Aaron and Randall had developed a work-around to their conversation flow like the radio operators of yesteryear.

Aaron: Hey brother. Everything is sunny here in Philadelphia. What's your status? Over.

A few seconds later, the response came back.

Randall: All good Aaron. Things are tight, but we are making progress. I heard you had some trouble with a shipment a couple weeks back. Everything ok? Over.

Aaron: Yeah. Ran into some heat that we had to dispatch. Nothing I couldn't handle though. If it was a regular shipment, I would have let it go, but we had some serious hardware in this shipment. In fact, it's headed your way tomorrow. You're gonna' like this one. Over.

Randall: Aaron. Listen up. I want you to keep that shipment. You're going to need it. Go to our file drop location and pick up the latest zip file. You'll see a new target. You make this score and get it in my hands, this conflict will be done and you'll be here like we discussed. Over.

Aaron paused, looking quizzically at the phone in his hands. Even though the app encrypted their conversation, he and his brother were careful not to divulge too much direct information in these monthly calls. Usually, he knew exactly what Randall was saying even using the evasive language. But this time, Aaron had no idea what his brother was talking about.

This shipment had more firepower in it than the last five combined; Randall should be drooling at the prospect of using the arms against the federal government. Also, what was the nature of this new target, that it would require that kind of firepower and bring a successful end to Texas' secession from the Union?

Only one way to find out.

Aaron: Copy that. Will receive the new target package and proceed accordingly. Over and out.

Aaron turned off the cell phone and removed the battery and sim card.

Then he turned in his chair and fired up his laptop. After a few minutes of navigating and entering passcodes, he downloaded the new target information.

Aaron opened the file and let out a low whistle. His brother wasn't joking. He would need the weapons in the last shipment and then some to hit this target. Getting into the building itself would be a challenge, but possible. The hard part would be to keep various law enforcement elements from responding to his raid and pinning him down. Even harder would be to transport the product from the building back to his headquarters. The building was nestled in Center City Philadelphia and Aaron's stronghold was on the other side of the Schuylkill River in Southwest Philadelphia, about two miles away.

Randall's idea for getting the package from Philadelphia to Texas was ingenious in its simplicity.

Aaron spent the next three hours studying and printing the floor plans of the building, the nearby street configurations, and the locations of the local, state and federal law enforcement agencies near the target.

Aaron's planning was interrupted by a light rapping on his office door. "Come in," Aaron called.

The door opened and Booker poked his head in. "Boss, some big cat calling himself Jackson wants to see you. Said you two go way back. What you want me to do?"

Several gears clicked into place all at once as Aaron thought about the possibility of Jackson joining the Southwest Militia. Aaron replied, "Booker. You done good. Show Jackson proper respect and bring him in."

Booker nodded and disappeared, closing the door behind him. A few moments later, there was a solid knock at Aaron's door and Jackson walked in. Aaron got up from his chair and the two men stared each other down. Booker started to tense up, not understanding what was going on. Just as Booker was about to draw his pistol, Aaron broke into a huge smile, lunged forward, and hugged the larger man. Jackson laughed and hugged Aaron back.

Aaron turned to the now visibly relieved Booker and said, "Thanks Book. Me and Jackie need some time for a parley."

Booker left the office for a second time. Aaron looked at Jackie and said, "Damn man. You're bigger than when I saw you after our last tour. I know you been fixing trucks for the City. Are you bench pressing them too?"

Jackson laughed again and said, "No, just been eating good and working out. You know what I'm talking about."

"Alright Jackie. That's good. Now why are you here? I thought you told me you were going straight. 'No nonsense' if I remember the conversation."

Jackie looked Aaron straight in the eyes. "I want back in."

Jackson was the best Marine he had ever seen in a firefight. Aaron recalled several times that Jackson's valor had seen his platoon through situations Aaron thought he would never survive. Jackson was also a monster in hand-to-hand combat. But most important, Jackson was a mechanical genius. He could fix or fabricate just about anything he got his hands on. That would tip the scales in Aaron's favor as he thought about the target package he had just been working on.

Aaron had made a lot of money in the Ukraine betting on Jackson when they were behind the front lines and had time to set up some mixed martial arts prize fights in the one camp they shared with a few units of Ukrainian irregular forces. Aaron would never forget the time Jackson knocked out a three-hundred-pound monster Ukrainian with one punch. Word was the Ukrainian was an Olympic wrestler (when they still did the Olympics), and the guy never saw the punch coming. Jackson hit him right on the button and the guy folded like a cheap pup tent. Aaron had made sure he took care of Jackson with some special goods he'd smuggled into the Ukraine and Jackson had provided Aaron the muscle he needed to grow his operations.

Aaron looked right back into Jackie's eyes. "I hear you Jackie. Are you good taking orders from me again? The landscape looks different, but the rules are the same."

Jackie smiled and said, "I hear you. I know the deal. You're the boss. You always had all the brains anyhow."

Aaron nodded and grabbed the folder from his desk containing all the information his brother had sent, along with his own notes. He took a moment to leaf through the dozen or so drawings before handing the folder to Jackson.

Aaron said, "I want you to study this building. In the basement level, the feds have decided to store something I want to take. I need you to figure out how to breach the building, secure it long enough to load about twenty tons onto a truck, and get a clean extraction."

Jackson took a minute to flip through the drawings himself. As he did so, the concern on his face grew. After a moment, he looked at Aaron and said, "Boss. This here is the US Federal Reserve building. This is going to be a tough nut to crack. I'm going to need some special equipment for this job, not to mention some serious firepower."

Aaron replied, "I figured as much. Take Booker and work with him on this. Only you two. Come to me with any requests for equipment. If we pull this off, it'll be well worth it."

"Alright boss, you got it. I'll get started right now." Jackson left Aaron's office and Aaron heard him speaking with Booker on the other side of his office door.

Twenty tons of gold. If his brother's intel was good, there was an incredible amount of wealth stored just miles from Aaron's headquarters. Doing the math in his head, twenty tons was forty thousand pounds, which converted to six hundred and forty thousand ounces of gold. The going price of gold—twenty-five hundred dollars an ounce—put the value of the gold at the Federal Reserve building at one point six billion dollars.

Getting that gold to his brother, after retaining a nominal percentage for himself, would allow Texas to purchase weapons systems that would make it too painful for the federal government to continue its siege. Or better yet, they could use the gold to pay for a country like Argentina or Peru to use one of its submarines to break the naval blockade in the Gulf of Mexico. Break the blockade, and Texas could sell all the oil it could pump to anyone in the world.

As for himself, he figured the folks in Texas wouldn't miss about fifty million dollars worth of gold. He had spent a weekend in Austin with his brother, and it seemed like a great place to set up operations. Plenty of people with a lot of money to fuel his extortion, prostitution, and drug businesses; incredible weather; and beautiful women.

Before now, there had been no way he could foresee breaching the Federal Reserve building to gain access to the gold. The place was too large, too solid, and had too many trained officers guarding it. He wouldn't even have thought of it without his brother's tip. But with that intel, and now with Jackson on the team, he was confident he would get a plan to breach the building. Then it would be up to his troops to storm the building and secure it. Even then, his biggest concern was holding a perimeter long enough to load the trucks and get them out of that part of the city. He had heard his raid on the docks had decimated the local Customs and FBI offices, but that still left the Philadelphia and Pennsylvania State Police forces in the game. Aaron had no control of the officers in the districts in and around Center City. Their response to an armed attack of the Federal Reserve would make successful exfiltration nearly impossible.

Aaron leaned back in his chair again and stretched his arms above his head. He frowned and said to his empty office, "What I need is a distraction. A really big distraction."

# CHAPTER 13

*Monday, October 30th, 2028*
*8:00 AM*

Julianne knew that fidgeting with her pen was putting her nerves on display, but it couldn't be helped. If it wasn't the pen, her feet would be tapping the floor or her legs crossing and uncrossing incessantly. Still rolling the pen from finger to finger, she took a moment to survey the other faces around the conference table in the mayor's office suite.

Nobody else seemed happy to be here either. Most of the department heads around the table were doing everything they could not to meet Julianne's eyes as she looked around at them. The exception was the chief of police, Emmanuel Braxton. He caught Julianne's eye and shrugged slightly, sending her a reassuring smile and a playful wink.

Chief Braxton was one of the most loved public servants in the city's recent history. He was also Julianne's favorite co-member on the cabinet and she enjoyed their monthly meetings to review his budget. The actual budget review only took a half hour; they spent the other half hour talking about local and global politics. Julianne appreciated Braxton's worldview.

Through their conversations, she'd also learned that he had lost his wife about a year ago in the worst of the early fighting on the Alaskan front. In a secret corner of her heart, she wished that he would ask her out to dinner, even if he was quite a few years older than she.

Maybe she should ask him out for coffee? Even if he was older by a bit more than a decade, from the way he filled out his uniform, he was still in good shape. And it would be good to have someone to look forward to spending time with—if she did, it might be easier to keep from working the extra hours she'd been logging lately.

That cinched it. After the meeting she was going to ask him to coffee.

It was early Monday morning, the first working day after the IOUs were issued alongside the reduced paychecks last Friday. To Julianne, the city seemed subdued but almost normal. Almost. The SEPTA bus she rode into work showed up ten minutes late. The driver explained that she was a manager and hadn't driven a bus for six years, but had to this morning because the transit workers had called in sick en masse. The driver's rustiness behind the wheel was evident from the curbs she clipped and the curses she spewed as she tried to navigate the narrow streets.

Entry into the Municipal Services Building, or MSB, as everyone called it, was a little different. Instead of the usual guards working the metal detectors at the entrance, Philadelphia police personnel were providing the security. When Julianne had asked a policeman why he was working there and not the security guards, he just shrugged.

She was interrupted from her thoughts as Chief Braxton cleared his throat and stood. The rest of the cabinet, including Julianne, followed his lead as Larry Roosevelt entered, followed immediately by the mayor.

Larry was wearing a black pin stripe suit with a matching vest, white shirt, and red tie. The mayor had a navy blue suit with a light blue shirt and metallic blue tie. Julianne recalled reading somewhere that the color blue put people at ease and was perceived as being trustworthy. She wondered if the mayor had thought about that while getting dressed for this meeting.

Larry clearly hadn't been going for "putting people at ease." His vest under his sport jacket reminded her of body armor. The way his eyes locked on to Julianne's from the second he entered the room didn't help the fact that the color of his tie reminded her strongly of blood. And from the intense stare and malignant smile on Larry's face, Julianne felt like the blood would be hers.

As the mayor took his seat, he asked the rest of the participants in the meeting to do the same. He shuffled some papers, then turned to Larry and said, "Before we begin the usual meeting format of department heads providing status updates, I would like to give Larry the opportunity to say a few words."

Larry's eyes bored into Julianne with the avarice of a predator about to gorge himself on a fresh kill. Then he frowned and addressed the entire table, "Ladies and Gentlemen, last week was, without contest, the darkest week in the history of our beloved city. In what I believe was a manufactured crisis by an inept financial manager, we devastated the lives of thousands of municipal workers by laying them off without cause and inflicted hardship on those workers remaining by only partially paying them. We are all owed an explanation of these actions by the person responsible for them, wouldn't you agree?"

Julianne was shocked that Larry would attack her so directly. Disheartened, she looked around the room and saw all the leaders of the city's government nodding in agreement except for one.

Chief Braxton, sitting three seats away from Julianne, immediately exclaimed, "Larry, what a complete load of bullshit. I'm sure the media soaks in your spin and half-truths, but we know better. The city is a mess. Even though the police department was spared in this round of cuts, I am down to under four thousand police officers, from sixty-five hundred four years ago. We are losing ground every day. We need more men and women in blue on the streets. But you don't hear me laying the blame at anyone's feet. Man up Larry. We're in this together."

Julianne looked at both Larry and Chief Braxton as they stared each other down. The other department leaders had their eyes on their notepads, scribbling nonsense to stay out of the fray. The mayor had an amused look on his face as he observed Larry and the chief square off.

Before Larry could respond to the police chief, Julianne spoke up. "Gentlemen, you were all copied on the emails I sent out that detailed the financial situation the City is in and the steps we—and I repeat, *we*—are taking to survive the crisis. This is a crisis long in the making. We have spent more than we've received and then taken out loan after loan to make up the difference. If you did that in your own home, you know it wouldn't work for very long."

Larry interrupted, "Why now? Any particular reason you're making it your mission to destroy the city on the Mayor Rhodes' watch?"

Chief Braxton erupted before Julianne could respond, "Were you listening to what she just said?"

Julianne continued, "Chief Braxton, it's okay. Larry asked a couple of questions. I'm going to answer them. First, why now? When I took over this job from my predecessor six months ago, the

City was in dire financial shape. We were spending more than we were bringing in. We were issuing bonds to pay for free benefits for our citizens. And finally, we couldn't make required payments to our pensions, which were already underfunded to start with. If you recall, at the time, I sat right here in this room and told you and the City Council that the City had to make drastic cuts, or we would run out of cash in less than nine months. And it looks like no one took my warning seriously, because here we are six months later, and we cannot make payroll."

Julianne paused and looked around the room. The mayor was looking out the window at the streets below. Larry's arms were crossed, and he was scowling with a slight shake to his head. However, the other six people in the room seemed to have reconsidered their earlier position and were now nodding their heads in agreement with her. Chief Braxton gave her a small thumbs-up gesture.

Julianne continued, "And as far as your accusation that I am destroying the city, that is laughable. I am doing everything in my power to save the city before it is truly destroyed. As you may or may not know, declaring bankruptcy would have been the best course of action—"

The mayor refocused on the conversation at this point and slammed his fist on the table, "Not on my shift! I will not go down in history as the mayor who bankrupted the city."

Julianne was not surprised by the mayor's outburst. She'd been hoping to get a reaction from him and he played right into her argument.

She made a point of taking a sip of her water and continued, "Correct. In lieu of declaring bankruptcy, I implemented, with the full lawful authority of the City Council and the mayor, two difficult policies last week. One was a twenty percent across the board reduction in city employees and the other a short-term fix to our low cash situation—that is, issuing IOUs for fifty percent of an employee's weekly paycheck. My financial models show us ending the issuance of IOUs and beginning to pay back previously issued IOUs in about six weeks. All of this information was in the memo I sent out last week."

Bob Torres, the head of the streets department, said, "I hear you, Julianne, and thanks for making the tough moves to keep us running, but I gotta' tell you, this ain't going to be easy. I got trash piling up on the streets without enough drivers and trucks to keep things clean. And that was before these cuts."

Larry looked at the mayor and said, "See boss, it's like I told you. Ms. Barnes' draconian measures are going to destroy the city. We need to make an example of her. Again, I recommend she be publicly fired to let the citizens of the city know she exceeded her authority by acting the way she did."

Julianne couldn't help her body's reaction to Larry's suggestion. Blood rushed to her head as a spectrum of responses played through her mind in rapid fire.

Before she could speak, Chief Braxton slapped the table and said, "This is bullshit and you know it. What are you going to do, fire her for doing her job? A job that clearly nobody else has the guts to do? We all need to be smart and figure out how to do more with less. Prioritize intelligently. For instance, I used to have over a thousand officers in the precinct houses that cover Southwest Philadelphia. Now I have under five hundred in that area and the crime rate is the lowest in the city."

Bob Torres added, "Yeah, things run smooth in the Southwest. That guy Aaron who runs that Southwest Militia runs a tight ship.

My drivers are never harassed, and he has the neighborhood kids stuff any loose trash bags into bins to make it faster for our automatic-loading trucks to get their job done more quickly. If I could get that level of cooperation from the entire city, I'd have no problem getting all the trash collected even after the cuts we just had."

Larry's head swiveled between Torres and Braxton. Julianne realized both men reported to Larry and she imagined he was none too happy to have this insurrection on his hands.

Larry finally turned to the mayor and said, "Sir, I swear to you, I had no idea these two men were colluding with a known criminal. In addition to firing Ms. Barnes, I recommend you place these two men on administrative leave until the ethics board can review this information."

Julianne exhaled the breath she had been holding as the mayor leaned back in his chair. He slowly looked at all four involved in the battle. Larry, the executioner. Chief Braxton, the hero. Torres, the naïve fool playing a game whose rules he didn't understand. And Julianne. She didn't know if she wanted to be viewed as the martyr or the street fighter. The two emotions of fight and flight were competing for dominance.

Finally, Mayor Rhodes spoke. "Larry, you are one ruthless cat. Always have been and I am glad you're on my team. It's good the feds don't know how quick you are to pull the trigger; they'd put a rifle in your hands and ship you off to Alaska. You'd have those red bastards running for their lives, that's for sure."

The mayor chuckled at his own joke and looked around the room to see if anyone else was laughing with him. Larry offered a polite chuckle, as did a few other department heads. Julianne did not join in. Neither did Braxton or Torres.

Continuing the mayor said, "I don't have a problem with trash truck drivers working with the community to get crap off the street more efficiently. As for Julianne, she is staying right where she is. Canning her now would be the worst thing we could do. She is now the face of the crisis. In addition to some television and streaming interviews I am lining up for her this week, there is a big event coming up I would love her to speak at if she would be so kind."

Then the mayor's demeanor became serious to the point of bordering on sorrow. He lowered his voice and said, "But I cannot allow the Chief of Police to collude with a known criminal. It looks bad for my administration and might even expose me to liability."

Looking directly at Chief Braxton the mayor said, "Chief, take the rest of the day to organize your office. Effective five p.m. tonight, you will be placed on administrative leave pending the next meeting of the ethics board after Thanksgiving. Hand off all your responsibilities to your deputy until this is cleared up."

The street fighter won the internal battle within Julianne and she exclaimed, "Are you kidding me? The chief never 'colluded' with anyone. You're going to discipline the chief because he redistributed his manpower in a way that reflects the needs of the city? This is ridiculous. Braxton is hands down the best chief of police this city has ever had. The people of this city love him."

The mayor raised an eyebrow at Julianne's outburst. Julianne realized she may have overplayed her hand, but she was outraged. Putting the chief on leave would weaken her position by removing her one strong ally in the city government. She also worried about her personal safety with the death threats, and the chief was very proactive about investigating the threats. She had even noticed a more constant police presence in front of her building last week.

Braxton stood up from the table and said, "If I may excuse myself, I have a lot to do before five o'clock."

Larry dismissively waved his hands in the chief's direction, "Sure Mr. Braxton, please do, and call me at the end of the day to make sure everything went smoothly."

Chief Braxton stood and looked at the attendees in the room. He grabbed his briefcase and walked to the door. Opening it, he turned and addressed everyone in the room, "Folks. The city is at a precarious crossroads. Please, do what is honorable and do right by the citizens of this great city. They are relying on you."

Julianne was speechless as Chief Braxton closed the door behind him and the meeting droned on with the usual status reports. She hoped that putting Braxton on leave was only the misguided reaction of two small-minded men and not the beginning death throes of the city she was fighting for.

# CHAPTER 14

*Friday, November 3rd, 2028*
*3:30 PM*

Jimmy breathed a sigh of relief as he tucked his new company-issued tablet into his new tool bag. Another day wrapped up and no sign of Dante.

Regarding the tablet, Nick had read him the riot act about "losing" the tablet. No sympathy for having been mugged and showing up to work Monday with a huge shiner and a swollen nose. Nick "graciously" allowed Jimmy to pay for the tablet with partial paycheck deductions over the next two months.

Jimmy had also used the time between two service calls on Tuesday to get his driver's license re-issued. It took three hours to get that, forcing Jimmy to work late that night.

Finally, Jimmy had to grab a new tool bag and hand tools. This time, he decided on a backpack instead of the kind of bag Dante stole. It would be much easier to carry up and down stair towers.

As for Dante, Jimmy had called the precinct building twice this week to inquire as to the progress of his open case. The first time he called, he spoke with a female detective from the robbery unit. She assured Jimmy that the case was in the process of being investigated and that the police department was tracking down the suspect.

The second time he called, on his lunch break today, he got bounced around the phone system until he reached an officer who introduced himself as Detective Green. Jimmy mentally replayed the conversation as he walked out of the building where he had just finished his service call.

*"This is Detective Green, Homicide. Who am I speaking with?"*

*"Jimmy, uh, James Brennan."*

*"What can I do for you, Mr. Brennan?"*

*"I'm calling to check on case number 10262018-42—"*

*"Standby, I'll bring it up . . . Oh."*

*"What's that mean?"*

*"Listen, sir. I work homicide, this is a robbery, I don't even know why they routed this call to me."*

*"Well, can you help?"*

*A pause. "Here's the deal, Mr. Brennan. You weren't killed and they didn't steal much from you. Count yourself lucky and move on."*

*"What are you saying?"*

*"I'm saying, this case hasn't even been assigned and probably won't ever be. We got bigger issues to deal with than this. Sorry, sir, but that's the way it is. Be careful out there and have a good day. Goodbye."*

Then all Jimmy heard was dial tone.

Maybe that detective was right. *Heck,* Jimmy thought, *the muggers didn't even get a chance to use my credit card before I was able to call the company and get it shut down.*

He'd had a pounding headache anytime he'd exerted himself earlier in the week, but that was fading with each day. Even the bruising around his eye was fading to a strange yellow-greenish color, and he could blow his nose without pain.

He crumpled up the police receipt that had his case number on it and threw it in a hallway trashcan. It was time to move on.

Back in the moment, Jimmy used his hip to push the panic bar on the front door of the building to exit. As he cleared the door and straightened out, his heart skipped a beat and then kicked into overdrive.

He was leaning against the building not ten feet away from Jimmy. The man had one foot against the wall and the other on the ground, smoking a cigarette in the classic Marlboro man stance.

"Hey Elevator Boy, I saw your truck posted up in front of this building and figured I'd pay you a visit."

Jimmy was speechless. This was the guy who'd mugged him. Dante. Jimmy quickly looked around to see if there was anyone he could call out to. The building superintendent was still inside the building. There were a few people loitering in the parking lot and sidewalk within earshot, but Jimmy could tell they were purposefully ignoring him and his situation.

Jimmy finally found his voice, "You . . . you're the guy who hit me and stole my stuff. C'mon, man, it's daytime and I'm just doing my job. Just let me go home."

Dante flicked his cigarette away and pushed off the wall. Approaching Jimmy with a menacing grimace, he said, "That's right, I am that guy. Can't let you go home just yet, cracker. You and me got a problem we need to settle."

Confused, Jimmy asked, "What are you talking about?"

Dante responded, "You called the cops. Big no-no around here." As he talked, Dante shook his head side to side with a mock-mourning expression. He stepped closer, wagging a finger in Jimmy's face and using his other hand to lift the front of his jacket. Jimmy could see the handle of a pistol tucked in Dante's waistband.

Dante continued, "You see white-bread, around here snitches get stiches. You got a beat down and lost your stuff, but you got to walk away. You should have counted that a win and gone home." He shook his head again. "But then you went and called the cops. That's bad. Real bad."

Jimmy's head was spinning. *Was this guy was crazy?* What else was he supposed to do after getting assaulted and robbed? Jimmy blurted out, "Well, if it helps, I called the precinct to check on the case number and a detective told me to forget it. They aren't doing anything about it."

Dante snarled as he placed his hand on the handle of his gun, "You dumbass redneck. What did I tell you about calling the cops? Of course they aren't going to do anything. We own these streets. Not them."

Jimmy involuntarily took a step backwards but was stopped by the closed door behind him. Dante took a half step forward to stay close to Jimmy.

"Here's the deal hillbilly. I'm gonna' cut you a break this time because you didn't know better. From now on, you gotta' pay me a tax every time I pay you a visit."

Jimmy asked, "What are you talking about, a tax?"

Dante laughed. "You know, a tax. Get your wallet out and give me all the cash. As part of our new deal, I'll let you keep your tools and tablet, so you can keep earning."

Jimmy was disgusted. This thug was going to steal his hard-earned money, so he could lounge around and terrorize normal, productive citizens? Jimmy imagined himself fighting Dante right here on the sidewalk. He would throw a roundhouse right followed by an uppercut. Then he would put Dante in a chokehold until he was unconscious. It worked on TV all the time.

Instead Jimmy sighed and unshouldered his backpack, explaining, "My wallet is in my backpack." Then he opened his wallet so Dante could clearly see the contents and removed all the cash.

Handing it over to Dante, Jimmy said, "It's twenty-eight bucks. It's all I have on me."

Dante snatched the cash from Jimmy's outstretched hand, tucking it into his front pocket, never once taking his eyes off Jimmy.

Dante snorted and said, "This ain't enough white-bread. From now on, I see you, the tax is forty. If you don't have it, I start taking tools to make up the difference."

Jimmy wanted to tell him to pound sand. Instead he nodded and answered, "I understand."

Dante quickly reached out to Jimmy, causing Jimmy to involuntarily flinch. Dante smiled at the reaction and patted Jimmy's cheek like a boss in a mobster movie. "Good boy. I'll be seeing you around."

Jimmy watched Dante saunter down the sidewalk and disappear around the building. Then he quickly walked to his van, started the engine, and slammed the door shut.

He pounded the steering wheel with his fist until he realized the van hadn't done anything to deserve a pounding.

He needed a plan. Jimmy put the van in drive and began his route home past the myriad of dilapidated buildings in Southwest Philadelphia.

Plan A was talking to Nick. The commute would suck, but maybe Nick could give Jimmy a territory in another part of the city or, better yet, Wilmington, Delaware. It would be a doable commute and there were plenty of tall buildings there. He'd try to talk to Nick about that today.

If that didn't work and Jimmy was stuck in this territory, he would have to implement Plan B. That meant two things. Doing something Jimmy himself didn't know if he could do, and calling in a favor—a big favor—with a man who could throw him in jail for even asking.

# CHAPTER 15

*Wednesday, November 8ᵗʰ, 2028*
*10:30 AM*

The robotic arm on Reggie's truck, equipped with machine vision system, was great at picking up heavy trash bins and it only required a driver instead of a two- or three-man crew. Reggie was the first city employee to volunteer to drive one of the new trucks even though some of his co-workers threatened to strike because of the reduced labor the trucks required. Reggie knew how things worked though. He knew sometimes you had to get on the bandwagon, because if you didn't, that wagon would roll right over you and leave you bruised and bleeding in a ditch.

Reggie liked working alone anyway. The radio was his constant companion. Today it was tuned in to the local news station. Traffic and transit on the twos. After you listened to the station for a half hour, it got repetitive. But Reggie didn't mind; he considered the radio anchors his friends, their voices his companions.

All week, but especially today, Reggie was having trouble on his route. Usually, to get a loaded trash bin in the truck, Reggie simply pulled his truck alongside the bin and hit the load button on his dash. The vision system on the robotic arm then activated and located the bin for the robotic arm to grab in its pincers, lift, and dump the contents into the hopper on the back of the truck. Usually quite simple. However, the whole system was foiled if the bin was toppled over. Usually on his route of twelve hundred bins, a few were toppled over. Reggie didn't mind hopping down to rake the refuse back in the bin then set the bin back upright for the robot to do its job. It gave him a break from driving and got him moving around.

But today, he was only three hundred bins into his route and he had already been out to upright bins over twenty times.

And as he came around the next corner, he found out why so many of the bins were toppled.

On the sidewalk, along the curb, four rough-looking youth ranging from about eight to fourteen years old were standing over a toppled bin, rummaging through its contents. The contents were strewn into the street and the youngest of the four boys was squatting down in the street, chewing on a discarded bone.

Reggie saw the whites of the boy's eyes flare as the truck bore down on him. As soon as he registered that the boy was in the street, Reggie immediately slammed his foot down on the brake pedal. Usually, when Reggie slammed on the brake pedal, the whole truck shuddered and the shoulder and lap belts bit into Reggie's body as the truck rapidly decelerated.

But this time, the truck bled its speed off at a leisurely pace as the brakes did about one-third the job they should have been doing.

The boy was frozen in place. Reggie could see, in startling clarity, the boy's tattered clothing and grimy face. Reggie spun the wheel to the left as rapidly as he could. The lumbering truck's front two tires bit into the asphalt, grappling for traction to make a maneuver it wasn't designed to perform.

The bumper passed within inches of the fright-frozen street urchin. Finally, the truck came to a stop and Reggie exhaled a breath he hadn't realized he was holding. He set the parking brake, opened the driver side door, and jumped to the ground. Fearing the worst, Reggie scrambled to the passenger side of the truck.

As he rounded the truck, his gut felt low and sick with fear. A mental image of the broken young boy gasping for life after the impact from the truck made his legs rubbery.

What he actually saw took a moment for him to process. The oldest of the four boys stood on the curb, one arm across his chest, the other hand by his side holding an empty glass jar. The other three boys were standing behind him. The youngest was unhurt but looking at Reggie with a mix of fear and hatred.

Reggie coughed out a laugh, both relieved and confused by what was going on. He said to the oldest, "Thank God you're alright! What are you boys doin' out here? You been knock'n them bins down? I thought so, now get over here and help me put the bin up right and pick up the mess so I can do my job."

The oldest boy looked at Reggie shaking his head and replied, "No. That one's got a lot of good scraps in it, we ain't done with it yet."

Reggie asked, "What the heck you talking 'bout kid? You ain't scrapping for food, I know the schools give you free breakfast and lunch. Been doing it since I was a boy, I should know, my taxes are paying for it."

The oldest boy shot back, "You don't know nothing, old man. The school stopped giving us food last week. Ain't no need to be going to school now."

Reggie again asked, "What about your folks? They should be feeding you."

A shadow of sadness darkened the boy's face, "My momma's high as a kite or out earning on the streets. She can't barely feed herself."

Reggie softened his tone and said, "Listen, I see you got it hard. I'm sorry for you. But I got a job to do and that is keeping these streets clean. You kids hit the bricks so I can do my job. And for Pete's sake, don't go sittin' in the middle of the road!"

The boy didn't budge. Reggie shrugged and turned to grab the rake from the side of the truck. An explosion of glass caused Reggie to flinch and tuck his chin against his chest as he felt glass shards pepper his gloves, the long sleeves of his jacket, and felt the biting sting as at least one piece found the exposed flesh on his face below the protection of his safety glasses.

Reggie yelled out in surprise and turned to see who had thrown the bottle at him. He saw the four boys digging frantically through the trash looking for more projectiles.

That was enough. He ran towards the front of the truck back to the safety of the cab as tin can ricocheted off the front fender just behind him.

He scrambled up the side of the truck, opening and closing the door as he settled into his seat. Putting the truck in gear he called out over the radio, "Dispatch, this is Reggie. I'm unable to collect the trash on the twenty-two hundred block of Earp Street due to kids looting the trash and assaulting me and my truck."

After a brief pause where Reggie idled the truck and watched the boys continued to rummage through the trash a half block away, dispatch responded, "Affirmative Reggie. Only pick up bins that are upright. If it's knocked over, skip it. Do not exit your truck again. You're not the only driver having problems. Please confirm."

Reggie couldn't imagine what some of the other drivers were dealing with. His route was in a decent area of the city known as Point Breeze. It was just across the river from Aaron's territory in Southwest Philadelphia and just south of the gentrified area in Center City. Reggie figured Aaron had things under control in Southwest. He wouldn't let a bunch of young punks dirty his streets or allow them to keep workers like Reggie from doing their jobs. Heck, he was probably feeding the kids now that they weren't getting food in school. But Reggie couldn't imagine how his co-workers in North Philly were doing. That area was a battleground of rival drug gangs. Once those kids got hungry, Lord only knows what they would do for a meal.

Reggie shook his head and keyed the mic, "Affirmative. Only load upright bins, stay in my cab throughout my route. Dispatch, one other thing. I need to call in a high priority maintenance request."

After a pause, the dispatcher's voice came over the radio in a rush, "Reggie, I'm gett'n hammered with other calls, turn in a work request at the end of your shift. Dispatch out."

Reggie looked at the radio at his hand and shook his head. He had a policy of doing things the minute they popped into his head, because if he didn't, there was a good chance he'd forget about it. Promising himself to remember to file the request before he punched out for the day, he eased the accelerator down and urged the truck onward to complete his route.

# CHAPTER 16

*Friday, November 10th, 2028*
*4:30 PM*

Jimmy had dropped off his service van at home and borrowed his mom's Crown Vic to drive over to a park not far from his house. He was leaning against the trunk of the car watching a group of four teenagers play a half-hearted game of two-on-two basketball. The court was across the parking lot from where Jimmy was, next to the woods on the north side of the park.

Jimmy was looking west, watching the sun as it made its nearly horizontal transit across the sky at this time of year. It was a clear, cold day but the sun was so low on the horizon, it shone a dull orange.

Jimmy's conversation with Nick to get assigned a new territory had gone over like a lead balloon. After listening to his well-rehearsed pitch, Nick made it clear that Jimmy either stick with his existing territory in Southwest Philadelphia or go work for someone else. Problem was, Jimmy didn't know "someone else." This was the only place he had worked since graduating high school. He'd interned here during his two years of trade school and then worked for them full time once he got his mechanic's license. Six years didn't seem like long compared to some of the old timers who had been working twenty or more years in the business, but for Jimmy, six years was longer than anything else he had done in his life.

On one hand, it made total sense for Jimmy to leave the company. His route was in a part of the city controlled by a militia and he was being harassed by a rogue member of the gang. On the other hand, if he left and couldn't find a job, who would pay for the food and heat and other things for him and his mom? No, leaving wasn't an option. He would have to figure out a way to deal with Dante.

Jimmy shook his head. No, he couldn't leave; that was why he was here, at this park, right now. Plan B.

He looked up. Pulling into the parking lot was an unmarked police cruiser. Jimmy slid down off the trunk of his mom's sedan and walked toward the newly parked car.

Unfolding himself out of the driver's side was a tall, thick man dressed in jeans and a black long sleeved mock turtleneck shirt that contrasted his blond hair and ruddy complexion. He had his badge clipped to his belt on his left side and his service pistol holstered on his right.

Jimmy smiled as he closed the distance and the men shook hands. Jimmy spoke first. "John, thanks for meeting me. I gotta' problem I need your advice on. I didn't want to speak about it over the phone."

John patted Jimmy on the shoulder and responded, "No problem Jimmy. I figure I owe you since you fixed all those radios for me this summer."

Back in July, Lieutenant John Brady, head of the patrol division of the Upper Darby police department, had stopped by Jimmy's house with three boxes full of surplus radios from the department of Homeland Security. He'd explained that he had scored the radios from a contact at Homeland Security who was about to throw them out because they were all old and in need of repair.

John and Jimmy went back to grade school; their fathers had played in a monthly poker game together. John was three years older than Jimmy, making friendship at that age impossible, but Jimmy had tried his best not to annoy John on the rare occasions that the families got together. John usually ignored Jimmy in school and, being three years apart, there were only a few years that they were in the same school together and for the most part, they didn't associate.

That had changed one October morning in high school. Jimmy was a freshman that year and didn't have many friends. He was a quiet kid who kept to himself. As usual, he was walking to the sprawling public school with his backpack and lunch bag, daydreaming about fixing a moped his neighbor wanted to get running and not really paying attention to his surroundings.

The three boys surprised him when he made a right on the sidewalk from Garrett Road to Lansdowne Avenue. They had demanded Jimmy's lunch and any money he had. Jimmy had tried to run away but barely made it a step before one of the boys grabbed his backpack and pulled him back. The largest of the three boys held him while the other two went through his backpack.

Then John Brady walked up. He stopped right in front of Jimmy, who was being held by the bully.

John looked at Jimmy and said, "Duck."

It took a millisecond for Jimmy to realize John wasn't talking about the animal. Jimmy crunched down as best he could while still being held as John's right fist came hooking in for the bully's face.

Jimmy felt the bully release his grip. The boy was sprawled on his back groaning in pain. The other two got the message and took off running.

John had picked up Jimmy's lunch bag and handed it to him, then said, "Why don't you walk the rest of the way to school with me, Jimmy?"

Jimmy took John up on his offer and from that morning onward, Jimmy would first walk to John's house and wait quietly on his front porch for John to walk to school. He and Jimmy didn't talk much, but Jimmy didn't care. Even walking a few steps behind John, Jimmy felt like a cooler kid.

This summer, when John dropped off the radios, Jimmy was glad to help. John had done Jimmy a huge favor in high school by protecting him his freshman year. Jimmy needed to make the ledger even. He was especially proud to help when John explained how badly the radios were needed, now that the department had to use extra foot patrols to keep an eye out for city dwellers coming out to the suburbs to steal what they couldn't find in the city.

Jimmy stayed up several nights diagnosing and then repairing the radios. Once he found the burned-out diode on the charging circuit on a radio, the repairs were simple. All the radios had the same problem; either they'd been hooked up to the wrong voltage to charge or, more likely, a spike in the voltage hit them while plugged in.

After fixing the radios, Jimmy felt like the ledger was balanced—or maybe even positive on his side of the account. That was why he was meeting with John this afternoon. To call in a favor.

The boys playing basketball nonchalantly grabbed their ball and cell phones and migrated away from the park. Nothing like an easily-spotted unmarked police cruiser to get a group of teens to clear out.

Jimmy continued, "I got mugged in the city while doing a late-night emergency service call."

John grimaced and said, "Sorry about that, you okay? Now that I'm looking, I can see a little faded bruise around your eye. When did this happen? About two weeks ago?"

Jimmy responded, "Yeah. That's about right. I got roughed up and they stole my stuff, but I'm all right. If that was the end of it, I would have taken my lumps and not bothered you with this."

John asked, "What do you mean?"

Jimmy paused for a moment then said, "What I mean is that I called the Philly police department several times to see if there was any progress on the case and they said to forget about it, they weren't going to do anything to find and arrest the guy who mugged me."

John sighed. "That's not surprising to me, Jimmy. I hear the Philadelphia police force is hanging on by a thread. I guess they don't have the resources to investigate anything short of homicide and major crimes."

Jimmy nodded, "Again, if that were the end of it, I wouldn't have called. The problem is the guy who mugged me, Dante, has me on his radar. As you know, my service van is a rolling billboard for the company; you can spot it a mile away. So now whenever he sees my van, he accosts me, in broad daylight no less, and demands I pay a tax for the privilege of working in his neighborhood."

John looked at Jimmy and scratched his scalp, then spoke. "Not that you don't know this, Jimmy, but this situation sucks. This guy Dante is probably in the Southwest Militia. That's why the police in Philly won't investigate. Heck, you'd have a better chance at getting him off your back by calling the militia leader, Aaron, than by calling the police. From what I hear, Aaron doesn't like it when people who maintain the infrastructure in his area get harassed."

Jimmy asked, "Okay, so how do I do that?"

John responded, "You don't. Guys like Aaron are dangerous. You're best off staying far away."

"Then what do you suggest I do?"

"Did you put in for a transfer for a different area to cover?"

Jimmy responded, "Yeah, I did. Shot down. Then I considered quitting and looking for a job with another elevator service company, but I don't know anyone. I'm not sure where I would go. Also, Mom and I don't have much saved up. I don't want to think about what would happen to her if I lost my job."

John said, "Okay, I hear you, but why did you call me to meet you here? What do you want me to do? This isn't high school anymore. I can't just punch a bully and make the problem go away."

Jimmy asked in a joking tone, "Any jobs open at the township? I can fix just about anything."

John shook his head and said, "No, we're not hiring right now, things are tight. We do have a bunch of volunteers on foot patrol around the township looking for looters from the city. Thanks to you for fixing the radios, those retired guys have been really effective at calling in bad guys before they do any damage. Unfortunately, those are unpaid volunteers. You can't pay the bills with that work."

Jimmy lowered his voice and looked down at his shoes, his voice barely above a whisper, "Then I need a way to protect myself." Looking John in the eye he said, "Do you have a Taser or something I can use on Dante next time he tries to get his 'tax' from me, or do you know how I could get one?"

John laughed, incredulous, and asked, "Are you serious Jimmy? That's a bad idea for a bunch of reasons. First of all, let's say this Dante guy accosts you and, just for the sake of argument, let's assume you're able to get a Taser out and successfully zap him. Then what? You think he's just going to forget about the whole thing? No way, next time he sees you, he'll kill you. No doubt about it."

"Then what should I do?" Jimmy asked.

John rubbed his scalp and walked away from the two parked cars. After a few steps he turned around, approaching Jimmy again. "Listen. I hate bullies. Always have and always will. That's why I helped you out in high school. No offense, you were a nice kid, but we were barely on speaking terms when I beat those punks. I did it, not because of any allegiance to you, but because I can't stand to see the weak get abused by the strong. It's why I became a cop."

Jimmy said, "I know, I understand. But I need help. Like you said, it's not high school anymore. I need to be able to take care of myself. I need . . . I need a gun."

John's voice hissed out in a strained whisper, "Are you insane? I could arrest you for even asking for a gun. Get another job, Jimmy. You're in way over your head here."

John turned to leave and get back in his car, but Jimmy grabbed the material on John's jacket and said, "No. I need to take a stand. I'm not going to let some thug tell me where I can and can't work. If I don't stand up to him, who will? If you don't help me, I'll just find someone else who can."

John looked Jimmy up and down, his expression unreadable. He released a big sigh and said, "Shit Jimmy. When the hell did you grow a spine? You're going to end up getting yourself killed trying to stand up to this guy."

"I'm no hero, that's true. And I don't want to die. But I have to take a stand, John. I'm tired of being a victim. I heard a quote when I was a kid. It went like, 'I'd rather die on my feet than live on my knees.' I can't go on living on my knees."

Jimmy paused as John processed what he had just heard. Jimmy could see the conflict roiling across John's face.

Finally, John made up his mind. He walked back to his sedan. Jimmy expected him to get in the car and drive away. Instead, he popped the trunk, and handed Jimmy an oily rag.

When John put the rag in his hand, Jimmy felt the weight of something solid in his hand. Unwrapping the cloth, Jimmy partially exposed a small, black revolver. He quickly wrapped it back up and looked up at John.

John spoke, "It's a twenty-two caliber magnum revolver. Point and pull the trigger. You're the smart one with mechanical stuff, so figure it out. I took it from a perp a few years ago and didn't turn it into evidence. Figured someday I might need the insurance. If this in anyway blows back on me, or my family, Dante will be the least of your worries. Got it?"

Jimmy responded, "Okay. I got it. I just . . . well, I wish it hadn't come to this. Feeling the gun in my hands makes this whole thing way too real."

John looked gravely at Jimmy and said, "If you pull this gun on a thug like Dante, it's going to get very real, very fast. I'm washing my hands of this. I don't want blood on my hands, yours or Dante's."

John shook his head, turned, and strode to his car. Jimmy stayed planted in the same spot, watching the headlights retreat and then disappear around the corner.

Looking at the gun in his hand, Jimmy hoped that Dante would have some sort of predator's instinct to know that Jimmy was now armed and had the ability to fight back. John's parting words bounced around his head. Of course, Jimmy didn't want to die. But he also didn't want to hurt anyone, even someone as despicable as Dante.

Who was he to sign Dante's death warrant?

# CHAPTER 17

*Monday, November 13ᵗʰ, 2028*
*4:45 PM*

Jimmy was getting nervous. He had finished his last service call of the day half an hour ago, but the superintendent of this building was still talking on his cell phone while Jimmy waited outside his office to get his tablet signed.

Jimmy wanted to get out of the city before it got dark. He'd parked his van two buildings over and planned on exiting this building by the back door to an alley that would lead him to the parking lot where his van was located. He didn't relish the thought of walking down the alley if it got dark out, even with John's revolver in his backpack.

He had decided on his new parking and egress strategy as a way to throw Dante off his scent and perhaps give himself a visual on Dante before Dante saw him. Jimmy figured if he saw Dante at the van before being spotted, he could call the police and have them escort him to his van. He didn't think the cops would let Dante mug him in front of their noses.

So far, the plan had worked great. No sign of Dante. Of course, that could be due to Dante being drunk or stoned or whatever he did during the day rather than Jimmy's new parking strategy, but that was alright. Anything to avoid Dante was worth it.

Finally, the super got off his phone and signed the tablet with a grunt. Jimmy asked, "You alright with me leaving out the back?"

The super raised an eyebrow and said, "Up to you pal, just don't let the door hit your ass on the way out."

Jimmy shook his head as he tucked his tablet into his backpack. He didn't understand why some people were rude just for the sake of being rude.

He walked down the maintenance hallway, pushed open the rear door, and came face to face with Dante.

Jimmy's breath caught in in his chest as the door slammed shut behind him. There was nowhere to run. Dante had him cornered between the side of the building and a chain link fence.

"Hey white-bread," Dante taunted, "I see you been parking your van further away from where you're working, using back doors. If I was a doubting man, I'd say you were trying to avoid me. You're not trying to avoid me, now, are you cracker-boy?"

Jimmy was frozen on the spot. He knew he had the gun in his backpack, but now, faced with the prospect of using it, he was unsure of himself. The indignant anger welling up in Jimmy made him want to whip out the pistol and shoot Dante right in the face. His upbringing and moral compass told him to pay Dante his tax then look for another job. Maybe he could find another job while he was still working so he wouldn't miss out on a paycheck.

Jimmy was shaken out of his moral and vocational contemplation when Dante shoved him against the wall and shouted, "I asked you a question! Are you trying to give me the slip?"

Jimmy's backpack cushioned his body's blow against the brick wall. Stuttering, he said, "No—no, I have your payment right in my backpack. Lemme' get it out."

Dante took a step back as Jimmy unshouldered his pack and opened the zippered compartment with his wallet in it. It was also the compartment with the revolver in it. Jimmy could see the dull black metal of the gun as he reached in for his wallet.

Dante laughed mockingly. "You gotta' pay double for try'n to avoid paying. Pay up or I take the whole pack."

Jimmy's gut fell as a wave of nausea coursed through his body. He didn't have enough cash to pay twice the 'tax' and if Dante took his bag, he would lose all his tools, the tablet, and John's gun. There was only one thing to do.

Jimmy gripped the handle on the revolver. Sweat beaded on his forehead despite the chill in the air. His gut felt greasy, his legs like putty. He swallowed, then pulled the gun out of the backpack and pointed it at Dante's chest.

Jimmy's voice was shaking as he said, "You need to leave me alone. I will shoot you if I have to. I have a right to earn a living without getting mugged."

Dante's eyes narrowed with menace. "You just made a big mistake, cracker."

Dante took another half step backward and slowly reached toward his back pocket.

Jimmy said, "Don't you move an inch, or I'll shoot. I'm serious, I'll shoot you."

Suddenly, Dante was lunging forward, reaching for the gun with his left hand and bringing a knife from his back pocket with his right hand.

Jimmy lowered the gun to keep Dante from grabbing it and pulled the trigger. Dante grimaced and flinched as the bullet hit his right leg.

Dante plowed into Jimmy, tackling him, and they fell together. Hitting the ground, he lost his grip on the revolver. It skittered over the broken asphalt, out of arm's reach.

Jimmy wanted to reach for the gun but in that instant he had a more immediate concern. Dante was on top of him, arcing the knife towards his neck. Jimmy shot both arms up and grabbed Dante's wrists to arrest the blade's descent.

The tip of the blade came slowly towards Jimmy's neck as Dante put all of his weight behind the knife.

Jimmy was assaulted by a litany of sensory inputs and thoughts as the steel approached his bare skin.

The red spiderwebs of Dante's bloodshot eyes. The clear droplet of sweat about to fall off Dante's nose. The sweet, rotten undertone of Dante's hot breath. The warm sticky feeling on Jimmy's legs as he struggled to get out from under Dante.

Jimmy's first thought was that he didn't want to die in a trash-strewn alley in a crappy neighborhood in Southwest Philly. Who would take care of his mom? And if he died here, he would never get a chance to convince Colleen to go on a date with him.

As he felt the cold steel of the blade touch the skin just above his sternum, Jimmy renewed his upward push. His arms burning, quivering with the effort, Jimmy knew that this was the end. Tears poured down his cheeks as he felt the pinch of the blade penetrating his skin.

The pinch turned into a hot stinging as the blade bit deeper into his flesh. A new wave of panic swept through his body as he struggled against the weight of the blade.

He pushed again with all his might and felt a lessening of the pressure on the blade and was able to push it up a fraction of an inch. He continued pushing until the blade was clear of his skin.

Not understanding how he was still alive, Jimmy focused on Dante's face and saw Dante's eyes roll up into his head as he lost consciousness. Jimmy was able to push Dante off him completely, rolling his body to the side.

Jimmy rubbed his neck where Dante's blade penetrated; his hand came back sticky with blood. He grabbed a shop rag from his backpack and applied pressure to his wound. He didn't know how deep the cut was, but he could still swallow and his breathing, while rapid, seemed to be working normally.

He then looked down at his legs and was surprised to see his pants soaked in blood.

Not yet understanding what happened, Jimmy rolled over to Dante. The man was breathing in shallow, panting breaths. His dark features looked ashen gray. Jimmy looked down at Dante's legs and saw blood soaking the man's pants. Jimmy figured his shot must have severed a major artery in Dante's leg. He was bleeding out.

With one hand, Jimmy rummaged in his backpack for another rag to hold against Dante's coursing wound to provide compression and stop the bleeding. Even though Dante had nearly killed him, he didn't want Dante to die.

As Jimmy pressed the rag against Dante's wound, Dante let out one last long, soft sigh and then he lay silent and still.

"Oh shit, oh shit, oh shit." Jimmy couldn't think. He had just killed a man. He reached for his cell phone on his holster to call the police.

Jimmy dialed nine. He dialed one. He stopped.

If he called the police, there was a high probability he would go to jail for shooting the man with an illegal handgun. What's worse, they would ask where it came from and that could get John in trouble.

The gun. Jimmy scrabbled on his one hand and knees and picked up the gun. Looking at it in his hand, he couldn't believe that this little black assembly of metal parts had just taken another man's life.

*No*, he thought. *I took the man's life. Not the gun.*

*I did.*

He needed a story about the gun. Jimmy sat next to Dante's body, staring at the gun and thinking. Nodding silently, he decided on the story. It was flimsy, but it might just work. The most important part was to keep Brady out of this nightmare.

He dialed one. He took a deep breath as the call connected. Nothing would be the same now.

Jimmy waited for the dispatcher to stop talking. He held the phone to his ear and said shakily, "This is James Brennan. I just killed a man."

# CHAPTER 18

*Monday, November 13th, 2028*
*5:15 PM*

Detective Green pulled his unmarked police sedan next to a cruiser with its lights flashing a blue and red beacon in the fading light of the early evening. He was just punching out for the day when he got a text from the Lieutenant that there'd been a homicide just a few blocks away.

It was a curious location for a homicide call. On the northern reach of Aaron's territory, the deceased was in an alley behind an apartment building just off Market Street. Detective Green put the car in park and pulled up the crime stats on his tablet. This was the first homicide in Southwest Philly in over a month. There were dozens of missing person cases open—Detective Green shuddered at the implication—but no homicides. Until today. It was why he was the only homicide detective in Southwest Philadelphia, effectively covering homicides for his precinct and the adjoining precinct, precinct 12. The police department officially called the precincts "districts," but nobody used that terminology. Police departments had been segmented into precincts since the dawn of policing, and you can't unlearn something like that.

Even more curious than the homicide itself was the fact that the perpetrator of the homicide called it in and was still at the scene.

Detective Green needed to get to the bottom of this in a hurry.

As Green got out of his cruiser, his right hand patted his service pistol in its shoulder holster on his left breast, an old habit. He did it every time he got out of his vehicle. He also grabbed his data tablet.

Green walked toward the scene and greeted a couple of uniformed officers at the police caution line. They pointed Green to the alley, where he could see the crime scene technicians had set up LED lighting on tripod stanchions, making the alley brighter than the strip in Vegas at midnight.

On the edge of the light was a lone figure sitting on a step with his hands cuffed behind his back. Looked to be a white male, average size, wearing work boots and pants with a jacket that looked like it was part of a uniform. His head was down and his hair messed up.

Green made eye contact with the sergeant in charge of the scene. It was Sergeant Walker, a veteran of the latest Middle East conflict like Detective Green. They got along pretty well when their spheres of influence overlapped, such as in cases like this.

As Walker approached, Green asked, "What do we have here Sarge?"

Walker tilted his head toward the white guy sitting on the step, "We got one . . ." he paused to look at the data tablet in his hands, "James Paul Brennan. Works for Pinnacle Elevator Service Company. He is claiming self-defense in the killing of one Dantrell, no middle name, Freeman. Street name is Dante, known associate of Aaron Mitchell, who as you know founded and leads the Southwest Militia."

Detective Green, usually a cool customer with a smooth poker face, couldn't hide his astonishment at what Walker had just shared.

"Whoa. Wait a minute." Green needed a moment to put together all the information he was just hit with. First, the perpetrator's name rang a bell. *Yes, that's right*, Green thought. He had taken a call from James Brennan—Jimmy, he recalled the caller saying—about being mugged and harassed by a street thug. Green recalled sitting as his desk and pulling the file up as Jimmy spoke to him, and recalled that the responding officers had listed the name "Dante" as the suspect in the mugging.

Green looked back at the police line. A crowd was gathering. That was bad news. Once Aaron heard that one of his soldiers was killed, he would act decisively for revenge. If he showed up with his posse, Green wasn't sure he would be able to bring Mr. Brennan back to the precinct building alive.

Green looked back to Walker and asked, "You talk to Brennan yet?"

Walker shook his head and said, "Nope. That's your job, big boy. I don't want to tread on your territory."

Green grimaced, "Thanks. Let's see what we got and then we need to get this guy outta' here. Once Aaron shows up, there could be trouble. Can you call in some more uniforms to provide us a show of force?"

Walker took off his cold weather cap and scratched his scalp. "Shit. I didn't think about that. Yeah man, keep your interview short or just take him to the precinct now. I'm too old to tussle with Aaron and his troops."

Green nodded and walked to where Mr. Brennan was seated. As he approached, the young man lifted his head. He was an average-looking white dude. Brown hair, blue eyes, maybe a little pudge on his face. Not the face of a cold-blooded killer, but hey, who knows anymore. He did have a gauze pad taped to the bottom of his neck just above the sternum. A little red blotch was visible on the outside of the gauze, but it looked like the bleeding had stopped.

"Mr. Brennan? I'm Detective Green. What happened here?" Detective Green watched as Mr. Brennan squinted his eyes and tilted his head to the side.

Then a look of hope emerged on Mr. Brennan's face as he said, "You can call me Jimmy. Everyone does. But, hey . . . I think I remember your name. You took my call about my mugging. Well, this is what happened—"

Green interrupted Jimmy, "Before you say anything, has anyone told you your rights?"

Jimmy shook his head and shrugged his shoulders, his hands still cuffed behind his back. "No, they cuffed me and treated my wound. Nobody has said anything except to sit and wait for you."

Green said, "Standard procedure kid, it's for your and the responding officers' safety until we figure out who's who and what's what." Green then read Jimmy his Miranda rights from memory.

Green spared a quick glance to the crowd and saw no change in its size or demeanor. He decided to get some information now while Jimmy was off-balance and everything was fairly fresh. He asked, "Now we got that out of the way, can you just tell me what happened here?"

Jimmy paused for a minute. Green wasn't sure if it was to get his story straight or if he was trying to remember exactly what happened. Usually when perps pulled a stunt like this, Green figured they were trying to line up their lies; but this guy looked scared and sincere.

Jimmy took a deep breath and spoke, "Before you read me my rights, I was telling you that we had spoken on the phone just last Friday."

Green said, "You know what Jimmy? You're right. I do remember that call. But that still doesn't explain how Dante is dead and you're in handcuffs. Please continue."

Jimmy nodded and said, "That's right. Good. I'm glad you remember. Dante mugged me, as you know, a few weeks ago. And since then, he's been stalking me anywhere I go in the city. With my service van lettered up like a rolling billboard, I'm not easy to miss. So after the mugging, he wanted me to pay a tax every time he saw me. I didn't have enough cash on me today to pay so he attacked me with a knife and I defended myself."

Green looked at the patch on Jimmy's neck, "Is that where he stabbed you?"

Jimmy again nodded, "Yes sir. He would have killed me. No doubt."

Green asked, "And why didn't he?"

Green watched as Jimmy swallowed and looked as his hands. Then he looked back at Detective Green and said, "I shot him."

Green let that sink in for a minute without saying anything. Then he clicked on his tablet a few times.

Looking up from the tablet, Green studied Jimmy's face and asked, "Jimmy, I don't show you owning a gun or having a license to carry a gun. Where'd you get the gun?"

Detective Green had been trained on police interrogation techniques several times during his career. There were several "tells" to look for when someone was lying. Not every person did the same thing, but almost everyone had a tell. The trick was to establish a baseline of questions and answers where the suspect answers truthfully before asking a critical question where the suspect may be lying.

In this case, Detective Green saw Jimmy blush ever so slightly. Usually, the tell has something to do with the eyes, but in this case the skin around his neck and cheeks flushed for just a moment.

Jimmy responded, "I found the gun right after my lunch break today in the stairwell of the building I was working in. I was going to call it in to the police once I got to my van at the end of my shift, I just never made it there because of Dante."

Detective Green thought about it. Not a bad lie, as far as lies went. The truth was probably that he bought the gun from a street dealer to protect himself after having been harassed by Dante. No way to prove either if the kid stuck to his story.

Green heard a commotion and looked back to the police line. Sergeant Walker jogged over, and, winded from the short exertion, spoke rapidly, "Aaron's guys are setting up a perimeter around the building and blocked the parking lot with some pickup trucks and several of his militia. I told you to get this perp outta' here quick. Now what are we going to do?"

Green thought through his options. There was no way Aaron would let Jimmy out of here alive, and at least half the cops working the scene were on his payroll and would probably help—or at the least, not hinder—Aaron in any attempt to grab Jimmy.

Green again looked to the police line and saw nervous expressions on their faces. There was no way out of this. Green reached for his radio to call for backup, even though he knew this conflict would be over well before any backup showed.

Green was surprised when Jimmy spoke, "My van is parked two blocks over, if we go out the back of this alley now, we could probably make it."

Green thought about it. The kid didn't seem violent and this was probably his only chance to get him back to the precinct building in one piece.

Green said, "Okay, kid. Here's the deal, I'm going to uncuff you, but if you try anything stupid, I will shoot you myself."

Green grabbed Jimmy by the shoulder and hauled him to his feet, then quickly spun him around and unlocked the handcuffs.

As this was happening, Jimmy said, "No funny business. I promise." Jimmy reached down and picked up his backpack, putting it on.

Green unholstered his service pistol with his right hand and grabbed Jimmy's jacket with his left as they crouched and ran from the crime scene and out the back of the alley.

# CHAPTER 19

*Monday, November 13ᵗʰ, 2028*
*5:25 PM*

Jimmy's head was spinning. It was barely half an hour since he had taken Dante's life and now he and the police detective were running for their lives from the Southwest Militia. If the police feared Aaron and his thugs this much, what hope did average people have against the man?

Leading the detective through the alley, the detective holding onto his jacket with one hand and pointing his pistol in his back with the other, scared the hell out of Jimmy. But since Detective Green was the only person keeping him from Aaron's gang, he wasn't about to do anything stupid to the one guy trying to keep him alive.

The alley was about forty yards long and Dante's body was near the other end of the alley. As they reached the back end of the alley, there was a uniformed police officer standing post, making sure no one came this way.

*Good,* Jimmy thought. Another police officer that could help protect him. He was on his cell phone, speaking in hushed tones.

Green motioned for Jimmy to stay put alongside the cold brick wall of the building.

Green crept up on the officer, pistol aimed at the back of his head. Jimmy watched in confusion as Green put the muzzle of the gun against the officer's head. The officer stopped talking into the phone and froze. Green said, "Drop the phone and slowly unholster your pistol."

The cop started to comply by putting his cell phone on the ground and slowly lifting his pistol from his holster. As he did so, he spoke, "Greenie. What are you doing? Just turn the shooter over to Aaron to deal with. You don't want to go down this path."

Detective Green reached out and took the pistol from the cop's hand. He said, "That's not the way it works, Aaron or not. I'm bringing this kid in and he will be processed per the law, not by the street."

Green kicked the officer's phone down the alley towards the crime scene and gave the cop a push toward the phone. As the cop started toward his phone Green yelled, "Run!"

Jimmy didn't need more encouragement. He sprinted across the street and heard both the pounding of Green's feet immediately behind him and shouts of exclamation back at the crime scene.

Jimmy ran straight across to the next alley. This alley was shorter than the one where Dante had confronted him. At the end of the alley, he paused to make sure Green was still with him and to see if he was being chased.

Green tackled him as a supersonic crack and a shower of bricks exploded right where Jimmy's head had been a moment ago.

Jimmy scrambled to a low crawl to get around the building as Green encouraged him onward with a steady stream of "Go, go, go!"

Jimmy regained his feet and ran straight to his van, which was now in sight. As he ran, he swung his backpack around and fished his keys from the compartment where he kept them.

Jimmy pressed the unlock button several times and was rewarded by the headlights flashing to indicate that the doors were unlocked. He opened the driver side door, hopped in, and started the van as Green was slamming the door on the passenger side.

Jimmy threw the gearshift into reverse and mashed the pedal to the floor as Green repeated his mantra, "Go, go, go."

Turning the wheel to the right, Jimmy backed the van out of his space and pointed it toward the parking lot exit.

Jimmy put the gear into drive and floored it again. The exit was clear and there was no traffic on the road. They would make it.

As the van picked up speed and Jimmy prepared to make a right onto the city street, he glanced in his side view mirror. He saw a man level a rifle at the van and several flashes erupt from the end of the rifle barrel.

An instant later, the mirror exploded, the van rocked, and the windshield spiderwebbed.

Instinctively, Jimmy jammed on the brakes. Green shouted, "No! You have to go. Go now!"

The shattered windshield was nearly impossible to see out of. How could he drive without seeing where he was going? Jimmy looked over as Green rolled down his window and stuck his head out to get a clear view of the road. Jimmy mashed the accelerator and the van lurched forward.

Green yelled, "Turn now, then straight."

Jimmy made the turn. The staccato of gunfire in the growing distance was followed by "Pang, pang, pang" as the bullets ripped into the back of the van where his service parts and tools were stored.

Jimmy rolled down his window and stuck his head into the face-numbing slipstream outside the cab as he navigated the van down the street.

Jimmy zigzagged through several side streets as he wove his way towards the precinct building per Green's instructions.

He tried to wrap his mind around his current situation. Driving himself to a police station with his head outside the window of his shot-up van. Crap, his van. What was Nick going to think about this? The thought of sitting in Nick's office trying to explain this situation without losing his job gave Jimmy the sweats even though his face was nearly frozen. But then why was he caring about a van when he could be arrested for homicide and go to prison for the rest of his life? Which probably wouldn't last too long, assuming Aaron had his minions there too.

Jimmy looked over at Green. He was talking into his radio, pointing his pistol at Jimmy, alternating his attention between the road and Jimmy.

Nope, no way out of this except to see it through.

Jimmy took a deep breath as they pulled into the parking lot of the police station. Green told him to park around the back of the building next to a door labeled "Employee Entrance."

Jimmy sighed as he put the van in park and killed the motor.

Green said, "Give me the keys and stay right there."

Jimmy waited as Green passed in front of the van, his pistol trained on Jimmy the whole time. Jimmy figured he was just putting on a show for any cops looking out the windows of the station. Jimmy wasn't going anywhere.

Green opened Jimmy's door and said, "If you keep cooperating like you have been, I won't cuff you again. Deal?"

Jimmy nodded and said, "Deal." He then slowly exited the van and gave Green his backpack as they entered the building together.

They were met just inside the door by a large black man in a fancier uniform than Jimmy had seen on the street cops.

This officer, clearly some sort of supervisor, spoke first, "So Greenie. Is this the young man that has everyone so excited?"

Detective Green nodded, "Yes sir, Captain Willis. I'm going to take him upstairs for processing, then we need to talk."

Captain Willis nodded and said, "Good job detective. You did the right thing here. We can't let men like Aaron make up the law as they see fit." Turning to Jimmy he said, "Young man, I don't know what happened earlier this afternoon or how you ended up in this predicament, but you are lucky that Green was called to the scene. Unfortunately, we have fewer and fewer men like Green willing to put their lives on the line to protect and serve."

Processing was a blur of fingerprints, pictures, and telling his story over and over to Green, Willis, and a very attractive Latina woman in a suit whose badge listed her last name as Hernandez. In addition to the struggle with Dante, they focused on the pistol. Jimmy stuck to his story about finding it that day and not having the time to turn it in. He figured they were probably checking on the last known owner of the gun. Jimmy hoped there was no way they could trace it back to John. If they could, it would spell serious trouble.

Finally, Green stopped back in. It had been three hours since he was brought into the precinct building. Jimmy was dozing off in the interview room.

He woke up as Green sat across from him and placed Jimmy's backpack on the table. Jimmy asked, "Detective Green, I don't know how all this works. Am I under arrest? Can I make a call?"

Jimmy was confused when Green shook his head and smiled at the same time. What did that mean? Finally, Green spoke. "No kid, you're not under arrest. I just spoke to assistant DA Hernandez. She said the homicide was justifiable self-defense. She wanted to press charges for illegal possession of a handgun, but I talked her out of it based on your cooperation in helping get us back here safely. I've never taken a turn on two wheels in a van and I hope I never have that experience again. You're a heck of a driver, kid."

Jimmy's heart exploded in disbelief at the thought of freedom. He couldn't wait to get home and hug his mom and sleep in his own bed.

Green continued, "But I wouldn't recommend you leave just yet. Since Aaron couldn't get you on the street, it looks like he decided to call the media in on it. There are several news vans outside right now, along with a couple hundred Black Lives Matter protestors. I recommend you let things cool down for a couple more hours. They'll go home soon and then you can go."

Jimmy asked, "Is my van . . . ?"

Green laughed out loud and reached across to pat Jimmy's shoulder, "No, your van's not drivable. And Hernandez wants to keep it for evidence to see if we can find the shooter and press charges. I told her that's a pipe dream, but she wants to try. You'll have to call someone to come pick you up."

Jimmy thought about it. He needed to call his mom so she wouldn't be worried. But she hasn't driven much recently and couldn't drive at night.

He also needed to call Nick and tell him what had happened to the van. But Nick lived out in the boonies, west on the PA Turnpike out in Morgantown. No way he would come all the way back here to the city to get him home.

There was no way he would call John. Jimmy wanted to keep his one kind-of-friend out of this situation.

That left Colleen. She didn't have a car, but Jimmy was sure she could drive his mom's old Crown Vic. There was a spare key in the kitchen. Logistically, the plan should work.

Jimmy had mixed feelings about asking for help from Colleen. On one hand, he was looking for ways to spend time with her away from his mom and her kids to see if there was any chance of them being anything more than neighbors. But these circumstances weren't ideal for having one-on-one time. He'd been hoping for something more along the lines of dinner and a movie.

Jimmy would have to call his mom right afterwards to explain that everything was alright, but for now he would tell her he needed Colleen to pick him up in the city because his van couldn't be driven. Which was technically true, so he didn't feel too bad about keeping his mom in the dark until he could tell her in person—or at least, have a longer conversation over the phone.

Jimmy said, "Thanks Detective. I'll call my neighbor and have her pick me up in my mom's car in a couple hours."

Detective Green became serious and said, "Look here Jimmy. This isn't the end of this. You and I are square, and the City is not pressing charges. But guys like Aaron won't let this go. Watch your back. Stay safe."

With that, Detective Green escorted Jimmy to a waiting area near the front of the building.

Jimmy sat on a chair lining the wall. He was the only one in the waiting area. He opened his backpack and fished out his cell phone. There were several voicemails from his mom. He'd call her in a minute. Instead of listening to them, he brought up the contact for Colleen and pressed send. It rang three times and Colleen picked up, saying, "Hey Jimmy what's up? Running late again?"

Jimmy let out a small chuckle of relief, "That's one way to put it Colleen. Actually, I really need your help . . ."

# CHAPTER 20

*Wednesday, November 15ᵗʰ, 2028*
*8:25 AM*

Julianne was reading the local news on her phone during the bus ride to work. There was bad news, and then there was really bad news. And fortunately for Julianne, the really bad news eclipsed the bad news.

The bad news was that Mayor Rhodes and Managing Director Roosevelt made good on their promise to make Julianne the face of the City's financial woes. As such, Julianne had been hounded by the press like never before in her career. It seemed like an evil band of paparazzi was following her every move trying to get a comment or a sound bite from her. Finally, she'd decided to hold an interview with a representative from each of the three major news outlets in the city.

The interview was recorded last night in her office—after all, if it was going to be three on one, she figured she might as well have home court advantage. At the time, Julianne thought the interview went relatively well. The questions were hard but fair and Julianne took her time to explain the situation, the changes made, and the path forward.

The interview was recorded but not videotaped. Three camera crews wouldn't have fit in her office anyway. They posed for some pictures at the end of the two-hour interview, shook hands, and called it a night.

But this morning, reading the articles based on the interview, Julianne was astonished at the news outlets' skill in spinning stories. Comparing her memory of participating in the interview versus reading the articles was like looking back in time through a warped lens that had been shattered then reassembled with Scotch tape. Julianne couldn't put her finger on a single instance of an outright lie, but the truth was so badly twisted and manipulated that it was unrecognizable. Every new article she read seemed to put her more at fault for the crisis than the last.

If that was the only news breaking this morning, Julianne was sure she would have been getting some ugly stares from her fellow commuters. But because of the really bad news, people weren't interested in reading a few long-winded, complicated articles about an interview with the City's Director of Finance.

The really bad news was that there had been a shooting in Southwest Philadelphia two days ago. Nothing news worthy about that in itself; there were shootings in the city all the time.

What made it news worthy was that the shooter was white, the victim was black, and they were letting the shooter go free because it was ruled a justifiable homicide in a case of self-defense.

Julianne would have thought that with everything facing the nation—an invasion in Alaska, Texas forcefully trying to leave the union, war in the Ukraine and Middle East, China annexing Taiwan, fuel shortages, high prices for food, and of course the City's finances tanking—the social warriors would have taken a break and been focused on something a little more large-scale and pertinent.

But the outrage machine was in full force this morning, with the shooting taking the headlines on all the news outlets and generating thousands of comments on the outlets' websites. People were outraged and demanded that the shooter's name be released. So far, Julianne saw no mention of the shooter's name. The district attorney explained that this was for the man's safety. It did leak out that the shooter lived outside the city in a nearby suburb.

Julianne had, in recent months, detected a subtle hostility from the surrounding suburban townships and counties. Never anything overt, but little things—like ways they used to cooperate that they didn't anymore. And she wasn't the only one who'd noticed: Chief Braxton had also mentioned it a few times in their recent conversations.

The bus slowed and brought Julianne's attention back to her surroundings. Her stop was next.

The bus lurched to a stop alongside the city government MSB building on 15th Street. Her eyes grew wide as she stepped out of the bus. She turned to get back on the bus, but the doors had closed behind her and it lumbered off, leaving her stranded.

There were hundreds—no, thousands—of protestors in front of the MSB building. Usually, Julianne hopped off the bus, bounded up the stairs two at a time, and strode across the concrete plaza to the front doors of the building. That wasn't going to happen today.

Julianne saw two flavors of protestors present in the agitated stew of humanity blocking the entrance to the building. The mix was about fifty-fifty—half of the protestors were holding up signs with the letters "BLM" and chanting, "Justice for Dante!"; the second half were holding signs that read "IOU" with the letters circled in red with a slash through the circle.

She decided to avoid that half.

Julianne pulled her winter cap down over her forehead and tucked her chin down. She was glad she was still wearing her winter boots and not her work shoes with heels; if she had to make a run for it, the boots were better. Her work shoes, lunch, and some papers were in her attaché case.

Instead of bounding up the steps, she weaved her way through the protestors who had spilled out to the sidewalk and made her way north on 15th Street, parallel to the MSB building. She hoped the protestors didn't know about the rear entrance.

Julianne had only taken a few steps when a woman to her left yelled, "Hey! That's the lady that fired my husband."

Julianne kept her head down and her pace steady as a loose, queasy feeling gripped her gut, while the muscles in her arms, legs, and butt tightened. Her breaths came in a quicker cadence, almost to the point of panting.

A hand reached out and ripped her winter cap off her head, allowing her straight ebony hair to fall past her shoulders. She immediately broke into what she hoped would look like a dignified jog. She didn't want to look like she was panicking, which she absolutely was, but at the same time she wanted to create some distance between her and the protestors. She knew there were usually security guards at the back door; all she had to do was make it a block north and make a right on Arch Street. The door was only twenty yards or so from that intersection.

A split second after her cap came off a shrill voice in the crowd screeched, "That's her! She's the one who gave us IOUs. Get her!"

The crowd was behind her now, but only by a few steps. Without turning back to see what the crowd was doing, she dropped her case and broke into an all-out sprint north on the sidewalk.

Julianne ran for her life as the crowd surged to pursue her, shouting angrily. Her long legs and lunchtime workouts proved to be more than a match for the pace of the pursuing crowd. A sprig of hope sprouted in Julianne's mind as she calculated that at this pace, she would be able to make the turn to the safety of the rear entrance before the crowd could catch her.

Legs and arms pumping, Julianne neared the end of the block and got her first view of the rear entrance. Her heart nearly stopped. There was a group of at least thirty protestors at that door, with the neither the police nor building security anywhere in sight.

Julianne slowed her pace to look for options. Unfortunately, this gave her pursuers time to close the distance her sprint had created. And by now, the protesters at the rear door were heading her way to check out the commotion.

Instantly, Julianne made her decision. She would keep running north on 15th Street to the lobby of the hospital just before 15th and Vine Streets. It was only two blocks away and would offer her at least a modicum of safety.

Shifting her weight forward to continue her sprint, she leaped down the sidewalk to the road surface and immediately had to stop herself as a sedan slammed on its brakes and swerved to miss her. As she was about to clear the hood, a voice shouted from the sedan, "Julianne, it's Braxton! Get in the car!"

Continuing with her forward momentum, Julianne leapt feet first and slid over the hood of the sedan. She was thankful she was wearing a pair of slacks and not a dress-skirt today. No way she would have been able to run, let alone pull a *Dukes of Hazzard* move over the hood, wearing a skirt.

As soon as Julianne cleared the hood, the crowd hit the car and surged around it. Julianne flung the passenger door open and rocketed into the seat. Without having a chance to close the door, Braxton hit the gas and the sedan leapt forward. No one was in front of the sedan, although one young man was thrown off the hood as he was in the middle of attempting the same move Julianne had completed mere seconds ago.

Braxton weaved the car through the incoming traffic on 15th Street and cleared the intersection heading east on Arch St. The traffic was light and Braxton slowed the sedan to a normal pace. Julianne looked in the side view mirror and saw that the crowd had not moved from its perch on the corners of 15th and Arch Streets.

Julianne let out a long sigh and performed a quick assessment. Obviously, she'd lost her cold weather cap. Too bad, she liked that one. It was made of faux fur and had the flaps that kept her ears warm with cute little tassels than hung down nearly to her shoulders. She'd also lost her soft-sided attaché case. It contained some paperwork, which wasn't a big deal, but it also had her lunch in it.

Then she patted her coat pockets. Her mom was never a purse-carrying lady—Julianne supposed it was a byproduct of being a policewoman—so Julianne had never carried one either. Her keys, cellphone, and wallet were still nestled in her coat pockets. That was great news.

Julianne looked at Braxton. His arrival on the corner couldn't have been a coincidence. "Chief, what . . . what the hell? How did you know to be there?"

Braxton glided the car to a stop and pulled over to let other cars pass. He looked over at Julianne with a sheepish smile, saying, "Sorry about that Julianne. I heard through the grapevine that our favorite pit bull, Larry, pulled the protective detail from you right after I was put on leave. Being on leave is boring, so I kept an eye on you to and from work."

He continued, "I hope you aren't upset. I just wanted to make sure you were alright. I couldn't let anything happen to the best Director of Finance in the history of the city."

Julianne chuckled at Braxton's reference to her support of him at the last cabinet meeting. She reached out and placed her hand on Braxton's shoulder. "No Chief, I'm not upset. I am happy to be alive. I can't believe the bloodlust in that crowd."

Braxton added, "Also, since I am on leave, it's probably not appropriate for you to keep calling me Chief. My friends call me Emmitt. It's kinda' short for Emanuel and goes back to my high school football days. There was a running back with the same name back in the nineties, so I guess the guys noticed the similarity and it just stuck. Having the nickname didn't make me anywhere near as good though." He chuckled, then became serious again. "And as far as the crowd goes, bloodlust is par for the course with an angry mob. What concerns me is the lack of police presence. I wonder if our friend Larry had anything to do with that, or with the lack of the usual guards around the outside of the MSB building."

Julianne thought about that. She couldn't believe Mayor Rhodes would have anything to do with this ambush, but she wouldn't put it past Larry. That man would do anything to further his agenda. She had a lunch with him and the mayor scheduled for Monday. Perhaps she would confront him then.

Julianne looked out the windshield at the people bustling by on the sidewalks heading to work. These people deserved the best public servants society could provide to serve their needs. Not cutthroats like Larry Roosevelt or self-serving eels like Mayor Rhodes. It angered Julianne to think that the bad elements in the city government could do so much damage despite the best efforts of those like Braxton and herself working earnestly on behalf of its citizens.

Julianne looked back at Braxton and said, "I don't have any way to prove Larry's involvement one way or another. Right now, all I want to do is to get into work so I can continue to serve this city and its people."

Emmitt nodded and patted the steering wheel, "That's the spirit. If you don't mind me taking your personal protection to the next level and working side-by-side with you, I've got an idea on how to get you into work without any problems."

Julianne smiled and responded, "I don't mind at all."

# CHAPTER 21

*Saturday, November 18th, 2028*
*8:25 AM*

The morning dawned bright and the sky was pale blue without a cloud in sight. A high-pressure front from Canada had swept down the East Coast, bringing with it clear skies and bitter cold temperatures. Reggie was thankful there wasn't any breeze, but it was the first hard freeze of November. The grass was frosted over and crunched with every step Reggie took.

The pastor had made his closing statement and his son's casket was lowered into the ground. Reggie had stayed by the grave for a few more minutes after the small group that had attended his son's funeral shuffled away. It seemed the thing to do. He knew he should have some deep thought for his son or say something like they do in the movies, but all Reggie could think about was how he wished his last words with his son had been kind ones. The last time Reggie had seen his son alive, Dante was slamming the door to his house after he had kicked Dante out.

Reggie plucked a red rose from the bouquet next to the pastor's podium and dropped it onto his son's casket. The petals scattered across the glossed ebony lid like the blood of so many young men on the black asphalt of Philadelphia's streets.

Two dark emotions swirled in Reggie's soul for dominance. One was guilt. He was the one who kicked his son out of his house and onto the streets. Dante made the choice to mug and harass people and that was his final undoing, but what if putting him out on the street was the tipping point? Would things have been different if Reggie had let Dante stay in his home?

*We'll never find out now*, Reggie thought to himself.

The other emotion competing for Reggie's heart was anger. His rage was focused on the police. How could they release the man who killed his son without charging him for the murder? Reggie thought that when a man did a crime, especially as big a crime as killing someone, that he was supposed to be charged with the crime and face a jury of his peers. Reggie wanted to see that man on the witness stand explaining to everyone why he saw fit to kill a man who was a son, a brother, a veteran, a fellow man.

*Now that man is scot-free and my son is dead.* That fact made Reggie more pissed off than he had ever been in his life. But what could he do about any of this except simmer in his own guilt, anger, and helplessness?

The thought of revenge was creeping in at the edge of his emotions. But revenge against who? The shooter who killed his son? The police wouldn't release his name and truth be told, Reggie admitted to himself, the man probably was defending himself. The police? The city government? The mayor? God himself? It all seemed so pointless and overwhelming.

His thoughts scattered from the darkness surrounding Dante and gravitated to the one remaining light in his life, Rose. Having her come home from college last night was the only good thing to come of this whole sorry event. Come to think of it, he should probably go find her and see if she wanted to grab lunch before he took her back to the train station to head back to school. As much as Reggie liked having his Roseate around, this whole ordeal was further confirmation that this neighborhood was bad news, and keeping her away from it was the best thing for her.

Reggie turned away from the grave and started walking to the parking lot where he could see a couple of groups congregating. Just before the ceremony began, Aaron, Jackie, and two of Aaron's henchmen had arrived. Reggie didn't recognize either of the other men. One was serious-looking and dark skinned, built like a sprinter. The other was tall and lanky with eyes protruding like a fish Reggie had seen at the pet store when he was a kid.

At first Reggie was surprised to see Jackie, a man he considered to be his friend, with Aaron. He hadn't seen Jackie at the truck yard since the day the City started issuing those IOUs. Reggie had asked a couple of the other mechanics where Jackie was and they wouldn't say. At least now his question was answered. As much as it saddened him, it made sense. Too bad Jackie couldn't stay straight and work a real job. Working for Aaron eventually led to one of two places: jail or right here, next to his Dante.

Aaron had brought a bouquet of white roses and he and his posse stood respectfully during the ceremony, so Reggie had no problem with them being there. There weren't but a couple other people at the funeral, so having Aaron and his people there made it feel like there was a little bit of a gathering. On the way to the cemetery, Reggie had shared a fear with Rose that it would only be the two of them and the pastor at the funeral.

As Reggie approached the parking lot, he saw that Rose was speaking with Aaron. Although he couldn't hear what she said, he saw her place a hand on his shoulder while talking to him.

He mentally withdrew his olive branch of goodwill.

Reggie's heart pounded in his chest as he walked up to the small gathering. He didn't want his Rose talking with these criminals even for a minute. Dante got killed running with Aaron's gang and Jackson was headed down the same path. There was no way he'd let his Roseate get tangled up with them.

Rose was a sweet young woman with a big heart. She put her trust in people and only saw the good in others. Reggie had seen how her naïveté had nearly gotten her in trouble in her teens; that's part of why he was so adamant she go away for college. When Rose was in her early teens, it was a constant battle to keep her away from the older boys who ran with Aaron. He was dangerous then, with his drug dealing and street violence. But his money and good looks made the neighborhood girls fantasize about being his girl, and the young boys dreamed of being in his posse.

The whole neighborhood got a huge break when Aaron got drafted to fight in the Ukraine. The unspoken, guilty hope (at least for parents like Reggie) was that Aaron would return in a body bag. But he came back on his own two feet, and Uncle Sam had given him the training and network to rule Southwest Philadelphia with an iron fist.

Reggie walked directly to the group, stopping next to his daughter, "Thank you for coming Mr. Mitchell. Dante'd be proud to know you showed him the respect to see him off." Addressing a street thug like Aaron by his last name chafed at Reggie, but he knew Aaron was a dangerous man. Best to show a man like that respect, then get far away from him as quickly as you can.

Aaron nodded, "You're welcome Mr. Freeman. Jackie tells me you're the hardest working truck driver in the city."

Reggie lowered his head and scuffed some pebbles with his shoes, "I don't know about that Mr. Mitchell. Jackie and I go back a ways. I got him out of a jam when he was younger."

Looking at Jackie, he continued, "I can tell you that we miss Jackson on the yard; in fact, the brakes on my truck could use him wrench'n on it to straighten them out."

Jackson shook his head and said, "There ain't no going back for me Reggie. Aaron takes care of his people. Something the mayor forgot when he decided to short pay me, you, and a lot of other hardworking people. If you had any sense, you'd be ask'n my boss if there was any need for truck drivers in his organization."

Aaron looked back and forth at the two men, raising his eyebrows. Then he focused on Reggie and said, "That's not a bad idea, Jackie. I can always use a driver that can negotiate a large truck in the streets of Philly. What do you say Mr. Freeman? You wanna' stop by my H-Q Monday and talk terms?"

Reggie wished he had the spine to rebuke Aaron. This was the man who used people up for his nefarious deeds. His son's death was the most recent example, but there had been hundreds before and there would be hundreds to come.

Reggie wanted to tell Aaron that he was a fool for thinking he would ever work in his gang. Instead, he said, "That's a mighty fine offer Mr. Mitchell. But I'm happy driving for the city even if they can't pay me everything they owe me right now."

Jackie grunted. Aaron shrugged and turned to Roseate.

Reggie looked at his friend and shook his head thinking, *Doesn't he know he'll end up in the ground next to Dante if he keeps working for Aaron?*

Reggie clasped his hand on Roseate's and added, "Speaking of right now, I'm looking forward to having lunch with my sweet Rose before she heads back to school."

Rose smiled and turned to Reggie and said, "Daddy. Aaron was telling me about some of his businesses he runs. He offered to buy me lunch and drive me back to college this afternoon. Is it okay if you and I take a rain check?"

A chill ran down Reggie's spine. He tightened his grip on Rose's hand and stammered, "No—no Rose, it ain't ok."

He quickly turned to Aaron while still holding Rose, "No disrespect, but I don't want my daughter knowing nothing about your business."

Then speaking to Rose, "Honey, you need to stay with me. Besides your old man, this neighborhood's got nothing for you now."

Rose rolled her eyes, "Dad, I'm all grown up now, you can't tell me who I can associate with."

Aaron's henchmen now took notice of the conversation and moved closer to the group protectively on either side of Aaron. Jackie uncrossed his arms, his gorilla sized hands resting near his belt.

Aaron furrowed his brow and spoke to Reggie, "You heard her pops. She's all grown up now and it sounds to me like she wants to have a meal with me before she goes back to school."

Reggie found his spine. Looking Aaron eye to eye he responded, "Don't matter how old she is. I'm her father and she's coming with me."

Reggie lightly pulled Roseate closer to him, placed his other hand on her upper back, and started to guide her away from Aaron, towards the train station.

Rose resisted Reggie's gentle push and protested, "Daddy! You can't tell me what to do."

Aaron glanced at his henchmen and said, "Books. Wilson. Escort Rose to my ride."

Reggie held his daughter closer and shouted, "No! Leave us alone. You already got my son killed. Now you want to take my daughter too."

Booker grabbed the hand that Reggie had on Rose's back and twisted his wrist back to a painful angle. While Reggie was distracted, Wilson grabbed Rose's hand from Reggie and pulled her away from Reggie.

Confused, Rose cried out, "What are you doing to my Daddy? Aaron, tell them to stop."

Instead Aaron shook his head as Booker and Wilson shuffled Rose past him.

Reggie took a step to pursue his daughter, but Jackson blocked his path. Reggie was crying out to his daughter as Jackson held him fast.

Aaron raised his voice, "Jackie. Time to prove your loyalty. Drop this old man."

Holding Reggie at arm's length like a parent would with a child in the throes of a tantrum, Jackie answered, "No contest boss. I'd take a bullet for you, this is a cake walk."

Holding Reggie firmly with his left hand, Jackson reared his right arm back and threw a lightening fast jab to Reggie's face.

Reggie's vision exploded in a white flash with red streaks of lightening arcing across his field of view. His legs lost all strength and he desperately clung to consciousness.

Jackson grabbed Reggie with both hands to keep him from falling. He turned to Aaron and said, "I'm gonna' drop this old man in the grass next to his son. I'll meet you in the car."

Aaron nodded and walked back to his SUV where the now frantic Rose was being forcefully shoved into the backseat.

Jackson lowered his voice and spoke into Reggie's ear as he shuffled him across the parking lot, "I pulled that punch old man. Otherwise you'd be dead right now. If you want to see tomorrow, do what I tell you. Pretend like you are knocked out and stay that way for five minutes after we leave. Then go home and forget this ever happened."

Reggie whispered back, "No. I gotta' get my Rose back."

Jackson lifted him up over the curb and roughly dropped him next to Dante's grave.

"Listen old man. I'll get Rose out as soon as I have a chance. Promise me you'll let me take care of this or I'll finish you right here and now and then roll you into the same hole as your boy."

Reggie looked past Jackson to the idling SUV holding his daughter. Letting out a breath he had been holding, Reggie nodded his head slightly, looked at his son's grave and said, "Don't let him kill my Rose, Jackie."

Jackie looked down at Reggie and rubbed his neck with his hands. Then he turned and quickly walked across the parking lot to the waiting SUV.

Ignoring Jackie's instructions, Reggie pushed himself up to his hands and knees and watched the SUV carrying his daughter, his Rose, his last remaining love, disappear behind a tenement building.

# CHAPTER 22

*Monday, November 20<sup>th</sup>, 2028*
*12:25 PM*

Julianne was usually enthralled by the Palm restaurant. Today she was on her guard, as she had been for the better part of a week, since the mob tried to kill her in front of her work place.

As she walked in, she wanted to be distracted by the caricatures of famous diners throughout the years that adorned the wall of the restaurant, but she knew she had to stay focused on the men she was having lunch with. It did comfort her to know that Chief Braxton—no, Emmitt, she reminded herself—who had escorted her to the restaurant, was waiting outside. They both agreed that there was no need for him to come into the restaurant. There was no danger of physical confrontation in such a public place, and they liked the idea of keeping Emmitt's role in protecting Julianne a secret. At least for now.

The official reason for this lunch meeting was still unclear to Julianne, but it had been called by David Berkowitz, the City Comptroller. Comptroller was an independently elected position whose job it was to make sure the City was spending the taxpayers' money in a responsible, legal manner. As comptroller, David was a thorn in the mayor's side and an object of hatred to Larry Roosevelt. Julianne's opinion was that David was more politically motivated than she would like, but she was able to work with the man. She found him to be highly intelligent, motivated, and fair.

As Julianne took her seat, Mayor Rhodes and Larry stopped their conversation to greet her. David was not yet at the table.

After the requisite greetings were completed, Larry added, "Julianne. I heard you had some trouble at work the other morning? What happened?"

Julianne looked directly into Larry's eyes. He was feigning concern, but his eyes betrayed the humor he clearly found in the situation. Julianne's temptation was to berate the man and accuse him of setting up the whole protest and mob chase. But that would be childish and inappropriate, and would only make her look like a fool in front of the mayor—besides the fact that she had no proof. Instead, she decided to lightly jab him back.

Julianne replied, "Oh, it was nothing Larry. Nothing a big girl like me couldn't handle on her own."

Larry grunted in response and turned back to the mayor to continue the conversation that Julianne had interrupted by her arrival.

"Bill, listen to me. You need to cancel the Thanksgiving address. The threat of violence is higher than any previous year and we have intel—"

Mayor Rhodes interrupted Larry mid-sentence. "No. The people need to see some stability in the city government. Cancelling a traditional address will show them we're just as scared as they are."

Larry said, "Okay, I agree with that. Why not release a video on YouView or something like that? As I was saying, I'm getting intel from law enforcement that several groups are planning on protesting, including disgruntled municipal workers, students, and your usual batch of anarchists. Look what happened to Julianne the other day. The people are restless."

The mayor responded, "Why is that any different than in years before?"

Larry answered, "Because this year, the city workers are getting IOUs instead of paychecks. They are very, very angry." He shot Julianne a glance and then continued. "The students are pissed because we aren't giving them free breakfasts and lunches anymore. And then there's the issue of our police. We don't have enough to keep the streets safe on a normal day, let alone a major event like this. Thefts, burglaries, and armed robberies are all at elevated levels since we issued the IOUs."

The mayor made a swatting motion with his right hand, "I hear similar complaints every year I give this speech. You have two days to get the security right. Make it happen, you always do."

Julianne saw Larry clench his jaw for a moment, then relax. He looked at Julianne and quickly added, "Ask Julianne," turning to her for the first time in their conversation, "Ask her, how are we going to pay for the police overtime to provide security along with the maintenance crews setting up and cleaning after the event? Ask her where the money is coming from."

Julianne shifted in her seat and spoke for the first time in the conversation, "I drafted a memo to cover the expenses by shifting the funds from the parks and recreation budget."

Mayor Rhodes smiled, "See Larry? Julianne has us covered. No problem there."

Julianne thought Larry was about to pound the table but instead, he placed his hands on either side of his place setting. "Julianne. I'm curious. What aspect of the parks and recreation department will lose funding to allow the mayor to safely make his speech?"

Treading carefully, she responded, "The plan right now is to shutter an additional twenty percent of the city's neighborhood pools this summer. That will pay for all the expenses incurred with this speech."

Larry looked like he was about to lash out. Instead he let out a long breath and said somewhat despondently, "That sucks. What are these kids going to be doing with their time instead of swimming and exercising? It just leads to more problems with crime and delinquency. Just do me a favor and keep the pool open in my neighborhood. My wife would kill me if that one closed."

The mayor clasped his hand on Larry's shoulder, "No problem Larry. We take care of our own. Well, now that we settled that, look who's here! The city's finest faithful servant, David Berkowitz."

David approached the table carrying a leather folding portfolio cover. He was a small man, not portly, but definitely overweight. Not the kind of overweight from eating too much, but from fifty plus years of not exercising. His body looked soft and his hair was receding from his forehead in the typical male balding pattern. David's dark suit looked a little frumpy and his smile was a little crooked as he approached the table, extending his hand to shake with the mayor. But one thing that stood out about David was his eyes. They were sharp, focused, and seemed to size up the three of them in an instant.

Once the usual pleasantries were extended and everyone was seated, David spoke. "Your Honor, Larry, Julianne; thank you for taking this meeting with me. It's my job to act as the 'Auditor-In-Chief' to make sure the taxpayers' monies are being used as efficiently as possible and to ensure that all laws are being followed with regards to the City's accounting procedures."

Larry interjected, "David, we all know what your job description is, please tell us why you wanted to meet."

David looked directly at Larry and said, "Very well. It began with a phone call I received last week from a friend of mine who now works at an investment bank in New York City." David paused. Julianne took a moment to glance at Larry and Mayor Rhodes. Larry's eyes were intently locked on David's, and the mayor seemed bored or amused or maybe a mix of both. In other words, clueless. Julianne was wondering where this was going so she kept quiet and continued to listen.

David continued, "My friend was calling to thank me for the recent loan the City had secured from his investment bank. I played along and told him no problem and requested he send me the finalized term sheets for my files. When I received the files, I understood why I received the thank-you call. The interest rate the City is paying for this money is off the charts. I also noted that a poor rendition of my signature signed off on the bonds. The only problem is, I never signed off on this debt issuance. I didn't even know we were going out to market for these loans. This is a major problem. By law, I get the final sign-off on any debt issuance by the City."

Larry leaned back and let out a huge breath. "Not my problem, sounds like a financial issue."

Julianne couldn't believe what she was hearing. Yes, she had put in the request for the short-term loan and yes, she knew the rate on the loan was high, but she would have it paid off in two months tops. It was a bridge loan to help keep the city running until her cost saving measures kicked into full force.

Julianne spoke up, "David, my office did request that loan and I know the rates were high, but I can assure you, it had all the required signatures on it before I submitted it to the bank."

David harrumphed and reached down to his briefcase on the floor next to his chair. He pulled out two pieces of paper. One was the signature page on the loan and the other a letter he had written a year ago to the mayor's office.

David placed the two sheets on the table side by side, "As you can see by comparing these documents, the signatures do not match. Not even close."

Julianne inspected the two documents. She was by no means trained as a handwriting analyst, but this was plain to see. The signatures did not match. The *David Berkowitz* on the letter was smooth, flowing, and somewhat effeminate. The *David Berkowitz* on the loan sheet was blockish, abrupt, and unabashedly masculine. Julianne imagined the writer on the forgery was either a man who used his hands to make his living or an athlete. Large and strong, like a football player or a wrestler.

Like Larry.

Julianne looked up from the document, directly at Larry. She recalled the events around securing the loan. She had gone back and forth with the bank a few times to get the rate down and remove the prepayment penalties. Then she had signed the loan signature page and sent it to the mayor's office. That was on a Thursday morning and she was hoping to have the docs back from the comptroller's office Friday at the earliest.

But her assistant had walked the papers into Julianne's office Thursday just after lunch. At the time, she was surprised that the document made it to the mayor's office, the comptroller's office, and back to her office within a business day, but she had so many balls in the air, she was just glad to have something done that could be crossed off the list. It also struck her as odd that David hadn't called to protest the terms on the loan—she'd had her arguments lined up—but again, she didn't want to look a gift horse in the mouth.

Staring directly at Larry, Julianne said, "David, I agree. Those signatures don't match."

Larry leaned forward towards Julianne, "Why are you looking at me? You were the one who submitted a fraudulent document on behalf of the City. I can think of half a dozen laws you broke with this stunt kiddo. This isn't going to end well for you."

Julianne was stunned. Larry had pushed her nearly to the breaking point. Julianne knew that Larry was the mayor's right-hand man and there was never daylight between the two of them, but this was too much. She was not going to let Larry steamroll her.

Julianne shook her head and turned to David, "David, I sincerely apologize that I submitted that loan with what I can clearly now see as your forged signature."

Larry interjected, "Sounds like an admission of guilt to me."

Julianne continued, "However, there are three points I would like to make before anyone starts knotting up a noose." She spared a sharp glance at Larry with that comment. He recoiled as if he had been slapped. Julianne didn't like to use the race card, but she needed to get Larry off balance and she needed time to make her points without him interrupting.

"First, the routing coversheet on the loan clearly stated the document was to go to the mayor's office then to the Comptroller's office before returning to me. It will be interesting to find that routing sheet and do a forensic analysis of the routing. Second, I don't analyze every signature that crosses my desk. I wouldn't get anything done if I performed that level of diligence. I must operate on good faith that when I receive a signature, the person whom it was intended for signed it. Finally, I propose all of us sitting here submit handwriting samples."

Larry erupted, "Don't try to deflect this onto us, Julianne!"

The mayor said, "Hold on Larry, no need to get all fired up. Julianne do you honestly think I had anything to do with this?"

Julianne responded, "No sir, of course not. However, I could imagine a scenario where after you signed it and placed in your out-bin that perhaps one of your close aids intercepted the document, forged the Comptroller's signature, then re-routed the document directly to my office. Or maybe even hand carried it over? I wouldn't be surprised if the video cameras were wiped clean in the MBS building the afternoon I got the loan document back."

Larry huffed and said, "Sounds like a criminal's fantasy."

Julianne didn't respond. She placed her now shaking hands in her lap and waited to see who would speak next.

David reached across the table and put the two sheets back in his briefcase. He then said, "I intend to refer this matter to the District Attorney's office tomorrow morning. We'll let him get to the bottom of this."

Larry held out his smart phone, "I have him on speed dial. Should I give him a call now? He is always up for a lunch at the Palm."

The mayor spoke up, "Gentlemen. Please settle down. Let's look at the bigger picture here. Two days from now is my annual speech and you gentlemen will be on the dais with me."

He then turned to look at Julianne, "Along with you, of course."

Looking back at Larry and David, the mayor continued, "The people need a to see a unified city government. Where we are all in the same boat, rowing in the same direction. Having this story hit right before the speech would be very damaging to the government and our citizens. After the speech is Thanksgiving weekend. David, may I propose that you pursue your investigation with full vigor on the following Monday?"

David shrugged and said, "Sure, I have no problem with that. However, if I find out that any of you used that time to destroy evidence, I will go loud with this on every social media platform I can find."

The mayor nodded and said, "Very well, I agree with that. You'll have my office's full cooperation."

David pushed his chair out and grabbed his folio bi-fold. "Gentlemen, Lady. I look forward to seeing on you at His Honor's speech tomorrow morning."

With that, he turned and left the three of them at the lunch table.

Looking at the two men still at the table, Julianne felt a growing sense of dread. The mayor was looking at the lunch menu detachedly, but Larry's glare was boring right through her. She could almost see the wheels turning in his mind as he worked out a plan to deflect the investigation away from himself, protect the mayor, and pin this on her.

Finally, the mayor looked up. "Well that sucked. What do you say we order some lunch?"

Julianne took a deep breath and responded, "Gentlemen, please excuse me. I need to get some fresh air." Julianne left the table, shrugged on her overcoat, and exited the restaurant to the sidewalk on Broad Street. Emmitt met her just outside the door.

To the left and one block north was City Hall. To the right, in the distance, was South Philly with its baseball, football, and hockey stadiums. Maybe if she turned right and just kept walking she could leave this city with its problems—her problems—far behind her. She took another deep breath and watched the mist dissipate as she exhaled.

She nodded at Emmitt, turned left, and they walked back to her office.

# CHAPTER 23

*Wednesday, November 22nd, 2028*
*11:41 AM*

Reggie was having trouble navigating his truck though his route. Tears streaked his vision. The forearms on both sleeves of his shirt were damp from wiping away the steady flow of heartbreak running from his eyes.

He couldn't believe he was totally, utterly alone. Burying his son was bad. It brought back the pain of burying his wife eleven years ago.

Except saying that wasn't even adequate. Losing Malynne had been a terrible shock but he'd had his son and daughter who still needed raising. Instead of breaking Reggie, it made him stronger, more resolute to get his act together and raise his children right. No, burying Dante was more like an earthquake. Reggie felt as if the ground beneath his feet was no longer reliable.

And then that last blow. After the funeral. Watching his sweet little Rose get stuffed into Aaron's car and leave with him. It had been four days since the funeral and Reggie hadn't heard from Rose at all. No text. No call.

Nothing.

Jackie hadn't returned his calls either, his promise just more words that didn't mean anything.

The reality that his daughter was gone swept Reggie's feet from under him and sent him careening into a chasm of despair.

Reggie had called the university that Rose attended and they said she hadn't been at class since the previous week and her dorm room was unoccupied.

Reggie could only assume the worst. When he called the cops and tried to issue a missing persons' report, they laughed at him. Rose being an adult and only being out of contact for four days didn't mean anything to the cops. They teased Reggie and told him maybe Rose was just having some fun that she didn't want him to find out about.

But Reggie knew better. If she was still alive, Aaron must have her doped up on heroin or something even worse. She probably didn't know where she was, what she was doing, or even who she was right now. First the government let his son's killer walk free and now they wouldn't help find his daughter. Reggie felt a swell of anger surge against the mountain of helplessness in his soul.

Whether it was the man upstairs pushing buttons in some game the Reggie didn't understand, or a more malevolent force stealing his loved ones for his sins in this or a previous life, Reggie didn't know. He just knew that he was alone and angry. Punch someone in the face if they looked at him wrong angry. He hadn't felt this level of rage since he was a young man.

And yes, much of his rage was focused on Aaron and his arrogant Southwest Militia.

However, as the questions swirled in his mind, a new target for his rage was coming into focus: the city government in general, and the police in particular.

Why couldn't the police find out who killed his son? Were they even trying? Why wouldn't the cops bring his Rose home? Reggie had heard that the police weren't getting any IOUs issued for their pay. They were getting paid in full and still couldn't do their jobs! Reggie was getting half his pay, had just lost his family, and still did his job.

The voice on the twenty-four-hour news radio program interrupted Reggie's thoughts with a live announcement: "The mayor is about to take the podium at his annual Thanksgiving address in Love Park."

\* \* \*

*11:42 AM*

Julianne did not want to be at the mayor's annual address. But the mayor had made it clear that it was an "all hands on deck" moment for his administration and she was going to be on deck. Even after the lunch at the Palm, the mayor had followed up with an email to Julianne.

"Your presence will reassure the people of Philadelphia that we have a plan to make our finances strong again," the mayor had written.

"What a crock of crap." Julianne whispered to herself. She and the other who's-who in the city government were all on the podium. Julianne was near the back of the podium. The mayor was in the front row flanked by City Council members. The deputy chief of police, the fire marshal, and various other department heads were in the middle row; and they were all in front of Julianne, who was seated in the back row at the rear edge of the podium.

Chief Emmanuel Braxton, or Emmitt, was not at the speech. He had wanted to be there, but she'd insisted he stay home. "It's just a boring bunch of speeches and there will be hundreds of cops around," she'd said. She argued further that with all the police at the speech protecting the mayor and other bigwigs, it would probably be the safest place in the city. Also, Julianne had noticed that Emmitt was looking tired and needed a break. He probably had family he wanted to be with, even if he didn't say so. After the speech, Julianne was planning on going to her mother's to spend the night and Thanksgiving Day with her.

"No one messes with Mama," she had told Emmitt last night after he dropped her off at her townhome. She recalled the exchange with a smile. She had surprised herself by leaning over and giving Emmitt a peck on the cheek and a quick hug before bounding away up the steps to her front door. Emmitt looked as surprised as she was, but Julianne was convinced she felt electricity between them when her lips touched his cheek. All she knew, as she sat bored, freezing her butt off listening to another pontificating politician's speech, was that she wanted more of that electric feeling.

The crowd was chanting, "IOU, IOU, IOU" over and over again. Because of the noise from the crowd, Julianne could barely make out the words of the President of the City Council as he bloviated on some self-serving topic instead of introducing the mayor, like he was supposed to. Julianne had never seen the crowd for this address so large and so very obviously angry.

\* \* \*

Jackson was standing behind the angry crowd at the mayor's rally with three of Aaron's foot soldiers. Jackson thought the assignment would've been better delegated to a subordinate with less experience, but he hadn't shared that thought with Aaron. He just said, "Yes sir," and got loaded up.

Their job was to make sure a bunch of city workers and high school age kids from the neighborhoods made it to the mayor's speech, and that they were fired up and rowdy. Aaron wanted the mayor's speech to go as poorly as possible. As it turned out, the people here didn't need much encouragement. They were pissed that the City hadn't been paying them properly and they were letting the mayor know by drowning out some speaker with the chant of "IOU" over and over again.

* * *

*11:43 AM*

Reggie stared at the radio. Time seemed to stop. In that moment, Reggie made up his mind. He was going to put an end to being a yes man. An end to being a puppet being pulled by invisible strings. It was time to make a statement.

Reggie wiped the tears from his face. The decision was made. He took a left at the next light toward City Hall and Love Park.

He was going to drop two tons of trash right in front of the mayor's podium. *Let's see how the folks living in the Ivory Tower enjoy a mound of trash under their noses.*

Two blocks later, the two-way radio in Reggie's cab squawked to life. "Reggie, this is southwest dispatch one. We show you deviating from route, please explain."

*That was quick,* thought Reggie. *How did they—*

*Crap.*

He'd forgotten they'd recently updated every rig with a GPS tracker.

Reggie paused for a moment, then replied, "Southwest dispatch one, this is Reggie. I'm having trouble with braking power." He hadn't so far today, but it was believable. "I put in a service req three weeks ago." That was true. He continued, "I'm closer to North Philly service depot, so I'm heading there." It was nearly a toss-up as to which maintenance yard he was closer to, but every block he went toward City Hall got him closer to the north maintenance lot and made his argument more feasible.

There was another long pause. Reggie started sweating. He didn't know what dispatch would do in this situation, but the last thing he needed was for them to call the police for an escort to the southwest yard.

Finally, the radio squawked again. "Copy that Reggie. Proceed to North Philadelphia maintenance depot. They have a spare truck there. Swap vehicles and complete your route. Out."

Reggie released the breath that he had been unconsciously holding.

He made the next right turn that put him on North Broad Street, heading straight toward City Hall. He could see the statue of William Penn on top of the old structure. It wouldn't be long now. Love Park was on the northeast corner near City Hall.

All he had to do was hook a right around City Hall, make a left on JFK, then dump the load. "I'm gonna' show them sons-a-bitches what happens when they jerk us around," Reggie muttered to himself.

# CHAPTER 24

*Wednesday, November 22nd, 2028*
*11:43 AM*

As the mayor was about to take the podium in Love Park, Detective Marcus Green was in the station house for the 18th district of the Philadelphia Police Department at 55th and Pine streets.

Green was pacing inside Captain Willis' office while the captain sat behind his desk scratching his scalp, trying to absorb what Green had just told him. Elizabeth Carter, the clerk who had worked on the case file for the shooting by James Brennan, sat facing Willis' desk with her arms folded across her chest, looking away from the two men towards the windows in the office, an air of defiance radiating from her person.

Finally, Willis spoke. "Shit, Lizzy. Is this true? Did you access the case file after we closed it? What for, Lizzy?"

Lizzy looked at the captain and responded, "I don't know what you and Green are talking about, Captain."

Green stopped pacing and exclaimed, "Bullshit. The IT department tracks all that stuff. I put a trace on that file so that if anyone opened it after it was closed, I would get notified."

Lizzy shifted in her seat and crossed her legs, switching which leg was on top. She looked out the window again and said, "That doesn't prove anything."

Green continued, now addressing the captain, "She's right. But then I pulled the camera feed from the interior and exterior of the building. Two minutes after she accessed the file, she left via the employee exit and stood in the vestibule texting on her cell phone."

Willis leaned forward, his belly pushing against his desk and causing the fabric on his white uniform shirt to strain, "Lizzy. Unlock your phone and hand it to me."

Lizzy slid her smart phone from the nearly invisible side pocket in her stylish knee-length skirt. She clutched the phone to her chest and responded, "Hell no Captain. Don't forget, I'm a clerk at a police station, I know how the law works. You need a warrant to search my phone."

Willis nodded and said, "If you want to stay a clerk in this office, you'll hand me that phone now. I don't need a warrant to fire your ass and make sure you never get another job in the city again."

Green watched the standoff. The captain was nearly as furious as Green was. Green didn't know if the captain understood what this leak meant; he was probably more infuriated with Lizzy's insubordination than he was regarding the implications of the leak.

But Green knew what it meant. There was little doubt in his mind that Lizzy was on Aaron's payroll, or somehow indebted to him. That meant that Aaron was now in possession of all relevant personal information for Dante's shooter, James Brennan.

Green had dealt with witness protection cases before in his career, where the witness had lived in the city and had to be kept safe for a short period of time before a trial. This was totally different. There was no trial, since the case was closed; and in this case, the citizen in danger lived outside city limits. Green supposed his first step was to contact the head of the police department where Mr. Brennan lived and tell those folks about the situation.

But he could do that after this meeting. Right now, they needed to get to the bottom of things with Lizzy.

# CHAPTER 25

*Wednesday, November 22nd, 2028*
*11:45 AM*

Reggie's trash truck was idling at the last light before he had to commit to his defiant plan. All he had to do to maintain his life as usual was turn right and head north on Broad Street to the depot.

But there was no "life as usual" anymore.

The light turned green. Reggie kept the steering wheel straight and pushed the accelerator to the floor, making the almost fully-laden trash truck surge forward.

In a matter of seconds, Reggie saw a huge problem with his planned trash-borne insurrection. The police had blockaded JFK Boulevard at Love Park with wooden sawhorses and were diverting traffic. Reggie had cars on his left, the curb and bollards for the park on his right, and the sawhorses less than one hundred yards ahead. On instinct, Reggie hit the brakes on the truck.

Nothing happened.

The brakes had finally failed.

\* \* \*

Jackson sensed a lull and saw that the fat-assed cracker who had been trying to talk was all done now and leaving the stage. Next, the mayor stood up and approached the podium.

* * *

*Finally*, Julianne thought. The Council President was done with his speech and the mayor was making his way to the lectern. The crowd did not cheer as it did in previous years. As the mayor prepared his notes, the chant from the crowd increased in volume and the people pushed forward against the police lines.

Julianne didn't know much about crowd control and told herself it was probably fine, but her gut clenched with a deep sense of foreboding.

* * *

Reggie continued to pump the brakes as the truck barreled toward the barricade. The female police officer at the barricade was waving her arms and yelling at him to stop. When she saw that the truck was not slowing down or diverting, she tried to draw her side arm. When she finally got the pistol clear of her holster, she didn't even have enough time to raise the weapon to fire before she had to dive away from the trash truck. During her less than graceful roll the pistol discharged harmlessly into the air just before the truck crashed through the barriers.

The barriers didn't slow the out of control truck. Reggie could hear the sound of more loud pops above the whine of the engine and the screech of the truck dragging the barricade under its chassis.

*Are they shooting at me?!* Reggie thought frantically.

He was about to turn the wheel hard to the left to get it away from the park and the crowds when he saw two holes explode in the windshield pane on the passenger side. Then he felt intense pain and heat in his neck. He took a hand from the steering wheel and placed it on his neck. Warm, sticky fluid was gushing through his fingers.

Reggie's sight dimmed, he slumped forward, and then Reggie was no more.

# CHAPTER 26

*Wednesday, November 22nd, 2028*
*11:46 AM*

The sound of a gunshot followed by a loud crashing and splintering sound snapped Officer Sanchez out of his near daze and into action. He was on a crowd control detail inside Love Park between JFK Boulevard and the podium. Before he even realized what he was doing, his pistol was clear of its holster. He quickly drew a bead on the driver of the out of control truck heading straight for the podium and started pulling the trigger. The first two bullets were on the passenger side of the windshield. His third shot was true. The bullet punched a hole in the driver's side windshield and hit the driver on the left half of his neck.

For a moment, he was amazed that his training had paid off and he'd actually incapacitated the driver. His amazement quickly turned to horror as the driver slumped forward and the engine revved as the truck gained speed.

The truck was on a beeline for the podium.

There was nothing Officer Sanchez could do but run out of the way of the rampaging truck and shout, "Move!" at the top of his lungs.

* * *

The mayor was just standing to make his speech when Julianne heard a female voice yelling "Stop!" quickly followed by the loud crack of a firecracker—or was it a gunshot? Then, immediately following the crack, came the sound of smashing wood. Being in the back row, she turned just in time to see a large trash truck heading toward the crowd in the park.

Then she saw an officer open fire and, on the third shot, hit the driver.

The driver slumped forward.

*Oh no.*

The truck suddenly accelerated and veered right toward her and the rest of the officials on the podium.

Without hesitation, Julianne's instincts took over and she sprang from her seat, turned to the back of the podium, and leaped as far from the platform as she could. The podium was about six feet above ground level. As she dropped, she was thankful to be wearing her boots again instead of the usual high heels she wore to the office.

Even so, her landing was not graceful. She barely rolled out of the way of the truck as it slammed into the podium. Wood and metal fragments became airborne, as if a bomb had gone off. As Julianne lay on the ground, she watched in horror as the truck plowed into the podium and flung bodies in all directions.

* * *

Jackson's attention was diverted by the sound of gunshots from stage left. He looked just in time to see a city trash truck careening toward the stands where the mayor and his staff were seated.

Just before the truck hit the stands, he saw a tall, athletic black woman jump for safety from the top back row of the stand. Then the truck hit the platform with an explosion of sound. Wood planking was splintered and went flying like a land mine went off. Chairs flew in all directions. Several bodies were mangled and strewn about the ground in front of the stand, only to be run down by the truck as its momentum carried it through what was left of the structure.

Jackson was momentarily stunned by the carnage the truck had wrought. Then he snapped out of it and yelled to Aaron's foot soldiers, "Get the crowd to charge the stands!" Then Jackson started pushing people forward toward the stands and shouting at the top of his lungs, "Charge! Go rush the stands! This is our chance to fight back against the man holding us down! They won't pay us, then we gonna make them pay! Go, go, go!"

It didn't take much encouragement. The cops on the police lines designed to keep the crowds away from the government had their backs turned to the crowd to see what had happened to the mayor, his staff, and guests. The crowd surged forward and caught the cops unaware. The line was quickly broken.

* * *

Julianne scrambled away from the wreckage of the podium on her hands and knees until she had enough sense to stand up. People were surging past her toward the podium. At first, she felt relieved, believing that they were first responders there to help the wounded.

But when she saw their faces, she realized that the crowd rushing toward the wreckage had bloodlust in their eyes.

# CHAPTER 27

*Wednesday, November 22ⁿᵈ, 2028*
*11:48 AM*

The crowd of over five thousand was now in open melee with anyone wearing a uniform or dress suit. They were using pieces of barricades to attack cops and government workers in a brutal beat down. The cops began to fight back with the standard riot control techniques of pepper spray and batons, but they were being overrun. A group of about eight police officers had formed a circle around the fallen mayor and several others who were now either writhing in pain on the ground or seated, stunned by what had just happened. The officers had their pistols out, threatening to shoot anyone who got too close. The mob swarmed around them to wreak havoc but wisely stayed away from the drawn guns.

Jackson flashed back to the day he received his first—and only IOU—after busting his ass all week fixing trucks in the repair yard. The anger he'd felt that day coursed through his entire being and in an instant, he knew what he needed to do. He grabbed Aaron's soldiers and shouted out the plan. Then the four of them approached the protective circle around the mayor with their pistols drawn and held down at their sides.

Using the crowd as cover, Jackson and his men surrounded the circle. Two officers were now inside the protective circle tending to the wounded and another was on his radio, frantically shouting instructions. Jackson noted that Aaron's other troops were in position then he took a step out from the crowd, leveled his gun at the first cop and pulled the trigger.

Time seemed to slow as Jackson saw the bullet hit the cop in the center of his chest. Usually, the standard issue bulletproof vest that the cop was wearing would have stopped the bullet. But Jackson had his standard issue FN five point seven pistol, firing a small projectile moving at more than twice the speed of sound. The bullet penetrated the vest and the shock wave caused massive internal damage before it severed the cop's spine and exited his body. The officer's legs buckled.

Time caught up with Jackson as he heard the other members of his posse open fire.

One of the cops focused on Jackson and raised his firearm. But Jackson was ready and faster. He pulled the trigger as the cop was still swinging his pistol toward him. The bullet caught the cop in the shoulder holding the pistol. The pistol dropped to the ground, Jackson fired once more, and the cop fell.

Jackson noted that the firing near him had stopped. There was still an occasional pop-pop-pop from shots being taken elsewhere in the plaza, but Jackson ignored them. Sitting upright in the middle of the circle of fallen officers was the mayor, grimacing in pain from a large piece of wooden shrapnel embedded in his shoulder.

Next to the mayor, standing protectively over him, was a bulldog of a man in a white collared shirt. Jackson recognized him from newspapers as the mayor's right-hand man. A white guy the mayor had grown up with, he was named after a president, Jackson thought, he just couldn't remember which one.

The bulldog had unbuttoned his cuffs and was now rolling up his sleeves. He looked at Jackson and called out, "Hey big man. You gonna' shoot me and the mayor in cold blood? How about you drop that gun and you and me have it out old school? Or are all those muscles just for show?"

Jackson didn't feel like wasting time with a fistfight when the mayor was stunned and bleeding a few feet behind the bulldog. But the man had called him out, and he didn't want to lose respect in front of Aaron's men. He would have to do this the old-fashioned way.

Jackson handed his pistol to the nearest Southwest Militia member, "Keep an eye on the perimeter and make sure the mayor doesn't move."

Jackson heard the mayor wheeze out a plea to the bulldog, "Larry, don't do this. Wait for the police, they'll rally soon and wipe these chumps up."

Larry ignored the mayor and took a step forward. Jackson wanted to rush in and pummel Larry to oblivion, but knew better than to over expose himself. Jackson noted that Larry had a nose that had been broken, some scars on his forehead, and a partially cauliflowered right ear. This guy was a fighter and even though Jackson towered over him by a good six inches and outweighed him by nearly a hundred pounds, he wasn't going to take any chances.

As quick as lightning, Larry shot forward and low to get a hold of Jackson's legs. Jackson crouched down and spread his stance to meet the charge, but Larry was able to get in under Jackson and get one arm around a leg, threatening to wrap his second leg, which would result in Jackson going down to the asphalt.

Jackson was shocked at Larry's speed and strength as Larry threatened to wrap his legs. Jackson could feel his weight lighten as Larry started to lift.

He'd had enough. He swung both fists in an arc over his head and landed a mighty blow on Larry's back.

To no avail.

Larry continued to work to wrap his left leg. Jackson repeated the blow with no effect. Just as he felt Larry lock his hands behind his left leg, Jackson bellowed and swung a final two-fisted blow with all his might. The blow landed with a resounding "Crack!" on Larry's back and Jackson felt Larry's strength falter.

Jackson shot an arm down between Larry's shoulder and his own leg and used his upper body strength to peel Larry off his legs and stand him up.

Once he stood Larry upright, he reeled back and threw a right hook that would have knocked out a large farm animal. Larry ducked under Jackson's fist and started landing a series of uppercuts on Jackson's midsection.

Jackson knew he needed to end this fight, and he also knew this guy was fast. Jackson allowed Larry to continue to pound his gut as Jackson used both hands to grab the back of Larry's neck. Simultaneously pulling down with all his might and bringing his right knee up as explosively as possible, Jackson ended the fight. Larry sagged unconscious to the asphalt, blood pouring from his wrecked nose.

Jackson accepted his pistol back from the militia member who said, "Nice work Jackie, I was wondering how long you were going to fool with him before you ended the fight."

"I hear you. Little cracker had some fight in him." Jackson said as casually as he could while trying to get his breathing back under control.

He strode directly to the mayor and pointed his pistol at Rhodes' forehead. The mayor looked up and through gritted teeth exclaimed, "Who are you? Stop pointing that gun at me and get me some help. Now."

Jackson smiled and said, "I'm the motherfucker you should have never paid with an IOU. Ain't nobody gonna' help you now."

Jackson pulled the trigger.

* * *

Julianne was on the northeast corner of the park, caddy-corner to where the stand was set up just off JFK Boulevard. The people were intent on charging the area around the demolished viewing stand, so they left Julianne alone. Now that she wasn't in immediate physical danger, her sense of duty returned. She saw a city ambulance pull up to the corner of Sixteenth Street and Arch Street. She approached the driver as he got out of the truck, medical kit in his hand.

"Hey!" Julianne shouted over the noise of the crowd as she approached him, "I saw where the mayor went down, I can lead you to him."

The driver asked, "Who are you?"

Julianne responded, "I work in the finance department. Now let's go."

At this point the passenger in the ambulance had joined the driver. She was holding an orange plastic spinal board in one hand and her medical kit in the other.

They looked at each other and nodded, The driver said, "Show us."

Julianne led them to the center of the square where the fountain used to be. There hadn't been water in it for years. As Julianne hopped up on the edge to get her bearings, a series of shots rang out nearby. Julianne crouched down instinctively. When the shooting stopped, Julianne cautiously straightened out and saw the mayor sitting on the ground sixty feet from her with a shard of wood protruding from his shoulder.

Policemen where strewn in a circle around him and Larry was shouting at one of the largest men she had ever seen.

Surprisingly, Larry charged the hulk and shot for a takedown. Julianne knew all the wrestling moves and terminology from when she dated a wrestler at Temple her junior year.

She found herself cheering for Larry. Larry, the man who almost had her killed by a rabid crowd and was working to end her career and destroy her reputation, was fighting to protect the mayor—and it looked like he might win.

Until she saw the hulking man land a series of blows on Larry's back. It didn't take long for the fight to end after that.

Julianne ran across the dry bed of the fountain in an unthinking charge to protect the mayor. She knew she didn't have a weapon, but maybe she could shield the mayor's body and talk the musclebound man out of making a big mistake.

Before she made it across the fountain, she saw the gigantic man aim a pistol at the mayor's forehead and end his life. The violent crack of the gunshot stopped her dead in her tracks.

She was too late. She wanted to collapse and cry. Her beloved city was tearing itself apart from the inside and despite all her efforts to fix what she could financially, a crazy man in a trash truck was able to destroy everything she was working for.

Knowing that she was in imminent danger, she turned away from the dead mayor, her boss, and ran back to where she had left the first responders at the edge of the fountain. They were nowhere to be seen, but there were two youths going through the medical supply bags she had seen the emergency medical technicians carry to the park.

Assuming the worst and realizing that more youth were pouring into the plaza with the blaze of anger raging in their eyes, Julianne knew she had to act fast.

She jumped over the knee wall of the fountain, sat down, and assessed her clothing. She had a cream-colored parka with a black turtleneck underneath. She was also wearing a wool skirt with thick black leggings underneath. Her black imitation Ugg boots completed her outfit. Even though the parka was scuffed up and dirty from the fall, she removed it. She also ripped her skirt down and kicked it out from under her.

Now she was in all black. She pulled her hair back in a ponytail. With her cell phone in hand, she shot up and ran right towards the heart of the mob, allowing the flow of the charging youth to carry her forward. As she approached the demolished viewing stand, she was able to veer off to the right and away from a scrum of the mob attacking a film crew.

She found herself on the south side of the plaza, the opposite direction from her home and her mom's place. She thought about jogging a few blocks around the plaza to the East and then looping North, until she heard an explosion in that direction and saw black smoke billowing up.

No, she was only a few blocks from a good college friend's condo. She would head there and figure out what was going on.

* * *

Mayor Rhodes' body fell forward. Jackson then fired two rounds into Larry's back. He turned to Aaron's men. "End the rest of these chumps. We gotta' roll." The foot soldiers followed Jackson's lead and pumped a round into each official in the circle.

Then Jackson and his men dispersed and Jackson jogged through the crowd southward on 15th Street. Once he got to Chestnut Street, the crowd had dissipated. People were still running around hysterically, but the density of the crowd had dropped significantly. Jackson slowed to a walk and pulled his hoodie up. As he walked, he took out his cell phone and made a call.

"Boss, you watching TV?"

Aaron responded, "No, but I heard about it from a couple of cops on my payroll. Shit, Jackie, I didn't think you'd get the crowd that riled up!"

"We had a little help, not sure why, but I'll take it. The city is tearing itself apart."

"Perfect. We're gonna exploit that. Listen, I just got the name and address of that cracker that whacked Dante. I was getting ready to grab some guys and roll out there to cap him. Lemme take care of this white-bread, then we'll meet at HQ."

"I hear you boss, but before you do that, I got one more thing to tell you—might change your plans."

"What?"

"I killed the mayor."

"Holy shit." Aaron paused. "You're right. Cracker boy can wait. Get back here ASAP. I'll get the troops ready. It's time to use all those toys you been building for me. We are going to bag us the payday of our lifetimes."

# CHAPTER 28

*Wednesday, November 22nd, 2028*
*11:51 AM*

Aaron disconnected the call from Jackson and paced in his office. His tactical training told him to put aside his bloodlust for Dante's killer. It wasn't easy for him to delay his desire for revenge, but it was the obvious choice, given the unfolding situation in Center City. Getting the kid would have to wait.

This was the distraction he'd been waiting for. Aaron would amplify the chaos of the riot in Center City by ordering his people in Southwest Philadelphia to attack anyone wearing a uniform and to storm any official building. He knew some businesses would be looted and that might impact his extortion earnings for a while, but if he could acquire the gold at the Federal Reserve, the loss of extortion earnings wouldn't mean squat.

He was also going to call some gangbangers he knew in North Philly. They didn't owe him much and they weren't reliable, but Aaron would encourage them to wreak as much havoc as possible. The breakdown in law and order in both Southwest and North Philly should keep the cops out of the game, or at least get them out of Center City, until he could get his perimeter established.

The next step would be to neutralize the police in his own backyard. Aaron's base of operations, where he sat now, was in Southwest Philadelphia in police district 12. The captain for this district and most of the uniformed officers and detectives were in his pocket in one way or another. No need to do anything there. They would play along with whatever Aaron told them to do.

District 18 was another issue. That district was in the northern edge of Aaron's territory, along the Market street corridor. The captain of that district had always stubbornly refused to play ball with Aaron. The man had no family to leverage and he lived in a high-rise condo building on the other side of the city in the Chestnut Hill area. His lack of family and his distance from Aaron's power base made him hard to crack. But he'd been anticipating having to do this the hard way—take down District 18 first, then make his play for the Federal Reserve Building. The plan was already in motion.

Aaron made a call and then went to join his men. It was time to pay District 18 a little visit.

\* \* \*

Detective Green and Captain Willis had spent the last five minutes trying to convince Lizzy to give up her phone. They hadn't made much progress. Captain Willis was losing his patience.

"Last chance, Lizzy. At this point you're fired anyway, but if you turn over the phone we might not press charges. Otherwise, we will get a warra—" Just then a uniformed officer poked her head into the office, interrupting the captain.

"Sir. You need to see this." She was a few shades paler than she should have been and her tone sent a chill down Green's spine.

Captain Willis immediately rose and followed her out of the office, asking Lizzy to "stay put" as he went. Green glanced out the door.

There was a group of uniformed police and detectives gathered in front of a wall-mounted flat screen television broadcasting some sort of turmoil, with a red banner scrolling across the top of the screen. Detective Green looked at Lizzy, repeated Willis' "stay put," and walked over to the crowd. He tapped the shoulder of the uniformed officer closest to him. "What's going on?"

The officer didn't take his eyes off the screen, just shook his head slightly and said, "Look for yourself. Center City is out of control."

Detective Green focused on the carnage on the screen. It was a street level shot of people running around and groups of young men breaking storefront windows and beating down bystanders. There was no aerial view—all commercial helicopters had been requisitioned by the federal government for help in one of the three or four wars being fought around the world right now. The news outlets couldn't loiter helicopters over crime scenes anymore.

The reporter on screen was trying to narrate the ongoing turmoil, to little effect. She was clearly concerned with her own safety and the cameraman kept panning away from her to show some other violence taking place. As Detective Green watched, the reporter paused, taking in new information from someone shouting at her off-screen. Her already harried expression broke into one of shock as she looked directly into the camera and announced, "I've just received an unconfirmed report that the mayor, his senior staff, and perhaps all of the City Council has been killed by this mob . . ."

Suddenly there was shouting just off-screen. The cameraman panned the camera away from the reporter again in time to see two uniformed officers fire their weapons into a crowd of youths. Two of them dropped immediately. Three more were able to launch their hand-held Molotov cocktails at the police with deadly accuracy. The glass bottles shattered at the feet of the officers and they were both engulfed in flames, dropping their weapons. The remaining group of youth then pounced on the burning officers with baseball bats. The cameraman stayed on the shot, showing the unfolding gore as the teenagers zealously bludgeoned the officers to death. As quickly as it started, the youths finished and looked directly at the camera.

The largest of the group walked directly toward the reporter with his bat held in two hands, lightly resting it on his shoulder in a menacing position. When he was about three feet away from the reporter, he swung his bat into her upper arm with all his force. The sound of the bone snapping in her arm sounded like a firecracker. She screamed and collapsed. The youth then looked directly into the camera and shouted, "We running the city now! We taking what's ours! Stand in our way and see what happens!"

With that the young man took a step back, cocked the bat, swung his hips, and ripped off a swing at the cameraman. The video feed went to static.

* * *

*11:59 AM*

Aaron watched as two of his drivers parked two of his dump trucks from his excavating business in blocking positions for the entrance and exit at the District 18 parking lot. He was riding in one of two "technicals" that he'd brought for this assault. A technical was a quad-cab pickup truck with a detachable stanchion mounted in the bed of the truck upon which an M60 thirty-caliber machine gun was fastened. He had acquired those weapons from a dealer in Syria he worked with. Jackson had devised the mounting system.

Aaron's technical truck was in between the two dump trucks blocking the exits. He had a direct line of sight to the employee entrance on the side of the building. The other technical was parked in front of the building, covering the public entrance on Pine Street. Aaron watched as his men spilled out from the back of the two dump trucks to set a perimeter around the building. These troops were some of his best. All had served in the military in various campaigns. They knew what they were doing and their movements demonstrated their prowess as they took cover behind vehicles and other obstructions all around the perimeter of the building. Aaron and all of his men were wearing black tactical uniforms.

* * *

In the station, the officers watching the television were stunned to the point of inaction. Detective Green was still processing what he had seen when three one-second tones sounded on the intercom, followed by the station chief's voice announcing, "All uniformed officers and detectives, report to the basement armory for tactical gear deployment."

Immediately, the group gathered in front of the television broke ranks amid exclamations of anger and fear, mixed in with questions from some of the younger officers. Detective Green surmised that, based on what he'd seen on the television, District 18 was going to be deployed to help quell the riot in Center City just a mile away.

* * *

Aaron got out his cell phone and sent a quick text, "Lizzy. Keep your head down."

* * *

As Detective Green hurried with a group of other detectives toward the stairwell to descend the two floors to the basement armory, he stole a glance out the window.

*That's unusual,* he thought. There were two large dump trucks in the station's parking lot.

And they were blocking both the entrance and the exit.

He stopped to look and process what was going on. The trucks were a couple hundred feet away from his location inside the station. He saw two men assemble something on the back of a pickup truck next to one of the dump trucks, and then a series of bright flashes leapt from the assembly. An instant later, the thunder of automatic machine gun fire assaulted his ears as the windows of the station imploded.

# CHAPTER 29

*Wednesday, November 22<sup>nd</sup>, 2028*
*12:01 PM*

Aaron's world erupted into the rapid-fire staccato sound of two thirty-caliber machine guns opening fire on the side and front of the building. Glass went flying and pockmarks of blasted brick appeared on the exterior of the building as the rounds slammed in.

At the same time, a team of five men approached the rear of the building and set two charges, one on the electric and communications feed for the building and the other on a backup diesel generator. The men then retreated behind a squad car in the parking lot and the charges went off nearly simultaneously. Aaron figured that would adequately cut the station off from the world and hamper the ability of backup from other districts to respond.

The machine gun fire quickly ended. The only sounds on the streets were a couple of car alarms going off. The station house was eerily quiet. Aaron reached over the special packages in the back seat of the truck and grabbed a bullhorn. Using the door as cover, he turned the volume up to maximum and announced, "Come out, unarmed, with your hands up, and we will spare your lives!"

Aaron saw movement in a second-floor window. He ducked down as a bullet shattered the truck window where his head was a moment ago.

Aaron keyed his radio and said, "Provide cover fire, I am going to deliver the special packages!"

Aaron heard the M60's light up again in short bursts along with several other AR-15 semi-automatic rifles providing him cover while he grabbed an AT4 anti-tank missile from the rear seat of the truck's quad cab. This version of the shoulder-fired missile was loaded with a highly explosive projectile instead of the armor piercing loads the military more commonly used. Aaron figured with the windows and doors already blown out, this one would work perfectly.

He deployed the shoulder brace and aligned the sights for a fifty-meter range. He then aimed for the second floor window where the police sniper had taken a shot at him and depressed the firing trigger. Aaron watched as the eighty-four-millimeter warhead flew directly in the center of the blown-out window he had aimed for. A bright flash blew shrapnel and debris out the window. A thunderclap of noise hit Aaron's ears immediately afterwards.

Without pause, Aaron grabbed the second rocket launcher and took aim at the gaping hole where the employee entrance door used to be. He fired and was rewarded with a second direct hit. The warhead must have gone further into the building this time before exploding; the blast escaping the building was not as intense and the sound of the explosion slightly muted compared to the first blast. Good. The more blast energy captured by the building, the more damage to its occupants.

Aaron keyed his radio one more time and shouted, "Breach, breach, breach!"

The M60's sporadically opened up again on any movement in the second-floor windows while Aaron's men approached the front and side entrances. Two of Aaron's men covered the rear exit door with M16's as a trap in case anyone tried to escape that way.

Aaron's troops approached the front of the building in a rapid low run. There were two squads with five men in each. Once each squad made it to the building, they flattened themselves along the brick exterior on either side of the front door. The lead soldier from each squad then grabbed a grenade from his shoulder harness, pulled the pin, and threw it in the door opening. In nearly perfectly choreographed timing, the grenades detonated and each squad entered the building in a cacophony of gunfire.

Aaron watched his men enter the building. From his position, he had a good view of the side and rear doors. It didn't matter, though; once his men entered the building, he couldn't see what was happening. His troops outside the building held their fire while the squads worked inside the building. The volume of gunfire would increase, then taper off intermittently. Aaron knew not to distract them with a radio check. If they didn't check in within two minutes, he would send in more troops.

Ninety seconds into the assault, the rear door opened and several uniformed officers made a run for it, pistols held at their sides. Once the lead officer was a few steps outside the door, Aaron's two troops opened fire, chopping down the group of six officers in a matter of seconds.

Okay. Two minutes were up. Aaron needed a situation report. He keyed his mic and asked, "Echelon group, hold your position at the rear door. Bravo One, SITREP?"

The response came back, "Bravo One here. All tangos down. I have a group of people barricaded behind a solid door to the evidence locker. Captain Willis is telling us to stand down. I'm about to set a charge to blow the door so we can breach the locker. Over."

Aaron thought about that information for a second, then responded, "Standby. Secure the area. I am coming in to speak with the captain."

Aaron and two of his men fled from their cover by the pickup truck and double-timed it to the employee entrance. They were greeted by a member of Aaron's posse. The soldier guided them through the wreckage to an area in the far corner of the station house. There were four bodies lying near the entrance with blood oozing from their ears and evidence of burns on their skin. Probably from the AT4 warhead explosion. There were more bodies in the hallway. So far, none of them were his men. That was good.

Finally, they arrived at a closed door where Bravo One's leader, Booker, and two other soldiers stood waiting. Aaron addressed Booker, "Great work. How many men did we lose?"

Booker replied, "One from my squad and two from Bravo Two."

Aaron winced then nodded, "Damn. Well, what do we have going on here?"

Booker again responded, "At least three to four people got in this room before we could get to them. The door is reinforced steel. Ain't no bullet going through that."

Aaron assessed the strength of the door. He knew he had to get in there before they made a bunch of phone calls, which they were probably already doing.

Aaron banged three times on the door and yelled in an authoritative voice, "Who's in this room! You have five seconds to comply before I blow the door!"

Aaron could discern faint discussion on the other side of the door. A man responded, "This is Captain Willis, I'm in here with a clerk named Lizzy and a traffic officer named Danielle. They have nothing to do with this fight, let them walk."

Aaron considered this information. He went to school with Lizzy and she had been a loyal source of information for Aaron in the Philadelphia police department for years, most recently with the morsel of info she had just fed him about James Brennan. For Aaron, loyalty was everything. He also knew he couldn't waste any more time here. He needed to move on to his primary objective.

Aaron raised his voice and yelled to the closed door, "Alright. Here is how it's going to work. Come out one at a time starting with Lizzy. Once Lizzy is out and secured, we will let you know to send out Danielle."

Aaron then turned to Booker and whispered an alternate set of instructions. He and his men nodded and readied themselves.

The sound of a sliding deadbolt came from the door. The door cracked towards Aaron and his men. It opened a bit further and Aaron could see the frightened, yet hopeful, visage of Lizzy. Her beige blouse and matching skirt were smeared with soot. Aaron reached into the doorway and grabbed her hand. As Aaron pulled Lizzy clear, Booker threw a M67 fragmentation grenade into the room and one of Booker's men slammed the door closed. The soldier remained leaning against the door with all his weight. Aaron could hear some shouts and sounds of scuffling. Two seconds passed, then the muffled blast of the grenade hit the door. The steel of the door stopped shrapnel from passing through, but it shook the soldier holding it shut.

Aaron quickly walked Lizzy down the hall as Booker and his men opened the door and stormed the room. Aaron heard four gunshots as his men dispatched Chief Willis and the traffic officer. A few seconds later, Booker's voice came over the radio declaring the evidence room clear.

As Aaron left the building, he saw his men loading all weapons, ammo, and body armor from the fallen police onto the beds of the dump trucks, exactly as they had been trained to do. Even better, firearms and crates of ammo were being loaded out from the armory.

Aaron had stockpiled a large amount of weapons and ammo from his black market dealings, so while he didn't need all of that material to keep his troops armed, he definitely didn't want the firearms lying around for other people to grab and cause their own mayhem. *And hey*, Aaron thought, *one can never have too many guns and ammo when going into battle.*

As rooms were cleared, other soldiers were splashing gasoline throughout the building. Aaron had instructed his men to take no survivors and destroy as much evidence as possible by torching the place.

Aaron crossed the parking lot with Lizzy in tow. At the dump truck, he grabbed a standard police issue nine-millimeter pistol, checked to made sure the magazine was full, and handed it to Lizzy.

"You're gonna' need this girl. Things going to get lively around here." Aaron said.

Lizzy took the gun, looked at it, and having nowhere to stash it in her current outfit stuttered, "O—Okay Aaron. Th—thank you. Can I go now or do you need anything else?"

Aaron laughed, then said, "Nah girl, you did good. I got some things to do around here, then I'll get that cracker you sent me the info about."

Lizzy held the pistol in two shaking hands, tight against her body. She looked from the nearly destroyed, smoking district house back to Aaron, then down at her now-bare feet, the high-heel shoes she had worn to work lost in the chaos of the fight. Tears fell from her eyes, cutting channels through the soot on her cheeks. She turned and walked haltingly away from the destruction.

Aaron watched her go for a moment. He was struck by the contrast of the scene: Lizzy's jet black hair pulled up and proper in a bun, her medium brown skin contrasted with the beige outfit, holding tight to her body a menacing black pistol, walking barefoot into a city that was increasingly filling with the sights and sounds of chaos and destruction.

Aaron turned back to the district police building. His men were clearing out. As the last soldier made his way out of the door, Aaron saw Booker light a cigarette. He took a deep drag, then flicked it into a puddle of gasoline just outside the employee entrance. The flames leapt to life like an angry animal let out of its cage and quickly spread into the building.

Aaron keyed his radio and told everyone to mount up and meet back at his headquarters. Now that his own backyard was secured, it was time to gather the rest of his troops and get them deployed to meet his next objective.

# CHAPTER 30

*Wednesday, November 22nd, 2028*
*12:08 PM*

Detective Marcus Green regained consciousness and immediately starting coughing. The heat where he was lying was getting unbearable and each raspy breath brought fresh agony to his raw throat.

He didn't know where he was or how he got here. He remembered seeing the trucks open fire and the windows of the station blow out as he scrambled to get off the second floor and down to the basement armory.

Then chaos. An explosion. He was on the floor and his ears were ringing. He had tried to stand, but became nauseous, losing his lunch, and falling back to his hands and knees.

He remembered being pulled off his feet and half carried, half pushed down a hallway to the roof access ladder. He recalled willing his arms and legs to obey his commands as the officers below him pushed him up. Then, nothing.

Looking around, it was obvious he'd made it to the roof. There was no one else here. He looked back to the opening in the roof where the access was and saw black smoke pouring upward like an angry volcano about to blow.

The sound of the roaring fire and the realization that the entire building below him was engulfed in flames hit him simultaneously.

Unsure of his balance, he tried to crawl on his hands and knees to the edge of the roof where the fire escape ladder was attached to the side of the building. He didn't make it three feet before he had to stop. The tar on the flat roof was starting to melt, threatening to burn his hands.

Pockets of flame started to erupt in patches on the roof as the fire burned with increased intensity.

Holding back the rising tide of panic, he slipped off his sport jacket and quickly ripped it down the seam. He wrapped the pieces of cloth around his hands and continued his crawl to the ladder.

As he reached the ladder and swung a leg over the side to mount it, the roof gave out under him. The heat singed his exposed skin.

Balancing with one leg on the ladder and the other leg hanging above the fire where the roof was a moment ago, Green strained his arms to swing himself back to the ladder. He quickly said a silent prayer that if God helped him back on this ladder, he'd never miss another workout again.

Finally, he had both hands and feet on the ladder and rapidly began his descent.

Then he froze.

What if Aaron's men were still at the building? He'd be an easy target silhouetted against the flames.

But there was nothing he could do about that. The building would collapse any minute, and if he stayed still, he'd go down with it.

Climbing down with a new sense of urgency, he reached the bottom of the ladder and dropped the rest of the distance to the ground, using his hands to brace himself as he landed.

Green scrambled next to a bullet-riddled patrol car and looked around. None of Aaron's troops were in sight. The few people he did see nearby seemed to be running back and forth with items in their arms. He assumed they were looting the nearby businesses.

As he got further away from the building, Green realized it was downright cold out. He did a quick inventory of his clothing. He knew his survival over the next hour depended on him not looking like a cop more than it did on him being warm.

He was wearing a white collared long sleeve shirt with a tie and dark blue slacks. He quickly lost the tie and rolled up his sleeves. He also had his shoulder holster with his service pistol thankfully still in place. He involuntarily gave it is customary tap with his right hand to satisfy himself it was there. Lastly, he checked his belt and confirmed his cell phone was still in its side clip holster.

First thing on his to-do list was to find a coat to cover his holster and keep him warm. Then he would call an old friend, find an intact precinct building, and get payback from Aaron and the Southwest Militia.

# CHAPTER 31

*Wednesday, November 22ⁿᵈ, 2028*
*5:00 PM*

After the chaos at Love Park, Julianne's instinct was to head home to her place in Northern Liberties, a neighborhood bound on the east by the Delaware River and on the other three sides by the Vine Expressway, Girard Avenue, and Sixth Avenue.

However, the direction she had escaped from Love Park put her even further away from that area. But she did have a friend in the area, Cassie, whom she had played basketball with in college. Cassie had become a successful lawyer and lived in Rittenhouse Square, a two-block square park anchored on 18th and Walnut Street. The buildings around the park were all high-end residential, commercial, and retail high-rises. It was where the elite in Philadelphia called home. Julianne now found herself on the fourteenth floor of one such well-heeled condominium building.

Cassie and Julianne were sitting together on a couch in the large open area in Cassie's unit. The television was replaying the footage of the carnage in Love Park. It was a local station that had several crews in various parts of the city trying to make sense of what was unfolding.

Julianne was wearing a black two-piece sweat suit of Cassie's with a built-in hoodie on the top. She was also freshly showered, with a hot mug of coffee warming her hands and her feet tucked under her.

Julianne was still processing the day's events. Her memory of her escape from Love Park was fragmented. One moment she was listening to the City Council President drone on and the next she was leaping off the grandstand to avoid getting hit by a truck.

Watching the news, she had learned that the truck that plowed into the stand was a city-owned garbage truck. Since it was still just a couple of hours after the event, the reporters had not learned who the driver of the truck was or why the person had targeted the mayor. The "experts" the network had found to interview about the truck hypothesized it could have been a disgruntled city worker, unhappy with the IOUs the city has been issuing; a Texas secessionist, targeting a major east coast city in some way to forward their cause (this made no sense to Julianne); or an agent from Russia, China, Iran, or Syria as an act of terror against our country. In other words, nobody had any idea.

The reports from other parts of the city were a mixed bag to say the least. North Philly, which was a poor section of Philadelphia north of the Vine Street Expressway along Broad Street, was in full riot and looting mode. Several buildings around the campus of the university along North Broad Street were burning and one camera crew was able to capture footage of intense looting of those buildings, with locals inflicting serious violence against the students and staff there. The university's own police force was clearly swamped and the Philadelphia police were trying in vain to control the streets.

Northeast Philadelphia, the large area of the city east of Broad Street, bounded by the Delaware River, and bordered by Bucks County to the north, was relatively quiet. That area of the city was a little less dense in population and was home to many of the working-class people of the city. Julianne thought that Northeast Philadelphia, often called the 'Great Northeast', was like a separate city unto itself. It sure felt that way when Julianne had visited. It looked more like an overbuilt suburb than a city. She remembered an odd fact—that the furthest north and eastern part of the Great Northeast was closer to the state capital of New Jersey in Trenton than it was to City Hall in Philadelphia. Julianne's mother was in an assisted living facility in that part of town. A quick phone call had confirmed that her mom was well and the area around the home was quiet.

A news crew from the Chestnut Hill area of the city reported some sporadic gunfire and looting, but the most recent report said the police had things under control there.

Surprisingly to Julianne, Southwest Philadelphia, which histori-cally had a high rate of crime and extreme poverty, was shown by a news crew to be quiet and under control. Julianne remembered back to the staff meeting where Emmitt was put on leave. She recalled the chief saying there was a crime boss who ran that section of town and kept things under control. Julianne wondered if the calm was due to that person's influence. She couldn't quite remember his name.

University City, the area of the city just west of the Schuylkill River, seemed calm except for the unconfirmed report of a police station on fire just west of the university's campus. For some reason, a reporter crew had not been able to access the area. However, the area north of Walnut Street, including Market Street, was a mess. The area had some rough neighborhoods in it, especially along Girard Avenue where the zoo was located. The news truck had been fire bombed before abruptly going off air. Many of the news stations were located on the west end of this part of the city, on its border with a Lower Merion township in Montgomery county.

Julianne thought about that border. The road was called City Avenue. It used to be called City Line Avenue, but it was renamed because someone felt the word "line" was insensitive. But it really was a line. On the city side of the line were Overbrook and Wynnefield, neither area very nice in Julianne's opinion. On the county side of the line were some of the nicest "main line" neighborhoods you could find, populated with large estates on manicured grounds. It was on that very line that the police department from Lower Merion was setting up roadblocks and checkpoints. The quick interview that Julianne had watched of the police chief from Lower Merion said that they were taking all precautions needed to protect their citizens and had no plans to enter the city to help in any way. The reporter asked the police chief if he thought the National Guard would respond to the growing emergency in the city. The chief looked at the reporter like she was joking and reminded her that the Pennsylvania National Guard had been deployed to Alaska.

Another crew in Delaware County had noticed the township of Upper Darby setting up similar checkpoints in an effort to keep the chaos within the city from spreading to their towns.

Julianne finally turned to Cassie and asked, "Have you seen any reports from Center City?"

Cassie was still in her business skirt, blouse, and jacket from work. She had told Julianne she had headed home a little early since the office was quiet the day before Thanksgiving. She was sitting in the same position as Julianne, with her feet tucked under herself on the opposite end of the couch. Cassie was seemingly hypnotized by the events unfolding on the television. After a pause, she turned to Julianne and said, "What?"

Julianne repeated herself, "I mean, we are sitting in a high-rise in Center City and we can hear gunfire around us and the occasional larger explosion. We can see smoke rising from several buildings, but I haven't seen any reports from this area of the city. What do you think is going on? Should we stay here and ride it out or try to get out of this part of the city to get somewhere safer?"

Cassie unfurled her legs and pushed herself off the couch. She was an incredibly tall woman. At six-foot one inch in height, she was considerably taller than Julianne, who was five-foot ten inches tall. Cassie was one of the few white girls who had played on the team when they went to college. She was descended from a Swedish mother and a Finnish father, and had red hair and a large bone structure. She had not done quite as good a job keeping the pounds off as Julianne had done, but Julianne suspected Cassie's job as a high-end corporate lawyer was more demanding on her time than Julianne's city job. Julianne watched as Cassie paced a few times to the window and back.

Night was falling. Julianne shuddered to think what could happen under the cloak of darkness in the city. History of urban rioting always showed the unrest getting worse when the streets were dark.

Finally, Cassie turned to Julianne with a pleading look on her face, "Jules. I think we should just stay here and ride this thing out. I'm stocked up with extra food because I expected my sister to take the train tonight to spend Thanksgiving with me. That's not going to happen now. Also, the electricity is on and this building should be secure. We have a doorman and you need a ID badge to get in."

Julianne got up from the couch and joined Cassie looking out the window. The sun was out of sight and the light was fading fast. Julianne could barely make out people running along the sidewalks and through the park at the center of Rittenhouse Square. As she watched, she saw a group of people smash the window of a bookstore across the plaza and begin looting.

Her gut told her to get moving. She remembered seeing a movie when she was in middle school about a zombie apocalypse where the hero said something to the effect that "Movement is life. If you stop moving they'll catch you and you're dead." While these rioters weren't zombies, she had already seen how a crowd could easily dispense death if whipped into a frenzy or if they believed there would be no accountability for their actions.

"Cassie, I hear what you're saying and if this were some storm or something like that I would agree with you. But I was at Love Park when the mayor was killed. I saw what can happen if you get caught by these crowds. I say we get going before we get boxed in or worse, they target this building."

Cassie looked down at her mug of coffee, "I just don't know. When I walked back home at lunch, everything was normal and now I'm safe and sound in my home. I think the best thing to do would be to stay right here. The police will have things under control before long."

Julianne was confused. Was Cassie watching the same reports on the television as she was? It seemed apparent to Julianne that the city was tearing itself apart and there was no cavalry coming to clean things up. Julianne looked at Cassie again. Could it be that Cassie was suffering from some sort of shock causing her to deny the reality of the situation?

Julianne was about to continue her argument for flight, when a commotion in the hallway outside of Cassie's condo unit caught her attention. She heard what sounded like a loud pounding on another unit's door. Then she heard a crashing sound and people shouting and laughing at the same time. A loud, distressed woman's howl assaulted Julianne's ear until it was cut off abruptly by the sharp report of a gunshot.

"Shit!" exclaimed Julianne, "They are here!" She grabbed Cassie by the shoulders and looked right into her eyes. "Do you have any weapons? Anything we can defend ourselves with?"

Cassie stammered, "Wh—what? No, no, of course not."

Julianne remembered a social media post she saw Cassie in a few months ago and asked, "You played softball in a league last spring, right? Where's your equipment bag?"

Cassie focused on Julianne and said, "Sure I did, but who cares? It's in my bedroom closet."

Julianne released her friend's shoulders and dashed to the bedroom. She slid the door to the closet open and there on the floor was the equipment bag with the handle to an aluminum bat sticking out. She unzipped the bag and grabbed the bat. It was a nice one, very well balanced. Julianne also saw a few pairs of sneakers on the floor of the closet. Deeming it good use of time she might not have later, she laced up a pair of Cassie's sneakers on her feet. They were a size too big but Julianne laced them up tight so they felt okay.

Julianne returned to the living area and found Cassie glued to the same spot, looking out the window with a blank expression on her face. Julianne held the bat in one hand and grabbed Cassie's hand with the other. Julianne led her friend to the kitchen, which was next to the exit to the hallway. Julianne then went around the condo unit turning off all the lights.

When all the lights were off, Julianne returned to Cassie's side. The only light was the glow from the microwave and oven timers and what little ambient light still came in through the windows.

Cassie whispered to Julianne, "What are you doing?"

Julianne answered quietly as she tried to steady her breathing. "Trying to stay alive. I think the looters are here on your floor. When they come in here, I'm going to hit them as hard as I can."

Julianne and Cassie stood together in the kitchen, ears straining to understand what was going on. Julianne remembered there were eight units on the floor. There seemed to be a pattern to what was happening in the hall.

There would be a tapping sound on a unit's door with a male voice announcing "Maintenance!" No one seemed to be buying that ruse, so there would be a pounding sound as something heavy repetitively impacted the door. Then the sound of the door smacking open followed by sounds of breaking glass and sometimes screams of occupants being assaulted or worse.

Julianne knew they were in a bad position. They were trapped without a great weapon against an unknown number of attackers. Still, something hot and angry welled up inside Julianne. She wasn't going down without a fight. Her desire to see Emmitt and her mother again pumped adrenaline into her system.

The rubber grips on the bat felt reassuring in her grasp as she tried to control her breathing and heart rate, knowing what was coming.

After two more cycles of what Julianne termed "smash and pillage," the tapping on the door to where Julianne and Cassie were hiding sounded through the apartment. Julianne turned to Cassie with her finger over her lip, silently communicating the universal "be quiet" symbol, then gently backed Cassie up a few steps further into the kitchen. She wanted plenty of room to swing the bat when the time came.

Through the door, she heard a muffled voice say, "We should wait till our boys are back up from running loot to the lobby before we do another one."

A deeper, more commanding voice said, "Nah. There ain't nobody even home at this one, no light coming from under the door. Ain't none of these rich crackers putting up any fight we can't handle anyhow. Bring that up and knock this door open. I'll go in first on this one."

The first voice replied, "Okay then, let's do this."

Julianne's heart was beating so fast she wasn't sure if she was going to faint or explode. Her grip on the bat tightened, she had her weight on the balls of her feet, and her knees slightly bent in a fighting stance.

BAM. Julianne jumped at the violent concussion from a large object hitting the door. In the dim light inside the apartment, Julianne noted that the door held up well.

BAM. Julianne was ready for this one. It didn't surprise her, but the door shuddered in a way it hadn't on the first hit.

BAM. Julianne saw the wood on the doorframe near the deadbolt start to splinter.

BAM. The door swung violently open. For a moment, nothing happened. Julianne's taught muscles in her arms, core, and legs vibrated with adrenaline-saturated energy. Then the dark silhouette of a man crossed the threshold.

Pivoting her front foot and rotating her hips, Julianne swung the bat with every ounce of her strength.

The bat connected squarely with the intruder's forehead with a sickening crunch that sent a stinging vibration up Julianne's arms. His forward momentum entering the apartment was immediately reversed from the impact of the blow and his legs crumpled as he collapsed onto the floor. Julianne heard something clatter to the floor from the intruder's now slack grasp.

Julianne heard the intruder's cohort exclaim, "What the . . ." as she stepped over the body of the first intruder to find the source of the voice. She knew she had to press the attack now or she would lose the element of surprise she had gained in her initial response.

Julianne stepped out into the hall to find a short, stocky young man wearing a black wool cap with the edges rolled up, barely hugging his head. He was reaching for a sledgehammer that was leaning against the wall right next to the doorway.

Not pausing a beat, Julianne took another step forward toward the second intruder and swung the bat again with all her strength. The bat connected with the man's left upper arm just above his elbow. The intruder grunted in pain and Julianne heard a sharp crack as the bat connected. The strength of the blow turned the man away from Julianne so that his back was facing her.

He dropped the sledgehammer and was reaching for something in his jacket pocket with his right hand. Before Julianne could get the bat reset for another swing, the intruder pivoted around with a knife in his hand.

Julianne would have liked to swing the bat down in a tomahawk chop motion to hit the hand holding the knife. Instead, she took a step back as the knife swiftly swung past her face with inches to spare. The momentum from the intruder's hasty swing carried his hand far past Julianne and exposed his left shoulder to her. His left arm hung limply by his side.

Julianne used the opening to swing the bat again. She didn't have time to set her stance or coil her hips, so she didn't have all of her strength behind this swing. She swung slightly higher this time.

The intruder saw the swing coming and tucked his head down to avoid the blow. It wasn't enough. The bat caught him just above the left ear. The rolled-up cap absorbed some of the blow but it still knocked him off balance.

Julianne cocked the bat and swung again. The intruder brought his right arm up to shield his head from the blow. The bat connected with his forearm with another thick crunching sound. This time the intruder shouted in pain as the knife fell from his grasp.

Without thinking, Julianne reared back with the bat and swung with all her might for the man's head. Simultaneously, the intruder decided to lunge at Julianne. The bat connected with the intruder's head right at his temple. Julianne saw the man's eye's roll up into his head as his body sagged to the left of her in the hallway.

The fight was over. Julianne felt as if she had been fighting for ten minutes. In reality, less than one minute had passed since the intruders first started knocking down Cassie's door.

Julianne checked the hallway for more looters. She didn't see anyone. With her heart still racing she took a few steps back to check on Cassie. Julianne reached in and turned on the light. Cassie yelped. Julianne noticed that Cassie had not moved from her spot in the kitchenette. She was looking at the floor directly in front of her feet.

"We need to go Cassie. We need to go now!"

Cassie, still frozen, didn't respond. Julianne placed the bat down and gently took Cassie's face in her hands. Lifting her chin, Julianne looked directly into Cassie's eyes and repeated, "Cassie. We need to leave. If we don't go now, we are dead."

Cassie, started to shake and muttered, "No, no, no. I . . . I can't go. This is my home. I can't." Just then, Cassie sat down on the floor right where she was, hugging herself and shaking.

Julianne recognized that her friend was in a serious state of shock. She decided to let her cool down while she checked out what was going on around her.

Julianne turned around and inspected the body of the first intruder. He looked like he fell asleep right on the foyer of Cassie's condo. One arm was splayed out in front of him, the other tucked at what looked to be an uncomfortable angle under his body. He was face down.

Julianne grabbed the bat again and used it to prod his body. He didn't move. Julianne bent over, grabbed his jacket, and rolled him over. She gasped when she saw his face. The bat must have impacted him above the bridge of his nose. The damage was grotesque. Julianne instinctively knew this man was dead.

In front of his body, she saw a black pistol. She didn't know much about guns, but she knew that right now, having one was better than not having one. She grabbed it and tucked it into her waistband at the small of her back. She then stood up and thought about what to do with his body. Knowing that the clock was ticking before more intruders came to this floor, she grabbed him by his shoes and dragged him in to the hallway.

She needed a plan. Leaving these guys in the hallway was dumb. She looked around. The door to the unit across the hall was slightly open. She could see the damage that had been done to the door and frame when it was forced open. She had no idea what carnage hid behind that door, but it did provide her with an idea about where to stash the bodies.

A few minutes later, Julianne returned to Cassie's condo. The first intruder's body was no problem, she slid it right into the foyer of the other condo. The second intruder was more of an issue. As Julianne finished dragging him into the condo across the hall, he started to moan. Julianne hadn't thought that he might wake up. Using the electrical cords from the blender and electric can opener in the kitchen, she bound the intruder's hands behind his back. She also bound his feet. By that point, he was regaining consciousness and was spewing obscenities at Julianne. She had enough of that. She grabbed his head and stuffed a dishtowel in his mouth and secured it with some twine she found in a drawer.

Julianne helped Cassie to her couch. Again, she said, "We need to go now. More bad guys will be coming up any minute."

Cassie finally took a deep breath and said, "Jules, you go without me. I'm just going to ride this out right here."

Julianne was growing increasingly frustrated. "Okay then, stay here. But I gotta' go. Take this gun to protect yourself."

Cassie looked at the pistol Julianne was offering her like it was a hot coal. Cassie's face scrunched in disgust, "I hate guns and everything about them. No way am I taking that!"

Julianne couldn't believe what she was hearing, "Did you not see the two men who tried to come in here to kill us? This is serious! If you don't do something, you will die."

Cassie looked back down at her feet and muttered, "No, I'll be safe if I just stay here."

Julianne leaned forward and gave her friend a hug. "Okay then. Goodbye. Once I leave, try to lock the door as best as you can and push this couch and anything else heavy against the door."

Cassie just nodded. Julianne got up and went to the closet in the foyer. She found a small backpack. She grabbed a couple of bottles of water from a case on the floor in the closet and put them in the backpack. She thought about grabbing another coat from the closet, but they were all light colors. It would be cold, but her black workout suit was probably the best thing for being out on the streets at night. She shouldered the backpack, put the pistol in the front pocket of her jacket, grabbed the bat with her other hand and headed out to the hall.

She walked away from the elevator to the stairs. As she neared the door, she heard the elevator make a "ding", indicating it had arrived on her floor. Julianne picked up her pace as she heard the elevator doors open and the sound of several male voices laughing and shouting. She quickly opened the door to the stairs, and closed it behind her. Listening for a moment, she didn't hear any exclamations of surprise from the voices at the elevator.

Julianne encountered no one on her descent to the ground floor. Before she opened the door that exited to the street she took some steadying breaths. She thought back to that cabinet meeting again. She remembered Emmitt telling everyone how a military vet turned gun dealer, drug dealer, and overall extortionist was running Southwest Philadelphia. Aaron. That was his name. Aaron. Julianne didn't know why the conversation came to mind at this time, but at least she'd remembered his name. That could be useful.

Then she thought about Emmitt again. She knew she had to get to him. He would know what to do in this situation. Although

Julianne wanted to get back to her apartment to rest, it was too far to go with too much mayhem in between. If she could make it to the Chestnut Hill section of the city where Emmitt lived, she would be safe and possibly useful. She knew the chief was still loved by the officers on the force and had contacts with the state government. Julianne briefly considered going to her mother's home in Northeast Philadelphia, but that would be an eighteen-mile hike. Emmitt's place was probably less than ten miles away.

That cinched it. She would go to Emmitt's house.

She opened the door and looked around. She was in an alley between Cassie's building and another. To the left, the alley led to Rittenhouse Square. She saw a few people running by and a fire burning in the park. She turned right, away from the park to a tight one-way street that provided access to the large condominium buildings.

At the corner of the alley and the one-way was a teenager with a two-way radio in one hand and a cigarette in the other. He was listening to voices calling information on the radio. As of yet, he showed no indication of noticing Julianne.

Julianne decided she would bluff her way past this kid. She casually rested the bat on her shoulder with her left hand and kept her right hand in her jacket pocket on the pistol's handle. Julianne strode purposefully toward the lanky teenager.

As she approached the youth, she greeted him. She finally had a reason to use the street slang her mother had never permitted. "Yo. You having fun tonight?"

The teenager squinted past the cigarette he was taking a drag from and looked at Julianne, assessing her from head to toe. He shook his head. "Nah. They got me watching this corner in case five-oh roll up."

Julianne laughed, "Ain't no five-oh rolling anywhere tonight. Aaron got them running for they lives! You should get in there and jack some crackers. It's mad fun."

The youth laughed back, "True, true." He looked up at the building with a contemplative gaze.

Julianne shrugged and answered, "Do what you gotta' do. I got called to meet my crew over by Vine Street. Keep it real." She walked by the youth who moved aside to let her pass. He took another draw on his cigarette. Julianne looked straight ahead and kept walking. Her heart was pounding in her ears. It took all of her control to combat the adrenaline-filled urge to break into a run. Once she turned the corner, she paced herself at a casual jog and set off into the chaotic night.

# CHAPTER 32

*Friday, November 24th, 2028*
*10:15 AM*

Jimmy couldn't blame Nick for firing him. Killing Dante and getting his van shot up was definitely outside the "acceptable employee behavior" section of the company's employee manual.

He had never been without work before. It was humbling. It was also scary and frustrating. After taking a couple of days to clear his head of the trauma of the shooting, his escape with Detective Green, and his subsequent release from police custody, Jimmy started his job search in earnest.

Since this was the first time in his adult life he had been without a job, Jimmy was in a mad dash to get back to work. He had either called or stopped by the five other elevator maintenance companies around Philadelphia, but none were hiring. He received shocking news from the technical manager at the last place he interviewed.

That manager had told him the owners of the firm Jimmy was working at had blacklisted him from the business. Word was out that while Jimmy was a great mechanic, he had broken policy by carrying a gun while working, killed a man, and got the company van shot up.

All of which was true, Jimmy admitted. He was pissed at the situation, but what could he do? As far as the local companies were concerned, he was done in the elevator business. He would have to focus his job search in a different industry. It would suck to start at the bottom again, but Jimmy wasn't about to complain. He was only twenty-four years old, with the added benefits of not being in jail or dead.

On the balance, Jimmy couldn't feel too sorry for himself. Also, his mom wouldn't put up with it. And he wanted to show Colleen that he could overcome this new obstacle to become a man who could provide for her and her boys.

Jimmy was sitting between his mother and Colleen at the kitchen table. He looked up from his ancient laptop, where he was working on his resume, to Colleen. She was mending a pair of one of the boys' jeans. From the small size, it looked like the younger brother, Douglas', pants. The material looked a little threadbare as a whole, but Colleen was fastidiously concentrating on hand-sewing a patch on the right knee. Jimmy didn't know how long the patch would hold, since the material she was anchoring it to didn't look very strong to start with.

Jimmy had also noticed that Colleen had lost weight around her face recently. Part of it may have been intentional; she had been working at the YMCA for the past six months; but Jimmy wondered if she didn't have enough money to pay the bills, feed and clothe the boys, then feed herself with what was leftover. Whatever the reason, Colleen—whom Jimmy had thought was beautiful before working at the Y—was now downright stunning. He found it hard not to stare sometimes.

He had noticed that she and her boys had been spending a lot more time at his house—well, his mom's house. At first, he hoped it might have to do with Colleen wanting to be closer to him. But the last time he was over there, he figured out why. A few weeks ago he'd carried the larger of the two boys, Jack Jr., back to his bed after he had fallen asleep in the living room.

Their house was freezing. Not freezing exactly—that would cause pipes to burst—but it was downright cold. After Jimmy had tucked Jack Jr. in, he said goodnight to Colleen and peeked at the thermostat on the way out. It was set at fifty degrees. That was cold, too cold for a six- and an eight-year-old boy to be comfortable unless they had a mound of blankets.

He'd told his mom about the temperature in Colleen's house and now she insisted that Colleen and her sons come over every night for dinner. Jimmy thought the idea was brilliant, until he lost his job. Now he was starting to feel the strain of keeping the heat on and paying for food. It had been only ten days since he was fired, so at the moment his finances were fine, but they wouldn't be for long unless he found a job. Or maybe two, in case the pay at one job was a lot less than what he made fixing elevators.

His mom noticed him staring at Colleen. She smiled at Jimmy, then excused herself to check on the boys playing with Legos in the living room.

Colleen looked up, absently thanked Katherine and got back to her sewing. Jimmy continued to look at Colleen, then asked, "Hey Colleen. Are there are any job openings at the Y?"

Colleen looked up from her sewing at Jimmy with her characteristic raised right eyebrow, "Actually, I had been meaning to talk to you about that. I asked around and the director of facilities there told me he wanted to talk with you."

"Wow, great Colleen, thanks. When should I go there to interview?"

"Not sure, I'll ask when I go in tomorrow. But don't get your hopes up too high—he mentioned he only has the budget for a part timer and, as you can see from the crappy mending job I'm doing on Dougie's pants, the pay isn't good."

Jimmy laughed and said, "I don't care how many hours they can give or what the pay is. I need to work, it's who I am. I like fixing things, it's what I'm good at." Then Jimmy paused. He blushed slightly, unable to control his body's response to the risk he was about to take.

"And, if I get the job and our schedules line up—it would be nice to walk to work together."

Colleen looked at Jimmy with her head tilted slightly. Then a smile broke out and she said, "I would like that."

There was an awkward moment of silence as they looked at each other without speaking when suddenly Katherine came back into the kitchen. "I shouldn't have turned on the TV. The news is crazy. They were just saying that New Jersey shut down all the bridges from Philly because they don't know what's going on. A bunch of townships, including ours in Upper Darby, have set up checkpoints at roads leaving the city into the township to keep looters from coming here."

Colleen added, "I stayed up late last night watching some YouView footage of the city. People are getting mugged everywhere, entire buildings are being looted, and that video of the attack of the police station near Market Street was insane. They burned it to the ground. It's no wonder our township is trying to keep the city's chaos in the city. It's a deathtrap."

Jimmy thought about what Colleen said for a moment, something about the police station tickled his thoughts. He remembered, "Wait a second, was that the police station you picked me up from?"

Colleen, surprised at the question, answered by asking, "What's that, why are you asking?"

Jimmy wasn't expecting another question in response—he thought briefly, *Why do women do that?* But he had much more pressing questions, and his mind was working faster than his mouth; so he stared at Colleen without speaking until she continued, "Yes, I suppose it was. Why?"

Jimmy knew that thinking Aaron attacked the station just to get Jimmy's information was a leap, but even if that wasn't the reason, could he have gotten it while he was attacking? Detective Green had promised Jimmy that he would personally see to Jimmy's information being kept confidential. But how could he keep it confidential if Aaron had total control over the police station?

Jimmy took a deep breath. That was crazy thinking. The station burned in the riots right after the mayor was killed. If Aaron did get his information, why hadn't anything happened yet? It'd been two days since the station was attacked.

Jimmy shrugged and answered Colleen, "No reason. Just curious, is all."

Then he added, "You're right about the city. I can't see anyone willingly going in there right now to maintain anything. The whole infrastructure was already being held together with duct tape and baling wire, especially with almost all our country's resources going to the military right now. I just wish someone would come forward and explain what's going on. I guess that truck and mob took out most, if not all, of the city government, but what about the Governor? What about the President? Why aren't they saying anything? It's been more than two days since the mayor was killed."

Katherine looked at him. "Jimmy. There is no cavalry to ride to the rescue here. Our state's National Guard is gone, trying to hold the line against the Russians north of Anchorage."

Katherine paused and placed her hand over Colleen's, "I'm sorry honey." Turning back to Jimmy, she continued, "The federal government's law enforcement is stretched thin with the whole Texas situation and making sure no other states join the Texas secessionist movement. Not to mention the attack at the docks a few weeks ago; word is they lost more than two dozen agents. And think about the state. Pennsylvania has world class state troopers, but a lot of them were called up to fight in the reserves and they need to make sure all the politicians in Harrisburg are safe, along with Pittsburgh and everywhere else. It's a big state."

Everyone was silent as they considered Katherine's points. Jimmy pondered the lack of reporting coming out of the city. There were some reports from Northeast Philadelphia that things were normal, and the western part of the city near Chestnut Hill seemed calm, but there was almost nothing coming out of North Philly, Center City, and Southwest Philadelphia. On a clear day, Jimmy could go out his front porch and see the tops of the high-rises in Center City. But not yesterday or today. There was a haze from the various fires, obscuring the buildings from view.

A chilling thought percolated to the forefront of Jimmy's consciousness. If he didn't land an infrastructure critical job in thirty days, his name would be added to the draft for the war efforts. He involuntarily shivered. There was no way his mom would be able to make it without his income. His thoughts were interrupted by the ominous droning beep-beep from the television, alerting viewers that an emergency message was forthcoming.

Jimmy followed Katherine and Colleen as they got up from the table and proceeded to the family room.

Jimmy was standing behind the ladies with his arms crossed when the alert screen was replaced by the visage of a middle aged black gentleman with a well-trimmed, thin mustache and a clean chin-strap beard. He was wearing a white button-up collared shirt with a tan sports jacket, topped off with a pink bow tie. The man was smiling, looking right at the camera.

"Good morning Ladies and Gentlemen. My name is Malik Aziz. I am the Philadelphia City Councilman for the Third District. My district covers the wonderful neighborhoods of Cobbs Creek, King-sessing, University City, along with parts of Overbrook, Parkside, Mantua and Powelton. I was not at the mayor's speech due to an illness in my family." Jimmy noted the speaker now pause and look off screen for a moment, allowing his smile to falter slightly. Then he re-engaged with the camera and cranked his smile back up to one hundred and ten percent. Jimmy perceived that the speaker's smile, which at first was warm and reassuring, now looked manufactured and less genuine.

The speaker continued, "Enough about me folks. I have been nominated by the surviving city government as the Administrator-In-Charge to provide you this critical information." Again, the speaker paused; Jimmy didn't know if it was for dramatic effect or just to make sure everyone was listening.

Now the speaker swapped out his smile for a very somber counte-nance, "I am very sorry to announce that the mayor, his senior staff, and the City Council were all killed Wednesday by the horrendous act of terror perpetrated by elements of the Texas Secessionist Movement. These cowards not only drove a fully loaded dump truck into the viewing stand where the mayor and his staff were seated; they then had several operatives planted in and around the crowd attack and kill any survivors."

Again, the speaker paused. Jimmy was confident he was doing so for effect this time. "We are fully engaged with the federal government to track down these terrorists and bring them to justice."

Another pause. Jimmy noted the speaker change back to his warm, friendly persona. It almost looked like the guy was trying to sell something. "There have been reports of looting and gunfire in the city. I am working with the police department and can tell you those reports have been overstated. We are in control of the streets. We will impose a curfew at sundown for tonight, Saturday night, and Sunday so that we can get the city back in working shape for Monday. We have a lot to do and we don't need people on the streets causing any mischief." He continued, "Finally, and this is important:"

The speaker took a moment to look down at some papers he was holding, "We have been made aware of a situation in the Center City Section of town from Second Street to 20th Street and from the Vine Street expressway to Walnut Street. The Texas terrorists have placed several sophisticated bombs on critical infrastructure in this area, including places such as gas mains, electrical transformers, and our subway system. Because of this, there are several checkpoints going in and out of those areas. We have been executing an orderly evacuation of civilians from that area. If you are in that area, stay put, our people will come get you. In addition, we ask that no traffic, commercial or otherwise, enter that area."

Jimmy then watched as the speaker lost his concentration for a moment and looked off screen with a somewhat puzzled expression. When he looked back at the camera, he regained his composure. "During the next day or two, we will be working to dismantle these bombs. You may hear explosions as we need to detonate these charges in a safe way as soon as they are removed from the infrastructure. Please stay away from windows and do not take it upon yourself to investigate. It is our primary goal to keep you safe. Just give us a couple days to clean this up and we'll have the city back to normal as soon as possible. Take care and peace be with you."

At that the programming returned to a female national news anchor, who was summarizing what Malik Aziz had just said. She was about to introduce two analysts with expertise in Homeland Security and municipal operations. Jimmy hit the mute button on the remote and said, "Something doesn't add up."

Colleen said, "I don't know Jimmy, I'm just glad that someone's taking charge."

"I hear you Colleen. But we all watched the YouView video of the attack at Love Park. Malik said it was a dump truck. I could clearly tell it was a City of Philadelphia trash truck. He also said that the Texas Secessionist movement was responsible for this. In the past, whenever the news does a story about those people, it's a bunch of white guys in Waco who have it out for Washington D.C. But, on the video I saw, it looked like the people rampaging after the truck attack were folks local to the inner city of Philadelphia, if you know what I mean."

Kathleen spoke up this time. "This is the kind of mayhem that breaks out when those hooligans in the city don't have other people there to keep them in line. I've been telling you for years to be careful around those people. One of them almost killed you a couple weeks ago and now they are tearing their own city apart."

Jimmy saw Colleen look at Katherine with her eyebrows lifted and a shocked expression on her face. Before this went any further, Jimmy stepped in and said, "Mom. We don't know the whole story yet. While I agree this is a bad situation, you can't go judging a whole group of people by the actions of a few of them."

Katherine didn't back down, "It's not a few of them. You saw the footage. It's the whole city. It's a mess. What's going to happen once they're done looting and stealing everything from the city? You think they're just going to stop? No. They will come here, Jimmy. They will come to the nearest suburbs and start attacking us."

By this time, Jimmy had guided his mother back into the kitchen so the boys playing with their Legos in the living room wouldn't hear her rant. Jimmy gently placed a hand on each of Katherine's shoulders and looked her in the eye. "Mom. You may be right. But getting hysterical about the situation doesn't help. There are more good people in the city than bad, you'll see. Things will calm down."

Katherine relaxed a bit and said, "Okay, Jimmy. It's not that I don't trust you. But I have a bad feeling about this. What if the leader of the gang with the man that mugged you wants revenge? You are the man of this house. You need to protect us."

Jimmy tried not to flinch when Katherine mentioned Aaron's desire to avenge Dante's death. He hoped that Aaron was too busy and distracted with everything happening in the city to concern himself with hunting Jimmy down.

# CHAPTER 33

*Friday, November 24th, 2028*
*9:00 AM*

The last forty-eight hours had been a whirlwind for Julianne. It started with her jump from the viewing stand at the mayor's speech as a truck barreled towards her. Now she found herself at a police station in Northwest Philadelphia with Chief Braxton trying to get the city back up and running.

The journey to Emmitt's house in the Chestnut Hill section of the city had been harrowing. Julianne had stayed off the major roads, instead using a series of side streets to get from Center City to Chestnut Hill. She figured it was about a ten-mile hike. She mostly avoided people. There were some looters and a few buildings on fire, but once she got far enough along on Germantown pike towards Chestnut Hill and away from the Wyoming and Germantown sections of the city, things calmed down appreciatively. She only had to brandish her pistol once. The baseball bat on her shoulder and her pissed-off expression seemed to be more than enough to keep away most of the punks out that night.

She got to Emmitt's house just as the sun was rising. He had mentioned which street he lived on, but never the number. It just hadn't come up in their conversations over the past ten days.

She did have Emmitt's cell number, but every time she tried to place the call, the automated message said the network was busy with unexpected volume, try again later. She stopped trying after three attempts.

Walking down his street, she saw Emmitt's police-issued unmarked sedan parked on the driveway of a handsome single-family stone home. Looking up and down the empty street for any other clue, she shrugged and marched up to the front door and knocked. She stood momentarily face-to-face with the barrel of a really large handgun before Emmitt recognized her.

A heartfelt greeting was followed by a shower, breakfast, and a change of clothes, courtesy of the chief's daughter who had just graduated college and now worked in Chicago. The chief's daughter wasn't as tall as Julianne, but the clothes fit well enough for the circumstances.

Julianne had then taken a nap in a spare bedroom and had woken up in the mid-afternoon on Thanksgiving Day to several voices in the living room. It turned out the captains from several of the police districts had gathered to implore him to re-assert himself as the chief of police. After a long discussion, he agreed to do so on a temporary basis until civilian governance could be re-constituted.

Now it was Black Friday and Julianne was in a conference room with Chief Braxton at the headquarters for the 14th police district. The building was a single-story box with offices in the front, a single conference room, a single interrogation room, and two cells in the back. The armory consisted of a locker with four sets of tactical gear and rifles. The building was located just off Germantown Avenue, a short trip from Braxton's home.

Julianne's cell phone sat on the table in the conference room on speaker mode. She was able to get a line and had coordinated a conference call between all the police districts that were available.

The chief continued, "—let me summarize what I have heard so far. Northeast Philadelphia is one hundred percent under control as is Manyunk, Roxborough, Mt. Airy and Chestnut Hill. North Philly is a problem because of looting and lack of police response. The police headquarters on North Broad is on lockdown due to low employee turnout and the gangs taking shots at the building itself. Also, someone cut power to the building and the neighborhoods around it are experiencing heavy looting and rioting. So effectively, the headquarters is off the chessboard for now."

"Chief. This is McNeal from the 8th District, Northeast Philadelphia. I'm hearing both Southwest Philly and University City are both completely off line and we have no idea what is going on there except for reports and a YouView video of a coordinated assault on the District 18 station."

Braxton continued, "Thanks McNeal, also all attempts at contact with the 12th District have been unsuccessful."

McNeal interjected, "Chief, we need to prioritize one thing: what the hell is going on in Center City?"

Julianne heard the speaker on her phone overload with a cacophony of voices responding to McNeal's question. The chief looked at the phone, scratching the black and gray stubble on his scalp. Finally, he spoke up. "Alright! Alright, let's quiet down. Here's what we know. Malik Aziz, the councilman for Southwest Philly, is a stooge for a thug named Aaron Mitchell. We believe Mr. Mitchell put Mr. Aziz on television to assert his control over the situation. Some of us are familiar with Mr. Mitchell, as he calls himself the leader of the 'Southwest Militia.' Mr. Mitchell is a veteran of the Ukraine conflict. He is known to be running a crime syndicate that covers all of Southwest Philadelphia that includes drugs, prostitution, gambling, and racketeering."

Julianne looked at a sheet in her hand, "I made some calls this morning. Mr. Mitchell also has some legitimate businesses such as trucking and construction. He is suspected of using those firms to hide his profits from his other endeavors."

Julianne flipped the sheet in her hand and continued, "The most disturbing information came from a contact I called in the FBI. Aaron is suspected of being a very successful black-market arms dealer. He runs a network, shipping arms from the Ukraine and Baltic states here to Philadelphia, and supplies the separatists in Texas with arms. He recently got on the feds' radar when they caught wind of a large shipment of heavy munitions coming into the Packer Avenue Terminal; we all know what happened there. That earned him a spot on the federal government's top ten most wanted list. They just don't have any resources to go after him. If they try to get him while he's holed up in Southwest, it'll be a bloodbath. "

Chief Braxton thanked Julianne. McNeal asked, "What does all this have to do with Center City being on lockdown?"

Julianne spoke again as Chief Braxton was taking a sip of his coffee "We believe Aaron's militia is responsible for the blockades preventing access to Center City. The blockades are manned by crews with—" Julianne took a moment to look at her notes, "—thirty caliber automatic machine guns mounted on the beds of pickup trucks and at least four-man crews, each person heavily armed with military grade weapons and body armor."

McNeal exclaimed, "Holy shit! How is that type of hardware landing on the streets of Philadelphia? We don't have the armor to take on that kind of threat!"

Chief Braxton spoke up this time, "Looks like Aaron didn't send everything he shipped in from the Ukraine to his customers in Texas. My contact also told me that the latest shipment may have had some shoulder fired anti-tank launchers, and there are a couple of Stinger missiles missing from the main weapons depot outside of Kiev. I am also acutely aware, as are you gentlemen, that the federal government has requisitioned all of our heavy tactical vehicles to keep the Texans from seceding from the Union. It leaves us without the ability to take a threat like this head on."

McNeal asked the obvious question, "So what's next Chief? I can start expanding my control to help out the situation in North Philadelphia, but there is no way I am sending any of my men to Center City to get chewed up by those machine guns. I was going to offer to use the one helicopter we still have—it's parked up at the Northeast Philadelphia Airport—to do some surveillance. But if Aaron has surface to air missiles, that would be a foolish thing to do."

Julianne watched as Chief Braxton used his fingertips to massage his scalp for a moment before answering, "Here's the plan. McNeal, proceed to expand your influence to North Philly and secure the Broad Street corridor first and foremost. Make sure that bird is fueled up and ready to fly with a flight crew on standby. Julianne and I have a call with the governor of Pennsylvania and the colonel of the Pennsylvania State Police. Also, the Director of Homeland Security will be on the line from Washington, D.C. I need to understand what resources they can muster to help us out here."

The chief paused for a moment as several of the captains on the line remarked about the low likelihood of the feds helping. At least one of the captains just chuckled in response.

The chief raised his voice once more, "Okay, Gents. That concludes this call. I will update you at seventeen hundred hours at our next call. Be careful out there and Godspeed."

Julianne ended the call and looked at Emmitt as he exhaled and rolled his shoulders. He looked back at her for a moment with a faraway expression painted on his face. Then Julianne watched as his eyes refocused on her and he smiled.

Julianne remarked, "Wow, Emmitt. I'd love to know what you were just thinking there."

His smile faded a bit as he responded to Julianne, "A lot of things all at once. What the hell is Aaron up to? What an incredible wing-woman you are. How did our country get to the point where a glorified gang leader can hold half of a major city hostage? And finally, once we get this mess cleaned up, you should be mayor."

The last comment caused Julianne to shake her head in disbelief. She responded, "Thanks for the vote of confidence. I just want to get the city back on its feet. I hadn't even considered what comes after that."

Braxton responded, "We shall see. Could you please set up the next call with the state and federal authorities while I hit the head and get a refill of coffee?"

A few minutes later, Julianne had Pennsylvania State Governor Fox and the head of the Pennsylvania State Police, Nicole Wilcox, on the line. The governor was an unabashed liberal who won the election by promising more spending in Pittsburgh and Philadelphia. His strategy had worked, as the turnout in those two cities swamped the electorate in the rest of the state. Julianne didn't agree with much that Governor Fox did except for the appointment of Colonel Wilcox as the head of the State Police. In her mid-fifties now, Wilcox had done two tours of duty flying Apache helicopters first in Iraq and then in Afghanistan. After the military, she worked her way up through the ranks in the State Police, taking any assignment they threw at her and excelling in each one as she climbed the ladder.

Also on the line was the Secretary of Homeland Security, John Asher. Julianne remembered that Asher was a controversial appointment who passed confirmation on a party-line vote. He was the son of the governor of California, and his major accomplishment before this very important appointment had been passing the bar exam in California (on his third try, Julianne remembered) and catching the best waves while surfing at Zuma beach. Everyone knew he was way in over his head, but since his father had delivered the state and all its electoral college votes to the President, Asher had his choice of positions in the current administration.

Julianne called the meeting to order. Chief Braxton provided a similar update to the one he'd given the police captains. As he was wrapping up, Asher interjected, "Mr. Braxton, as chief of police in Philadelphia, how did you let this security situation escalate? The sixth largest city in the United States is being terrorized by a gang leader on your watch!"

Julianne saw Braxton take a deep breath and straighten his shoulders to respond, before he did so, a deep alto voice interjected, "This is Colonel Wilcox, Pennsylvania State Police. Mr. Asher, what Chief Braxton did not tell you is that he was relieved of duty by

Mayor Rhodes three weeks ago for providing what I understand was sound council. The captains of the various districts in Philadelphia unanimously voted that he re-assume his role as chief during this crisis until the city government can be reconstituted. What we need now are solutions; not the finger-pointing, ass-covering politics that are endemic in the Capitol."

Julianne had never heard anyone actually "Hurrumph" before, but that was pretty much the sound that came over the line from Secretary Asher.

There was a brief pause on the line. Finally, Governor Fox spoke up, "Secretary Asher, are you prepared to tell us what assets in personnel and material the federal government can provide to help us bring this city back under control?"

Julianne could hear Secretary Asher breathe out a loud sigh into the receiver of the phone on his end. Then he responded, "Ladies, Gentlemen. I know this is not a secure communication line, but time is of the essence here and I need to read you into a situation you are not aware of that may be relevant to the current situation in your city."

Julianne hit the mute button on her cell phone and turned to Chief Braxton, "What the hell is this guy talking about?"

Braxton looked at her and said, "I don't know, but I have a feeling this is about to go from bad to worse."

Julianne unmuted the phone and listened as Asher continued, "Approximately three weeks ago, the United States Treasury transferred twenty tons of gold from our repository in Fort Knox, Kentucky, to the Federal Reserve Bank of Philadelphia. This wasn't the only transfer made, but it is the only one germane to this situation. These transfers were done for two reasons: one, to move our holdings further away from Texas and their sympathizers in the South; and two, to prepare to pay for arms and other logistical support from our allies in Europe, specifically Germany."

Governor Fox broke in with a laugh and said, "I was wondering when the rest of the world would realize our currency isn't worth the paper it's printed on."

Secretary Asher found his voice again and said, "Hey. I'm not in charge of the Treasury, so don't blame me for what's going on there. What I just told you is strictly confidential. We have not informed the public that we are using our gold repositories to pay for several ongoing conflicts around the world. I am not sure our financial markets could handle that information right now."

Julianne spoke up this time, "So connecting the dots here. The feds park about two billion dollars' worth of gold at the Philadelphia Federal Reserve Bank building at Sixth and Arch Street and try to keep it hush-hush. Somehow, Aaron Mitchell, who has a well-armed illegal militia headquartered not four miles away from the Reserve Bank, catches wind of it. Now Aaron has the whole Center City area, which includes this building, blockaded from anyone getting in. Damn, this just did go from bad to worse."

Asher spoke up again, "That's not all."

Julianne responded, "What do you mean that's not all? Isn't this situation bad enough?"

Asher continued, "I need to make you aware of Aaron's motive."

"Do you mean in addition to Aaron being a maniacal sociopath who deals drugs, prostitutes women, runs extortion rings, and imports military grade weapons?" Julianne asked.

Asher confirmed, "Yes. He has a brother, Lieutenant Colonel Randall Walker of the illegal Texas Secessionist Army. They were separated by youth services as children and never reunited until about five years ago. Turns out they both were overlapped for a couple weeks at a joint services base in Texas."

Julianne let out a breath. "And I thought Aaron named his militia after the part of the city where he operated, Southwest Philadelphia. With the connection to Texas, it may have another meaning."

Asher continued, "Correct. We suspect that Aaron returned to Philadelphia with the explicit purpose of supplying arms to the separatists in Texas through his brother. We also have intel that shows the Texans caught wind of the gold move. We assume that Randall has tasked his brother to retrieve that gold and deliver it to Texas. If Texas gets that gold, it will be a tipping point in their quest to break away. We won't be able to stop them."

Wilcox from the State Police spoke up again, "Asher. We need to know what assets the feds can give us to help Chief Braxton break through the checkpoints this guy Aaron has set up. Governor Fox and I have spoken about this and we can augment the city with one hundred troopers. That's five percent of our active troopers, which are already depleted from the forty-five hundred or so troopers we really need to patrol the state properly. But we don't have any munitions larger than AR-15 rifles and our heaviest vehicles are the special tactics vans, which are not up-armored at all."

Secretary Asher spoke again, "Okay. I did speak with the chairman of the Joint Chiefs of Staff here in DC. He's got two first generation armored MRAP vehicles in Harrisburg. They were about to be upgraded with a cold weather package and sent to the Alaska theater. He will let us . . . borrow them to help you punch through Aaron's blockades. These MRAPs are slow as hell and bulky, but they can resist the thirty caliber rounds from the blockades that this Aaron character is using."

Braxton asked, "That's a good start. Anything heavier? What do you have at Willow Grove Naval Air station?" That base was just a short ride down Route 611, which fed right into Broad Street.

Julianne could almost hear Asher nodded as he responded, "Good thought chief. Just a few months too late. We mothballed that base and moved all the assets to Joint Base McGuire in central New Jersey. I believe there is a Bradley fighting vehicle stationed there to protect the airfields. I'll inquire about its status and availability, but I seriously doubt we'll need it. Aaron won't be ready to handle those MRAPs when we roll them down his throat."

Julianne looked to Braxton for confirmation of Asher's last assertion. He glanced at Julianne and responded with a shrug.

Wilcox interjected, "What about eyes in the sky? It would be nice to know what we're coming up against. Braxton, I heard you still have a bird available at Northeast Airport. How you kept that off the feds' military appropriation radar is beyond me."

Braxton paused, looking at Julianne. She hit the mute button and said, "Emmitt, if we send that helicopter up and Aaron has those Stinger missiles, it will be a death trap for the pilot and spotter."

Braxton nodded and said, "Let's see if the feds have anything that can help first."

Julianne hit the mute button again and Braxton addressed the people on the line, "Yes, we have a mid-1990s Rotorway Exec Ninety that a private citizen donated four years ago. It didn't fly when we first got it, so when the feds requisitioned equipment for use in the war efforts, it was passed over. We had a mechanic who got it in flying shape, but it's only a two-seater and has pretty limited flight time before it needs to be refueled. We could put it in the air to do some recon, but we heard a rumor that Aaron might have received surface to air missiles in his last shipment. Secretary Asher, can you confirm his acquisition of those munitions and if so, are there any unmanned or satellite assets you can deploy?"

Asher responded with a belligerent tone, "What the—how did you hear about—I can't comment on the possibility of missing Stinger missiles from our military and it concerns me that you are even aware of the possibility. Also, no. We do not have any air-based assets. As you know, when China decided to annex Taiwan, the first thing they did was knock out any satellites we had capable of imaging. They only left the GPS satellites up, because they use them also. As far as drones are concerned, we could use ten times more than what we are able to produce today. No, if you want eyes in the sky, you need to provide them yourself."

Julianne sat back as the logistics for the assault on Philadelphia was planned out. She couldn't believe that the city she'd grown up in and served as an adult was going to become the scene of an urban war.

She thought about her mother. What would Mama do in this situation? She wouldn't back down, that's for sure. She would find Aaron's weakness, then use it to bring him to justice. Aaron's weakness. That was the key. But what was it? Something in her gut told her going head-to-head against Aaron was a bad idea. She didn't understand half of the technical terms being discussed on the line right now but her instinct told her that Aaron would be ready for anything they threw at him. Somehow, they had to hit him where he wouldn't expect it. The only problem was that Julianne had no idea where that was.

As the call wrapped up, she disconnected the various parties from her cell phone and looked over at Braxton. "What's next boss?"

Again, Chief Braxton massaged his scalp with his fingertips, looking up at the stained and warped acoustical ceiling tiles above the conference room. He stopped working his scalp and laid his hands on the table, looking now at Julianne, "I know this cat, Aaron, pretty well. When I was chief, we had an unspoken treaty. I wouldn't dig too hard or press him too hard and he would keep violent crime in Southwest Philly to a minimum. It worked for years. The districts covering his territory repeatedly reported the lowest murders, assaults, and property crimes in the city. That allowed me to redeploy my extremely understaffed patrol divisions in other parts of the city to fight crime where things were out of control. I'm telling you this not because I wanted to police in this fashion or because I wanted to aid and abet Aaron's gang, but to tell you that he operates a level far higher than the typical gang leader. His command structure is based on military hierarchy and most of his people are war-hardened veterans. "

Julianne, not reassured by his comments, replied, "I'm concerned we're being overconfident here. Do you think this could actually work?"

Braxton replied, "I hope so, but I got a bad feeling about this planned assault. Wilcox and Asher are relying too much on the advantage those MRAPs are going to provide. And if Aaron wants that gold bad enough, there ain't nothing we can do to stop him from getting it."

# CHAPTER 34

*Friday, November 24ᵗʰ, 2028*
*11:45 AM*

Aaron was pleased with how the operation was unfolding. His blockades around the perimeter of Center City were holding. At a few points, the Philadelphia police had probed the strength of the blockades, but a few short bursts from the M60 machine guns mounted on the beds of the pickup trucks he had stationed there had deterred them from getting too close.

It was late Friday morning and he was standing with Booker and Jackson on the north end of the roof of the William J. Green Federal building, overlooking the Federal Reserve Bank building. In typical government fashion, the WJ Green building's construction unapologetically prioritized function over form. The building was a large concrete block with narrow windows. On the south side of the building, a small annex housed the Internal Revenue Service. South of the annex sat the Federal Courthouse. The three structures took up an entire city block.

It had taken most of Thursday to secure the block. Aaron knew he had to neutralize the remaining federal law enforcement officers in the area if his operation to infiltrate the Federal Reserve Building, just across Arch Street from the building he was standing on, had any hopes of success. He took no pleasure in having to kill the dozen or so agents in the WJ Green building, but he couldn't have them flanking his operation. He did enjoy ransacking and burning the Internal Revenue Service's annex building. The annex itself was unoccupied by the time Aaron's men entered the building. It didn't take much gasoline to get the annex cooking—there was paper everywhere. So much for going digital.

The courthouse building south of the annex was another story. Again, Aaron had no use for the building itself, but it needed to be clear of anyone who could attack his flank once the assault on the Federal Reserve Bank started. His men had breached the building and secured the first floor, basement, and sub-basement. In the sub-basement was the city water supply for the fire protection sprinkler system in the building. Jackie knew which valves to turn to disable the system so that no water would flow from the sprinkler heads. Then Aaron's men distributed about a dozen fifty-five gallon drums of gasoline, kerosene, and other petroleum distillate products they had 'requisitioned' from the refinery in Southwest Philadelphia near the airport.

The ensuing blaze was fearsome. The accelerants on the first floor created an incredible amount of heat and smoke that rapidly engulfed the upper floors. Aaron had six to eight men stationed at each stair tower exit door on the streets, and they mowed down any panicked agents or officers attempting to flee the building. People stopped attempting to flee to the street level exits soon after they realized that certain death awaited them outside the exit door. A group of agents from the building had made it to the roof, looking for some sort of airborne escape. No help arrived. Aaron's snipers, perched atop the

WJ Green building, quickly dispatched them. That was the end of that fight. Aaron assumed the remaining people in the building died of smoke inhalation. *Crappy way to go*, Aaron thought, *but nothing is going to stand between me and the gold in the Fed's vault.*

The pale, late November sun was low on the horizon trying to shine through the remaining haze from the smoldering fires in the city. Aaron had allowed his core group of thirty soldiers to get a few hours of sleep so they would be sharp for today's assault. It was time to strike the final blow. He knew that holding this much territory with the number of troops he had was not sustainable. He was up against local, state, and possibly federal authorities. He would eventually lose the game.

But only if he took too long.

Aaron walked away from the edge of the roof overlooking Arch Street toward the roof access door leading to the stairs, flanked by Jackie and Booker.

As Aaron was about to open the door to exit the roof, his cell phone buzzed. Aaron looked at the caller ID. It was the spotter they had stationed at the interchange of the Schuylkill Expressway and the Roosevelt Expressway on the western approach to the city.

"Boss. We got trouble rolling your way on the Schuylkill. I got two MRAPs followed by about eight SWAT vans from the state police. Crawling along at about twenty miles per hour. They going be on you in ten minutes tops."

Aaron was prepared for this contingency. He hadn't known what direction the assault would come from and the timing was shitty, but they could handle this.

Aaron turned to Booker and said, "You and I need to get to the Vine Street Expressway ASAP and set up our ambush."

Turning to Jackie he said, "I need you to stay here and finish prep for breaching the Federal Reserve. You gotta' make sure that flatbed truck gets here and is ready to load. Once me and Booker stop this assault, we'll be back to start the final phase of the plan."

Both men nodded their assent and then the three of them hustled down the stairs to get to ground level.

Aaron's truck was parked at the corner of Arch and Seventh. It did not have an M60 mounted in the bed—Aaron wanted his truck open for supplies or men that might need to be repositioned around the city. This was one such time. Aaron double-checked to make sure the AT4 rocket launchers were still on the back seat of the quad cab of the truck.

He counted six of the lethal tubes. He had used two of the eight that came in on the last shipment on the police building. His two Stinger surface-to-air missiles were deployed with his soldiers—one in Southwest Philadelphia protecting his headquarters and the other with a two-man team on the top of a high-rise building at Ninth and Vine St. He would have liked to have more of each, but in a couple hours, he could fall back and not be so extended.

By the time Aaron had stowed his AR-15 rifle in the back seat of the truck and was starting the vehicle, Booker had eight heavily armed troops in the bed of the truck. Aaron could feel the added weight of the men and munitions on the suspension of the truck.

Aaron turned to Booker, now sitting beside him in the front passenger seat of the cab. "How many men did you leave at the Federal Reserve building?"

Booker responded, "Two at each corner on a technical and a four-man crew at the front and back, so a total of sixteen. I got eight in the back with us and six more following in another technical truck.

Two of the men in the back of the truck have the fifty caliber Barrett's we got from the last shipment and four of our men have the M249 squad machine guns."

As he drove, Aaron visualized how to deploy his troops to maximize the impact of his ambush. The convoy would be coming into the city on the Schuylkill Expressway. For a main artery that fed traffic into and out of a major city, it was woefully narrow. Just before reaching Center City, the Schuylkill Expressway crossed the Schuylkill River, where it was renamed the Vine Street Expressway. The Vine Street Expressway was a cattle chute, narrow with high sidewalls and several overpasses where city streets crossed the expressway.

That was where Aaron would spring his trap.

# CHAPTER 35

*Friday, November 24ᵗʰ, 2028*
*11:52 AM*

Aaron drove his truck to 15th Street and used the ramp up from the Vine Street Expressway to 15th Street to access the expressway. It was amazing how small the city was and how quickly he could traverse it with no other traffic on the roads. His men had all access points blocked with disabled heavy vehicles. He had the blockades at small streets manned by two-man crews with AR-15's and the major arteries manned with the technical trucks Jackson had made. His manpower was stretched thin as hell, but he only needed it to hold for a few more hours.

Aaron barked orders at his men in the truck to deploy to various points along the Vine Street Expressway. He then got on the radio and ordered the two technicals nearby to position themselves on the 21st Street overpass above the Vine Street Expressway. He sent two riflemen to spots the trucks couldn't cover.

One of the riflemen positioned himself in the small grassy area just north of the wall of the expressway. The other set up his rifle in a small parking area just past the expressway's south wall. Since the expressway was recessed below the city streets, each shooter had an elevated shooting position.

Aaron left his truck near the on-ramp to Broad Street on the expressway. Then he and Booker grabbed their rifles and two of the AT4 grenade launchers. Both launchers had the acronym HEAT spray painted in yellow on the side: High Explosive Anti-Tank. Aaron was saving these launchers for the possibility that heavier armored vehicles would be deployed in this conflict. During his time in the Ukraine, the HEAT launchers couldn't do much against the monstrous T-14 Armata tanks the Russians used; but for lighter armored vehicles, they were deadly. The MRAPs the authorities were using, while providing a lot more armor than a standard HUMVEE, were nothing like a main battle tank. Aaron was looking forward to seeing what carnage the AT4 could inflict on the approaching vehicles.

Aaron and Booker made their way towards the underside of the 20th Street overpass. This was the widest of the city streets that crossed over the Vine Street Expressway, which had been constructed below grade to allow the city streets to pass overhead with adequate truck clearance. They had to walk around quite a few abandoned and looted vehicles—it seemed the wave of youth he'd unleashed on the city to sow chaos had improvised. That was fine with Aaron. The abandoned vehicles would slow the convoy as they approached Aaron's ambush point.

As Aaron and Booker were about to walk under the overpass, which was so wide it felt like a tunnel once you were in it, Aaron heard the distinctive thump-thump-thump of an approaching helicopter.

Aaron paused and scanned the sky. With so many high-rise buildings in this vicinity, he couldn't determine the location of the bird. He keyed the radio clipped to his shoulder harness. "Stinger One, this is Alpha-Mike, do you have eyes on the approaching bird?"

After a short pause, a voice on the radio replied, "Alpha-Mike, this is Stinger One. Affirmative. Two-seater, state police markings, coming straight down route ninety-five corridor to your location."

Aaron keyed the microphone again, "You are cleared to engage the target then exfiltrate to the primary objective." Aaron wanted them to down that bird before it got a visual of the ambush he was setting. Since the Stinger was a one-shot ground to air missile, Aaron had instructed the two-man crew to get to the Federal Reserve to help in the upcoming assault after deploying the weapon.

Aaron and Booker stopped walking, turned, and looked east down the Vine Street Expressway to where it and Route 95 intersected, just west of the Delaware River. Within seconds, the helicopter appeared around an apartment building, barreling down the Vine Street Expressway about fifty feet off the ground.

Immediately after first seeing the bird, Aaron looked at the building where his Stinger fire crew was positioned. Aaron was surprised that the missile had not been launched. He would have popped the shot off right then and there. The helicopter was flying at full speed with its rotor and body tilted forward in an all-out sprint. Within seconds, it was past the building with his fire team. Aaron was about to shoulder his AR-15 to pop some shots off at the approaching bird when it happened.

As the helicopter passed the building at Ninth Street, it leveled off and started to gain some altitude. At that very moment, a streak of smoke reached out from the top of the building. The warhead from the missile targeted the hot engine on the top of the cockpit. When it got within thirty feet of the helicopter, a proximity fuse in the warhead activated and hundreds of pieces of small shrapnel peppered the flying craft.

The effect on the helicopter was immediate but not catastrophic. Aaron always chuckled when he watched a movie and a missile totally obliterated the aircraft it hit. He guessed that made for good movies. In this case, the helicopter shuddered and listed to the right while losing altitude and belching grayish smoke.

Aaron watched in fascination as the helicopter struggled to stay airborne. The craft continued to pull right, veering off its path above the Vine Street Expressway. Despite the efforts of the pilot, the helicopter smashed into the Mormon tabernacle building which had been constructed about ten years ago just north of the Vine Street Expressway, between 17th and 18th Streets. The building had been meticulously maintained and seemingly immune to the blight that had affected so many other buildings in the city. The craft disintegrated into thousands of pieces as it collided with one of the two spires that rose above the building proper.

Aaron was momentarily mesmerized as he watched the spire slowly tilt, then accelerate as gravity worked its magic and brought the spire and the golden bugler atop it crashing down.

Booker clapped Aaron on the shoulder, bringing Aaron back to the moment. Booker was laughing as he said, "Oh shit Boss! Now we did it. We done pissed off the Mormons. We might as well pack up and go home now."

Aaron chuckled and responded, "You're right Books. Them Mormons didn't like us to start with, now we just gave them a reason to be really pissed off. But we got bigger fish to fry. Once we take care of business today, we can buy our own damn church. Let's do this. That convoy'll be here any minute."

Aaron and Booker jogged under the overpass. The total span of the covered area was longer than a football field. They stopped about halfway in and took a position behind an abandoned four-door sedan with all four tires slashed and flat. The midday sun from either end of the overpass did not provide much light at their position. It wasn't pitch dark, but it was about as dark as a city street at night. Each man grabbed a launcher and positioned himself with his elbows resting on the hood or trunk for stability.

Aaron said, "Booker. There are two MRAPs. I'll take out the first one, you try to get a bead on the second one."

Booker kept his eyes on the road ahead of him, "Affirmative."

Aaron heard the rumble of diesel engines before the hulking vehicles became visible. The Vine Street Expressway elevated and turned as it crossed the river. Aaron first saw the MRAPs as they were making their way down the decline that would put them in the cattle chute of the expressway. The abandoned cars on the road slowed their progress. The MRAPs would avoid those they could but several times, Aaron watched the lead MRAP slow to make contact with a car and then rev its engine and push the car out of the way.

Finally, the lead MRAP rolled into the lighted area between the 21st Street overpass and the overpass where Aaron and Booker were waiting. It was about a one hundred foot stretch of road open to the sky. The lead MRAP looked like a giant off-road vehicle made of plated armor. The front bumper rode a good three feet above the asphalt with huge tires and exposed suspension below it. Aaron set his sights in the center of the front engine grill. He figured the armored grill would laugh at the twenty-two caliber rounds from his rifle or even the thirty caliber bullets from the M60s on his technical trucks, but not the warhead from the AT4. He depressed the trigger and felt the satisfying recoil of the projectile leaving the launch tube.

Aaron's aim was true. At nine hundred and fifty feet per second, the projectile impacted the grill of the lead MRAP a fraction of a second after being fired. The projectile penetrated the grill and impacted the top of the iron engine block, disabling the engine. The momentum of the destroyed engine components and shrapnel from the original projectile deflected upward at a shallow angle and breached the next layer of armor protecting the driver and passenger in the cockpit. Both men were killed instantly as the white-hot shrapnel scattered through the confined space of the truck's cab.

The MRAP shuddered then rolled forward and to the left until it hit the dividing wall between the east- and west-bound lanes of the expressway. The second MRAP revved its engine and lurched forward just as Booker fired his AT4 launcher. The second projectile impacted the surging MRAP just above the front bumper. Again, the projectile penetrated the front grill but this time the momentum of the weapon was arrested by the bulk of the iron engine block. Several of the internal components of the engine where obliterated so that the engine immediately stalled, but the driver and passenger were unharmed as the integrity of the cab had not been breached.

Both trucks were stalled in the pale morning sun between the two overpasses. Aaron keyed his radio, "Engage! All troops, engage the vehicles."

Just as Aaron lifted his thumb from the radio, the driver side window on the second MRAP exploded in a shower of glass. Immediately after that, Aaron heard the booming report of one of the fifty caliber rifles that his men were firing. The pink spray on the front windshield showed Aaron that the armored glass of this version of the MRAP could not hold up to such fast, heavy rifle rounds. The second rifleman fired at the passenger side of the MRAP's cab with similarly devastating results.

The fifty caliber shooters continued their assault on the rear troop transport area of each MRAP. Aaron almost felt sorry for the people he imagined huddled back in each compartment. Each hoping the next bullet didn't find him and wondering if he were safer hunkered in the armored box or out in the street.

Immediately after the first fifty caliber shot, Aaron heard the distinctive chug-chug-chug of the M60 machine guns on the technicals opening fire. These shooters concentrated their fire on the unarmored SWAT vehicles closest to the overpass. The goal was to create a kill zone of disabled vehicles on the east and west end of the clearing between the two overpasses.

Aaron and Booker had to keep their heads down and their bodies protected behind the vehicle they were using as cover due to the stray rounds of machine gun fire ricocheting off the surrounding vehicles. Aaron was able to see that six of the eight SWAT vans were caught in the trap he had set. Two of the vans were still under the 21st Street overpass, out of the line of fire. Black clad troops were starting to disgorge from the rear of each of the unharmed vans.

These men stepped out into the final phase of Aaron's ambush. He had four M249 machine gunners positioned on the 22nd Street overpass. This overpass was to the west of the 21st Street overpass, where the technicals were set up, by about one hundred yards. The machine guns opened fire on the emerging troops with a relentless hail of bullets. Most of the men fell immediately. Some were able to crawl to the front of the vehicles to find cover from the bullets pouring in.

After another minute of an angry cacophony of machine gun and large caliber rifle fire, the volume of shooting started to trail off.

Aaron keyed the microphone on his shoulder holster and yelled into the receiver, "This is Alpha-Mike. Provide SITREP from 21st Street overpass!"

The response came back after a quick pause, "This is Papa-Tango four. All SWAT vehicles are disabled. No movement visible."

Aaron's hearing was starting to normalize, so he didn't shout into this mic this time, "Thor Three, Four, report."

Aaron's soldier assigned to the fifty-caliber rifle in the parking lot overlooking the Vine Street Expressway responded, "Sir, Thor Three and I put twenty rounds each into the passenger compartment of each MRAP using our armor piercing rounds. I can't imagine any one being alive in either vehicle."

Aaron keyed the microphone one more time, "22nd Street overpass, report."

A deep bass voice with a heavy Jamaican accent responded, "Alpha-Mike, we popped each truck so they aren't going nowhere, but we have three or four tangos huddling on the other side of the trucks away from us hid'n behind the engine blocks. If Thor could swing his hammer our way, he should have a clear shot."

Aaron keyed the mic again, "Thor Three and Four, see what you can do. After that, two troops from 21st Street get your boots on the expressway, dispatch any survivors, and salvage munitions. Booker and I are heading back to the primary objective. Alpha-Mike out."

With that, Aaron and Booker stood up and walked away from the massacre on Vine Street.

# CHAPTER 36

*Friday, November 24th, 2028*
*12:05 PM*

The truck ride back across Center City was quiet. Aaron noticed a few people looking out the lower floor windows of various buildings, only to quickly back away from the glass and disappear into the darkened interior as Aaron's pickup truck and the following technical truck drove by.

Aaron reviewed the assault plan in his head one more time. The Federal Reserve Bank building was a large structure about half a city block in size and six stories tall. The front of the building facing the Independence Center had a secure entrance with a huge five-story atrium. If the security inside the Fed had its act together—and from the intel he got from his brother, they would—the atrium would be a free fire zone for the defense of the building. Aaron's men would have to run a gauntlet of bullets, as the defenders would have the high ground and several defensible points to shoot from.

That left the back door. Aaron parked his truck a block away. He and Booker exited the cab as his men dismounted the back of the truck. Aaron and Booker checked over the remaining AT4 launchers. These were marked, "highly explosive." Not good for penetrating armor, but would wreak havoc in enclosed spaces. Aaron figured they would work just fine for his attack on the Fed.

Aaron looked up as he saw Jackie and ten of his troops jog to his position. Aaron nodded to Jackie and asked, "What's the situation on the flatbed and Fed building? Are we good to go?"

Jackie nodded, "Yeah boss. Flatbed is parked right outside the vehicle elevator on Arch Street. It's idling with the driver in the cab and four troops securing it. We were able to peek some at our assault point in the building. They got it bunkered up pretty tight. Wilson said it looks like they got a mini-gun set up behind some sandbags in front of the elevator lobby entrance inside the building."

Aaron turned to a lanky dark-skinned soldier in his early twenties with large bulging eyes. Aaron remembered this kid was in grade school when he graduated high school. Aaron knew he was one of the few to return after a tour in Alaska, but looking at him it was hard to believe. Wilson nodded his head like a bobble head toy in an earthquake and said, "That's right bossman. It's hard to tell because they built the bunker inside the building underneath where the inside parking lot is, but I'm pretty sure I saw that mean-ass barrel poking up over the sand bags."

Aaron leaned into the group and said, "Alright, here is how we're gonna' crack this nut . . ."

# CHAPTER 37

*Friday, November 24th, 2028*
*12:15 PM*

Julianne was still processing the information. The news pouring in on the radio from various police spotters north of Vine Street was disastrous. Aaron had destroyed both of the MRAPs and killed all of the elite state police troopers sent in to stop him.

Emmitt was so upset by the additional loss of life and failed mission that he excused himself from the conference room. Julianne assumed he was pacing the halls of the precinct building. Although she had only just begun to spend time with him, she surmised that he would be back once he worked through the problems in his own way.

Julianne looked down at the cell phone in her hand. She didn't want to make the call, but she knew time was of the essence. There was nothing else to stop Aaron unless Asher could come through with that Bradley fighting vehicle.

She knew that Asher would go apoplectic once he got the news of his MRAPs being destroyed. But she had no other option; Asher had skin in this game too.

She considered the situation. *If he needs to lash out at me so be it. I've dealt with more abusive men than Asher. Larry makes this guy sound like a toothless Chihuahua.*

Then she caught herself. *Jesus, Jules—you saw Larry die at the hands of Aaron's thugs not twenty yards away. Stop feeling sorry for yourself and do what needs to be done.*

Julianne dialed Asher's number and waited for it to connect.

"Asher here. Julianne, please give me some good news."

Julianne inwardly winced and said, "I can't do that Mr. Asher. The reports are that Aaron disabled the MRAPs and killed all the state police troopers in the MRAPs and escort HUMVEES."

Julianne held the phone away from her ear at arm's length while Asher barraged her with a litany of expletives, just as Chief Braxton re-entered the room.

He looked at the phone then to Julianne, "Asher?"

She nodded to Braxton and as Asher paused to catch his breath, she quickly put the phone on speaker mode and said, "Sir, I understand and share your frustration and anger but this is a time for action. We need you to get that tank rolling from McGuire right now."

Asher quickly responded, "First of all, it's not a 'tank'. It's a Bradley Fighting Vehicle. Secondly, this is total bullshit Ms. Barnes. You people locally need to step up and make some sacrifices here."

Braxton's complexion darkened as he raised his voice, "Listen John, we have lost over three dozen city officers since this crisis began and those were our state troopers we lost in a failed assault attempt. And you're telling me about sacrifices!"

Julianne reached out and gently held the chief's arm, turned to the phone and said, "Mr. Asher, what the chief is saying is that we are doing all we can. We need your help. We are on the same team here. You want to keep Aaron from stealing your gold and we want to keep Aaron from ripping our city apart."

"That's better." Asher quipped. Julianne saw that Braxton was about to unload on Asher and she added a slight amount of pressure to her grip on his arm in a silent gesture for him to stay quiet.

Asher continued, "I'll get the Bradley rolling along with any troops they can spare."

Julianne released the breath she didn't know she was holding and smiled at Braxton.

Her smile faltered as Asher continued, "But I am personally going to hold you responsible, Ms. Barnes, if a single ounce of that gold is missing once I get it back."

# CHAPTER 38

*Friday, November 24th, 2028*
*12:25 PM*

After Aaron briefed his men, they dispersed to take their assigned positions. The assault began when two technical trucks converged around the back of the building simultaneously. Both trucks' gunners fired into the depths of the Federal Reserve building where the sandbags were set up.

Aaron and Booker were crouching low behind a knee wall directly across the street from the Federal Reserve building's rear entrance. He could clearly see a sandbag bunker located about fifteen yards inside the building. The rear entrance had drive-in access for an indoor parking garage for employees. The drive-in entrance to the building was blocked with lift gates and deployable bollards. Aaron saw glass shatter on the building as the M60 rounds went wild, shooting from a moving platform. Once the trucks were close enough together to get a clear line of fire on the bunker, they stopped and the M60 gunners started to aim their fire directly at the bunker.

The moment the rightmost truck came to a stop, a tongue of fire erupted from the bunker with an ear splitting high-pitched buzzing sound. The mini-gun had opened up and unleashed a torrent of fire from its six Gatling gun style barrels. The truck shuddered, glass exploded, and the two soldiers manning the machine gun on the back of the truck were shredded by dozens of bullets.

Aaron didn't hesitate. He popped up above the knee wall and depressed the trigger of his AT4 rocket launcher directly at the source of the deadly stream of bullets coming from the bunker. Six feet from Aaron, Booker fired his projectile at the same target.

The two projectiles exploded on the sand bag bunker protecting the mini-gun in a devastating one-two punch. Aaron thought there was no way the machine gun or its operators were still functional. He stood up and yelled at the top of his lungs, "Go, go, go!"

Twelve of Aaron's men charged into the open area at the rear of the building. On either side of the open area, before the glass doors that led to the building's elevator lobby, there was a ramp allowing access to and from the upper levels of the enclosed parking garage. On each ramp, high enough not to be seen from outside the building, was another sand bag bunker.

As Aaron's men got about halfway through the open area, light machine gun fire from each bunker opened on Aaron's exposed troops. Three of his men went down immediately. The remaining nine found cover behind nearby columns or the waist high wall of an elevated garden in the middle of the passenger drop off area.

Aaron swore under his breath. These bastards weren't messing around. He'd lost a few men assaulting the Albert Green building complex, but the security here was way more organized and determined than the other buildings. Aaron figured the people that handled all the money for the country could buy whatever level of security they wanted.

He called Booker and Jackson over for a quick meeting. "Look. We gotta' get past those two nests and do it quick. We gonna' pop a bunch of smoke and run through the gauntlet, wrap around, and neutralize those nests. Booker, you take Wilson. Jackie, you and me will get the other nest."

Booker and Jackson exchanged a look. Jackie spoke up first, "Boss. Let me take another man. We need you calling the shots out here, not dodging 'em in there."

Aaron stared Jackson down. "Negative. I'm in." Then Aaron keyed the mic on his shoulder rig, "Pop smoke in ten seconds then provide suppressing fire."

Aaron saw the leader of the squad pinned down behind a concrete planter key his mic twice, indicating he received the message. Four of the troops pulled the pins from canisters on their bandoleers and began rolling them out. When the smoke provided adequate cover, Aaron keyed his radio and yelled, "Now!"

His troops opened fire on the two flanking sandbag bunkers. The return fire from the bunkers also increased in intensity and then quickly tapered off as the troops dug in behind the sandbags found cover from the return fire.

That was the opportunity Aaron was waiting for. He and his three men ran full-speed in a crouch with weapons at the ready. Aaron led his men based on his memory of the layout of the parking area before the smoke obscured everything not three feet from his face, negotiating the parking bollards and skirting around the elevated garden. The mini-gun bunker had been built on the other side of the garden, so that the nest only needed a few more layers of sandbags on top of the concrete wall of the garden to create the bunker.

Once he cleared the bunker, the smoke was starting to thin out. He made an all-out sprint for the man-doors leading to the elevators. As he did so, he felt and heard the supersonic crack of a bullet just missing his head.

As he approached the glass doors, he raised his rifle and fired two three-round bursts to destroy the glass pane next to a set of doors. The glass shattered, leaving a gaping hole large enough for even Jackson's hulking frame to pass through. Aaron took a knee next to the leftmost wall and looked for targets. He saw some distant movement past the glass doors on the other side of the elevator lobby leading out to the huge five-story atrium. He depressed the trigger and saw the glass of the far doors pucker from the bullets passing through.

Aaron noted that Wilson took up the same firing position on the other side of the elevator lobby. He was methodically taking shots at any movement. He yelled out, "Bossman! We need to move, looks like they sending reinforcements from the front entrance!"

Aaron cursed again to himself and checked behind him to see Booker covering Jackson while Jackson used a huge crowbar to open the controller access door to the stairwell. As Aaron watched, Jackson jammed the long end of the bar just above the locking mechanism. Then he got on the other side of the bar and pulled with all his might. Muscles strained and veins on his exposed arms expanded and pulsed like a fire hose at full charge. With a large crack, the door violently swung open as the locking mechanism was shorn in two.

Booker yelled, "Go!" and Aaron and Wilson fired a quick salvo of shots into the atrium, then ran to the breached door, following Booker and Jackson up the stairs.

They met no resistance on the quick sprint up the stairs. At the landing, Jackson opened the door and Booker threw a fragmentation grenade through the opening. Jackson quickly closed the door and the four men flattened themselves against the concrete walls. A moment later, a crunching blast detonated on the other side of the door.

Wilson opened the door while Jackson and Booker took firing positions on either side of the door looking for targets. There were none. The floor looked abandoned. The grenade had peppered the walls and ceiling of what looked like a reception area. The elevators were just to the right through another set of glass doors. Aaron tapped Jackie's shoulder and motioned across the floor to what he hoped would be an access door to the parking garage on the south end of the building. Then he pointed to Booker and Wilson for them to go to the garage access door for the north end of the building.

Aaron and Jackie proceed south along the building. The office was full of shoulder-height cubicles. Aaron hated conditions like this. There could be twenty men hiding behind those cube walls waiting to spring an ambush or they could be empty. Part of him wanted to stop and empty his remaining three magazines of ammo into the cubicle walls. The thought quickly passed as he and Jackson reached the door that accessed the south end of the indoor parking area. Randall's intel hadn't shown much on this floor since Aaron had been more interested in the first floor and, most importantly, the basement.

Aaron whispered to Jackson before they opened the door. "Jackie. We gonna' do this quiet. The door won't be locked because they gotta' let people get out the building in emergencies. We gonna' sneak up on their position and open fire. Got it?"

Jackson nodded. Aaron gently pushed the panic bar on the door and slowly opened it. The sound of gunfire increased, the door no longer muffling the sound of the back and forth still taking place below them. Aaron knew he needed to hurry before the security at the front of the building redeployed to where his men were pinned down. If they opened fire on his men from a third position, his men would be slaughtered and the assault would be over.

Aaron slow crouch-walked to where the south-end down ramp was located. He and Jackson made it to the top of the ramp with no resistance. Aaron peeked his head around the structural column he was hidden behind. He saw four men manning the sand bag barrier, their backs turned to Aaron and Jackson, oblivious to their presence. Aaron caught Jackson's eye and held up his right hand with four fingers. He didn't need to tell Jackson which two to shoot. Jackson nodded and Aaron turned back to his targets.

He placed the front sight square in the middle of the leftmost man and pulled the trigger. A single bullet felled the man. He quickly sighted in the next man to his immediate right. The soldier was turning when Aaron shot him in the side. The man was still swinging his rifle to bear on Aaron, so Aaron shot him again, this time in the chest. Aaron shot several more bullets into each man to make sure they were dead. Jackson had similarly dispatched his two targets. The bunker was out of commission.

Aaron keyed his mic, "Booker. Status."

After a pause, Wilson's voice came on the radio, "Bossman. Booker dead. Sonnabitch got a lucky shot off and popped Books in the neck. Nuttn' I could do 'cept kill the fuckers. Is clear though."

Aaron looked for something to punch and couldn't find anything. He sure as hell wasn't going to punch Jackie. Probably break his wrist if he tried to hit anywhere on his bulk. Instead, he keyed the mic, "Damn. Alright. Scavenge the weapons and ammo and exfil to the elevator lobby. Troops on ground floor, secure the elevator lobby. It's time to go for the gold."

By the time Aaron and Jackson made it back to the lobby, his troops had created two temporary firing positions near the doors leading to the atrium. Things were quiet for the moment. Aaron left four men to keep the lobby secure, then took the other six along with himself and Jackson down the steps to the basement.

At the bottom landing, Aaron spoke to his men, "Listen up. Jackie's gonna' pop that door with the crowbar. Once he does that, I want Wilson and Leonard to throw two frags through the door. Then we go in. Just like we practiced up in the mountains. Any questions?"

The troops shook their heads slightly. Wilson's head bobbled up and down a few times, which Aaron took as his way of saying he understood and was ready to go.

Jackie approached the door and inserted the crowbar between the door and the frame where the lock was located. The badge reader to the left of the door was glowing red, indicating that the door was locked. Jackie again strained against the crowbar. Aaron could hear the metal in the lock groaning against the near superhuman force Jackie was applying.

Just as Aaron thought the door was about to give, a muffled shot rang out. A bullet penetrated the door from the vault side. Aaron turned to see Wilson sitting on his butt with a surprised look on his face. Aaron heard some shouting on the other side of the door to the effect of holding their fire. Jackie took a break from the door as Aaron reached down, grabbed Wilson under the armpits, and pulled him away from the door behind the shielding of the cinderblock walls.

Aaron said, "What the fuck, Wilson, you hit?"

Wilson bobbled his head and his normally bulging eyes were even more bug-like as he looked at his chest and then back up to Aaron. Then Wilson smiled, reached into his shirt, and pulled out a ballistic plate with a puckered little dent right in the middle of it. "Just stole this off them bastards that killed Books." He brushed the remnants of the bullet off the front and put it back into his vest. Then he looked up at Jackie, "Quit mess'n with that door and pop it. It's payback time."

Aaron quietly laughed and clapped Wilson on the shoulder, "No wonder they call you the human cockroach, ain't nothin' can kill you."

Jackson grunted as Wilson and Leonard got into position with grenades ready. Jackson laid into the door once more. The lock sheared violently and the door flew open. Jackson quickly flattened himself against the cinderblock wall away from the opening.

Wilson and Leonard pulled the pins on their grenades and threw them into the opening. Immediately, the defenders on the other side opened fire with a fusillade of bullets. Leonard was stitched with several bullets from his abdomen to his chest. Wilson rolled to the side as one of the men on the opposite side of the door from Jackson kicked it closed.

A second later, the grenades detonated with a fraction of a second between the two crunching explosions. Wilson was the first through the door in a low crouch with his M16, firing rapidly. Two more of Aaron's troops followed. One was immediately cut down. The next five troops hustled through the opening, alternately breaking right or left immediately after clearing the door. When his troops were all through, Aaron followed Jackson through the opening.

From the plans Randall had given Aaron, he knew the general layout of the basement. It was a large open area divided into several smaller areas with large chain-link walls that went from floor to ceiling with secured man-gates controlling access to each caged off area. Some areas were as large as twenty feet by forty feet. Others were smaller. Some areas were dedicated to sorting coins and others had paper currency. The whole basement itself was huge, having the same footprint as the building itself—about half a city block.

Aaron quickly saw that the defenders had found impromptu firing positions by crouching behind bags of coins of various denominations. Aaron's men were already in two-man teams taking cover behind structural columns. Aaron saw another one of his men sprawled out about ten feet beyond the door, unmoving. The defenders had his remaining men pinned down behind the columns.

Aaron was about to shout out commands above the sound of gunfire when his men responded per their training. One man would spin left from the column and lay out a barrage of covering fire while the other soldier spun to the right and threw fragmentation grenades at the defenders' firing positions.

After five volleys like this the volume of fire from those defending the vault tapered off significantly. Then Aaron heard a familiar voice shout out.

"Bossman, hold off them Christmas Crackers, I got this." Then three shots rang out. About ten seconds later, four more shots echoed off the walls. "Okay, boss! All clear!" Wilson came walking down the main aisle towards Aaron and his troops, his head bobbing and his eyes scanning for any remaining Federal Reserve security guards.

Aaron saw that Wilson had an access badge on a loop around his neck. He said, "Wilson, where'd you come from?"

Wilson nodded and responded, "I got this badge off them troops upstairs too. I was gonna' tell Jackie, but he was hav'n too much fun ripping that door off. Then I got shot in my chest plate and got mad. When I went through the door, I stayed low and found a service corridor that looped around to the back of the basement. Then I scanned my way back in this part and ended up behind everyone shooting at you. Then it was like shooting ducks in a barrel. I went to town on 'em and here we are. What's next?"

Aaron shook his head and said, "Now it's time to load the gold up in that caged area over there. You can grab whatever paper money you can carry and still fight. Jackie, it's your show now. Load us up and get us out of here."

Aaron watched as Jackie walked away from the cage with the gold towards a large stainless steel platform that sat flush with the floor. Next to the platform was a simple lift controller with up, down, and stop buttons. The platform was large enough to hold an armored truck.

Jackie keyed his radio and said, "Flatbed crew, prepare the forklift and move it to the vehicle lift door." Aaron followed Jackie to the platform. He figured it was better to watch topside and make sure the gold got on the truck and that the truck was secure. Also, even with sections of the city burning, it was better than the thick stench of cordite and the coppery acrid smell of blood from the dead bodies in the Fed's basement. As the lift ascended, he watched his men strip the Fed's security guards of ammunition and firearms. Then they started stuffing paper currency anywhere they could in the pockets of the military surplus uniforms he'd issued them years ago.

Aaron rode the lift up with Jackie. Jackson said, "Boss, this is going to take a while. The flatbed can haul forty thousand pounds, which is exactly how much gold is down here. We'll leave the forklift here to lighten the load."

Jackson continued, "The forklift can only handle about four thousand pounds so it's going to take about ten loads. Figure about thirty to forty minutes."

Aaron nodded, "I understand. I'll stay topside to make sure the flatbed and our egress path stay secure."

As the lift stopped at the ground floor, Jackson reached over and pushed a button on the wall mounted control box for the large truck-sized overhead door. As the door opened, Aaron could see the forklift waiting to drive in. He could also hear distant sirens, screams, and the occasional staccato of gunfire.

Aaron stepped aside and out to Arch Street, then started speaking into his radio to get status reports from the crews running the technicals at the roadblocks around Center City. Most of the reports were quiet, but there were two exceptions.

The crew holding North Broad Street crossing the Vine Street Expressway was experiencing exploratory fire and encroaching movement from a determined foe. While Aaron was on the radio, he heard the chugging report of the M60 thirty caliber machine gun mounted on the bed of the pickup truck as his troops targeted some unlucky soul. That didn't concern Aaron. They could keep things buttoned up for another half hour. They could fall back to JFK Boulevard if necessary and keep the flatbed's escape route on Market Street to Southwest Philly secure from there.

The next call, from his crew on the Benjamin Franklin Bridge, was more concerning. At the onset of the chaos when Aaron saw the opportunity to make the score of a lifetime, he knew he would have to secure a perimeter around Center City. The Benjamin Franklin Bridge was one of five bridges that spanned the Delaware River between the Philadelphia area and New Jersey. This particular bridge made that connection just a few blocks away from where Aaron was standing. While he didn't think New Jersey had any assets to bring the fight to his troops or the desire to tangle in a problem on the other side of the river, Aaron couldn't have a surprise on his rear flank. He'd instructed a four-man technical crew to park a couple of loaded dump trucks to block the road and shoot anyone who was stupid enough to approach. The roadblock and fire team were located mid span on the bridge, at the apex, to have the high ground on anyone approaching from the east.

"Hector, Aaron here, how's it looking on the Benny?"

The response came through after a brief pause, "Boss, I was just about to call in. I think we got a problem."

Aaron was surprised. The bridge had been quiet to this point. It'd seemed like the Delaware River Port Authority cops didn't want any of this fight. "Alright, whatcha got?"

The response came back, "Hold on. Hand me those glasses . . . alright. I got some binocs and it looks to me that the Jersey boys aren't messing around. Yup, they scrounged up a Bradley fighting vehicle. They've got a couple Humvees too. What do you want us to do boss?"

Aaron replied, "How close are they?"

Hector responded, "They're on the Admiral Wilson Boulevard maybe three miles from the tolls leading to the bridge. We been watching Camden for the past couple days and the hoods there took it on themselves to try to loot what they could and burn what they couldn't. There's a lot of burned out cars on the road so it's going to take a little while."

Aaron, trying to keep his temper in check, keyed the mic again, "Hector. I need more info than that. How long in minutes until they get to your position?"

The answer came back. "Fifteen, maybe twenty minutes."

Aaron looked at the forklift lifting its second load onto the truck. Checking his watch, he verified that each load took three and a half minutes. He needed twenty-eight minutes to finish loading and then another two minutes to clear out. He thought about his options. The thirty-caliber machine gun on the technical wouldn't do anything to the Bradley except make a bunch of noise for the troops inside the armored troop carrier. If they had ammo for the twenty-five-millimeter cannon on top of Bradley, Aaron's troops would be dead before the M60 on the technical was even in range.

Aaron doubted they had ammo for the cannon. Those munitions were in a dire state of short supply. Even if the Bradley only had its thirty-caliber machine gun operational, its armor would give it the upper hand over Aaron's troops. And if it came directly at his technical in a frontal assault, the angled front of the Bradley would make any incoming fire even less effective. He needed to get a broadside shot at the Bradley.

That gave him an idea.

"Hector, I need you to hold that bridge for another thirty minutes. Standby, I'm going to get you some assets that will help." Aaron changed the channel on his radio and keyed the mic on his shoulder holster, "Thor Three and Four, I need you to confirm that you can be on the roof of the Chocolate Works building on the two hundred block of Third Street in under fifteen minutes." That building sat directly to the north of the Ben Franklin Bridge. From its roof, you could watch cars descend the decline of the bridge to the streets of the city.

After a short pause he heard the panting reply, along with metal jingling in pace with his soldier jogging at three quarter speed, "Yessir. We'll just make it. What's the objective?"

Aaron responded, "Incoming Bradley fighting vehicle. Need you to hold it for thirty minutes from now. Confirm you have A-P rounds with you."

"Affirmative. Another twelve rounds between us. The remaining load out is full metal jacket. We'll do what we can," the sniper responded.

"Ten-four, Aaron out." The third pallet had just been loaded on the flatbed. This was going to happen. Once he got this truck back into southwest Philly loaded with nearly two billion dollars' worth of gold, he would be unstoppable. Nobody would dare think about mounting an assault on his headquarters there because of the embedded firing positions he had on every approach and the overwhelming support of the locals. It would be an urban warfare nightmare. He just needed to get there before this Bradley ruined his party.

About fifteen minutes later, he heard the distant chugging sound of the M60 machine gun firing at full automatic from the Ben Franklin Bridge. Then he heard the rat-a-tat-tat sound of the turret-mounted machine gun on the Bradley responding.

Aaron did not hear the thumping percussion of the twenty-five millimeter cannon on the Bradley open fire. That was good news. That cannon would make short work of the technical even with the protection of the dump trucks stationed in front of it.

Eventually, the chugging of the M60 fell silent. After a few more seconds of the distinctive rapid staccato of the machine gun on the Bradley, he heard a crunching explosion. That was probably the fuel tank on his technical. Aaron looked at the flatbed. The sixth pallet was on and the forklift was in the basement getting the seventh load. There wasn't going to be enough time.

A few seconds later, Aaron heard the booming reports of the fifty caliber rifles stationed on top of the Chocolate Works apartment building as his snipers opened up on the Bradley. The roof of the building was level with the bridge, about one hundred yards up the incline of the bridge from where it landed on the Philadelphia side. Each sniper was using a Barrett model 82A1 fifty caliber rifle. Each rifle had a magazine holding ten rounds. At the rate of fire, it almost sounded like a single, fully automatic fifty caliber machine gun.

Aaron hoped that the Bradley would stop and engage his shooters. That would buy him more time. The price would be two more of his men, but this score was worth it. No doubt about that.

Aaron was disappointed. The Bradley's engine was getting closer without pause. He could hear his snipers still firing, either at the Bradley or the following Humvee's, he wasn't sure. He was out of time. He looked back as the forklift emerged from the basement with the seventh pallet. The rational part of his mind told him it was time to cut and run. Twenty-eight thousand pounds of gold at the current market rate of twenty-five hundred dollars per ounce still put the haul at over a billion dollars.

No. His brother had been clear, the entire stash was what he needed to free Texas from the grip of the federal government.

Aaron reached for his mic. "Technical crews Charlie and Delta, dispatch immediately for Race Street to intercept incoming Bradley vehicle." These were two of the three technical trucks still outside the building. The fourth had been destroyed by the mini-gun at the back of the Federal Reserve building.

His trucks couldn't stop the Bradley, but they could slow it down. He wasn't going to lose this gold.

Any of it.

Aaron looked around and saw Wilson behind a large concrete bollard with his rifle slowly scanning the windows of the surrounding high-rises. Aaron yelled, "Wilson, you ever fire an AT4 before?"

Wilson jogged over to where Aaron was standing next to the end of the flatbed. Paper currency fluttered behind him as some of the bills stuffed into his pockets found their way into the breeze. "Yeah boss. But only in training once. They didn't want us in the penal battalions to have anything we could turn against our own."

Aaron looked at Wilson with a raised eyebrow, "Someday, Wilson, you're going to have to tell me how you survived being cannon fodder in that battalion during the siege of Anchorage and got yourself all the way back to the hood. For now, I need you to come grab a launcher and help me take care of this incoming Bradley."

# CHAPTER 39

*Friday, November 24ᵗʰ, 2028*
*1:50 PM*

Aaron and Wilson each grabbed a launcher and hustled up Sixth Street. There were two ramps down from the bridge that dumped into Race Street. Earlier, Aaron's men had parked several tour buses at the bottom of the ramp that dumped out a block to the east, near the United States Mint building. Maybe an M-1 Abrams tank could get through that roadblock, but not a Bradley. The other ramp connected to Race Street right at Sixth Street. That's where Aaron's technical trucks were waiting. Aaron sprinted and slid behind an abandoned car on the northwest corner of Sixth and Race Streets. Aaron saw Wilson scramble behind a knee wall on the southeast corner of the intersection.

Just as Aaron unfolded the handle on his launcher, the Bradley came into view, barreling down the ramp. The normally light gray exhaust was pitch black and the engine sounded rough. It was good to know the fifty caliber rounds did some damage, but not nearly enough. The Bradley had gravity on its side as it came down the slope of the bridge.

Simultaneously, both machine gun operators on the technical opened fire at the rapidly approaching Bradley vehicle. Aaron saw the exhaust from the Bradley double in volume as the driver accelerated toward Aaron's trucks. At the same time, the machine gun on the Bradley opened fire on the rightmost technical.

The Bradley was about a hundred feet from his trucks and only one hundred and fifty feet from his position when Aaron fired his AT4. He aimed low at the treads and was rewarded by a direct hit that destroyed an axle and caused the tread to derail in a catastrophic grinding, slinging mess of tread parts. Immediately after Aaron's shot, Wilson fired his AT4. Wilson's projectile impacted the turret on the opposite side of the vehicle from Aaron.

Immediately, the Bradley veered hard right towards Aaron's position. Aaron dropped the tube and ran back down Sixth Street toward the Federal Reserve building. The Bradley crushed the car Aaron was hiding behind as it crashed to a stop.

Aaron ducked behind a different vehicle to look at the aftermath of the ambush. His men were pulverizing the remaining Humvee that was following the Bradley with heavy gunfire. As for the Bradley itself, it was bellowing black smoke from every crack and orifice. Anyone in there was cooked. This fight was over.

Aaron and Wilson jogged back around the corner to the flatbed and his pickup truck. They watched the last pallet being loaded. He jumped in his pickup truck and keyed his radio. "Objective is secured. Exfiltrate now." This was the last phase of his plan. His men were to pull back the roadblocks and join the convoy as it lumbered to the docks in South Philadelphia via Broad Street.

Aaron started his truck and slowly followed the flatbed Jackson was driving. In less than twenty minutes, the gold would be on a container ship, headed for his brother.

# CHAPTER 40

*Friday, November 24ᵗʰ, 2028*
*3:35 PM*

This time, Julianne thought her phone would melt because of the vitriol emanating from her cell phone. She, Emmitt, and their impromptu city government were still in the police barracks in the Mt. Airy section of the city near Emmitt's home. They had finally pieced together the activities in the city that morning, including the loss of the police helicopter; the catastrophic ambush of the convoy of state police vehicles and personnel; the failed attempt to use the Bradley fighting vehicle from McGuire air base; and finally, the issue that had Homeland Security Chief John Asher so upset: the raid on the government's gold holdings at the Philadelphia Federal Reserve.

Finally, Asher's tirade lost its energy and Julianne spoke up, "Mr. Asher. We all have lost people and assets today. All of these losses are the result of Aaron Mitchell's criminal enterprise. What are you asking us to do?"

Julianne could hear Asher take a deep breath. The other participants on the conference call included Wilcox from the Pennsylvania

State Police, Governor Fox, and the head of emergency management in the state of Pennsylvania, John Ritter.

Asher responded, "I'm not asking, I am demanding that you put together a task force to go into this Aaron's warehouse and get the gold back. That is the property of the United States of America and—"

Chief Braxton interrupted Asher mid-sentence, "John. Were you listening to the status report we provided you at the beginning of the call? We have confirmed that after the raid on the Federal Reserve, Aaron is holed up at his headquarters. This guy has some heavy munitions. He took out two MRAPs, a Bradley fighting vehicle, and a police helicopter. All while holding territory outside of his base of power. If we launched an assault into his territory, it would be a bloodbath. We would need a couple thousand troops along with armored vehicles and air support. Are you telling me the federal government has the troops and assets ready to assist in this operation?"

Asher quickly responded, "Of course not. You know we are pouring everything we have to keep Alaska from falling completely into the hands of the Russians. Not to mention Taiwan, which is holding on by a thread against being annexed by China. My resources are tapped trying to keep the situation in Texas from creating a domino effect with neighboring states. You need to get me that gold ASAP or we could very well lose Texas and Alaska because we won't get needed military supplies from Germany in time."

Julianne looked up at Emmitt with raised eyebrows, hit mute and said, "Son of a bitch! I can't believe, first, how screwed our country is and, second, what he's sharing over an unsecured line!"

Julianne hit the mute button again to turn on her phone's microphone.

A woman's voice came on the line, "This is Wilcox again. We have absolutely nothing to offer at this time except some logistical support. We lost some of our best men in that ambush. Braxton, why can't we just send someone in to assassinate this Aaron character? I know it's not a lawful way to resolve this, but this is an extraordinary situation. My thought is chop the head off the snake and the whole thing could unwind."

Braxton thought about it for a minute, "We have no undercover assets placed in Aaron's organization. He only recruits returning veterans that he either knows from his neighborhood or who can be vouched for by one of his closest people. If we tried to sneak someone in, they would be caught before getting within a half mile of Aaron. The guy has a whole section of town on his side and they're all eyes and ears for him. It wouldn't work."

Everyone on the conference call was silent for a few moments. Just as Julianne was reaching for the phone to end the call, a new voice spoke up.

"This is John Ritter. I have an idea that could turn the neighborhood against Aaron and get him on the move. Chief Braxton, Ms. Barnes. How quickly can you meet me at PMJ's headquarters in East Norriton?"

Chief Braxton raised an eyebrow. Julianne hit mute on her phone and explained, "PMJ is the electrical power grid operator. It originally covered Pennsylvania, Maryland, and New Jersey, hence the name. It has grown to cover more states since its founding, but they never updated the name."

Braxton asked, "Why does he want to meet us there?"

She replied, "I think I know. Let's find out." Julianne pressed a button on her phone to turn the microphone back on.

"Mr. Ritter, are you suggesting we cut the electricity to Southwest Philadelphia just as winter is approaching?"

Ritter replied, "That and more. We cut the power and turn off the supply of natural gas. No lights, no heat. For that matter, no running water, since the pumps will be shut off. I don't know anything about fighting wars, but I do know how long it takes people in dense urban environments to get desperate without modern conveniences—two days at the most."

Julianne shook her head, looked at Braxton, and said, "I don't like making innocent people suffer. Do you think this could work?"

Braxton replied, "I think it will, especially if we broadcast that Aaron is the reason for the outage. We have to communicate to the people that once he leaves the city, the power will be re-established."

Julianne weighed her desire to capture Aaron against the welfare of the citizens in Southwest Philadelphia. Once again, painful short-term measures had to be taken to harvest long-term benefits. Bringing Aaron to justice was in the best long-term interest of the city, even if it caused pain for a few days.

Julianne nodded and said, "Chief Braxton and I are going to stop by a TV station to make an announcement. Then we'll meet you at PMJ. Give us three hours."

John Ritter replied, "Sounds good. It'll take me a couple hours to get there from Harrisburg. See you there."

# CHAPTER 41

*Friday, November 24th, 2028*
*6:05 PM*

Watching herself on a streaming news outlet was disconcerting for Julianne. She would have liked to have gone home before the announcement to use her own cosmetics and pick out a blouse from her own closet. But that couldn't happen, both because of the urgency of the announcement and the danger in her neighborhood.

Police Chief Emmitt Braxton drove his police SUV while Julianne critiqued the video on her smart phone screen. When she told Emmitt she thought her face was pudgy on the video, he countered that TV cameras do that to everyone. When she noted that the station's makeup made her look jaundiced, he countered that it was the colors on her phone's screen.

One thing she didn't complain about was the message itself. It laid out the facts and affixed the blame for the death and mayhem in the city directly on Aaron and delivered the ultimatum that he had until six p.m. this evening to call the police to arrange his surrender or the power and water to the area around his headquarters would be shut down.

No phone call had been received and now Julianne and Chief Braxton were standing with John Ritter in front of a huge wall of floor to ceiling video monitors, which showed a dynamic representation of the power infrastructure in the states of Pennsylvania, Maryland, New Jersey, Delaware, and parts of New York and Ohio. The monitors were about twelve feet square. Three of them were mounted side-by-side, creating a video wall more than thirty feet across. On a recessed floor in front of the monitors, several operators worked on computers with quad monitors. They were focused on a small, more detailed section of the panoramic on the wall.

Julianne and her companions stood on a raised floor behind a guardrail. Four steps down a small flight of stairs would take them to the area where the operators were working. The entire command center was five stories below ground under a nondescript building in a mundane office park about fifteen miles from the city line.

Ritter explained, "This is the command center for the electric grid and natural gas utilities for a wide area centered in Pennsylvania. In fact, in this very command center, operators stopped a massive blackout from spreading up and down the East Coast over twenty years ago. Ohio and New York got hit but other states were spared due to the efforts of individuals just like those you see here."

Julianne asked, "What exactly are we seeing on these video monitors?"

Ritter responded, "All the flow of electric power and natural gas for the areas we control. Water utilities are not part of this command center, but," John turned to Julianne and Braxton and shrugged his shoulders, "not much water will flow without the pumps running. And they run on electricity."

Julianne said, "I don't like this. It may cost innocent people their lives."

Braxton reminded her, "Julianne, we talked about this on the drive out here. There is no other way. Any type of assault would result in bloodshed on a level ten times what might happen by doing this."

Julianne said, "I know Chief. I agree with you, it's the right plan. I just don't like it."

A woman in her mid-forties walked up to the trio holding a single paper in her hands. She wore a dark skirt and a matching jacket with a white blouse underneath. Her black hair was up in a bun. Julianne's first impression was that she was a secretary, but when she saw a few operators look over at her and give her a little salute or thumbs up, Julianne quickly updated her impression of this woman as the person who ran the command center.

John Ritter made introductions, "Lucia, it is wonderful to see you again."

Lucia extended her hand and shook his, then replied, "You too John, although you only come to visit when there's some sort of impending disaster."

John nodded, "Comes with the title I suppose."

He continued, turning to Braxton and Julianne, "Chief Braxton of the Philadelphia Police Department and Julianne Barnes of the Philadelphia city government, this is Lucia Cerale, Operations Director of PMJ corporation."

Lucia took a deep breath and said, "It is a pleasure to meet you and under normal circumstances, I would take the time to provide you a tour of this state-of-the-art facility to show off our team, processes, and as you've already seen, some of our technology. But these are not normal circumstances."

Julianne motioned toward the paper in Lucia's hand and asked, "Is that the order from the governor?"

Before Lucia could respond, Ritter interjected, "I hope it is, I pulled a ton of strings to get that order on the governor's desk in record time."

Lucia nodded and responded, "It is. I just want to summarize it here with all of you present to make sure this is what you want to do."

Chief Braxton added, "Ma'am. Trust me. We don't want to do this. This guy has left us no choice."

Lucia looked down at the paper in her hand and said, "Very well. Here it goes. This order is to de-energize all electrical substations and transformers in the City of Philadelphia west of the Schuylkill River to the border with Delaware County. Since the airport is on a separate feed, we can isolate that and keep it up and running. We are also to isolate this section of the city by closing several remotely operated valves of the natural gas branch lines to approximately the same geographical area." She looked up. "The areas don't exactly match, but it's close enough to do the job."

Lucia held onto the paper and let her hands drop to her sides. She looked sternly at the group and said, "You do realize there are several hospitals in this area, including a pediatric hospital. Do you have a plan to evac those patients?"

Julianne noted that Chief Braxton looked around to make sure no one was eavesdropping on their conversation. Old military habits die hard. He looked directly at Lucia and replied, "We have established a perimeter around the university and pediatric hospitals. As we speak we are delivering bio-diesel to keep their generators running so they can have their patients shelter in-place."

John agreed with the chief and added, "Also, we don't expect this siege to last long. Aaron's people won't be happy without electricity, heat, or Internet access. He has no idea how quick those folks will turn on him once they lose what they're used to."

Julianne said, "The media outlets have already started running a recording we made that Aaron is behind the chaos in the city and is responsible for the power and gas being shut off."

John said, "We'll use the emergency notification system to let every cell phone user on that side of the city know that their power and gas have been cut off due to the actions of the outlaw Aaron Mitchell."

Braxton finally added, "We're hoping these measures will smoke him out quickly."

Lucia sighed and said, "Understood. Okay folks, please follow me."

She led them down the short flight of steps to an operator's station in the middle of the crescent shaped work area. She handed the sheet to the operator and said, "Ramesh. Here is the order we spoke about. Please implement this immediately. May history judge us kindly."

The operator nodded and typed at a controlled but rapid pace. Julianne looked up as the large monitors zoomed in from their usual multistate view to a detail of the city. A thin yellow line demarcating the area to be affected by the order appeared on the screen. As she watched the screens, several green icons that identified substations and pumps changed from a solid green on the monitors to a blinking red. Next, several icons in the shape of valves did the same thing.

The operator looked up at Lucia and said, "It's done. The area inside the yellow border is dark and cold."

The monitors became blurry to Julianne, and she realized the swell of sadness that had been building in her heart was finally trying to escape. She dabbed at her eyes with the back of her hand and looked at Braxton, "Getting Aaron out will just be the beginning of our problems. The temperature is in the thirties now and forecast to drop tomorrow. We are going to have a refugee crisis right in our own city. The children and the elderly—it's going to be problematic."

Braxton put a hand on Julianne's shoulder and responded, "I know Jules. That's why the city needs you to help us restore order once Aaron is gone."

# CHAPTER 42

*Saturday, November 25<sup>th</sup>, 2028*

*8:35 PM*

Louis Cordrell had spent the majority of his adult life wearing orange coveralls. That's what they issued at the Curran-Fromhold Correctional Facility. The CFCF was Philadelphia's largest prison, shoe-horned between Route 95 and the Delaware River on the eastern edge of Northeast Philadelphia, not too far from the Bucks County line.

Louis was a bad man—emphasis on was. During his last stint at CFCF, for aggravated assault—the guy at the bar did look at him wrong—he found Jesus. Or Jesus found him, he wasn't so sure who found who first. When many of the other inmates were turning to the false teaching of Islam, he was saved by the sweet balm of the Gospels.

Which was how he found himself, seven years after being released from prison for the last time, wearing a white collared shirt and black pants in the basement of the church he pastored.

Getting ordained as a Baptist preacher while holding down two jobs wasn't easy, but God never said following Jesus would be easy.

Look what he made his own Son go through. If He was willing to let a hurt'n that bad befall his only begotten, how could we expect to live without some pain and hardship every now and then?

Pastor Louie, as his flock called him, didn't mind shouldering the pain and grief that often afflicted his flock; in fact, he carried it with joy. It felt like, by taking it on himself, he was making penance for his own past sins.

But this was enough.

It was time to open the eyes of his flock to the evil that had permeated his neighborhood and led them astray. It was time to rise up against the man who had brought them to this point.

Pastor Louie could feel the despair in the room. It loomed like a dark cloud hovering over his people. The dim glow from the last of his emergency candles cast shadows through the room of over a hundred men, women, and children. Their faces reflected the fear and disbelief of refugees who never imagined war would come to their hometown.

The candles were down to inch-tall nubs on paper plates. When they burned out, the congregation would be cast into darkness. The last meal of chicken broth and crackers was served at breakfast today. Now the cupboard at the church was empty. The room they were in was above freezing, thanks to the body heat, but the stench from the buckets in the bathroom was becoming overpowering, and he had run out of bleach yesterday.

On Wednesday, when the looting started, all the stores were closed and deliveries of any sort—most importantly, food—had stopped coming into the neighborhoods.

Pastor Louie had opened the doors of his Thanksgiving soup kitchen to find twice the usual crowd. He and his elders scrambled to make enough food, dipping into the church's emergency storage cabinets.

Word must have spread, because the huge crowds at Friday's breakfast and dinner nearly wiped his stores out.

The power went out just before dinner was served yesterday. He had put his candles out, thinking it was just a normal problem that would be fixed quickly.

That was more than twenty-four hours ago. Soon after dinner was cleared last night, he turned on a battery-powered radio and heard the truth. The city was under siege and the man who had been revered in this neighborhood, the man who had brought order to the streets of Southwest Philadelphia, the man who brought jobs and money to the homes in these neighborhoods, was the very man responsible for tearing it all apart.

And even though it might serve as his death warrant, it was time to tell the people the truth.

Pastor Louie grabbed a stepstool from the kitchen and placed it in front of the food serving counter. He stepped up the two rungs and held onto the bracing bar in front of him, a poor man's lectern.

"Friends! Settle down and listen to a word from our Holy Scripture."

The crowd quieted even though the hush was interrupted sporadically by a hacking cough or an infant whining in complaint.

"Throughout history, God's people have been no stranger to trouble. Remember Moses; fleeing the tyranny of the Egyptians only to wander the desert for forty years. Remember our Lord and Savior Jesus; beaten, whipped, then crucified. Remember the twelve apostles of the early church, eleven of whom were either crucified or beheaded for spreading the Gospel."

This was followed by some quiet "Amens" and nodding of heads from those gathered.

"No friends, we are no strangers to trouble. And this trouble is no different. Just as the serpent deceived Eve in the Garden of Eden, so have we been deceived. Our deceiver came in the form of a man who brought calm to the streets, jobs to the unemployed, and money to the poor. But there was a dark side to his gifts. He sold drugs to our addicted, ran casinos for our compulsive, and killed those who questioned him."

Many of the men in the crowd were now casting their eyes downward, uncomfortable with the implication of the pastor's words.

"Now friends, his ambitions have brought the current troubles down on all of us. He used his might and his men to take something from our government. I don't know what he took, but I do know the government needs it back. Needs it back so bad, that they had no choice but to turn off the power in our neighborhoods. No power, no heat, no water."

From this he got some heads nodding even though some in the crowd did not want to look directly at Pastor Louie.

"I've heard you, and some of you blame the government. What kind of government would do this to its own people, you ask? I will answer you, a desperate government. A government unable to defend its own borders or help friends in faraway lands."

The question was reflected in the eyes of those in the basement.

"Friends, the government is not to blame. No. Just as one man, Judas, betrayed our Lord Jesus, so is one man to blame for our troubles. That man's name is Aaron Mitchell."

A murmur spread through the crowd at the speaking of Aaron's name. Pastor Louie knew he was a dead man now. Word would get out that he spoke against Aaron, but he didn't care anymore. His flock was dying. If he had to sacrifice his own life to spare even one of his sheep, it would be worth it.

"That's right friends. Aaron Mitchell. He and his militia have brought this trouble upon us. As Christians, we are taught to turn the other cheek, to do unto others as you would have them do unto you. And those are good lessons, spoken directly from Jesus' mouth to our hearts."

The shock of calling out Aaron had subsided and now he had the people nodding again.

"However, there is more to our story as a people. Sometimes God calls us to do more. Sometimes He calls us to action. That time is now."

Now more people were nodding, and he began to see the glimmer of hope in some of their eyes.

"After wandering the desert for forty years, God led his people across the river Jordan to the promised land. The Israelites had finally arrived at the land of milk and honey. There was only one problem. There was already people on this land. And on that land, was a great walled city of Jericho. Did the people of God turn the other cheek? Did they cower in fear in the basement? No. God spoke to Joshua, a mighty warrior, and told him what he needed to do to tear down those walls and take the city for themselves."

He got strong response of "Amen" as the people were now sitting straight in their chairs, their attention glued to Pastor Louie.

"Now I don't have no trumpets to hand out and I'm not going to tell you to march around Aaron's headquarters praying that the walls will fall down. But I am going to tell you, just like Joshua told his people, we need to act, we need to fight, we need to push back against the one who deceived us and take back what is rightfully ours."

The crowd cheered exclamations of "Amen!" and "Preach it brother," among other exhortations.

Pastor Louie stepped down from his stool and walked back to the kitchen. There he shrugged on his winter coat and donned his hat and gloves. He reached under the serving counter and grabbed his baseball bat. He had never used it but sometimes a hopped-up druggie would need a visual reminder to wait his turn.

He stepped back in front of the crowd and placed the bat on his shoulder.

"Friends, God is calling us to rise up against the deceiver! I ask all able-bodied men and women without children to follow me as we fight for our own Jericho."

# CHAPTER 43

*Monday, November 27ᵗʰ, 2028*
*8:35 AM*

Chess was the only game Aaron enjoyed. He learned it from his case worker as a child, getting bounced from one foster home to the next. There were several times when Aaron had to sleep in his case worker's office because they couldn't find a home to place him. That's when he learned the game.

He lost the first two games as he learned the rules and used passive, defensive strategies. Then his true nature came out and attacked. He won the third game versus his case worker and every match after using an aggressive strategy that stunned his opponents to inaction.

He found himself in the midst of a chess game now. His opponent, the various government agencies allied against him.

He had opened this match aggressively—striking the enemy multiple times in enemy territory and securing the gold.

Then his enemy got lucky. Sheer dumb luck. The Coast Guard intercepted the cargo ship that Aaron was going to use to get the gold out of Philadelphia. On his drive to the docks, Aaron placed a cell phone call to his contact and got the news that the ship never made it to the docks. There was a Plan B, but it would take a few days to put together. That day was today.

Aaron didn't like to react, but he'd had no other choice but to hole up at his headquarters until a barge with radioactive medical waste could make it to the docks in Chester, Pennsylvania. Chester was a downtrodden industrial city just south of Philadelphia along the Delaware River.

No one would suspect that buried under a mound of medical waste was twenty tons of gold. Aaron would hop a ride on the tugboat pushing the barge to Louisiana where Randall would arrange ground transport for the quick hop to the Texas border.

He was low on ammunition, water, and food, and his men were in low spirits.

Cutting the power and natural gas to Southwest Philadelphia was brilliant. It was turning the local population against him and made it difficult to communicate to his troops. His cell phone only worked for twenty-four hours after the blackout.

Jackson had explained that all the cell towers had backup batteries in them for temporary power outages. Once the batteries ran out of juice, the cell towers would stop transmitting, making all cell phones in the area useless.

It was time to make the next move. A move his own people would not understand. He would have to continue to shroud his intentions in secrecy. None of them, not even Jackson, knew that he had a brother or that his intention was to get the gold to him and start his operations anew in the free republic of Texas.

He wished he had more vehicles and especially ammunition. He would have to make do with what he had. Getting through the blockade that the local townships and state had put on all the major exits from the city would be a challenge. Once he was clear, he was confident he could make the short drive to Chester.

Feigning that his fury was at the plight of his surrounding neighborhoods, he paced back and forth across the floor of the warehouse he'd used to store the flatbed with its treasure and two of his technical trucks.

Seated at a card table near the flatbed were Jackson, Wilson, and Dantrell. The three men had proven themselves in loyalty and ferocity over the past few days. Aaron felt no remorse about betraying two of them when he skipped town. Who knew, maybe they could build their own gang and rule the streets for themselves. They sat and watched Aaron pace back and forth, moving only their eyes.

Aaron finally approached them and looked at the water bottles on the table. They were starting to form ice crystals from sitting in the cold air of the warehouse. It had been more than forty-eight hours since the government had cut the power and gas to his territory.

*I wonder if they know we don't even have running water?* He thought. Sure, the water was gravity fed from a reservoir up on City Line Avenue, but when the pipes froze, no water could flow through them.

He pulled his chair out, turned it around and sat down with the back of the chair in front of him.

Aaron took a deep breath to calm himself and looked at Dantrell, "What's the status on the streets?"

Dantrell looked at Aaron, "It's not good boss. People were hunkered down just fine Friday night and Saturday. Then Saturday night people started mobbing our patrols. Our men had to open fire to defend themselves. The crazy thing was, that didn't put an end to it. I even heard of a couple Militia men getting their houses ransacked while they were out on patrol. We also had someone throw a Molotov cocktail at one of our technicals. Ended up torching it and killing one of our guys."

Aaron asked, "Is someone in the neighborhood behind this, or are people just pissed about the power?"

Dantrell said, "I was thinking the same thing so I questioned a couple boys we caught trying to climb a chain link fence around our truck yard. They said Pastor Louie from the church on Hazel Street was talking smack about you."

Aaron lifted an eyebrow at this information.

Dantrell continued, "So I paid Pastor Louie a visit myself. He was jabbering some nonsense about deceivers, Jesus, Joshua, and Jericho before I popped him. He won't be a problem no more."

Jackson spoke up, "Then what about last night? The people tried to burn this building down with Molotov's. I had to open up with my M16 to get them to scatter. I never seen anything like it around here."

Aaron rubbed his neck and said tersely, "The explanation is, Dantrell martyred the pastor and that pissed the people off more. I know you wanted to silence the pastor, but it would have been better to detain him and persuade him for a while instead of outright killing him."

Dantrell nervously added, "Sorry boss, I thought I needed to shut it down. Tonight, when the sun goes down, will be bad. I don't know what's going to happen. There's too many desperate people to keep a lid on things."

Aaron shook his head and turned to Wilson, "What about the checkpoints the state and local police set up?"

Wilson nodded a couple times. "I checked 'em out myself bossman. They got us bottled in pretty good. I guess we kicked a hornets' nest and now they are *pissed*. The Schuylkill is blocked up, so is Route 95. No way to go north back into the city, we'd never make it, too slow. I even went up to City Line, and they got a bunch of civilians with hunting rifles posting up on the checkpoints. They ain't messing around bossman. Best bet is south. Through the suburbs. The roadblock on Market Street into Upper Darby isn't too heavily guarded and once we break through, there are dozens of routes we could take to get some distance from the city."

Aaron rested his chin on the top of the seat back. He took a moment to think. The most direct route to Chester was route ninety-five. Wilson's findings gave him a new idea—blasting through the roadblock into Upper Darby would put him south of the city. From there he could use a variety of routes to get to Chester and stay off of the highways. It was definitely the way to go.

Decision made. Now it was time to put the pieces together.

Aaron straightened up and cleared his throat, "Dantrell. Get twenty-three of our best soldiers. Give them the best body armor you can put together. You and them are going to report back here at three p.m. ready to roll. I need six men to have the M249 squad autos, the rest of the guys can have regular load-outs. Scrape together all the ammo we got and distribute it to these troops."

Dantrell got up from the table. "You got it boss. That's gonna' leave us threadbare at home to cover the streets and HQ. You okay with that?"

Aaron nodded and said, "Yeah. That's part of the plan. Don't worry about what happens after we roll. My man Wilson here will take care of that."

Dantrell nodded and excused himself from the meeting, then jogged across the warehouse floor to the exit.

Aaron looked at Wilson. "Wilson, listen up. I would have you infiltrate our Thor snipers into position to help us get through a checkpoint, but the checkpoint I want to run doesn't have anywhere good to set up. I need you to do the hardest part of this plan."

Wilson nodded a few times and said, "Sure bossman, you know me. I'll do whatever it takes."

Aaron said, "I knew I could trust you. What I need you to do is stay put."

Wilson's head stopped bobbing up and down. Shocked, he asked, "Bossman, what are you talking about? I'll fight anywhere, anytime you want me to."

Aaron patted Wilson on the shoulder, "I know Willy. But the time for fighting is over. We need to retreat and regroup so we can fight another day. I need you to cover our rear. Basically, once we roll out, spread the word that I skipped town. I need our troops and the public to believe it, so set this building on fire once we're out. We gotta' get the state to turn the power back on and get life back to normal. Once everything calms down we can work to re-establish our operations. I need you to keep our troops in line for a few weeks while I lay low. Can you do that?"

Wilson nodded his head, "Sure, sure Aaron. Like I said, you need something done, I get it done."

Aaron squeezed Wilson's shoulder, "I knew I could rely on you. The caravan is leaving here at four p.m. today. I want to hit the checkpoint before it gets dark just in case we need to shoot our way out. Start the fire at five p.m. and get the word out after then. Once they know they flushed me out, the government will get the power back on. We can't operate in territory so demoralized and hostile anyway. We'll come back when things calm down."

Wilson bobbled his head in understanding and stayed seated at the table.

Aaron asked Wilson, "How 'bout you skip out? I gotta' talk to Jackie for a bit. Don't worry Willy. I'll see you again in no time."

Wilson nodded one more time and excused himself from the table.

Now it was just Aaron and Jackson. Aaron looked the big man right in the eyes. It was good to have him by his side for this mission. "Jackie. I need you to drive the tractor pulling the flatbed. I'll be riding shotgun. You good with that?"

Jackson nodded, "You bet Aaron. I'll make sure the old girl is ready to roll."

Aaron said, "Also, since we have a few hours to prepare, is there anyway to add some armor or steel plating to the truck we're driving? It's going to be pulling our treasure, I would hate to have it disabled by a stray bullet."

"I don't know boss. That old diesel is pulling for all she's worth with the load on her. She's overloaded as it is with the gold. That shit is heavy. If I add any more weight, I'd be afraid of smoking the clutch and then we ain't going nowhere."

Aaron conceded the point, "I figured as much. Well, I need you to do a couple things before we roll. Get backpacks loaded for you and me in the cab of the truck. In addition to what we would need for a couple days on foot, load each with twenty pounds or so of the gold. Just in case."

"Got it boss, what else you need?" Jackson replied.

"I need to tell you about my brother." Aaron answered as he casually lowered his right hand from the table to his lap.

"What?" Jackson exclaimed. "You have a brother? I never knew that. Where is he?"

# BANKRUPTURE

Aaron answered, "By the time you moved to my neighborhood in high school, I was living in my sixth foster home. The city separated us when I was eight and he was twelve; he was long gone before you and I connected. His name is Randall and he's a colonel in the Texas Secessionist Army."

Jackson scratched the stubble on his cheek, "Why are you telling me this now, boss?"

Aaron replied, "Because once we get to Chester, we are taking the gold to him."

Jackson's brow furrowed. "Why? What's the play? You've been tell'n all of us that this gold would make us the biggest, strongest, richest gang in the country."

Aaron replied, "I know. I was going to let you and Booker in on the plan on the way to the docks after the heist. But Booker died and that ship got delayed. Now we have a way out on a barge out of Chester and I'm telling you."

Jackson asked, "We going to Texas?"

"That's right. We're going to deliver most of the gold to my brother so Texas can be free and clear of the US government. Then you and I are going to set up shop again in Austin."

Aaron paused. Jackson used one of his massive hands to rub the back of his neck while he pondered the decision. Aaron kept his left hand where it was on the table. He slowly crept his right hand toward his pistol in his holster. He knew if Jackson didn't agree to come with him, he would have to kill him right here and now. It might not be easy, but he wouldn't hesitate to kill his closest comrade in order to keep his plans intact. Having Jackson know the plan without being part of it was unacceptable.

293

Jackson finished rubbing his neck and looked directly into Aaron's eyes with an intensity Aaron had only seen on the battlefield. Aaron tightened the grip on his pistol. Even with the gun, Aaron didn't like his chances of coming out on top of a fight with Jackson from the close proximity across the table.

"Shit boss. I told you I was back in one hundred percent. I'll follow you anywhere. I don't owe this city anything."

Aaron removed his hand from the grip of the pistol. Then he reached his hand out to Jackson to shake the large man's hand. "My man! I knew I could count on you. Trust me, getting this gold to Texas will serve up a huge helping of revenge to Uncle Sam and this city for what they've done to you, in the Marines and in the sanitation department."

Jackson clasped Aaron's hand in a solid grip and responded, "That's right boss. Now, I got something I got to tell you."

Still in the midst of the handshake, Aaron asked, "What you got Jackie?"

Aaron felt Jackson's grip tighten slightly on his hand. It wasn't uncomfortable, Jackson could crush every bone in Aaron's hand if he wanted to, but Aaron understood the implication. If he tried to withdraw his hand, it would be a sign of weakness. Aaron locked eyes with Jackson and waited for him to speak.

After a pause, he did. "I been keeping an eye on the girl from the funeral in the basement—keeping her fed, hydrated, and clean in that room you got her locked in."

Aaron's eyes grew wide, "Oh shit. I forgot about her. I don't want any loose—"

Jackson interrupted, "Boss. I want to let her go. Her old man is dead, if we skip town, there ain't no harm she can do to us."

Aaron thought about the girl, Rose, locked up in the basement. He had a few days of fun with her before her father had a screw come loose and drove his truck at the mayor and his cronies. He knew Jackson owed the father from his childhood. Could his authority as a 'superior rank' over Jackson force him to go to the basement and kill the girl? Maybe. But why put his loyalty to the test so soon after his last demonstration?

A new idea quickly came to mind that could meet both men's desires.

Aaron nodded and said, "I understand you owe that old man and I don't want to get between you and your debt. But I don't want any loose ends left behind."

Aaron continued, "How about we bring her with us? She'll fit between you and me in the cab of the truck and if something goes haywire, we could use her as a hostage."

Aaron saw lines emanate in Jackson's brow as he contemplated Aaron's proposal.

Jackson released Aaron's hand and nodded, "Ok, boss. I like that plan. That feels right to me."

Aaron answered, "Glad we have an agreement. Let's get to work. We have less than eight hours until we hit that checkpoint."

Jackson excused himself, leaving Aaron alone at the table. He pulled a folded printout from his back pocket and smoothed it out on the table. It was a map of Upper Darby he had printed before the power went out. A small red circle showed James Brennan's house in the middle of the page.

Aaron removed a pen from a breast pocket on his tactical vest and circled the police checkpoint in the lower right-hand corner of the printout. He drew the route from the checkpoint to Brennan's house. A mile and a half, tops. A four minute drive, about twenty on foot.

They would be making a small detour before disappearing.

# CHAPTER 44

*Monday, November 27ᵗʰ, 2028*
*4:02 PM*

It'd been a rough few days for Detective Green but as he sat against the brick façade of an abandoned building in Southwest Philly, freezing his ass off, wearing third or maybe fourth-hand clothing, there was no other place he would rather be.

After his fiery escape from the doomed 18th district police building, Green's immediate instinct was to go home and nurse the blisters on his hands and knees. Within a millisecond, he dismissed that thought.

Instead, he made his way on foot to the 19th district police building about two miles away from the 18th's destroyed building and more than a half mile north of the northern edge of Aaron's territory. The 19th was based in a hardscrabble part of town just off Girard Avenue between the Haddington and Overbrook sections of the city.

*It's funny*, Green thought, *half a mile doesn't mean anything to someone in the suburbs or the country*. But in the city, a lot could change in five city blocks. You could go from a bad neighborhood to a gentrified one; or, in this case, you could go from enemy territory to a safe harbor.

On the way to the 19th, he had called Chief Braxton to tell him what had happened with the assault on his precinct building. Green had served under the chief in North Philly and they still had each other on speed dial. Braxton had insisted Green get himself to a hospital. Green declined and instead told him to make sure the boys in blue at the 19th knew he was coming.

Green wanted payback.

Which is why he was sitting with newspapers stuffed in his over-sized pants and jacket for additional warmth and urban camouflage. His dirty, grease-stained knit cap was pulled down, nearly covering his eyes. His nearly empty bottle of malt liquor had the consistency of a slushy in the cold, late November afternoon.

His squatter's location was three blocks away from the gate in the chain link fencing surrounding Aaron's headquarters. As soon as the call went out for a volunteer to infiltrate Aaron's territory and get eyes on his HQ, Green volunteered. He had another two hours until it got dark, when he would work his way back to the 19th for a shower, meal, and sleep. His hands and feet were starting to get numb, but there was no way some discomfort was going to get Green to take his eyes off that gate.

The power had been off in this neighborhood for more than forty-eight hours. Green wasn't sure if this plan to smoke Aaron out would work. Nobody had intel on what type of emergency rations and stores Aaron had for himself and his troops. The possibility that Aaron could be holed up here all winter nagged at Green. He didn't want to keep coming out here to survey Aaron's headquarters every day—but at least he had somewhere else to go. The toll on the residents was becoming obvious.

As Green reached down to shimmy some more cardboard under his butt to keep it from losing heat to the sidewalk, he saw movement from the corner of his eye.

The gate was retracting and the sound of a diesel engine rumbled from the yard. Green watched as four pickup trucks with machine guns mounted on stanchions on the trucks' beds rolled out of the gate at a low speed. Then a large tractor trailer lumbered through the gate followed by two more pickup trucks, again with machine guns in the backs of the trucks.

Green spotted a driver and passenger in each pickup truck, along with a man operating the mounted machine gun and another man with a hand-held machine gun in each truck bed. There were two men in the cab of the tractor trailer, a driver and passenger.

Once the trucks cleared his field of vision, Green shambled to a standing position. Using the wall as a brace, Green stayed in character as he drunkenly stumbled along the wall, around the corner into an alley.

Once he got to the alley, he sprinted at full speed, the bottle of malt liquor smashing against the asphalt and newspapers flying out of his ragtag clothes. He sprinted the full eight blocks to where he had stashed his unmarked sedan inside an abandoned garage.

He had parked this far away for two reasons, the first obvious: driving an unmarked police sedan around here was a suicide mission. But this was also as close as he could get to Aaron's headquarters and still get a signal on the police department eight hundred megahertz radio system. Since most repeaters in Southwest Philadelphia did not have power right now, Green had to find a location where he could make this call.

He grabbed the key from under a pile of brick rubble in the corner of the garage and unlocked the car. He started the car and cranked on the heat. Then he grabbed the police radio, keyed the mic and said, "Squad Nineteen calling in a 10-54, repeat 10-54."

# CHAPTER 45

*Monday, November 27ᵗʰ, 2028*
*4:11 PM*

"I promise you will get paid, I just need you to get those trucks with water and ready to eat meals in position as soon as possible."

Julianne sat at the conference table in the police district building in Chestnut Hill, pausing with the phone at her ear to let the Chief Executive Officer of the largest commercial food distributor in the state of Pennsylvania respond.

"Good, good, that's right. Have the trucks report to the 19th district police building. We'll escort them into the affected neighborhoods once Aaron is out of there or neutralized."

Julianne thanked the CEO and ended the call. Looking across the table at Emmitt, she sighed and said, "I have the food, water, and other supplies en route for our citizens once Aaron clears out. Now we just need him to take the hint and leave. Any news from your embedded friend?"

Chief Braxton shook his head in worry. "No. No word and I just got another call from the feds. Their patience is running out. They said they have the authority to federalize our officers and send them in to assault Aaron's headquarters. That weasel Asher said we have until tomorrow morning to get his property back or he'll be hand delivering the executive order and taking over our cops."

Julianne was enraged. That level of bloodshed was what they were trying to avert. She stood up and asked, "How could they, after all—?"

Just then the radio in Braxton's hand squawked, "Squad Nineteen calling in a 10-54, repeat 10-54."

Braxton stood up at and pushed the talk button on his radio, "Affirmative Squad Nineteen. We have received your 10-54. 10-24 to base."

Julianne asked, "What happened, what do all those codes mean?"

Braxton said, "10-54 means livestock on the road. Green and I thought that would be a good code to use when Aaron left his HQ since we've never heard that code used, ever, during our careers. And 10-24 instructs him to get back to the district house."

Julianne asked, "What's the plan now?"

"We have a few other spotters in the city. Need to figure out which checkpoint Aaron's going to try to get through. We gotta' give them a heads-up. Then our force is going to roll up behind him and bottle him in so he can't escape back into the city if he can't break through the checkpoint."

Julianne watched as the chief shrugged on his cold weather issue police coat. She grabbed her coat and went to follow him as he made his way out of the conference room which had served as the impromptu seat of the city government over the past few days.

"Where are you going, young lady?" Braxton asked with a raised eyebrow.

"I'm going with you. You had my back for the past few days, now I need to have yours. Also, I need to see this through. Aaron and his thugs have done their best to tear the city apart. I need to be there the moment we start putting things back together."

Julianne defiantly squared up across the table at the chief with a hand on her hip and the other hand resting on the handle of the holstered pistol she had made a habit of wearing since Thursday.

The chief returned the stare.

Until he lost the staring contest and started laughing.

"Damn girl. You are one tough nut, that's for sure. Okay Jules, saddle up. Just keep your head down and stay in my SUV until the shooting stops."

With that he turned and grabbed the riot shotgun propped against the doorjamb.

Julianne's heart raced in her chest as she closed the door behind her.

"It's payback time," she whispered under her breath as she followed Braxton to the squad room.

# CHAPTER 46

*Monday, November 27th, 2028*
*4:25 PM*

The streets of Philadelphia were eerily quiet. Aaron could see the after effects of the past five days on the city as his caravan slowly rumbled past. Several of the storefronts along Market Street were destroyed and burned out. Some buildings were still smoldering. There were people of indistinguishable sex huddled around fifty-five-gallon drums with fire and smoke belching from the barrels. They didn't look up as Aaron passed them on the street—if anything, they huddled tighter together.

The caravan crawled toward the city limit. Up ahead, Aaron could see his lead technical pause at the intersection of 63rd Street and Market Street. The intersection marked the end of the city. After that intersection and a brief stretch of woods maybe a hundred yards deep, the suburbs began.

His caravan consisted of six technical trucks, four in front of the tractor trailer Jackson was driving and two behind. As they past the technical watching the intersection, it pulled in line and took the rear position in the line of vehicles, making three technicals behind the tractor-trailer.

The trailer was the same one from the raid of the Fed. With the exception of the gold stashed in the two backpacks at Aaron's feet, all of the gold taken from the Federal Reserve was still on the trailer. Jackson was the only person Aaron allowed access to the trailer. During the time the trailer was in the warehouse, Jackson had put all the gold into wooden shipping crates, than lashed the crates to the deck of the trailer with locking chains.

Aaron sat in the passenger seat in the cab of the semi, watching the machine gunners in the lead technicals cover the intersection as they crossed the final boundary into the suburban Delaware County, leaving the relative safety of the city and his power base.

Roseate sat wedged between Aaron and Jackson. Jackson had cleaned her up nicely with fresh clothes, but must have given her a large dose of heroin or who knows what before they left. Even though her eyes weren't overly dilated, it was clear to Aaron she was high as a kite with an absent grin, humming a slow melody, while she slipped in and out of consciousness.

Aaron checked the safety on his M16. He moved the selector to "fire." He also moved the fire selector on the rifle from "semi" to "burst." This mode would cause the rifle to fire a three-round burst with a single pull of the trigger.

Aaron looked over at Jackson. The big guy's face was calm and stoic, but the rippling of the corded muscles on his forearms as he held the truck steady showed his nerves.

Aaron said, "Jackie, when the shooting starts, keep your head down. I'll be your eyes and tell you where to steer. The technicals you built are going to hit these boys so hard they'll be running for cover by the time we roll through."

Jackie just nodded without taking his eyes off the road and replied, "You got it Boss. Thanks for taking me back in. It's been a good ride."

Before Aaron could respond, the first technical reached the clearing at the end of the wooded buffer between the city and the suburbs. Even though Aaron and Jackie were in the fifth vehicle in the caravan, the heavy rapid-fire percussion of the powerful thirty caliber machine gun on the first technical nearly caught Aaron by surprise.

Aaron looked ahead and saw the police at the checkpoint dive for cover behind the bollards and concrete traffic dividers that they had set up to channel the traffic at the checkpoint to a single lane.

The lead technical sped up toward the chute. The gunner on the back braced himself for the acceleration but was temporarily unable to fire his machine gun, as he was working hard to stay in the truck. The second gunner in the bed of the truck was sitting against the cab and had braced himself so that he could continue to lay down suppressing fire.

The plan was not to engage in a long firefight, but to hit the checkpoint with a withering amount of automatic gunfire and run through the gauntlet as quickly as possible, leaving two technicals and crews behind to hinder any pursuit.

The lead technical was now entering the cattle chute, gunners firing. The other technicals had also opened fire. The volume of fire from the four machine guns was intense.

Finally, the technical directly in front of the tractor trailer leapt forward to begin its run. Immediately, Aaron felt the vibrations of the engine as Jackie jammed his foot down on the accelerator. Aaron was pushed back into his seat and Roseate's head snapped back, waking her up from her reverie.

In the fading light of the late afternoon, Aaron could see flashes of return fire behind vehicles or next to buildings. He and Jackie sank lower in their seats as a bullet punctured the door of the cab and another popped through the windshield above Aaron. The bullet through the door missed both Aaron and Jackie but Aaron did feel the glass from the windshield pepper the exposed skin on his face. His helmet and ballistic glasses protected the rest of him from the flying glass.

Roseate yelped from the flying glass. Jackson reached over and pushed her down on the bench. Her legs slid forward with her upper torso on the seat, her head propped up on the seat back.

Aaron shrugged off the glass and yelled over to Jackson, "Keep going Jackie, straight ahead, push through!"

Aaron peeked over the dashboard and looked out through the spiderwebbed windshield and still-intact side window. The lead technical was through the cattle chute and was pulling to the left of the road to set up a firing position. The second technical was almost though the chute, firing to the right as it progressed through. The next two technicals were approaching the chute with machine guns blazing.

Aaron had no idea what the three technicals behind him were doing, but he heard a lot of machine gun fire from that direction.

Aaron saw several police cars from townships other than the Upper Darby police converging on the checkpoint from the suburban side. He also saw more and more flashes as the police put up more resistance.

Through the driver's side window Aaron saw a fire truck racing down a side street perpendicular to the road they were on. It was a brilliant strategy on the township's part. Allow Aaron to commit his truck to the cattle chute and use the fire truck to ram his truck just as it exits.

But they miscalculated the timing of their trap. From his truck's speed and the distance through the cattle chute, Aaron's quick mental math told him he would be through in a few seconds. The fire truck would pass harmlessly behind him. It would cut off his trailing technical from exiting the cattle chute, but by then he would be long gone. The momentum was on his side as the tractor trailer entered the cattle chute of the roadblock even as the intensity of the incoming fire picked up.

Aaron hollered a cheer of victory as the front of the tractor cleared the chute, pulled even with his two technicals parked on either side of the chute, and pulled past them. He was free, this was going to work!

\* \* \*

Chained to a steam pipe in the boiler room last week, Roseate couldn't believe what she had heard on the radio Jackson had given her. Before the power went out and the radio went silent, she had learned that her father was the man who had driven his truck into the viewing stand at the mayor's speech. Her father, her rock. A man who never raised a hand to her and had the patience of Job with her older brother. He was the killer who had allowed Aaron to unleash hell upon the city.

That pain was worse than anything Aaron had inflicted on her with his "sessions" over the past week.

Roseate was now fighting the effects of the drugs Jackson had given her. He had been kind to her throughout her imprisonment in that room in the basement of Aaron's headquarters. She had spent her time trying to engage him in conversation when he stopped in to drop off food, bring bottles of water, and provide her a clean bucket for her waste.

That was why she felt so betrayed when he held her down this afternoon and plunged that poison into her body using a syringe in her arm. She was no actor, but the second he started to depress the plunger, she rolled her head back and moaned in pleasure. Her goal was to get him to inject her with a low dose so that she would have her wits about her.

It had paid off. He fell for the act and stopped the plunger after only injecting a quarter of the contents into her.

*Don't get me wrong*, she thought, *I'm high as a falsetto note at a helium-sucking contest, but I am in control of myself.* Her goal was to continue to act high and see if there was an opportunity for her to escape.

She knew once she left the city with Aaron, her chances of survival were zero. Jackson wouldn't protect her, as he'd proven when he drugged her to make her easier to transport.

Roseate heard the bullets hitting the side of the truck and then felt the truck accelerate. Jackson reached over and slammed her down on the bench seat of the truck. In front of her was a yellow knob labeled "air brake." She had noted at the beginning of the ride that Jackson had pushed the knob in and then put the truck into gear before leaving the headquarters. She didn't know if the button would do anything while the truck was driving, but it was time to take a chance.

Roseate heard Aaron holler in celebration. Hoping that he and Jackson were distracted, she quickly reached out, grasped the yellow knob, and pulled.

She was immediately rewarded as the truck shuddered and slowed dramatically, tossing her into the passenger's footwell.

\* \* \*

Aaron caught a flash of movement from Roseate, then he felt the truck shudder and slow significantly.

He was reaching for her hair to pull her away from the dashboard, when she slipped into the well next to his boots.

Aaron turned to look out of the driver's side window and then braced himself as a wall of glass, chrome, and red paint rapidly approached the driver's side of the tractor's cab. His shout of warning to Jackson was in his throat as the impact rocked him to the side and the world went black.

# CHAPTER 47

*Monday, November 27ᵗʰ, 2028*
*4:27 PM*

**D**etective Green pushed his sedan to its limits on his mad dash back to the District 19 station house. His goal was to meet up with those officers before they left as part of the contingent to trap Aaron's caravan from the rear.

Driving through the mostly empty streets, had to wait until he was halfway to the district building before he could get a cell signal. Then he called in other details about the number of trucks and their armaments.

As he pulled into the station's parking lot, his heart sank. He could tell from the lack of vehicles in the parking lot that they had mobilized and left without him. He couldn't blame them, time was of the essence, but he was disappointed nonetheless.

He was about to vent his frustration by punching his steering wheel when the rear door to the station opened and an overweight civilian administrator poked her head out.

Green opened the door to his car and she shouted, "Detective Green. Hurry up! They left you a set of tactical gear and told me to tell you to saddle up and join the party!"

Detective Green clapped his hands together in a silent prayer to a God he rarely thanked for anything recently. He sprinted across the asphalt to the open door of the station. While he was undercover, he didn't carry any weapons, money, or ID. He also didn't want to leave any weapons or gear in the car, just in case it was found. His clothes, shoulder holster, pistol, and wallet were in a locker the station chief had assigned to him; now he had a set of tactical gear to go with it.

Inside, Green looked at the set of gear.

He grabbed a ballistic vest, his pistol, and the only other weapon available to him: the standard issue police semi-automatic shotgun. He loaded five rounds in the shotgun and put extra ammunition in the side pocket on the vest. He stowed his pistol in a belt holster he found in the locker room. He would return it later, there was no way he was going into battle without a pistol, even if it wasn't in his customary shoulder holster.

Green sprinted back to his cruiser and floored the accelerator as he spun the vehicle out of the parking lot. Radio discipline seemed to have been abandoned and several voices clamored over each other in panic as the officers who were engaging Aaron's convoy encountered the sustained, accurate, and powerful firepower of thirty caliber machine guns operated by men trained in years of combat.

Green kept the pedal down as he weaved through the light traffic on North 63rd Street. He was heading due east towards Market Street, which ran north-south. Aaron's convoy was on Market Street heading out of the city to the adjoining township of Upper Darby in Delaware County.

When Green was three blocks out from Market Street, he could see about a dozen Philadelphia police trucks and cars in various states of destruction from the machine gun fire. Some were fully engulfed in flames, others missing windshields or simply riddled with bullet pockmarks.

Instead of driving directly into the line of fire of the machine guns at the rear of the convoy, Detective Green turned the steering wheel of the sedan hard to the right. The tires complained as the sedan made the turn onto Gross Street, a small residential side street a block short of Market Street, which backed into the Cobbs Creek Park that separated the city from the suburbs.

The sedan kissed the curb as it halted to a stop. Green propelled himself out of the driver's seat, shotgun in hand. He went to tap his chest to verify his pistol was in his shoulder holster and remembered that this time, it was in a belt holster. He slapped that holster to be sure it was there, and was rewarded with the cold familiar grip of his service pistol.

The light was fading, but it was still bright enough out to navigate the uneven ground, trees, and old concrete pads that were in the park. As he advanced, the sound of gunfire grew in terrifying intensity. The violent percussion of the thirty caliber machine guns was the strongest by far, but the higher pitched staccato of rifles and pistols filled out any gaps in the sound of the heavy machine guns so that Green's world was a total assault of gunfire.

Green slowed as he approached the edge of the woods. As he knelt to assess the situation, the trunk of a tree twenty feet to his right splintered as a heavy bullet smacked into it.

Up ahead, he could see three technical trucks on Market Street pouring fire into the police huddled behind vehicles. Green cursed. If he'd had a rifle, he could pick off those machine gunners from their flank without them knowing he was even here. But the tree line he was hiding behind was a good seventy to eighty yards away from the fight. He knew he couldn't shoot that far with his pistol and hit anything and if he remembered his training, double-ought buck shot was only effective to about fifty yards.

Green spotted a waist-high concrete wall about fifty yards from his position. It would put him in a great firing position to flank the machine gunner from their broadside, if he could get there alive.

Green looked back at the fight and saw one of his comrades get shot by the machine gun even though the officer had taken cover behind a sedan. Without further thought, Green launched himself from behind the tree line and sprinted headlong to the barrier wall.

Two steps into his sprint, Green looked up to focus on the barrier he was approaching. Further ahead on Market Street, he saw a fire department ladder truck approaching Aaron's flatbed tractor trailer. It looked to Green as if the fire truck would miss Aaron's truck. Then Aaron's truck inexplicably slowed, a cloud of white smoke billowing from the rear tires.

The fire truck slammed into the cab of Aaron's truck in an explosion of sound, metal, and flying plastic parts.

The Militia men operating the machine guns on the technicals all turned to see what had caused the crash.

Green used the distraction and slid behind the wall without being spotted. At least, that was his conclusion as he hunched below the wall catching his breath. If he had been spotted by any of the machine gunners, he wouldn't need to be catching his breath. He'd be dead.

Every second he waited, he knew he was putting his fellow officers at risk. This was his moment. It was payback time. Green thumbed off the safety on the shotgun and double checked that there was a shell in the chamber.

He sprang up from behind the barrier and placed his sight on the nearest machine gunner. Pulled the trigger.

Not pausing long enough to see the effect of his shot, he swung the barrel to the next machine gunner and pulled the trigger. His aim didn't have to be perfect; with the three-inch twelve gauge shells he was using there were fifteen thirty caliber pellets in each shell. He swung the gun to the location of the third and final machine gunner and pulled the trigger.

Green then quickly dropped down behind the barrier as bullets from the other men in the trucks flew toward him. Green stayed low and crawled to a position behind the wall twenty feet to his right, toward the trucks with the machine guns.

As he crawled he didn't hear the pounding of the heavy machine guns. His aim must have been true. He could also hear more small arms fire, meaning the police were able to return fire more effectively without the threat of the heavy guns.

Green knew that if he were one of Aaron's troops, his top priority would be to get those heavy guns shooting again. Green loaded three more shells into the shotgun to replace those he had fired.

Gathering his breath and his courage, Green popped up again to fire on Aaron's troops. This time, one of the troops in the back of the lead technical was waiting for him to pop up, but Green didn't pop up where the Militia man expected him. As the Militia soldier swung his muzzle to compensate for Green's new position, Green fired. The shot peppered the side of the truck and killed the man. Green stayed up this time and continued to fire at drivers or other

Militia men scrambling to get to the machine guns in the beds of the pickup trucks.

After five shots, Green huddled behind the barrier and reloaded. He decided to stay put and stand up again from this position when he noticed a difference in the firefight.

The heavy machine guns still had not started up since he had first broadsided the gunners, but now he thought he noticed a reduction in the volume of gunshots.

Then he heard a word shouted by an officer that was music to his ears, "Truck one. Clear!" Followed by a pause then, "Truck two. Clear!"

This time, instead of standing up to fire, Green peeked over the wall just enough to see what was going on. The other officers had secured the last two trucks in the convoy and were approaching the third. Green saw a Militia man tucked in front of the bumper of the truck waiting to ambush the approaching officers.

Unwilling to use his shotgun for fear of the spreading pellets accidentally hitting one of his own, Green pulled out his pistol and braced it against the stone wall. Using a two-handed grip with his forearms resting against the wall, Green centered the Militia man in his sight. The shot was at the far end of his effective distance. At the shooting range at sixty feet, Green had trouble keeping his groups tighter than a large pie plate.

But he only had seconds before this thug would ambush three or four of his fellow officers. He knew he had to take this guy out now. Green steadied his breathing and slowly pulled the trigger. The gun bucked in his hands, the officers were startled and stopped in their tracks at the driver and passenger doors of the truck, and the Militia man slumped backwards, dropping his rifle.

Green stood tall and held up his badge making sure the officers knew he was a friendly. The he hopped the wall to join his colleagues in ending the threat.

# CHAPTER 48

*Monday, November 27ᵗʰ, 2028*
*4:34 PM*

Gunfire. It was the Ukraine. Aaron was taking cover behind sandbags in a blown-out storefront in the shelled-out city of Donetsk in Eastern Ukraine. Aaron and his platoon had just successfully carried out a raid on a Russian ammo dump, setting charges and blowing it and two old T-14 Russian main battle tanks to smithereens. In doing so, they had kicked up a huge hornets' nest. The bear was pissed and he wanted revenge.

Aaron was pinned down with incoming fire coming from three positions. He couldn't understand why the floor was tilted. Or what was holding him, pinned against the wall.

As the cobwebs cleared Aaron realized he wasn't in the Ukraine, the floor was tilted because the truck's cab he was in was in precarious danger of falling over to crush the passenger door, and he wasn't pinned to a wall, it was the seatbelt holding him fast to his chair.

The gunfire was real though. That reality was punctuated by a round coming though the windshield, impacting to his left. Aaron heard a weak grunt after the unmistakable sound of the bullet impacting flesh.

The cobwebs clear, Aaron quickly looked to his left to see his friend Jackson clinging to life. Jackson had taken the brunt of the impact from the fire truck that Aaron now saw had broadsided his tractor trailer. Aaron also saw three bullet wounds on Jackson's arms and shoulders and several pockmarks on his ballistic vest where rounds hit but didn't penetrate.

Jackson looked over at Aaron with his one working, bloodshot right eye. The left eye was hideously swollen shut. Jackson smiled with blood red teeth and whispered, "About time you woke up Boss. I'zz about to start smacking you around to get you moving."

Aaron checked himself for wounds and didn't find any. He looked back at Jackson and asked, "Jackie, how long I been out? What's our SITREP?"

Jackie coughed up some blood and weakly spit it out, soiling his vest, "Just a minute Boss. We in deep shit. You gotta' move—now."

Aaron said, "Alright Jackie, let's get moving."

Jackson responded, "I ain't going nowhere Boss. Fire truck busted up my legs bad and I'm bleeding out. Get out now before I frag your ass myself."

Aaron wanted to laugh at the thought of Jackson "fragging," or exploding, a hand grenade to kill Aaron, mishap that had happened to a few clueless officers in the Ukraine.

Instead he reached out and grabbed a spot on Jackson's shoulder where there were no wounds and said, "Jackie, best day of my life was when you walked back in to my office. I'll see you on the other side, my brother."

Jackson only had the energy to nod before he closed his eyes for the final time.

Aaron braced himself against the frame of the cab and unclipped his seat belt. At the angle of the cab, gravity was threatening to spill him against the door and down to the concrete. Instead, Aaron reached down to his backpack, heavy with gold, and grabbed two canisters labeled "M18 smoke yellow".

He popped the tabs on both canisters and threw them in front and to the side of the tractor trailer's cab. The canisters started to spew copious clouds of smoke.

Aaron counted to five, then unlatched the passenger side door. Roseate tumbled onto the concrete. He couldn't see any wounds on her, but she didn't respond to the fall; he figured she was dead. He quickly shouldered his backpack, making a conscious decision not to bring his rifle, and crawled to the front of the cab.

The smoke covered his movements well enough that no rounds were impacting near him. The silence of the M60's told him this battle was nearly over, and he had lost. Part of him wanted to stay and kill as many of these country bastards as he could, but he knew that would result in him ending up like Jackson. Now was not the time to fight. It was time to run.

In between the wreckage of the cab and the fire truck was a triangular gap near the ground wide enough for him to crawl through. Through the gap, Aaron could see the woods of Cobbs Creek about twenty yards away.

Aaron popped his last canister of smoke and threw it through the opening. Then he shimmied his way through the gap, pushing his backpack in front of him, with his pistol drawn.

Once through the gap, he shouldered his backpack, stood up in a cloud of smoke, and using the mental map of the next twenty yards he'd created before the smoke obscured his vision, sprinted to the safety of the woods.

His immediate priority was to get a car and get to Chester, Pennsylvania, where he could still hop on that barge and start over in Texas. His need for revenge for Jackson and his other men was still tugging at him as he made his way in a low crouch through the darkening woods.

Then it hit him. He could get a measure of revenge and secure a car at the same time.

Pausing in the woods to get his bearings, Aaron adjusted his path, grim determination on his face.

# CHAPTER 49

*Monday, November 27ᵗʰ, 2028*
*4:48PM*

Julianne had never been to a warzone before and she hoped she never would again. She and Chief Braxton pulled up behind one of a dozen ambulances on Market Street. Several police officers were being treated by paramedics for a variety of horrific wounds.

The chief gave some of the men on gurneys an encouraging word as he quickly strode by them. He was looking for the incident commander, who was also the captain of the 19th district. A policeman in full tactical gear pointed the chief in the right direction and Julianne nearly had to jog to keep up.

Chief Braxton approached Captain Jack Higgins, who was calling into a radio for immediate prisoner transport. Captain Jack Higgins had been on the force for twenty years and Julianne had learned on the ride over that he and Braxton had worked together on some task forces earlier in their careers, but didn't know each other that well. Higgins was of Irish descent, as was evident from his ruddy complexion.

Next to the captain was another officer in full tactical gear. This officer was pointing his shotgun at a group of four men with their hands tie-wrapped behind their backs. The men on the ground were wearing the uniforms of the Southwest Militia. Three of the four were suffering from gunshot wounds and the fourth's face was swollen. The officer watching them seemed to be hoping one of the prisoners would do something stupid so he could shoot them.

Higgins lowered the radio from his mouth and greeted the chief and Julianne.

Braxton asked, "What's the situation?"

Higgins answered, "We recovered a barely conscious woman named Roseate Freeman from the cab of the tractor trailer. She was the one who popped the air brakes that allowed the township guys to ram the tractor trailer. She also confirmed Aaron was in the cab but escaped using smoke canisters. He is currently on the loose."

Julianne interjected, "This may sound brash, but please tell me those crates I see on the back of the trailer are the federal government's gold?"

Higgins answered, "Yes ma'am. I thought you might be interested in that. I have four patrolmen stationed to secure the load now."

Julianne let out a sigh then looked around, "How were you able to stop Aaron's men? I can see the heavy machine guns on the pickup trucks. Aren't those the same ones that Aaron's troops used in the city to hold us at bay while he raided the Federal Reserve?"

"Good questions. Braxton's boy Green went freaking Rambo and flanked Aaron's rear troops just as they were putting a hurting on us with their machine guns. Greenie took the air out of their sails and we were able to advance and clean things up."

Braxton asked, "Where is Detective Green?"

Higgins pointed past the city line in to Upper Darby where the mangled tractor trailer sat at a forty-five degree angle with the fire truck pressing against it.

"He's up there looking for Aaron."

Braxton patted Higgins on the shoulder and said, "Great work here Jack. Secure those crates on the back of that trailer. I'm going to find Green."

Julianne also thanked Captain Higgins and then followed Braxton toward the trailer. Braxton had his badge out and presented it to a township officer who was inspecting the cab.

Around the front of the cab, Braxton found Green speaking quickly with a tall, white officer from the township.

"I can't believe that son of a bitch snuck past all your men. I'm not blaming anyone, I just can't freak'n believe it." Green said while pivoting to look at the wreckage and the surrounding area.

Braxton walked up and said, "Detective Green, did I hear you correctly? Aaron isn't here?"

Detective Green turned. "Hey Chief." Then, reminded of his manners, he said, "Chief Emmanuel Braxton and City Coordinator Julianne Barnes, this is Lieutenant John Brady. He is the commanding officer in the township, since their captain was injured piloting this fire truck. They also lost some good men in the fire fight."

Julianne was the first to offer her hand to Lieutenant Brady, "Thank you for what you did here. I'm very sorry for your losses."

Braxton agreed then added, "What's the status on Aaron, any leads?"

Lieutenant Brady responded, "He could be anywhere right now. We put out an emergency text message with his photo to all of our citizens' phones, but no hits so far. Based on the time since the fire truck crashed into Aaron's truck, if he was on foot at a jog he could be about a mile away. We are working on setting up a perimeter, but our boys are still shaking off the shock of being fired at by large caliber machine guns and we have wounded to attend to."

Julianne nodded her head as she took in the information. Then she looked over at Green, who was deep in thought, tapping the left side of his chest with his right hand. Julianne thought maybe he was suffering some form of post traumatic stress disorder when all of sudden he straightened up like electricity was coursing through him.

"Oh shit! I think I know where Aaron's going."

Green ignored the chief and Julianne and he grabbed Lieutenant Brady by the jacket and said, "Car, car. I need a car. I know where Aaron is going!"

Without pausing to ask what Green was talking about, Lieutenant Brady replied, "My cruiser's over here, come on."

Julianne watched as Green and Brady ran towards an idling cruiser with its light bar fully illuminated.

Braxton took a step towards the men to follow. Julianne grabbed his hand and before he could pull away said, "Emmitt. This isn't your fight. Your men need you here. The press will be here any minute and we are going to need you to reassure our citizens that this nightmare is over."

Braxton stopped and turned to face Julianne. His eyes were troubled. "You're right. I just hope Greenie remembers to have Lieutenant Brady call for backup. We're not in the city anymore."

Then he looked quizzically at Julianne and asked, "What do you mean *I* have to handle the press? You've been doing a great job of that over the past few days. They love you."

Julianne whipped out her cell phone and replied, "No worries Emmitt, I'll work with you on handling the press. But first I want to call Secretary Asher at Homeland and tell him the good news. His gold is secure."

# CHAPTER 50

*Monday, November 27ᵗʰ, 2028*
*5:04PM*

Jimmy couldn't wait to tell his mom about the incredible day he had.

Colleen had arranged an interview with the maintenance director at the YMCA where she worked. The interview was going okay, but not great. Then the radio on the director's hip blared out news that the chair lift in the main pool was broken and there was a handicapped woman in the pool who couldn't get out.

The director ended the interview and began showing Jimmy to the door. Jimmy offered to get his tools from his car and see if he could help. At first, the director declined because Jimmy wasn't an employee. Jimmy responded by telling him to consider it a free service call. The director agreed and after Jimmy got his tools, they met at the pool.

Jimmy and the director worked together to fix the device and got along "swimmingly," sharing stories and generally having fun while they fixed the lift.

After an hour, the lift was fixed and the woman was able to get out of the pool, shriveled skin to be sure, but no worse for the wear.

Colleen had stopped down then to see the fruits of Jimmy's labor just as he was putting his tools away. Word had gotten out about Jimmy's repair to the lift. She gave him a hug, followed by a peck on the check. Of course, he blushed—the director was still on the pool deck with them—but Jimmy didn't care. He loved it.

Jimmy went to shake the director's hand and see himself to the entrance when the director told him to come to his office to fill out some paperwork and get on the clock.

Jimmy did so and he was given a blue YMCA collared uniform shirt. Even though the pay was about half his previous job, Jimmy was so excited and thankful to have a job again, he didn't care about the money.

Jimmy pulled the Crown Vic to the curb and put the gearshift into park. He took a deep breath and gave thanks for how grateful he was that everything was turning out so . . . well, so incredibly great.

The shooting was behind him, he had a job again, and he was convinced Colleen liked him. Really liked him. Once he was done telling his mom about his day, he was going to see if Colleen wanted to go on a date this weekend.

All the pieces in his life seemed to be coming together. But the situation in the city, just a couple miles from this quiet neighborhood, was falling apart.

The radio, which had been tuned to a music station, had just broken into a special alert report as Jimmy cut the ignition. He had heard so many special alerts on the radio and TV lately that he had become numb to them. No need to listen to another one.

The lights were on in Mom's house and dark at Colleen's. That meant Colleen and the boys were over for dinner, as had been the routine for over a month now.

Jimmy walked to the front door, he looking forward to sharing his news with everyone.

Jimmy unlocked the door and stepped inside. The TV in the front room was playing a cartoon and the door to the kitchen was closed. Jimmy checked his watch. A little early for dinner, but not outside the norm. That would explain why the boys weren't in the front room.

But Jimmy couldn't figure out why the kitchen door was closed. It was almost always open, to allow the heat from cooking to help keep the front room warm.

Jimmy turned off the TV and walked towards the kitchen. As he did so, he called out, "Hey Mom, Colleen, I'm home. Smells good, what's for dinner?"

He opened the door to the kitchen and froze as he attempted to process the scene.

The first thing he saw was a military helmet sitting on the kitchen table like an inert upturned turtle, next to a drab green backpack.

Sitting at the kitchen table, there was a light-skinned black man in military garb. It took a second for Jimmy to recognize that this man was Aaron, the head of the Southwest Militia. He had the chair turned backward, so that the back was at his chest. He was aiming a sinister, black pistol at the center of Jimmy's chest.

To his right and on the floor against the wall near the sink were Mom and Colleen sitting cross-legged, with Jack Jr. in Mom's lap and Dougie in Colleen's lap. The ancient wall phone that Mom insisted on keeping active even though everyone used cell phones today was ripped off the wall and lying at Jimmy's feet. In his shock, Jimmy found himself thinking he'd need to fix that once he got a chance.

That thought was broken when the military man said, "Well this must be the man of the hour, James Brennan."

Jimmy slowly nodded as he raised his empty hands in a sign of surrender. "It's—just Jimmy. I—I know you. You're Aaron Mitchell from the Southwest Militia. Why are you here?"

Aaron shook his head and pointed the barrel of the gun at Jimmy's face, "You're not so dumb for a country-ass cracker are you? Well, if you're smart enough to know who I am, you ought to be able to figure out why I'm here."

Jimmy felt tears well up as the realization of Aaron's purpose hit him like an emotional freight train. Jimmy slowly shook his head and said one word, "Dante."

Aaron slapped the table, causing Colleen and the boys to yelp in surprise. Aaron barked out a quick laugh then became quiet as he steeled his eyes at Jimmy, "That's right Jimmy boy. It's payback time."

"I thought I would just kill you before I moved on, but I hit the treasure trove here. So here's what's going to happen. I'm gonna' kill these little white boys first, followed by their momma, then your momma, then you. How's that sound, Jimmy?"

Jimmy's mind raced. He looked at the wounds on Aaron's face, at the backpack. He knew something was going on more than Aaron just seeking payback. Maybe there was a way out of this predicament.

Aaron waved the gun at Jimmy, "Be a good boy and get over there with your people, so I can kill you all nice and orderly."

Jimmy knew he had to act now. He thought about the alert he'd ignored on the radio and decided to take a chance.

Jimmy didn't move. Instead he said, "Wait. Just wait a second. I know you're on the run. You're alone and don't have any transportation. I can help you out. I have wheels—and I can—"

Aaron interrupted Jimmy, "You don't know shit boy. I was planning on killing all of you then taking your wheels anyway, now get over there or I'll shoot you first."

Jimmy added, "Wait. I can drive you out of here. The police won't be looking for a white guy in an old sedan. You can hide in the back seat with the pistol pointed at me the whole time. Then, when we get somewhere safe, you can, you can—"

Again, Aaron interrupted, "I will kill you. Not a bad plan, kid."

Jimmy added, "I'll only do it if you leave my family alone."

Aaron reached into his backpack and brought out a pack of wire ties. Then he said, "Fine kid. Secure your family with these so they can't call anyone or run next door once we leave. You do a good job and I won't kill any of them."

Jimmy did as he was told. He felt fear radiating from his mom and the boys. Colleen looked at him with a mix of fear and appreciation, tearing up. . He didn't want to die, but he could see no other way out of this.

His life for theirs. The math made sense although his fear induced a nausea that threatened to upheave the contents in his stomach.

Jimmy straightened up after securing everyone and turned to Aaron.

Aaron said, "Nice job kid. Let's go." Aaron shrugged on his backpack and left the helmet on the table. Then he grabbed Jimmy by the jacket with his left arm and held him at arm's length. With his right arm, he kept the pistol square in Jimmy's back. Jimmy knew one wrong move and he would be dead.

Jimmy opened the back door and stepped down the two steps to the ground. Then he cautiously walked around the house to the front walk where the car was parked in the street.

Jimmy slowly unlocked then opened the front driver's side door, all the while feeling the pressure from the muzzle of Aaron's pistol in his back. He hit the unlock button on the door and moved to open the back door.

Aaron shrugged off his backpack and stowed it in the backseat.

Jimmy was moving to the driver's door to get in the car when he heard a voice call out, "Stop right there and put the weapon down!"

# CHAPTER 51

*Monday, November 27ᵗʰ, 2028*
*5:10 PM*

On the hectic ride to James Brennan's house, Detective Green and Lieutenant Brady agreed to park a block away and approach the house on foot. Brady had also called for backup and it was only a few minutes out. The hope was that they could beat Aaron to the house and secure the property before he showed up.

As they turned a corner, Brady stopped the vehicle. Both men got out and Brady used hand signals to indicate to Green which way Brennan's house was located.

Both men had their service pistols drawn as they jogged down the sidewalk. The light of the day was fading, but it was still bright enough to see the details of the neighborhood.

Green was amazed at how orderly and clean everything was out here. He was only a mile away from the city line as a crow flies, but it might have been a different universe judging by these tidy single-family homes on postage stamp sized parcels.

Green saw two men about to get into a car about forty feet away from him. One of the men threw a bag into the backseat, and when

Green saw the distinctive black silhouette of a pistol in the man's hand, he shouted, "Stop right there and put the weapon down!"

The man with the pistol reacted immediately by grabbing the other man and using him as a shield against the two approaching officers.

As Green pulled up to a stop with Brady about twenty feet to his right, he could clearly identify the gunman as Aaron and the hostage as James Brennan.

Green and Brady instinctively spread out in a flanking procedure to make it harder for the perpetrator to track their movements and allow them to get a clean shot if needed.

Aaron called out, "Stop moving now or I'll kill him!"

Green answered, "Aaron, I don't care about some white boy in the suburbs. You killed a lot of my friends, there is no possibility of you getting out of this one."

Aaron jostled James Brennan in front of him to position him towards Green.

Aaron said, "Me and Jimmy are getting in this car now, you try to stop me and he gets capped."

Green said, "One more step and I shoot."

Brady called out, "Jimmy. Mallard."

# CHAPTER 52

*Monday, November 27th, 2028*
*5:12 PM*

Just like ten years ago, it took Jimmy a millisecond to understand what John had said.

Jimmy let his body go inert and fall to the ground. As he was falling, he felt a hot piercing pain in his upper back and chest. Then he heard several gunshots as he hit the ground.

Lying on his side, Jimmy saw Detective Green to his left, lying in the middle of the street moaning in pain. Jimmy was alongside the Crown Vic. Aaron was just in front of him in a crouched position with his pistol braced on the trunk of the car. He was shooting at John, who was pinned behind a tree planted on the thin strip of grass between the road and the sidewalk.

It was obvious to Jimmy that the tree wasn't big enough to work as a barrier and it would be a matter of another shot or two before John was in serious trouble.

Jimmy tried to understand what was happening to his body. His upper back felt like someone impaled him with a hot poker. He had foamy blood coming from his upper right chest and he was having trouble breathing. He just wanted to lay right here and rest. Just for a little while.

He started to close his eyes when he remembered that the lives of his friend John and the detective who'd saved his life were on the line.

Willing himself to all fours, Jimmy gathered his resolve. He didn't have any weapon on him so, he did what he could.

Propelling himself with his legs, he drove his left shoulder into Aaron's back. Aaron lost his balance from the unexpected blow and rolled out past the Crown Vic's trunk. Exposed in the middle of the street.

Jimmy heard two shots and Aaron sprawled out flat in the road. Jimmy watched as Aaron tried to raise his pistol to fire at John. John calmly walked up to Aaron and said, "Drop the gun. You're under arrest. It's over."

Aaron ignored him and continued to lift his gun.

Jimmy was fading out as he heard John say, "I hate bullies."

The gunshots from John's pistol barely registered to Jimmy as he slipped away.

# CHAPTER 53

*Wednesday, December 20ᵗʰ, 2028*
*10:30 AM*

"What do you mean the City of Philadelphia owes the federal government for the unrecovered gold? How about I send you an invoice for the damage caused to the city due to your choice to store the gold here unbeknownst to us and with insufficient security?"

Julianne paused as the Treasury Secretary responded.

"I've told you already—we looked everywhere. His personal residence, his headquarters, stash houses, all his vehicles—we still come up twenty pounds short."

Again, she waited as he stated his argument. Then she exploded.

"What? I cannot believe this! You cannot hold me personally responsible for the missing gold! That's nearly a million dollars, I won't be able to cough that up in thirty days or thirty years for that matter."

Julianne ended the call. She wanted to slam the handset down on the phone on her desk but thought better of it. She already owed the Treasury almost a million dollars, she thought it best not to owe the city for a new desk phone.

Regardless of the trouble with the feds, Julianne was proud of the accomplishments her team had made putting the city back together over the last few weeks. One thing she didn't let anyone spend a penny on was this office. Looking around, she was glad the looters had destroyed all the furniture and stolen what was easy to carry. Instead of the rich leather chair and mahogany desk her predecessor had sat behind, Julianne sat on an ordinary office chair behind a card table with a laptop on it. She liked the message this furniture projected. This was a time for hard work and harder choices. Not a time for luxury and trappings of wealth.

The furniture wasn't what made this office a burden. It was the nature of the job. After Aaron was killed and his empire torn down and raided, she was nominated by the surviving department heads to be the interim mayor. She declined that job—or at least, the title—but accepted the title "Administrator." Her first act as Administrator was to announce elections for the mayor and city council positions.

That had been three weeks ago and the election was next week. Julianne didn't spend a minute campaigning for the job even though her name was on the ballot. It was an open election. Anyone receiving the most votes, got the mayor's office. This office. She did participate in the only scheduled debate at the prodding of her boyfriend, Emmitt.

She'd been on the stage with five other people who wanted the job. After a few rounds of bickering and empty promises, the mediator shushed the other participants and asked Julianne what would be her first act as mayor. She looked right at the camera and said, "Require the city to file for chapter nine bankruptcy." The other contestants guffawed as Julianne continued, "The people of this city have been through a lot. But they know the jig is up. We can't spend our way out of this predicament. It's time to buckle down and work on what really matters and do without the freebies. Previous leaders have been too cowardly to give our city the medicine it needs to be healthy again. And to continue that metaphor, this doctor has rounds to make. So, if you will excuse me, I need to get back to work." With that Julianne unclipped the lapel mic and walked off the stage. The moderator and the other contestants were aghast.

Her aides told her she had just shot herself in the foot. They argued that a politician couldn't be that honest with the voters. That the only way to get elected was to make more promises. Julianne fired those advisors. Then the polls came in at the end of that week—Julianne would've carried seventy percent of the vote if it had been held that day.

Her rare quiet moment was interrupted by a light rapping on the door. "Come on in," she called out.

Chief Braxton came in to the office looking worried. Julianne furrowed her brow. "Emmitt, why the long face? I thought you were looking forward to today? I know I sure am."

Braxton showed Julianne the manila folder he was holding and responded, "I am. Or was—I need to run this by you before we bestow the award on our hero."

Julianne sighed and motioned Braxton around the card table and said, "Lay it on me Chief, it can't be worse than the conversation I just had. You're not going to tell me that the man our city—heck, the whole country—is crediting with ending Aaron's maniacal terrorism spree is a Russian agent or something?"

Braxton didn't smile at Julianne's joke, "No, but it is a complication you should know about, and I don't want you to get blindsided."

Julianne looked at Braxton, "What are you talking about? Show me what's in the folder."

Braxton opened the folder, he explained the contents "These are files recovered from the server of the 18th district police station that Aaron attacked right after the riot at Love Park. My tech was able to partially reconstruct the file and he only showed me the contents. I told him to keep quiet about this until I spoke to you."

Julianne looked over the contents. "Please get to the point Chief, we're doing the award ceremony here in the office in a few minutes."

Braxton sighed and said, "Bottom line. Detective Green arrested and then released James Brennan for the killing of a young man named Dantrell Freeman."

Julianne thought aloud, "Freeman . . . Freeman. Why is that ringing a bell? Wait, wasn't that the last name of the woman we recovered from the cab of Aaron's truck? She's the one credited for activating the air brakes, slowing Aaron's escape, right? Is she doing okay?"

Braxton reminded her, "That's correct, and she is recovering well. She was also the daughter of the municipal worker who ran the trash truck into the mayor's viewing stand at the annual address—Reginald Freeman. Dante's father."

Julianne's eyes widened as she thought about the ramifications, "Do you think the loss of his son was what drove Reginald to lash out at the mayor?"

Braxton shrugged, "Who knows? It turns out Aaron also kidnapped Reginald's daughter a week or so before everything hit the fan—that's why she was in the cab during his escape. The kidnapping, Dante's death, along with those IOUs that were being issued could have pushed Reginald over the precipice. We'll never know. Reginald was shot and killed by one of our patrolmen as his truck approached the viewing stand."

Julianne remembered all too well hearing the gunshots before the truck rammed the stand.

The city, state, and even the federal government was holding up James Brennan as a symbol of what one ordinary, average citizen could do in the service of his country. While Mr. Brennan was recovering from surgery, the story spread of how he, with a near-fatal gunshot wound through his right lung, was able to tackle Aaron during a gunfight with Detective Green and Lieutenant Brady. If it weren't for Mr. Brennan's actions, both officers believe Aaron would have killed them and gotten away.

The release of this information would destroy the narrative. No, Julianne decided, this file was not to see the light of day.

Julianne closed the file and looked at Chief Braxton for a while. Finally, she spoke, "This information does ruin the narrative. Even though Mr. Brennan's killing of Dante was deemed justifiable homicide, it wouldn't take too long for the press to connect the dots and conclude that Dante's killing might have pushed Reginald into such a state of despair that he drove his truck into the speech."

Braxton added, "I'm more worried about it blowing back on you, Julianne."

Julianne shook her head, "No Emmitt, it's not about me. It's about hope. Jimmy's act of courage in the middle of a gunfight where he was the only one without a gun shows what an ordinary person can do in extraordinary circumstances. Our citizens are living in unimagined circumstances every day as this city, and hopefully our nation, tries put itself back together. They need a hero, and right now that hero will be James Brennan."

"As for the file—I want to hold on to this file until after the award ceremony. Then you and I can have a conversation with Mr.

Brennan. If the conversation goes the way I think it will, bury this file. Don't burn it, I want to keep it as insurance, but bury it deep so only you and I know about it. If that technician who reconstructed the files has a problem with it, have him speak with me as well so I can explain the situation."

Chief Braxton nodded and said, "I figured that's the call you'd make. I'll put it in a file cabinet in my basement at home. Nobody goes down there but me."

# CHAPTER 54

*Wednesday, December 20ᵗʰ, 2028*
*10:45 AM*

Jimmy beamed with pride as Administrator Julianne Barnes slid the purple silk necklace attached to a gold medallion around his neck. He was flanked by Lieutenant Brady and Detective Green, who had both been given citations of bravery to add to their uniforms.

Jimmy had requested that the ceremony be done in a low-key location. He didn't want the attention and he still was recovering from his gunshot wound.

Jimmy's mother, Katherine, had tears in her eyes as she held the hands of who would soon be his adopted sons, Jack Jr. and Douglas. Jimmy could tell the boys were antsy and bored from waiting outside the mayor's office, but they were behaving since it was better than being in school for the morning.

Colleen stood next to Jimmy, her arm protectively looped through his elbow. He was still a little short of breath from his wound and this was his first outing.

Administrator Barnes said some nice words about bravery and service for the benefit of the film crew that had been called in.

Then everyone posed for a few photographs to release to the online news outlets.

As Jimmy and his family were about to leave the mayor's office, Ms. Barnes addressed him, "Mr. Brennan, would you mind staying for a moment? Chief Braxton and I have a few details to cover with you. Nothing critical." Then she smoothly addressed Green and Brady, "Detective Green, you are dismissed, Lieutenant Brady, would you please wait for Mr. Brennan outside? This will only take a minute. Thank you."

Detective Green swung forward on his crutches to thank Julianne and Chief Braxton. Detective Green had taken two bullets from Aaron during the gunfight. One hit him square in the ceramic plate in his ballistic vest. If it had hit anywhere else on the vest, it would have penetrated and killed him. The other bullet got him in the meat of his thigh. It didn't hit anything critical, but it hurt like hell and was still healing.

Detective Green turned to Jimmy and said, "Don't be a stranger kid. You and I have been through a couple rough patches. You ever need anything, you give me a call." Then he excused himself and used his crutches to exit through the double doors.

Lieutenant Brady paused and lifted an eyebrow at Jimmy.

Jimmy said, "It's cool. I'll be right there."

Brady nodded and excused himself to wait in the reception area outside the mayor's office. He had gotten hit with some shrapnel from the tree he was hiding behind while Aaron fired at him, but the wounds were all superficial and had healed since the gunfight.

Colleen, Katherine, and the kids were still standing beside Jimmy. Jimmy noticed that the Administrator and Chief were looking at him expectantly.

He got the hint and squeezed Colleen's hand, "Colleen, I think they want to speak to me alone for a minute. I'll be okay. Could you give us a minute?"

Colleen was about to protest but Jimmy leaned over and gave her a kiss on her cheek, "It's okay. Honest."

Colleen nodded and said, "Alright. We'll be just outside the door."

Then she and Katherine took the boys out of the room, closing the doors behind them.

Jimmy blushed a little and said, "She's been very protective of me since I was shot. That was a tough night for all of us. Now she won't let me out of her sight."

Julianne responded, "I understand, we all have our scars from that episode."

Julianne grabbed a file from her desk. She handed it to Jimmy.

She said, "I am going to cut right to the chase. This file contains the digital notes and documentation from District 18's server."

With all the events of the past few weeks, Jimmy had nearly forgotten that he had killed Dante.

Jimmy opened the file and saw that Dante's last name was Freeman. He hadn't known that before now and for some reason, that rung a bell, but Jimmy couldn't figure out why.

Jimmy handed the file back and said, "I already admitted to killing Dante in self-defense. I was the one who called the police after it happened. Detective Green and the prosecutor said it was justifiable."

Chief Braxton grabbed the file and said, "We know kid. That's not the problem. The problem is that Dante's father was Reginald Freeman. Does that ring a bell?"

While Jimmy had been recovering in the hospital he had read everything he could about the five days of terror that had enveloped the city. He knew that the driver of the trash truck was an older municipal worker named Reginald Freeman. Everyone assumed he snapped over his daughter being kidnapped and the IOUs the city had been issuing.

The realization shook Jimmy to the core. He involuntarily inhaled and grabbed the back of the chair in front of him for balance. He felt as if he may get sick to his stomach. Working to control his breathing, he arrived at the conclusion that his action that day defending himself had led to all of the chaos and hundreds, if not thousands, of people losing their lives.

It was his fault.

Jimmy couldn't stop the tears that pooled up and spilled down his cheeks. He whispered, "I had no idea." Then, looking directly at Julianne with tears streaming down, "I am so very, very, very sorry."

Jimmy reached up with his left hand and lifted the silk necklace off his shoulders.

Julianne stared at Jimmy for a few seconds then nodded at Chief Braxton.

She said, "You are keeping that award. The people need a hero. They won't find out what's in that file."

Jimmy let the silk fall back to his shoulders, "I don't understand. I started this whole thing. I should—"

Chief Braxton interrupted Jimmy, "Stop talking and listen."

Julianne continued, "Okay, here's the deal. Chief Braxton and I are the only ones who know what is in the file. I have instructed the chief to bury the file. Know that the file is being buried, not burned. If I hear anything about you from this day forward that makes me second guess my judgment in this matter, this file will be in the hands of every streaming news service. Your reputation will be ruined and you could very well face charges for illegal possession and use of a firearm. Am I clear?"

Jimmy cleared his throat and took a moment to gather himself. He stood up and straightened his shoulder as best he could with his wound. He looked both Julianne and Chief Braxton in the eyes and said, "Yes ma'am. Sir. You can count on me, I owe you—big time."

# EPILOGUE

*Sunday, January 14th, 2029*
*8:30 AM*

Tomorrow would be Jimmy's first real day at his new job at the YMCA. They agreed to hold his position for him while he healed. His breathing had returned to normal, although he could feel some tightness in his chest and shoulder if he pushed himself too hard.

Colleen and Katherine wanted him to stay home and rest for a couple more weeks, but he was going stir crazy. His innermost-self found dignity at work. His fifteen minutes of fame had passed and it was now time to get on with life.

He also needed to get back to work because they were running out of money. Colleen and the boys had officially moved over to his house. It was tight and it was noisy at times, but it was right. So right that even though they hadn't been dating long, Jimmy proposed to Colleen for her hand in marriage. When you know, he figured, why wait around? She had agreed, and now wore the engagement ring he fabricated from copper wires and silver solder on her left hand. He promised to get her a proper ring, once he could afford it.

It was also the first time they would be going to church together, as a family.

Jimmy offered to go out and start the Crown Vic to let it warm up before loading everyone for the ride to church.

Jimmy hadn't driven the car since the night of the shootout in front of his mom's house. There wasn't anywhere he needed to go and the women in his life wouldn't have let him go anywhere if had he tried.

Jimmy unlocked and opened the driver's side door. A swatch of olive drab cloth on the floor of the back seat caught his eye.

Curious, Jimmy opened the rear door and looked in.

Instantly his mind flashed back to the night of the shootout. He recalled Aaron throwing his backpack into the backseat before Green and Brady showed up.

He hadn't thought about the backpack until he saw it sitting on the back seat.

Jimmy reached in for the pack and grabbed a strap. He was surprised at how heavy it was. He should probably just leave it there and call Green to turn it in. Maybe there was something in it Green would want for his investigation.

But maybe just a look? Surely that wouldn't hurt.

Curiosity got the better of him.

His eyes opened wide.

Jimmy looped the strap over his good shoulder and walked back to the house.

He called everyone to the kitchen and emptied the contents on the kitchen counter.

Katherine gasped. Colleen shook her head in surprise. The boys cheered and each grabbed one of the gold bars now on the table.

Colleen asked, "Where did this come from? What are we going to do with it?"

Jimmy said, "I had forgotten Aaron threw his backpack on the back seat of mom's car before the shootout began."

Jimmy held his hand out and looked at the boys demonstratively. They reluctantly placed the two bars back in his hand. Jimmy placed them back on the table.

"I'd love to use some of this to get you a big fat rock to put on your finger, Colleen, and it is tempting to keep this gold and make all of our financial woes disappear, but I can't."

Jimmy paused, looking at the dull shine of the gold bars on the table, "I owe a new friend a big favor."

With that he opened his phone and placed a call. Once it connected, he smiled at his new family and said into the phone, "Ms. Barnes, I found something you may be interested in."

## THE END

# ACKNOWLEDGEMENTS

Thanks go to my family for encouraging me in so many ways during the writing of this novel. While I take full responsibility for any errors or typos, I would like to thank Trinity Huhn for her editorial services. Her insight and feedback were priceless. Finally, I am extremely appreciative of the efforts of my beta readers, Richard Oliver, Chip Roach, and Rick Groves.